J. E. REED

THE SACRED AND THE TORMENTED

Cover Design: Story Wrappers

Interior Formatting: J.E. Reed

Title Page Flower Design: ProMagicCreations

ISBN: 978-1-967835-00-3

Visit the author at jereedbooks.com

Also available in ebook, hardcover, and audio.

To my family, for always being there when it mattered most.

Books by J.E. Reed

The Chronopoint Chronicles

Running with the Wolves
Rise of the Wolves
Feral Magic

The Fae of Alastriona series

The Divine and the Cursed
The Revered and the Pariah
A Fate so Cruel
The Sacred and the Tormented
The Exalted and the Forgotten

PRONUNCIATION GUIDE

Characters:

Aiden - AY-den
Alec - AL-uhk
Arianna - ahr-ee-AH-nah
Avalon - AV-uh-lon
Cara - KAR-uh
Conall - KON-uhl
Eimear – EE-mer
Ellie - EL-ee
Evelyn – EV-uh-lin
Gavin – GAV-in
Kirian - KEY-ree-an
Kaylee – KAY-lee
Lan - LA-on
Laoise - LEE-sha
Lillian - LIL-ee-uhn
Máili - MAH-lee
Maya - MY-uh
Myrna - MUR-nuh
Niall – Nye-ul
Raevina - Ray-vee-nuh
Rion - REE-on
Róisín - ROH-sheen
Saoirse - SUR-sha
Sive – rhymes with "hive"

Talon - TA-lon
Vairik - VAY-rik
Whelan – WEE-lin
Zylah – ZIE-lah

Places:

Alastríona - al-as-TREE-na
Ashling - ASH-leen
Brónach - BRO-nah
Fiadh - FEE-ah
Levea - le-VEE-ah
Móirín - MUY-rin
Nàdair - nay-DEER
Pádraigín - PAH-druh-geen
Púróg - pure-AHG
Ruadhán - ROO-awn

HUMAN LANDS
ASHLING
PÁDRAIGÍN
ASHLING
RUADHÁN
PÚRÓG
FIADH
MÓIR

SEA
NÁDAIR
VILLAGE
BRÓNACH
FERNSWORTH
WHITERIDGE
LEVEA

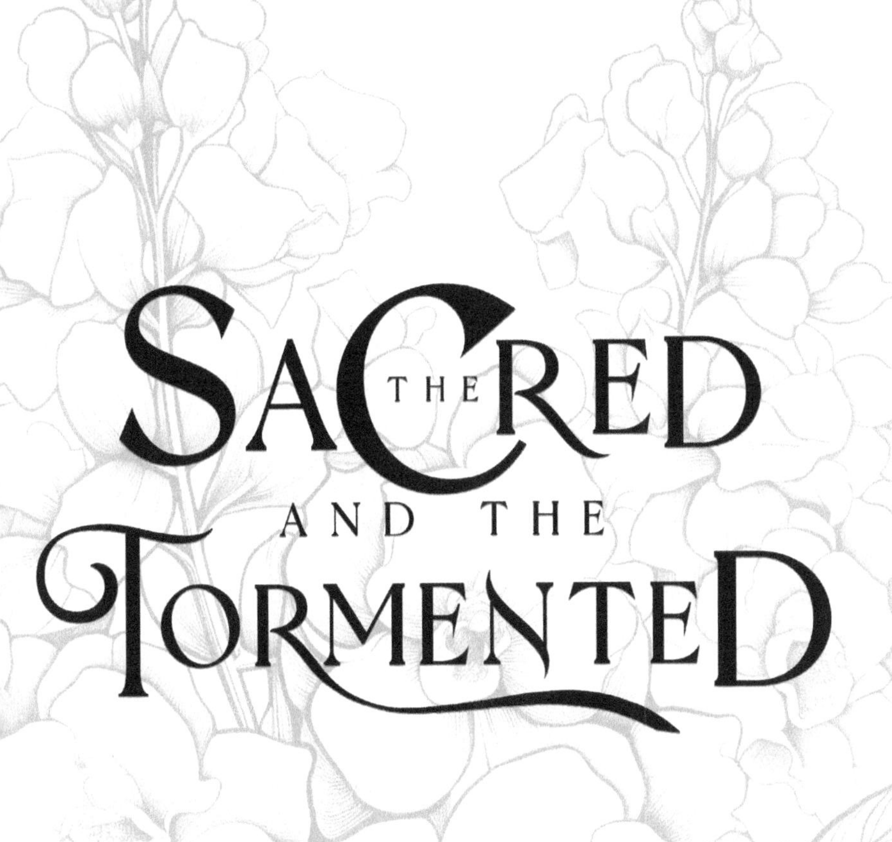

THE SACRED AND THE TORMENTED

J. E. REED

CHAPTER ONE

ARIANNA

A scream shattered the night, tearing through shadow and silence. Arianna bolted up in bed just as the warm body beside hers fled the safety of the silken sheets.

Thunder cracked outside and lightning flashed through the dark curtains, illuminating her mate and the storm circling his body.

He'd retreated to the far wall, bare chest rising and falling in rapid succession. Wild, green eyes scanned the space from top to bottom before his anguished gaze landed on hers.

Landed and didn't settle.

Instead of a refuge for him, Arianna's presence had become a nightmare all its own. Rion hadn't elaborated on all the ways Niall had tormented him, but she'd pieced together the fact that Niall had used her as a focal point in her mate's torture.

Which was exactly why he was staring at her now, uncertain of himself or his reality. She saw the doubt flicker in his gaze. He was questioning everything: her, the room, himself.

Rion might be free of his physical chains, but the damage Niall had inflicted remained. Rion's mother, the High Lady of Nàdair, wasn't faring much better.

Every night. Every single night since he'd escaped Niall's grasp, Rion woke screaming. He couldn't be reasoned with, and though he never struck out, Arianna didn't push her luck by approaching. She knew a caged animal when she saw one. Not that her own fear helped.

Even now, as his magic snaked across the floor, Arianna's pulse pounded in her ears. She didn't want to be afraid, but her body betrayed her.

During the day, Rion was careful around her, keeping his magic and temper in check as best he could. But they were all on edge and she hated every second they couldn't just relax in one another's presence.

They were mates. The relationship between a bonded pair wasn't supposed to be like this.

It was all Niall's fault. Or maybe it was hers for allowing herself to be manipulated. If she'd just paid attention, she might have seen through the illusions. Rion wouldn't have suffered. Ruadhán might not have even fallen.

Her fists clenched. She should have driven that iron blade through Niall's throat, not his stomach.

Rion's heart slowed and his magic settled a fraction. His glazed eyes seemed to focus and Arianna reached for the bond, running a gentle fingertip along the cord that tied them together.

Her mate stiffened, his body locking up all over again.

Their bond had changed. It was stronger, deeper than it'd ever been. Sometimes, Arianna swore she could hear Rion's thoughts. And right now, she could feel the storm inside him as if it were her own.

She knew he could sense her fear, too.

Arianna swallowed hard and rose, the cool air prickling her bare skin as the sheet fell away. She stood before him, vulnerable, just as he was.

Rion's nostrils flared as he scented her, then wrapped his mind around the bond like a cat brushing up against its owner.

Arianna dared a step closer, watching for his retreat.

It didn't come.

She slowly closed the distance separating them, the rain still beating on the rooftop and thunder rumbling through the sky.

Rion just stood there, staring, his eyes half full of hope and half full of fear, likely wondering what he might see next. Maybe someday he'd tell her about those nightmares. Maybe someday they wouldn't haunt him.

Arianna lifted a hand and placed it on his chest, right over his heart, just as she'd done at the cabin. She didn't know if Niall was able to access memories. Maybe he'd tainted all their best moments together and nothing would ever be the same.

"This is real," she whispered in the dark. Lightning flashed through the room again. His brows were drawn together, jaw locked as he studied her. She knew he didn't believe her. She could feel it down the bond. But Rion's lips parted anyway as he looked her over, still seeming to wait for something to happen.

"This is real," Arianna repeated.

Rion clasped her hand, closed his eyes, and pressed his forehead to hers. Arianna rubbed soothing strokes up and down his arms. He'd already put on more weight and his skin had regained its color.

He didn't embrace her. Instead, Rion pressed a kiss to her forehead, then walked beyond her reach. Arianna crossed her arms over her chest and watched as he tugged on yesterday's pants and shirt.

Her heart pulled. "Stay," she whispered. Begged.

Rion froze with one hand on the wooden bed frame. She watched his jaw work, then he slowly shook his head. An ache radiated down their bond. *Please*, it seemed to say.

She relented, then sent down reassurance that she wouldn't hold it against him when he returned. How could she?

Rion fled into the rain outside, closing the door behind him. Arianna padded to the window and watched her mate break into a sprint, ignoring the downpour that soaked through his clothes in seconds. He hadn't even bothered with shoes. He never did this early. Something about the earth against his bare feet seemed to comfort her mate.

He reached the perimeter and turned, moving beyond her line of sight.

Arianna sighed and let the curtains fall back, once again shrouding the room in darkness. She leaned her back against the wall and slid to the floor, wrapping her arms around her knees before resting her head against them.

Every day.

Tears welled in her throat. Every. Single. Day.

She remembered the first night he'd run. She'd feared he wasn't fully awake and that he'd wind up hurting himself or someone else.

He hadn't.

She followed him the second time to be sure. By the third, she simply stood by the window, checking the bond to reassure herself he was still alive.

He never acknowledged her. Never pulled back in comfort and Arianna had eventually just let him be.

A tear slid free.

She knew he wasn't doing it to hurt her. His actions during the day proved his devotion. But her mate was in pain and she couldn't do anything to comfort him.

Twenty-five days.

Twenty-five days since the fall of Ruadhán. Twenty-five days since her sister's disappearance.

Arianna wiped the tears away and pulled herself up. She'd done enough wallowing. She couldn't allow herself to break down again. For Rion's sake and for Ellie's.

Arianna dressed, pulled on a cloak, and marched out into the pouring rain. It battered against her hood, and she pulled the material tighter. Her guards stood to attention, ready to follow their queen anywhere.

They reported to her father and one had likely already run off to tell their High Lord that his daughter was up and moving. Her father never seemed to sleep. Not that she was one to judge. Sleep only seemed attainable in the stolen hours between meetings.

Talon claimed she was pushing herself too hard. Rion said she didn't have to shoulder the responsibilities alone. Arianna briefly wondered what Ellie might say. Her throat tightened and emotion swelled through her chest again. She stamped it down. No more.

A light flickered in the window of a little building down the street that served as their temporary kitchen. Those running it were always up early, preparing breakfast for the masses, the half-breeds included. Arianna refused to let anyone show favoritism, especially where meals were concerned. Between her father's and Saoirse's resources, there were plenty of supplies and more arriving every day.

They were rebuilding, forming a new life one step at a time. She just hoped Niall didn't show up to tear it all down.

Arianna stepped inside and a fresh wave of heat washed over her. Those preparing the breakfast plates welcomed her when she removed her hood. Water pooled at her feet and Arianna grimaced, half wondering if she should grab a towel to clean it up.

She likely wouldn't be the last one trekking water inside, though.

"Good morning, My Lady." A female with a broad smile, full figure, and wild brown curls greeted her from one of the stoves. She set down a large paddle laden with fresh rolls, and Arianna's mouth watered at the scent.

"Morning." Arianna returned.

"I have everything wrapped up and ready to go." The female crossed the room and pulled out two small boxes. She stuffed a few fresh rolls into another before approaching, then hesitated. "Are you sure you don't want someone to carry these for you?"

"Thank you. But I can manage." Arianna took the boxes, feeling the heat from the fresh meals inside. "I appreciate it."

The female bowed her head slightly. "Anything for you." Her smile fell. "Have there been any changes?"

Arianna averted her gaze. "Not really, but Saoirse is hopeful."

The female wiped her hands on her apron. "Perhaps a little taste of home would do her some good. Have Lady Saoirse make a list of her mother's favorite meals. Perhaps I can work something out."

Arianna looked around the room, watching the volunteers flit between pots, stirring and adding ingredients before returning to chop or knead something else.

"I think you have your hands full with enough."

The female waved her off. "Nonsense. If there's something I can do to help, I'd like to. It's not every day a High Lady resides in our presence."

Never mind the fact that Brónach's ambassador, Móirín's High Lord, and their queen were there, too.

Arianna shifted the boxes. "I'll ask."

The female beamed. "Off you go then. We don't want that growing cold."

Arianna pulled her hood up and wrapped her cloak around the boxes, then she darted back outside.

Her guards followed, ever the silent, watchful guardians as she moved through the dirt streets at a brisk pace.

Arianna veered toward the outskirts, squinting through the dark for a sign of her mate in the distance. He never went far, but having him out in the storm still made her uneasy.

A few candles flickered in various windows, but the world was mostly silent, as if the storm were a famous musician that had taken center stage and no one dared to interrupt.

Arianna sloshed through the puddles toward the single house that stood at the end of the short road.

Guards patrolled from a distance, all ready to defend their once lost High Lady. Candles illuminated every window. Saoirse never let them go out. Because the second The High Lady had been safe, she'd nearly lost her mind.

The first time had been violent, with her screaming and kicking and clawing at any who drew near. She'd almost gouged out a male's eye, screaming for Niall to come fight her himself.

Thankfully, Arianna had been able to heal the guard, but as far as Eimear's mind went, there was nothing to be done.

The healers claimed it was a normal result of isolation. They were confident, given enough space and time, the High Lady would make a full recovery. Their words gave Arianna hope for her mate as well.

Arianna padded up the stone stairs on silent feet. She didn't knock and Saoirse came to the door quickly, cracking it open enough for her to slip inside. She knew her father's guards didn't like it, but it was better for everyone if they gave Eimear space.

Arianna's presence never seemed to bother the female. Neither did Zylah's or the healers', so long as they were all female. After the incident with the guards, the only male who ever entered the space was Rion. The little house was a refuge of sorts, at least until they could figure out what to do with her.

Arianna didn't know why she did it, but she'd made a habit of bringing Eimear and Saoirse breakfast. Zylah always brought lunch and dinner, though Zylah never lingered. Arianna still hadn't gotten around to asking about their strained relationship. Not that it was any of her business. There were too many other things that required her attention anyway.

Saoirse and Arianna silently crossed the small living space and entered a second bedroom on the right. Saoirse gently closed the door, then pressed her back against it and sighed.

Arianna set the food on a small table and shrugged out of her cloak. She kept her voice to a hushed whisper. "Long night?"

Saoirse rubbed her temples. "She just fell asleep about an hour ago." Arianna noted the bags under Saoirse's eyes, then followed her gaze to the window. "How is he?"

Arianna plopped into the chair, feeling her own exhaustion wash through her. "He was up early."

The two females had bonded over their loved ones' shared pain. Neither knew what to do aside from being present when they were needed. It never felt like enough.

"When do you think this ends?" Arianna asked.

Saoirse grabbed the kettle from the middle of the table and poured them both a cup before sinking a bag of tea leaves into each.

"When Niall is dead." She handed one to Arianna and Arianna

wrapped her fingers around the warming mug.

"What happens if the High Lord is involved, too?"

"Then we take him out as well."

"Do you think it'll be that simple?"

"Nothing in war is simple."

"Do you think Rion can handle it?"

Saoirse fell silent, eyes flicking to the window. "I think he needs it." Arianna watched her carefully, waiting for her to say more. "When we marched to Ruadhán, both he and our mother were fine. It's this sitting around and waiting that's driving them both insane."

"They're not the only ones."

Saoirse looked back at her, then to her own cup. "Maybe we've waited too long." Her fingers drummed against the side. "We've gathered little to no information and there's no telling if those seeking it have been manipulated by Pádraigín's magic anyway."

"So what do we do now?"

Saoirse shook her head. "Always seeking answers from someone else. I thought I told you to stop that."

"You're an ambassador with far more experience than I have. Call it seeking council."

Saoirse smirked, sipped her tea, and said, "Perhaps you are learning."

She had been, thanks to Saoirse. In the hours before dawn, the female had taken to teaching her all the things that would be required of her as a queen. How to speak, when to listen, and most importantly, when to act.

Arianna had been trying to implement all of them while dealing with the aftermath of Ruadhán's fall. The issues with the slaves. The discourse between half-breeds and the Fae. The increased need for supplies to house and feed the masses. The nobles and their endless demands. Trying to locate her sister. The Dark Fae that were suddenly roaming the land at night.

Arianna sighed and stared down into her cup, watching the leaves that'd fought their way free and now floated on the surface. "Have you decided what you're going to do?"

They'd been discussing The High Lady's relocation for the better part of a week.

"She needs to be back in Nàdair. I think the familiarity will help, but it's getting there that will prove problematic." Because of her nightmares and the fact that Saoirse would have to go with her. "I can have my second remain in my place and give him the authority to make decisions on Brónach's behalf."

"Rion still doesn't want her to go."

"No, Rion just wants to come with us." It was true, he wanted to keep his mother safe. He wanted to keep Arianna safe and at the same time, he wanted to hunt down Niall and rescue Ellie. But he couldn't do it all at the same time.

"I'm sure if you're—" A high-pitched scream jolted Arianna enough that the cup slipped from her hands and shattered all over the wooden floor. Tea went everywhere, splashing up Saoirse's legs, but the female was already out of the room, sprinting for the door across the small living space. Arianna followed.

They found Eimear pressed against the far wall, her eyes wild and teeth bared. She hissed when Saoirse entered the room and Arianna remained in the doorway.

Eimear's heart beat so hard and fast that Arianna wondered if she would pass out again. Eimear's hand went for the iron around her wrist, but instead of ripping it off, as Arianna had seen her do, she spun it in nervous circles. Eimear had commanded Saoirse to put another bracelet around her ankle, one that couldn't be easily removed. Just in case.

"It's me," Saoirse whispered as if she were calming a wild animal. It reminded Arianna of Rion. The fear. The uncertainty. Tears welled to the surface and Arianna had to bite the inside of her cheek to keep them from falling.

Saoirse crept closer and lowered herself to one knee before her mother. She gently took the female's hand and Arianna watched the tension leave Eimear's shoulders.

Then the front door burst open. Arianna stepped aside as Rion swept in, soaked from head to toe. His breath was ragged as he took in the scene. His mother. Saoirse. Her. He rested a gentle hand on Arianna's shoulder, met her gaze, then brushed past and into the room.

Eimear dropped her head into one hand and clenched her other fist, struggling to ground herself to the present.

Arianna's heart swelled, then Rion's arms were around his mother and Eimear desperately clung to both her children, drawing them close.

She understood why Rion was so reluctant to let Eimear travel without him. Sometimes, he was the only one who could bring her back.

Pain lanced through Arianna's chest and she backed away. She wasn't needed here. Not in this moment. Two steps, then she slipped into the rain, letting it wash away her own haunted memories.

CHAPTER TWO

SAOIRSE

The rain let up before sunrise and Eimear left the safety of their little house, opting for some fresh morning air. It was good for her, especially since she spent so much time cooped up, fearing the outside world. Eimear needed to see more than just a set of four walls. She needed to get out around other people. She needed to learn that she wasn't still a captive of that monster.

Saoirse clenched her fists and watched from a nearby hill as her mother played with the village younglings, two of whom never left her side. Kaylee, the young half-breed female who had tended to Eimear while she was imprisoned, and Wylan, the young male who also possessed the ability to see into the future—and the past.

A dozen others circled Eimear, bringing her flowers and handmade offerings. Eimear laughed at their jokes and all the things younglings so innocently told adults.

Eimear claimed it was a special sort of magic to experience life all over again through the eyes of a child.

Saoirse sighed and lowered her head into her hands, rubbing her tired eyes. She'd barely had three hours of sleep over the last two days. She needed rest. And a drink.

Footsteps crunched in the grass, and Saoirse glanced over her shoulder to find the last person she expected to see.

Zylah walked up the slope, her gaze directed toward Eimear and the younglings.

Zylah's attention over the last few weeks wasn't lost on her. It made Saoirse's heart race with hope, no matter how slight. Zylah claimed to hate the royal family for everything they'd done, or rather, hadn't done. That hatred should have extended to Eimear, but for some reason, it didn't—not if the meals and medicines were any indication.

Zylah settled down beside Saoirse but kept her distance. A youngling screamed in delight as they chased another and Eimear clapped her hands in encouragement. Saoirse had missed her mother's smile above all else.

"Today is a good day."

Saoirse only nodded. It *was* a good day. She'd shared a decent breakfast with her mother and Rion. They'd talked about the ways Nàdair had changed over nearly a century and the many things that remained the same. Then they'd discussed their experiences and all the things Eimear had missed. Her mother's eyes had misted, but she'd urged them to continue. She wanted to know everything about her children, down to the smallest detail.

Saoirse supposed she should be thankful that her mother's memories were intact. At least Niall hadn't been able to destroy those. So long as Eimear was calm, like today, she would remember everything they told her. Saoirse just wished she could figure out what changed from day to day to make some better than others.

Eimear had a smile on her face now, but Saoirse knew the darkness wasn't far off. Her mother would revert back to her fearful state soon and Saoirse would likely spend another night watching over her.

"Here." Zylah extended a small bag and Saoirse took it, peering inside to find a few unlabeled vials. "It'll help you both sleep tonight."

Saoirse thought about making a lewd comment regarding what else might help her sleep, but she didn't have the energy for it.

"Thank you," Saoirse said, setting the bag down between them. "But I can't take it. I need to watch her."

"You'll both sleep like the dead. Gods know you need it."

I need you, she wanted to say, but didn't. Not physically, but mentally. Saoirse craved Zylah's presence like one craved water in a desert.

"And I can't just drug my mother."

"Ask her while she's lucid. I'm certain she won't say no."

"And I'm certain she can hear you." Saoirse thought she saw her mother smile, though Eimear didn't turn. She wondered if her mother already suspected what Zylah was. Or perhaps her abilities had already told her, iron or no.

"I can stay tonight. If you'd like."

Saoirse straightened and turned to look at Zylah. The female was entirely serious. "I thought you hated the Fae from Brónach."

Zylah turned away again, her jaw working. "She's suffered far more than anyone should."

Saoirse flexed her fingers, itching to reach out and rest them on Zylah's hand. Anything to convince the female to stay once this was all over.

"I have a condition."

"If you're going to make some comment about—"

"I want to train you."

Zylah sighed. "I've told you already, I'm training with the other half-breeds."

"Then I'll train them, too." She'd worked with Zylah once, before everyone had marched on Ruadhán, but since then the female had declined further training.

Zylah arched a brow. "You'll train half-breeds? That's not beneath you?"

Saoirse *knew* her mother was listening now. "Not anymore." Zylah fell silent again. She shifted her body, then settled, still staring at Eimear and the younglings. "War is at our doorstep," Saoirse said.

"It could happen any day, and if reports are to be believed, we're not just going to be fighting Fae. I just—" Saoirse crossed her legs, leaning forward. "I just want to know you're okay."

"I'm a healer."

"That didn't stop you when we were in Ruadhán. I think your words to Arianna made it clear how much you want to fight."

"So, if I agree to train with you, you'll sleep tonight?"

"If you agree to train with me, I'll sleep whenever I'm commanded."

"Fine. But no lewd comments from you, or I quit."

"Deal."

The pair fell silent as they continued watching the younglings play. If only the games could remain so simple.

CHAPTER THREE

ARIANNA

Arianna stared at the desk and the stacks of papers waiting for her. She'd already visited the infirmary tent for an hour to heal any who needed it. Most were small wounds from training exercises. She always chastised the warriors to be more careful and they'd bow their heads in shame.

She settled into the chair and picked up the first pile. It was the simplest of the bunch, with handwritten requests from the village elders asking for approval of any changes they wanted to make. She honestly didn't know why they needed her input at all.

The next stack was a series of reports that she rarely got to read. Rion usually filled her in. It was everything from attacks on nearby towns to the location of Dark Fae that'd been spotted roaming the roads at night. Then there were the reports of movements from any large forces that seemed like they could be problematic. Thankfully, all those groups were still too far to the north, likely just patrols. She hoped. The other reports regarding decimated villages concerned her more, but her father said it was outside their territory and there wasn't much to be done.

Unseating the High Lord of Pádraigín would do a lot of good, but they had a long road to travel before then.

One report from two nights ago claimed Talon would return today, hopefully with news about her sister. If he came back empty-handed again, she wasn't sure what their next move would be.

They'd been sedentary too long, stuck in a limbo of indecisions.

Her father wanted her to convince the village elders to move to Móirín where they'd be safer and better able to defend the masses. But Levea still had a crowd of refuges outside its border that would need to be brought inside if they hoped to fortify the area. Adding more mouths to feed would only serve to stress the already overpopulated community. She supposed they could scatter them between the various villages across their territory, but that would be unfair to those villages, and she couldn't be in fifty places at once. Not to mention, splitting up friends and comrades didn't seem like the best move when they might be on the brink of war.

Arianna sighed and rubbed her temples. Not to mention the fact that village elders didn't want to move at all. She'd thought about leaving, just to make this place less of a target, but if she chose to move silently, as everyone would advise, then Niall would still think her here, which would defeat the entire purpose.

Arianna picked up another handwritten request. A group of nobles was asking for housing to be built on the far side of the village, outside the wall, followed by another wall to be erected around them. They'd been asking for the same thing for weeks, but Arianna knew the real reason. They wanted to be separated from the half-breeds. Her father said it might be best to let them have what they wanted in order to keep the peace. Just temporarily. But if she gave in to the segregation now, then it would continue and thrive until they were right back to where they started.

There'd only been a few small skirmishes between the nobles and half-breeds, but what would she do if it escalated? What would happen if someone was killed like the noble in Ruadhán? Not that he hadn't deserved it.

She set the note aside unanswered and moved on to the next. A request for where to place farmland. Right, because clearly *she* was the expert. She didn't know the first thing—a shrill alarm cut through the mid-morning bustle.

Arianna's heart leapt into her throat, but she remained still, listening for another. It didn't come.

One alarm. That meant an unfamiliar group had been spotted approaching the gate.

Arianna let the paper fall from her hands and marched outside. Her guards had their weapons drawn. People had paused everything and were staring toward the northern gate, wondering if it was just a passing traveler or someone more sinister.

Many watched her and she could scent the fear floating through the air. They had little more than a wooden fence as a means of defense. Something they desperately needed to change. Perhaps she could work with Rion on creating a stone wall around the village instead, though they'd also have to teach the villagers how to properly man it in the event of a siege.

Arianna's magic sparked at her fingertips, already creating a trail of frost in her wake as she marched toward the edge of the village. She'd taken one step up the stairs when she felt her mate beside her, his magic mingling with her own.

Her heart skipped a beat, then their eyes met. For reasons she couldn't explain, her magic quelled her fear. So long as the beast lurking in her veins was awake, she could tolerate the presence of Rion's magic. It practically purred in her mate's presence, drawing him closer. His magic answered in kind.

Rion allowed her to walk in front of him. The guards parted, and she peered over the edge, only to find a lone figure walking with a cloak obscuring their face and hands held up in surrender.

Alone. Why in the gods' name would anyone be traveling alone right now? The factions were in an uproar and the entire continent was on the brink of civil war. Then there were the Dark Fae themselves. Creatures they hadn't even been able to name, let alone understand how to deal with.

Her heart jumped with the possibility of Niall, or worse, the High Lord of Pádraigín himself. Both could likely level this place in an instant. But if they'd planned to attack, they wouldn't announce themselves. Unless they just wanted her.

The wind shifted and Arianna scented the air, her shoulders stiffening when she found Pádraigín's magic floating through the breeze.

No, no, they weren't ready.

The warriors beside her drew their weapons and magic tore from their bodies, all preparing for a fight.

Arianna glanced behind her briefly, wondering how fast they could evacuate the villagers into the underground safe houses. Were the supplies ready? Could they get to them fast enough? Would it even matter in the end?

She turned back right as the figure pulled their hood down and everything in Arianna's body relaxed a fraction.

Gavin.

But Gavin was—she didn't have time to react as a fierce snarl ripped from Rion's throat. Then he was moving. The earth came up to surround his body, rocks floating in all sizes and shapes as he closed in on the male faster than she'd ever seen him move.

Anger flooded the tiny room containing the bond and Gavin stepped back, fear plainly written across his face as The Demon of Alastríona barreled toward him.

Gavin stepped back and Arianna had the sinking feeling that Rion wouldn't show the male any mercy.

Gavin had disappeared the same night Ellie had gone missing. Their only conclusion had been that Gavin helped Niall escape, or, in the best-case scenario, was forced to go back with him. But Gavin could lie. He'd admitted it himself. There was the possibility that Gavin had never been on their side to begin with. Regardless of his loyalty, he'd know whether Niall had Ellie.

Arianna yanked on the bond hard enough that she saw Rion falter. It wasn't a movement anyone else might have noticed, but she saw the way his magic jerked all the same.

Don't kill him yet, she tried to convey.

Rion's fist collided with the side of Gavin's face and a resounding crack echoed across the field, followed by Gavin's howl of pain. He tried to fall to his knees, but Rion grabbed him by the collar of his shirt and lifted him up, slamming another fist into the male's torso.

No one dared intervene, not even her, though she wasn't sure she wanted to. If Gavin had helped Niall escape—if he were the reason Ellie was taken—she might very well kill him herself.

Rion struck him again and Gavin fell to the ground, scrambling backward away from The Demon, his face pouring blood. He held one hand up, begging Rion to listen.

Rion growled in response and made to lunge for Gavin again, but ice tore across the ground at Gavin's feet. Rion jumped back, his magic drawing closer around his body as he searched for the threat.

Then Arianna saw Talon jogging across the field. His clothes were torn around his legs and left arm. Blood stained the fabric. Even so, her friend kept moving until he stood between Rion and Gavin.

Arianna's heart tightened all over again as she remembered the last time Rion and Talon had been at one another's throats. She placed one hand on the edge of the wooden fence, prepared to leap over the edge in order to separate them.

They stared at one another, then Talon turned toward the male on the ground. Gavin almost looked relieved, then Talon planted his boot in the male's face.

FOR THE briefest of moments, Talon feared Rion might outright kill Gavin, but he should have known the male was more calculating than that.

Gavin might very well be the only one able to tell them where Ellie was being held.

Talon had looked around for Arianna and was surprised to find her standing at the top of the wooden wall, looking down on them. She'd given Talon the briefest of nods and his chest swelled with the trust. She'd always trusted him, but he'd been failing her at every turn. To know he might finally be able to bring her some good news was a relief.

Rion grabbed Gavin by the back of his neck, ignoring the male's pleas for mercy. This *was* mercy as far as Talon was concerned.

Talon turned to the warriors in his unit and gave them the signal to freshen up. His second would inform Avalon of their findings, which amounted to pretty much nothing, at least where Ellie was concerned, but there were other things Avalon needed to know about. Like the amassing Dark Fae and all the destruction they'd caused. And where they were likely headed.

Arianna was already gone by the time he looked back, likely preparing herself to tend to the warriors in his unit. There was only one who could use her help. The other two had been lost on the way home, bleeding out long before their arrival.

Rion was a brewing storm the likes of which Talon hadn't seen since they'd fought in Levea. He followed in silence, almost relishing in the fear pouring from Gavin as they moved away from the village. If the male had hoped to plead his case before Arianna, he'd been sorely mistaken.

When they were far enough away that a wandering villager wouldn't overhear their conversation, Rion slammed the young male's back against a flat rock and stood with his hands at his sides, fists clenching and unclenching.

The old Rion might have very well already taken off a leg, Talon had seen his methods before. But again, he was a calculated male and likely thinking about the possibility that Gavin might have to lead them to Ellie.

But if Gavin proved useless, well, Talon wouldn't be hanging around to find out what Rion had in store for him.

A traitor. That's exactly what Gavin was to them now. He might have helped everyone escape Ruadhán, but if he were involved with

Niall, there was no sparing him.

"Where is Ellie?" Rion growled.

Gavin cowered on the ground, trying to staunch the blood gushing from his broken nose. "In Ashling." Tears rolled down the male's cheeks and Talon wondered if he'd ever been struck before.

"With Niall?" Rion spat the name.

Gavin did a poor job of shaking his head. He gasped for air through the pain. "Worse: she's with the High Lord."

Talon's stomach dropped. He'd hoped she'd escaped the High Lord's notice, but it had been a fool's hope from the start.

"Why are you here?" Rion demanded. Gavin's next answer would likely seal his fate.

"I-I was branded a traitor. The warriors who saw me leave with Evelyn and the half-bred reported to Niall. He put a warrant out for my arrest."

Talon crossed his arms. "So you turned tail and ran? How heroic."

"I came for help," Gavin sneered, showing the first real sign of aggression. He regretted it immediately when Rion's boot collided with his face. "Why do you keep hitting me?" Gavin shouted. "I haven't done anything wrong!"

Rion grabbed the front of Gavin's tunic and slammed him against the rock again. "You left with Niall, who conveniently escaped and took Ellie with him. You expect me to believe it was a coincidence?"

"They had Evelyn, what was I supposed to do? I couldn't just leave her."

"You're here now," Talon said, his own anger threatening to boil over. A tinge of fear accompanied it, wondering if the reason Gavin had left—

"Because I need your help. If you'd stop punishing me for a second, I could explain."

"Explain faster," Talon warned. "Before you're not able to talk at all."

Gavin eyed the two males, then began talking as fast as Talon had ever heard anyone speak.

"Niall was already out of his bonds when I brought the civilians back from Ruadhán. He was hurt, thanks to Arianna. He said we needed to get back to Ashling as quickly as possible. I couldn't refuse, you know how strong he is." Gavin glanced between them and sat up slowly, his back against the wall. He looked away.

"That's when I saw Evelyn in chains. Niall already knew she was my mate. I almost slipped up. Almost ran and begged him to let her go. But somehow he didn't know about my betrayal yet. Or maybe he thought I was doing everything for his benefit. I don't know. I stayed in control and played the part he wanted to see. I thought that maybe I could unlock her bonds on the road, but Niall kept her unconscious the whole time. The half-breed was instructed to care for her. I didn't dare show that I might be concerned lest Niall feel my loyalty was threatened. So I waited, but there was never a good time and Niall had her under his magic. He'd know if I moved her and then we'd both be in chains.

"Then we got to Ashling. I thought he'd take her to the dungeons, but she went right to the High Lord. Even her cell was too closely guarded for me to break her free." Rion had turned a shade paler. "If you thought Niall was bad, he's nothing compared to the High Lord." Gavin was shaking now. "I promised her I'd find help."

"You talked to her?" Talon asked.

Gavin nodded.

"What did she say?"

"To rot in the deepest pit of hell."

Talon couldn't stop the small smile that spread across his face. "Well, I'd say she's hanging in there."

"She's not." Talon's smile fell. "He—he's doing things to her."

"What things?" Rion growled. Talon's stomach turned sour.

Gavin tapped his head. "He's messing with her mind. She's not right. She's different. You have to get to her before—"

Thunder rumbled overhead and Talon glanced at the cloudy sky before he scented a familiar magic. He turned slightly to see shards of ice crackling around the High Lord of Móirín as the male marched toward them.

The very air pressure seemed to shift, reminding Talon of Arianna's magic when she lost control. The first raindrops started to fall and Talon stepped to the side.

Avalon's guards marched at his side, each with fury written across their faces. Ellie was their future High Lady. She'd known each of their names by heart and had made a point to get to know their families, too.

If Gavin thought Rion was the worst of them, he was sorely mistaken. Talon gave Gavin a sympathetic look. "Good luck."

Gavin visibly paled as the Avalon closed the distance. He was only a few feet away when he demanded in a menacing tone, "Where is my daughter?"

CHAPTER FOUR

ARIANNA

Arianna healed the cuts and bruises across Gavin's body, then reset a broken arm and put three fractured ribs back in one piece.

She'd given all three males a harsh look when they'd half dragged Gavin through the gate, bloody and screaming as if the trio still had plans to put an end to him. None bothered to mention they were bringing him to her.

He'd nearly sighed in relief, even after Rion had clamped an iron bracelet around his wrist. She knew if it weren't for her past, it would have been a shackle instead.

Arianna reset his nose and he yelped. It wasn't that she was being particularly cruel, but Arianna wasn't making an extra effort to be gentle either.

Rion, her father, and Talon had informed her of everything. Gavin hadn't betrayed them and Niall didn't have her little sister. The High Lord did.

Her blood ran cold at the thought. Ellie was deep in enemy territory with only Kirian as her ally. Gavin claimed the half-breed had still been alive when he'd left. Given that Gavin was wearing iron, Arianna supposed she didn't have to wonder if was lying.

But Ellie was hurting and that made her heart ache even more.

"You'll help us break in?" Talon repeated for the third time.

Gavin let out an exasperated sigh. "For the last time, yes. I want her out of there just as much as you do." Arianna couldn't tell if the reasons were purely selfish or if he actually cared about her little sister. The two barely knew one another and Ellie had called him a pompous ass.

Avalon studied the map hanging on the wall. "If what you claim is true, then we don't even have an accurate map to know how to navigate the terrain."

"I know the map. I can point out the landmarks."

Avalon raised a brow at him and Gavin swallowed. Apparently her father had been the one to break his bones, which surprised her considering Rion had gotten a hold of him first.

"I'm Niall's nephew, remember? Do you really think he'd let me anywhere near him if I were uneducated?"

"I'm wondering why he'd trust you with a true map of Ashling's location at all."

"Everyone in Ashling knows the truth. It's part of the pride they carry as a city, but it's also the reason so many aren't allowed to leave."

"Meaning many aren't allowed in either."

Gavin's lips stretched into a thin line and her heart sped.

It wasn't just that Ellie was in the middle of enemy territory. According to Gavin, everything they knew about Pádraigín's main city was a lie—another fabrication from the High Lord.

Instead of a small port city that traded with the humans for their own kind, an abomination Arianna still couldn't comprehend, Ashling was actually a large, thriving city full of guards that wielded iron weapons.

Arianna glanced at her mate. He and Eimear had suffered in the hands of Niall. A seven hundred-year-old male with powers beyond anything she'd ever seen. But his father was far older, and as a result, more powerful. He was a male who'd manipulated their entire history and he was willing to tear the land apart to get what he wanted. He'd killed countless innocents.

And he had her sister.

"What now?" she asked the question everyone seemed to be sitting on.

"We organize a team to infiltrate and Gavin will be our guide," Rion said. She noted the spark in his gaze. An anger she knew all too well.

"I'll join you," Talon said. To her surprise, Rion nodded in agreement. The two had been spending a lot of time together since Ruadhán. She hadn't been privy to their conversations, but their relationship had definitely taken a positive shift.

"As reluctant as I am to do it, I'll remain here and see to the village's care." Avalon turned to Rion. "And I'll make sure your mother gets back to Nàdair safely. We might have to move her to Levea first, given her condition, but she'll be well cared for. As will Saoirse."

"Thank you." Silence fell over the space as the two males stared at one another. Two who might have been allies had their worlds not been turned upside down.

"I'm going with you." They all knew she wasn't speaking to her father.

Avalon sighed. "Arianna, you're needed here."

"For what? To tell people how to do things they already know how to do? To play the part of a pretty queen so everyone else can feel better?"

"You're a symbol to the people. Don't underestimate that."

Arianna stood. "Ellie has been gone for three weeks."

"And there's nothing you're going to be able to do that Talon, Rion, and an experienced team won't be able to accomplish." She cringed at the word experienced, knowing full well she'd barely scratched the surface of qualifying to move with an organized team.

"I found Rion," she challenged.

"Because you are mates. The bond led you to him."

"Ellie is my sister—"

"And she's my daughter." Arianna fell silent and watched her father bite his tongue, struggling to control his anger. His voice was softer when he spoke again. "Don't you think I want to join them as well? Don't you think I'm worried sick, wondering what that evil bastard is doing to my youngest daughter?" Arianna didn't respond. "But I'm a High Lord and I know where I'm needed. You're the queen of this continent and you're needed here as well. A war isn't won from a single battle. We need to strategize and prepare for the conflicts to come."

Again, Arianna didn't speak. She bit the inside of her cheek, feeling the familiar emotions well up within her. Trapped. Caged. Useless.

Avalon ran a hand through his hair and it was the most frustration she'd seen in him these last few weeks. Her father's face had turned haggard and large bags hung beneath his eyes. They weren't the only ones pushing themselves hard.

"I'm going to speak with the village elders again. I'll threaten to pull my warriors out if I have to, but we need to relocate everyone to Levea. It's not safe here anymore."

"Have there been more attacks?" she asked.

Avalon shook his head. "Don't worry about it right now. Take the day to yourself. We'll regroup in the morning."

No one moved and it took Arianna a moment to realize her father was waiting for her approval. Right. She still wasn't used to that.

"Okay."

Avalon nodded once, glared at Gavin, then stormed across the room and let the door click shut behind him.

Silence filled the space. Gavin shifted and she could sense him wanting to speak, yet holding back.

"So, when do we leave?" Talon asked.

Arianna's head shot up. "What?"

Talon shrugged. "You said it yourself, you're useless here."

She looked between Talon and Rion, but both males just stared at her.

"What do we tell my father?"

Talon shrugged again. "Don't tell him anything, or leave a note if you prefer. We can pack and leave tonight. Worst-case scenario, we come back empty-handed."

"Or don't come back at all," Gavin added.

All three of them glared at the male and he shrank away. Arianna looked between Talon and Rion again before shaking her head, a smirk creeping to her lips. "And here I thought you were the reasonable one among us."

"I've been reasonable long enough. Besides, I have to take some of the responsibility of mischief maker without Ellie to fill the role."

"And you," Arianna addressed her mate, "you're okay with me going?"

"Have I ever held you back?"

No. No he hadn't. Because he'd met her in the middle of a war camp when she'd already been fighting for her life. He'd seen her take down seasoned warriors despite her inexperience. And he'd stood with her against Ruadhán.

"Are we going alone?" she asked.

"I'll gather a unit of my warriors, and I'm certain Saoirse will spare a few for the cause."

"My sister will stay to care for our mother."

"What about Raevina?"

Talon bristled at the name. "Do you want her to come with us?"

"Do you?"

"She's strong," Rion reasoned. "But can she be trusted not to run to your father?"

"I don't think Raevina is the reasonable type, either." She turned back to Talon. "But if you'd rather not—"

"I'll ask her tonight."

Arianna nodded. She wanted to ask more questions, but didn't quite feel it was her place to do so. Talon would talk when he was ready. Perhaps on their journey to Ashling if Raevina decided not to accompany them, which wasn't likely.

"Don't I get a say in this?" Gavin asked.

"No," they all replied in unison.

"Tonight then?" Arianna clarified, feeling a jolt of excitement spark through her.

"I'll gather the supplies," Talon said. "Rion can sneak us out underground and we'll be long gone before anyone becomes the wiser."

Arianna glanced at the stack of paperwork she still hadn't sifted through. "Do you think they'll be alright?"

"Avalon will manage. If all goes well, we'll be back with Ellie to help you sort through what you left behind."

"And if it doesn't?"

If they all just ended up captured … or worse.

"Then we take Niall and the High Lord down with us," Rion finished.

ARIANNA CONTINUED to work through the paperwork she deemed important. She answered questions regarding the slaves and wrote up an entire paper on how she wished for them to be treated. With her gone, her father would be responsible for keeping their affairs in order. She wasn't sure if a document would hold much merit, but she hoped the nobles would respect it, at least.

Avalon would likely send out teams to search for her, that was almost a given. If they caught up, she supposed she'd give them a choice to either return to her father with a message, or join her in their mission and rescue their future High Lady. Arianna already knew which option the warriors of Móirín would choose.

A light breeze shifted papers on the desk and Arianna took the moment to breathe in the fresh air. She kept the window open as much as possible, just to get a little piece of the outside world while she worked.

Arianna could almost feel a growing storm outside, as if the world were charged and ready to shake the very foundations of Alastríona. She wondered if the feeling had something to do with her magic, volatile as it was. Her father regularly had his warriors accompany her outside the village just so she could release it, otherwise it spilled out of its own accord. Even now she could feel it tingling at the edges of her skin, begging for release.

She still didn't understand why her body wouldn't just shift. Maybe it was waiting for something. The elders were just as baffled. With everything she'd faced, her body should have given itself over. But no one really knew how her magic worked either, given that the previous Divine had destroyed the knowledge.

Arianna thought back to the statue still seated in the rubble of Ruadhán. Some of the fanatics had flocked to the area, the nobles included, though they'd been more than disturbed to find a statue of someone with Rion's magic beside it. It made them question everything they'd been taught.

Some of them, anyway.

Others were worshiping the gods as they'd not seen in centuries. They were the ones who claimed her as their queen, but they'd also grown aggressive with their teachings, going so far as to publicly execute any who spoke out against her.

A war was slowly forming between the rebel factions and the religious zealots.

And that was just one of their current problems.

She'd almost been glad to hear the religious leaders were freeing humans and half-breeds as she'd demanded until she'd also learned that they were beheading those who still owned slaves despite her decree.

Arianna rubbed her temples. "How has everything gotten so out of hand?"

Rion peered up over the document in his hand. "You're here to reshape the world."

"I didn't think that meant it needed to break first."

"The world has been broken for a long time. You're just yanking on the jagged edges and people are getting cut."

"Do you think it'll all be worth it in the end? The death?"

Rion looked away. "Honestly, I can't say." He leafed through another paper, then set it on the desk in a pile they were leaving for her father to deal with.

Raevina burst into the room then, clad from head to toe in battle leathers. Knives were strung across her body in a menacing display.

Those who were her most trusted warriors waited outside. Rion stood to attention, his body shifting slightly to stand before Arianna. She scented his magic trying to form, but knew he held it back for her sake.

"What's wrong?" Arianna asked. The female rarely sought her out for anything. She usually just sent a messenger.

Raevina had taken on the role as her interrogator and head of security. She made sure regiments followed a strict rotation and that all parties were ready in the event that Niall or all of Pádraigín retaliated.

Raevina held up an envelope and Arianna almost groaned. She was sick of paperwork and couldn't wait to get out of here. "My father sent word."

Arianna straightened. Her father. The High Lord of Fiadh.

"Is he sending aid?" Talon asked, marching in right behind her. Arianna wondered if they'd had a chance to talk yet. Maybe he'd been following her, looking for an opportunity before she walked in.

Arianna refocused. Her father had sent word to Alec in Nàdair and the High Lord of Fiadh. Alec had responded immediately, likely because Saoirse was with them. But they hadn't heard from Fiadh and her father's council feared he might have sided with Pádraigín.

Raevina slowly shook her head and Arianna's heart fell. "What does he want then?" she dared to ask.

"Me," Raevina rolled her eyes. "He says he's grown impatient with my failures and demands I return to Púróg at once." Right, because Raevina had been sent to assassinate her. A fact Rion certainly hadn't forgotten.

"Will you?" Rion asked, his tone a bit more aggressive than Arianna thought necessary. She scented another wave of his magic and her heart rate accelerated.

Raevina scoffed and met Rion's glare with a sneer of her own.

One that Arianna was certain made other Fae retreat. "I serve my queen. I go where she commands." Her attention returned to Arianna. "He also says he won't assist in anything involving the false monarch, that his boarders are closed, and lethal force will be used if anyone attempts to cross them."

"Did he mention anything about the Dark Fae?"

Raevina's face shifted at that. "We already had issues with the Dark Fae before I came. It's increased in the last few years, so much so that we can't even venture to the mountain's peaks for fear of them picking us off."

"Do you think they escaped the transports?" Arianna asked. Rion had filled them in on Ellie's findings about the Dark Fae being moved between the strait that bordered Fiadh's western coast.

Raevina shrugged. "Now that I know about them, I'd venture to say he likely approved their release to roam the lands. He made it forbidden to kill them."

"That confirms it then. He's working with Pádraigín."

"Is. Was. Hard to say."

"Either way," Rion said. "They're an enemy now."

"Which means the continent is split right down the middle."

"We've always been the stronger two nations," Saoirse said, stepping inside, causing Arianna to start. Rion moved closer and wrapped a reassuring hand around her shoulders. Were they all stalking one another today?

"I beg to differ," Raevina said.

"I'm being objective, not offensive," Saoirse countered. "We have greater numbers, land, and resources."

"You don't know what my father has been cultivating in the shadows."

Saoirse's face turned a shade paler. "You have more weavers."

"More than we've ever had in the history of our people."

"He's kept them hidden?"

Raevina nodded, her expression almost smug. "My father knows there are spies in his midst. He's arrogant, but not a fool, much to our disadvantage." She turned to Arianna. "The attack on Levea wasn't a one-time deal and had nothing to do with my brother trying to start a revolution. It was a test of Levea's defenses."

"A successful test," Talon said.

"Do you think he'll strike soon?" Arianna asked. There were still so many refugees on the outskirts of Levea.

Raevina shrugged. "Perhaps. With the fall of the royal city and Avalon away, it would be the perfect opportunity. I'd warrant a guess that my father wants me to lead the attack on the city myself. To test my loyalty."

"If you don't return, he might retaliate against this village just to make a point," Rion said.

Raevina's face turned grim. "I have no doubt. He'd sooner see me dead than risk my betrayal."

"Can you send a letter and buy us time?"

She shrugged. "I can try, but the Fae in Fiadh don't … delay. It would take me two days to travel back. If I don't arrive in that time frame, it's likely that he'll move."

Niall, the Dark Fae, the factions, and now Fiadh. "We're too vulnerable here," Arianna said.

Rion gave her arm a reassuring squeeze. "You should call another meeting with the elders. They might listen to you this time if you fill them in on the situation."

Arianna shook her head. "I've tried. Even with the threat of the Dark Fae, they refuse to budge."

"Try again," Raevina said. "The Dark Fae still seem like a myth to most. An army from Fiadh is a real threat. And I assure you, my father will come."

"Maybe we should consider sending you back," Rion said.

Talon's head snapped toward him, but Arianna replied before her friend could. "He'd punish you, wouldn't he?"

Raevina grimaced. "It wouldn't be anything I've not faced before and certainly not permanent. But yes, he would."

Arianna saw Talon's fist clench at his side, then she shook her head. "I won't send you back to endure that." She squared her shoulders. "I'll speak to the village elders again, see what comes from that first." Her heart was pounding. She'd thought they would be leaving to find her sister tonight, but if Fiadh was marching on them—

Her father entered next and paused on the threshold. His gaze roamed to her first and the way her arms were crossed with Rion's hand holding her close. Then it drifted to Talon, then Saoirse, and finally Raevina. She grimaced at what this looked like. A meeting he'd been excluded from.

Avalon maintained his composure and cleared his throat. "We have a problem."

Arianna sighed. "Tell me something I don't know."

Her father ignored the comment and unrolled the map in his hands, laying it out across the desk before her, heedless of the important papers beneath.

Everyone moved in to examine the circles drawn across the map. Circles that followed a path traveling south, right toward them.

"Attacks?" Rion asked.

Avalon nodded. "Messengers just arrived a few minutes ago. The villages were destroyed. There's nothing left." No one spoke. "The Dark Fae have … organized."

"What do you mean?" Saoirse asked.

Avalon handed her a document that Arianna could only assume was the reports mentioned. "They're moving together. As a unit."

"How is that possible? Wouldn't they just kill one another?" Raevina said.

"We can worry about the how's later. If they keep moving at the same speed, they'll be here tonight."

"Tonight?" Saoirse said, her face draining of color entirely.

"You're sure?" Raevina asked.

Avalon nodded again.

"Why haven't we spotted them before now?" Saoirse asked.

"Because they're moving at night and any who have come across them paid the price for it. They don't leave much behind."

"But where are they hiding?" Saoirse gestured to the documents in her hands. "Someone would have noticed a horde this size moving across the land."

"Underground," Avalon said. "They found caves and claw marks, along with anything the creatures left behind. One of the messengers barely escaped and she's beside herself."

Arianna glanced outside to the sun. It was still high noon, but even so, that only left them half a day to prepare. They wouldn't have enough time to evacuate the citizens, and the wooden wall wouldn't do much to protect them from hordes of monsters.

There were younglings, elderly, and humans who couldn't defend themselves against such creatures.

"Do your messengers believe Niall is with them?" Rion asked, his voice laced with venom. If the Dark Fae had been organized, then he might have used his magic to—

"No." Relief flew through Arianna. "My reports say he hasn't left Ashling."

"And you believe those reports?" Raevina asked.

"I do." There was no malice between them, just two leaders sorting through the little information they had.

"This is revenge, isn't it?" Arianna asked.

"Only the beginning of it," Avalon answered. They all stared at the circles along the map for a moment, then her father straightened. "Raevina, Talon, Saoirse, organize your forces and get them into position. Arianna," she startled at the commanding tone in his voice. "Find your half-breed healer and inform her of the situation. Have her get beds prepared in the underground safe houses and have her assistants start preparing bandages and medicine."

Avalon let the map fold in on itself. "I'll inform the village head."

No one argued. They nodded, then filed out, running in different directions to prepare.

This was really happening.

Avalon turned to Rion once they were alone. "See what you can do about delaying them."

Arianna's magic stirred beneath her skin as the full weight of what was about to happen settled over her. They were under attack. The Dark Fae were coming. And she wasn't sure if anyone was truly prepared to face them.

Chapter Five

Arianna

Arianna stood atop the wooden curtain wall that circled the village, her mate at her side. Silence enveloped the space as they watched the sun slowly disappear below the horizon. Shadows from the trees stretched toward them like eerie, clawed fingertips and the sun cast hues of pink and orange through the clouds as if offering one final glimmer of hope before darkness descended.

The wood groaned beneath her feet as Arianna shifted her weight. She loosed a breath. Her magic pulsed beneath her skin, eager and restless.

That magic was exactly why she wasn't below ground with Zylah right now. It craved release and healing wouldn't even begin to scratch the surface.

Everyone close to her knew how powerful her magic had become and none shied away from having her on the front line. Well, aside from her father, but he'd relented with the knowledge that Rion would remain at her side. Avalon knew her mate would protect her at any cost— not that she'd ever leave him to fight alone.

None of them had anticipated a battle like this. They had expected Niall to retaliate eventually, but the realization that monsters from legend were marching straight for them was almost unbelievable. Some had even scoffed, claiming the witnesses were simply being influenced by Pádraigín's magic.

She wished that were the case, but the reports said otherwise and those grieving lost loved ones said even more.

Arianna clenched and unclenched her fists, trying to ease the stiffness in her joints. The wooden planks beneath her feet began to freeze over and Arianna could see her breath in the warm air. It felt as though ice were forming in her veins, waiting to pounce like a predator.

She hoped it would be enough.

The last sliver of sunlight disappeared and a hushed silence fell over the vicinity. No lights burned. They were shrouded in complete darkness; their first line of defense.

Those from Pádraigín who'd sworn their loyalty to her were shielding them from view, hoping to avoid a confrontation altogether. It was a fool's hope, perhaps, but one they had to try.

Arianna listened closely as the Fae, humans, and half-breeds surrounding her drew their weapons. They kept their magic at bay, conserving their energy until Rion and the other commanders gave the signal. If they all survived to see the sun rise, then they'd flee to Móirín. But they had to make it until then first.

When Arianna had informed Zylah about their situation, the female had visibly paled. Arianna had watched a myriad of questions play through her friend's eyes before Zylah had collected herself and set to work.

The female had come so far since her captivity in Rion's camp. She'd been spotted in Ruadhán's library, reading everything available while also seeing to her duties with the former slaves.

She was equal parts healer and half-breed representative. Arianna was willing to bet the female had learned even more since Ruadhán's destruction.

Ruadhán. The silken sheets and fancy dinners all felt like a lifetime ago. Survival was the only thing that mattered now. Again. It was always about survival. For her. For her family and friends. For the innocents who looked up to her.

Arianna glanced down the line, studying those preparing for the inevitable conflict. Many exchanged uneasy glances with their comrades while others stood with their hands gripping their weapons.

She wondered how many had actually seen battle and how many more wouldn't live to see another.

Talon stood several yards away and she could just make out his form in the fading light. His gaze was locked on the landscape, eyes searching for any signs of the dark creatures said to be coming for them.

Though Arianna couldn't see the female, she knew Raevina stood on the western side with her own warriors. Avalon had taken the eastern side, and they'd stationed the humans and half-breeds willing to fight at various intervals throughout.

Teams stood just inside the wall as well, ready to take on anything that slipped over or through. The archers were ready. The warriors, too.

Here they were again, the four nations all working together alongside humans and half-breeds.

All because of her. Or so everyone claimed. But if it really came down to it, wouldn't they all stand together anyway? Surely pride wouldn't prevent them from protecting their families?

Then again, they wouldn't even be here if it weren't for her. She was reshaping the world, sure, but she was also the cause of so much conflict. And she had no idea how to sort through it all.

Arianna kept her voice low as she leaned toward her mate. "You set the traps?"

"Several." Rion watched the horizon just as intently as Talon. "There are trenches and pits. It'll buy us time."

"But won't stop them."

"No, I doubt anything would stop them entirely."

Arianna stared at the giant earthen wall Rion had erected thirty yards ahead. It circled the entire village, acting as a second curtain wall.

Brónach's forces had wrapped the entire thing in thorny vines and poisonous plants.

The children, elderly, and those unable to fight had been stationed underground with Zylah. Arianna knew her friend would force every able-bodied person to assist her when the time came. Even the children wouldn't be spared from witnessing the devastations of war. There was no way to separate them while also keeping them safe.

Saoirse had opted to guard the door to the underground safe house. She'd refused to leave Zylah's side and no one had reprimanded her for it. They needed someone powerful just in case things took a turn for the worst.

"Do you really think the numbers are right?"

Rion's jaw worked. "I doubt your father's warriors were exaggerating."

Her voice lowered enough that only Rion would be able to hear. "What if Niall *is* with them? He knows where we are, if his intention is to eliminate us—"

"We won't lose," Rion said simply. "If Niall is here, then I'll deal with him myself." Arianna studied the resolve in his gaze, then felt his determination flood their bond. It fueled her own and she returned her attention back to the dark horizon.

"Just promise me you won't face him alone."

"I won't leave you," Rion assured, and her heart swelled. They were doing this together. If they lived, it would be at one another's sides. If they died, it would be in each other's arms.

An hour passed, dragging by so slowly, it was as if time himself were mocking them. Some relaxed and leaned against the wooden railing, while others kept their eyes glued to the outskirts.

Another hour drifted by. Arianna slid down the wall and watched over and over as frost coated her hands, only to melt away again.

Rion never moved.

He was like a statue. A guardian that stood vigil over the village below.

Something shifted. She couldn't explain exactly what. It was in the air. Like the tense moments before a thunderstorm.

Arianna hardly dared to breathe, straining to listen.

Silence.

Silence.

There.

The sound was so faint at first. Nothing more than the rustling of grass in the wind.

Arianna stood and focused on the horizon once again.

Something drew closer, and a strange noise kept repeating itself, over and over. She heard the wind shift, moving rapidly. Beating.

Her heart plummeted. Warriors around her shifted uneasily on their feet.

Wings. Massive bat-like wings were moving against the dark sky, heading straight for them. Arianna glanced sidelong at Rion, but if he were worried, he showed no signs of it. No increased heartbeat. No shift in stance. Just a general assessing the threat before him.

Arianna waited, counting the seconds until their bodies came into view.

Humanoid. Somewhat, at least. Their skin had a strange hue, slick and dark like oil. Claws extended from their fingers and bird-like talons curled from where their toes should have been.

The Dark Fae moving along the ground were slower, though from the sound of thunderous feet, she could tell they were itching to catch up to their airborne brethren. Likely so they wouldn't miss a meal.

Arianna shuddered and watched their advance. They weren't veering away, which either meant they could smell them or Niall had somehow commanded the vile creatures to do his bidding.

Heartbeats spiked and pressure built in the air, magic ready to unleash itself into the world. She clenched her own fists, feeling the beast writhe beneath her skin.

"Steady," Rion's deep voice commanded those around him. It settled her somehow. It settled the others, too.

He was a general, she reminded herself. This was his element. He'd been fighting a war for a decade before she'd come along. He'd know the best time to strike; her only job was to wait and follow his orders.

Arianna drew her sword, and others around her adjusted their grips, all ready to fight and die at their queen's side.

She looked down the wall to see Talon, weapon in hand, frost already coating his blade. He turned to meet her gaze and gave a subtle nod. He'd fought in the recent war, too.

They could do this. They'd survive the night and show Niall just how powerful they could be if they stood together.

Her magic pushed against its invisible cage, begging for freedom. It promised destruction on the Dark Fae closing in and on any who dared to threaten her mate.

Arianna took a deep breath and steadied it, coaxing the creature to wait just a little longer.

Rion's magic stirred at their feet then, rising up from behind as small grains swept over the wooden structure. It brushed against her skin, but she didn't flinch away. The creature within her kept the fear at bay.

Somehow Rion knew it, too. His magic rose higher, circling their bodies with pebbles and grains, like a serpent ready to protect its den.

The wingbeats drew closer. Arianna swallowed against the dryness in her throat. They'd face a fight to the death today. The Dark Fae had swept through other villages without much resistance, devouring everything in their path.

Not tonight.

Not here.

The flying creatures were closer now and Arianna swore she could hear their deep guttural growls in the distance.

Someone shouted, then fires lit up the entire area, momentarily blinding her. Her eyes watered but she blinked it away, willing them to adjust.

Phase two, then.

Laid out before them on both sides of the far wall, large piles of wood burned bright. Each had been strategically placed to act as a funnel that would lead to various traps.

The Dark Fae yelped and snapped their teeth as they scattered to avoid the fires popping up in their midst. Arianna hadn't realized Fiadh's magic could reach so far, but Raevina had said small sparks were easy from a distance. It was maintaining the flames that would cause too much strain.

But those fires wouldn't need to be maintained. They were solely for the purpose of guiding and illuminating the enemy.

The numbers before her did nothing to ease her nerves. Fear coursed through her as she studied the masses. Counting was of no use.

Rion's fingers threaded through her own and she startled before closing her hand around his. He didn't look at her, but she could feel the comfort he tried to convey down their bond.

Arianna took another steadying breath as they waited.

The seconds seemed too long and too short all at once.

The winged creatures surged past the outermost wall just as those on foot tumbled into the pits. Howls of pain filled the air and she cringed at the sound.

Seconds. They had seconds.

Were there a thousand of them? Two? Did she even know what a thousand bodies looked like?

Rion remained still. An immovable force. He didn't balk at the numbers and neither did Talon, nor the other seasoned warriors positioned along the wall. Arianna was certain their steadiness was the only thing keeping the others from fleeing. They trusted their commanders. Which was exactly what they needed if they hoped to win.

She jolted again when a male's voice pierced the air and several Fae standing among them raised their arms. Rion squeezed her hand again. She'd been with them when they'd gone over the plans, but her heart was racing too much to remember everything.

Wind tore through the air, whipping her braided hair around, before it converged in a wave and shot out, slamming into the flying creatures so hard, they were shoved back into the others.

Wings folded in on themselves and they plummeted to the ground, screeching the whole way before they landed in a heap of crunching bones. The beasts snapped their jaws at one another, some going so far as to tear their comrades to shreds as if they were the cause for the sudden outburst.

Animals. They were nothing more than animals.

She watched them scramble to their feet and howl in frustration and pain when their wings wouldn't respond. How had Niall directed them at all? They clearly held no intelligence of their own, or maybe the male had corralled them somehow, or planted a scent no one could detect.

Another blast of wind went out, striking the flying creatures again. They rained down, landing on their comrades. Some didn't rise again.

Hope began blossoming in her chest. If they could take them all out from a distance, then—part of the outer wall Rion had erected came crashing down. One second it was standing, the next large chunks of rock were falling as it crumbled apart.

Dark Fae were crushed beneath the weight of the stones but more were spilling through. So many more. The sheer mass of them continued to pull the wall apart, crumbling it bit by bit.

A collective gasp went through those beside her. One stepped back, ready to run.

"Steady," Rion called again. The command echoed down the line.

Arianna could scent their fear rising, but none turned to flee.

Pits swallowed creatures as they scrambled to avoid the strengthening fires. Arianna knew the bottom of those pits contained spikes and poisonous plants. The Dark Fae's howls proved they were effective.

Another gust of wind pushed forward, hitting another line of the flying creatures.

Those below were closing in fast.

The fires erupted outward, sparks scattering as the flames shifted into great beasts of prey that consumed everything in their path. Shadow creatures joined them, singeing flesh and melting bodies before her eyes. Some even took flight, burning through the membranous wings of the Dark Fae as they brushed past.

Three stepped beyond the fires. It was the last stretch of land separating the Dark Fae from the curtain wall. A wall that seemed so flimsy now, especially in comparison to the rock one the creatures had all but barreled through.

What hope did they have of it standing?

Firelight danced off leathery hides and reflected in yellow eyes. Some creatures she recognized from studying the books in Ruadhán's library. The hounds that had come after Rion among them. But there were others she'd never seen before, too.

Rion's magic whipped out and crushed the three Dark Fae in seconds. Their bodies writhed on the ground before falling still. Five more crossed that invisible line and Rion crushed them, too.

She gaped at her mate and watched as he did it again and again and again. Those standing on the wall around her stared at the male who hadn't even moved. Only his eyes darted back and forth as he tracked the creatures advancing on them all.

He hadn't released her hand either.

Talon called her name above the chaos and her head whipped toward him. He only had to point before her heart was sinking all over again. Because stepping through the wall, completely unfazed by the beasts surrounding them, were the ones with ashen skin and ice at their fingertips.

The very creatures that had run them into a river when she'd been hunting for her mate.

A shiver ran down her spine as the creatures' gazes roamed across the top of the wall. They were assessing. Forming a plan.

She'd thought them incapable of such reasoning, but what kind of conclusions could she really draw from one encounter? They'd attacked her and Talon as a unit. Perhaps it had all been planned from the start.

Her blood ran cold. Niall might not be directly leading them, but if the creatures could be reasoned with, they could very well be here on the male's orders.

Their dark eyes didn't display an ounce of fear. Not from the Fae currently bringing down their winged comrades. Not from the fire searing through their lines, and not from the massive pits where beasts still howled in pain.

A test. That first line of Dark Fae had been a test and a battering ram to break through their defenses.

Shit.

The ice wielders were climbing the wall now and landing on the other side, their teeth clicking in a strange pattern. She never imagined there would be so many of them.

"There," Arianna pointed with her free hand. "Focus on them first."

Rion followed her finger. "Raise your voice."

"What?"

"Raise your voice."

Arianna turned to find a few Fae staring at her, waiting for the instructions they hadn't heard. She'd had no intention of leading anyone in battle. She'd never wanted the position. But eventually, sometime soon, she'd have to make a stand. It was either here or wait until she was face to face with Niall and the High Lord.

Arianna steadied herself for what seemed like the hundredth time and raised her voice. "Focus on the Dark Fae in the back. The ones that look human. Use heat to burn their skin and stop their magic."

Arianna heard the creatures hiss and could have sworn it was directed her way. Could have sworn they … understood.

Those on foot were crossing that invisible line en masse now. Rion couldn't hold them all back by himself … or so she thought. Her mate raised one hand and a chasm that stretched from one end of the field to the other yawned open. It swallowed the Dark Fae in a matter of seconds. They screamed and clawed at one another, desperate to reach the edge, but the chasm closed again, trapping them and their screams below the surface.

The overturned dirt didn't move again, but more Dark Fae were coming. Sweat rolled down Rion's face, but rather than look exhausted, he appeared … exhilarated. More alive than she'd seen him in weeks.

He was ready for this. He craved the fight. And maybe her mate needed this battle in order to chase away the nightmares left by Niall. Maybe he needed to relearn his own strength in the wake of that torment.

Arianna had no intention of holding him back.

The next line of Dark Fae closed in and Arianna inwardly broke the imaginary chain holding her magic back.

Finally, it seemed to whisper before bursting from her body in a wave of cold air.

Frost coated her skin, making it shine in the firelight. It wrapped around her mate's arm momentarily before pulling away of its own accord and spreading around their feet.

The wooden structure became cold and slick as power enveloped her body and soul.

She was elegant and beautiful and ready to tear down anything in her path.

Arianna watched the creatures approaching with renewed vigor. She let her magic lash out and dance before it solidified overhead, forming into a dozen thick crystalized spears.

"Fire," Rion roared the command. It echoed down the wall and magic came to life in a symphony of sounds and smells and colors.

Bow strings snapped and a barrage of arrows plunged into the tender flesh of the winged creatures. Vines and trees with sharp thorns ripped from the ground, snatching anything in their path. Roots reached up to drag those unsuspecting into cold darkness.

Arianna kept battering them with ice and those with similar abilities did the same. She watched the jagged pieces tear through muscle and bone and pin others to ground while they were still alive.

They thrashed in pain and frustration.

They were doing it. With everyone working together, they were holding the line.

Ice and fire erupted from the enemy's rear line and Arianna watched in horror as it came barreling toward them.

She threw up her arms, erecting a shield. Rion's magic joined hers, as did others. Her mate wrapped one arm around her shoulders to hold her steady as the enemy's flames and ice slammed into their own.

A resounding boom echoed from the impact and Arianna covered her face with her hands, half expecting her shield to shatter, but it hadn't so much as cracked.

She wished she could say the same for others.

Arianna's gaze roamed over those who had fallen. Most were scrambling back to their feet. Some had minor injuries while others no longer moved.

She stared at a male body with an icicle through his chest.

Her breathing accelerated. Her hands trembled.

Dead.

Dead.

Dead.

How easily could it have been Talon or Raevina or Rion?

One second they'd been fine, and the next—

Arianna glared toward the rear wall where the ice wielders stood. She swore they were smirking. Her cold gaze shifted to the ugly Dark Fae at their sides. Creatures that stood on all fours, with thick bodies and flat noses. Molten fire dripped from mouths full of pointed teeth.

The ice wielders pointed and it began all over again. Warriors and Dark Fae pitted their magic against one another in a match to the death. Everything was a kaleidoscope of colors taking form only to wink out again.

The Dark Fae kept advancing, coming closer and closer until they slammed their bodies against the wooden wall.

Arianna stumbled forward from the sheer force of the impact. Rion gripped the top of her arm hard and pulled her back, placing her body just behind his own.

She frantically searched for Talon and found him leaning over the edge, hand half outstretched in what looked like an attempt to catch someone.

The creatures below had already piled on top of the unfortunate soul.

She didn't know if they were Fae, human, or half-breed, but she recognized that scream of terror. The one that came right before death.

The series of noises that followed had her stomach turning. She saw a limb fly but couldn't bring herself to turn away as the victim was devoured alive.

Gone in a matter of seconds.

The Dark Fae fought one another, pulling at scrapes of the body until there was nothing left.

Then a scream followed. A delayed grief-stricken howl that sent shivers down her spine.

Screams of fury echoed up and down the wall. The wood groaned against the weight of the Dark Fae pushing in, then ice began crawling up the planks, consuming it. Arianna's gaze snapped back to the ice wielders.

Talon shouted commands and Arianna finally stepped away from her mate. Steam curled from her skin, momentarily clouding her vision before she spun and hurled a sizzling sphere across the field.

The steaming mass collided with an ice wielder's chest and the being screamed in agony, falling to the ground in a heap as it rolled in an attempt to be rid of the pain.

More spheres followed, then Fiadh's flaming creatures and shadows turned on the ice wielders too, ready to eradicate the threat entirely.

Another group slammed against the wall as if they'd been commanded to, and a warrior toppled over the edge.

No one hesitated this time. Three of his companions leapt down with him, using magic and sword to beat back snapping jaws and jagged teeth.

A creature grabbed one of the male's feet, its fangs sinking deep.

Two more jumped from the wall, their magic blasting in all directions, creating a small space for them to stand while others rescued their companion.

They killed the beast and dragged their friend back. Then Talon jumped and she was moving. Arianna's magic burst from her body, knocking three of the winged creatures from the sky before they could snatch anyone else. She shot more spears of ice down on those trying to crawl up the wall, killing them as she ran.

The Fae followed her and she leapt, landing at Talon's side with magic flying in all directions, beating the Dark Fae back from the only structure separating this village from the creatures ready to devour them whole.

They pressed forward, killing and dancing with the magic flying from their fingertips. Rion pulled them parallel to the wall and she followed, creating a path for more to jump down and join the fray. Arrows and magic still rained down from those above, striking those in the distance.

Rion's magic coiled around her, shielding her from unseen threats. She was doing the same, neither willing to allow injury to come to the other. They wouldn't be parted again.

One of the large creatures with a leathery hide shifted its massive head in her direction. She planted her feet right as it reared its neck back and a stream of molten fire flew in her direction. Arianna yanked her magic up and shoved it forward, not just to block, but to destroy.

Ice engulfed the fire, freezing it in the air before her frost crawled straight into the creature's mouth. It tried to retreat, but was encased instead, her magic streaking across its body until it was a glimmering statue.

Another rushed up from behind and used its giant mace like tail to shatter its companion into a hundred pieces. Arianna's magic froze that one, too. And the next and the next.

Rion remained close, their abilities working in tandem.

The Dark Fae were thinning. Slowing. Her magic caught another as it leapt for Talon, and she threw the creature back.

They were going to win.

Someone screamed in warning but before she could turn, a thunderous boom echoed across the area. Every head whipped toward the sound of splintering wood.

Then Arianna watched, horror freezing her in place, as the Dark Fae poured through the broken wall.

CHAPTER SIX

TALON

Their line broke. Warriors scattered, and in what seemed like seconds, their imminent victory faded to nothing more than a dream.

Commands were shouted and ignored. Those stationed behind the wall fled as the winged Dark Fae swooped in and snatched victims from behind, burying their talons deep before carrying them off to be devoured midair.

Those stationed atop the wall leapt down to fight those who were pouring through. It left the front line too vulnerable. Too weak.

These were the moments that tipped the scale toward victory or defeat. These were the moments when Fae decided who or what they were willing to put their trust in.

And right now, no one trusted anything.

Talon met Rion's gaze. He could see it, too. They needed to regain control and somehow redirect those who were turning inward.

A piercing cry shattered the air, and they all turned in time to see a large creature with a flat horn across its head barreling straight for the wall. It screamed in terror and swung its massive head, hitting both Dark Fae and warriors as it tried in vain to outrun some invisible enemy.

Talon felt a pang of sympathy for the creature.

"Inside," Rion yelled over the chaos. Talon nodded and moved, understanding Rion's meaning with that single command. He was reluctant to leave Arianna's side for any reason, but they needed to separate if they hoped to regain control of the situation.

Rion would ensure it happened on the outside, evidenced by his magic rising up to block the warriors trying to leap from the wall. Rock and dirt turned the startled Fae back around before he shouted orders to the other commanders.

Remember your stations, Talon willed them. *Hold your line.*

Talon vaulted over the wall with his magic, taking out one of the flying beasts as he sailed past. He rolled in the damp soil, refusing to acknowledge exactly why it might be wet—blood, piss, water. One never knew. His eyes scanned the chaos and he spotted his second, Aiden, locked in combat with a reptilian creature that slithered across the ground.

Its legs were nearly too short, like it had been born wrong.

Aiden jumped away when the beast lunged for his throat. The creature hissed when its jaw snapped nothing but air. It swiped its heavy tail out next, determined to knock its opponent off balance, but Aiden wasn't a novice. He dodged before plunging his blade into the side of the creature's neck.

It thrashed, twisting and turning its body from side to side before falling still. Aiden glanced up briefly, met Talon's gaze, then was blind-sided by another of the reptilian creatures.

Talon lunged forward, his magic zipping across the space. It collided with the beast, sending it sprawling back.

Two others drove their spears through its head.

Aiden clutched his bleeding hand. His quick reflexes were the only reason the creature hadn't torn through his throat instead.

Talon took advantage of those gathering around and grabbed Aiden by the shoulders. He leaned close and raised his voice above all the noise.

"Direct any who will listen back to the wall. Secure it by any means necessary." Aiden nodded. They hadn't lost yet, and Talon wasn't about to back down just because things had fallen out of their favor. Aiden ignored his bleeding hand and sprinted straight for the break in the wall, grabbing another warrior by the arm as he ran. No words were needed, just gestures.

Talon trusted his second. Aiden had led enough battles at Talon's side. He'd get the job done.

Even so, Talon grabbed another warrior and gave him the same instructions.

Another large creature was running toward him like its life depended on it. It stood on all fours, its grayish, smooth skin covering a thick body and strong legs. The perfect beast for tearing through a fortified line. The flat horn across its nose crashed through another house, shattering it on impact. Fae came running out and Talon moved, cursing the villagers who had opted to stay above ground.

They should be with Zylah.

A female ducked low to avoid the magic flying in all directions. Talon blocked a winged creature from grabbing her, then shouted for her to get below ground.

She obeyed, then Talon let his magic fly. It zigzagged across the ground, avoiding his allies before latching onto one of the creature's thick legs. The beast screamed and fell to its knees, trapping a warrior underneath its massive weight. Talon cringed but didn't let his magic relent as it climbed up the beast's body, encasing its entire front.

Others finished the job, leaving him to turn his attention to the Dark Fae above. He shot out a dozen spears, then headed for the break in the wall.

Trees with thick trunks were already rising up to seal it shut. Dark Fae were climbing them, clawing at the bark as they fought their way through. Fire sparked in the air, throwing them back. Wind hit Talon's back and the creatures above him ran into one another, toppling to the ground.

Talon shoved his blade through a throat, then a chest, before grabbing another warrior by the forearm and hauling her to her feet.

"Get to the break in the wall. Secure it, then return to your post."

The female nodded and was off.

Thunder cracked from the eastern side, and Talon turned to find a storm brewing above. Avalon. Some called him The High Lord of Storms due to the wild nature of his magic. Talon had never witnessed the magnitude of it with his own eyes.

Dark clouds hung over that single area and Talon could already see the torrential downpour. Those from Móirín would take advantage. He almost found himself envious that he couldn't be amidst that power himself.

Even so, he could feel it feeding his own, coaxing it out, as if the land itself were calling to him.

He blocked another set of snapping teeth and plunged his blade into the creature's thick flesh.

Saoirse fought in the center of the village, moving elegantly with vines and trees as her partners in a deadly sequence of movements. None would get to the villagers so long as she stood.

Injured Fae were carried through the door by the dozens, some screaming as they made their way down the narrow stairs. Talon wasn't sure how much more room they had for bodies.

Fire sparked before him, twisting around another creature, and Talon shifted his attention westward toward the female he'd been trying not to focus on. Raevina fought on the other side of the wall alongside her comrades, wielding flames and shadows. He wished he could see her, just to reassure himself she was all right. But there wasn't time.

Another crack splintered the air. Fae were hurled from the wall as another section blasted apart. The dark creatures flooded through.

Talon rooted himself, letting mist billow up around his body, effectively drawing the attention of the Dark Fae nearest to him. A droplet of rain landed beside his feet, Avalon's storm ever-growing.

One of the lizard-like beasts snapped its jaws at him and rushed forward, legs rapidly carrying it across the ground. A spike of ice shot up, piercing the creature through its torso, leaving it hanging to writhe midair. Others turned to him next.

On his left stood two fire-breathing Dark Fae, their bodies large and corded with muscle. To his right were the flying beasts with long, bloody claws. Their wings had already been shredded.

Talon didn't wait for them to move; he struck first, sending a line of water flying at them so fast that it sliced right through their bodies.

Another of the lizard creatures jumped at him from behind and Talon burst a quick cyclone of water and sharpened ice from around his body, effectively ripping the Dark Fae to shreds.

A shout, and Talon's head whipped around to find a swarm of beasts converging on Saoirse. His eyes scanned the area, trying to find—the blood. Of course. They were transferring all the injured below ground, it was basically an invitation. A lure.

Talon summoned glistening tendrils of icy water and whipped them out to slice through everything surrounding him in one quick movement, then sprinted toward the Ambassador of Brónach. A beast lunged for him in passing, but Talon shot ice below the creature, then dropped to his knees, sliding beneath its hulking frame. Another tried to latch onto his arm, but Talon grabbed the creature's snout, then ripped the water from its body, leaving it as nothing more than a papery husk.

He skidded to a halt just short of Saoirse's line, where she and her warriors were cutting down Dark Fae one after another. Steam rose from Talon's body as he joined the fray, sword swinging, slicing open flesh. Boiling water blinded those who drew too close. Ice spread in a semi-circle around Saoirse's group of warriors and the Dark Fae slipped, falling to the ground before vines and branches crawled over and through their bodies.

More swooped in from above, and Talon shot the steam upward. Flesh peeled away from their bodies and they came crashing down, tangling around their comrades before they tore one another apart.

More Fae were screaming from the reforming wall and Talon

watched another section crack. He plunged his blade through yet another winged creature then prayed that Rion could regain control of the outside line before it was too late.

CHAPTER SEVEN

RION

*B*eautiful was too small a word to describe his mate in this moment. He'd seen her magic take control, causing her to forget herself and those she desired to protect. But the bond told him she was in control now—that the magic radiating from her was of her own free will.

And it was intoxicating.

Electrifying.

Addictive.

Rion smiled for the first time tonight, confident they just might pull out of this mess. There were too many poorly trained warriors. Too many who had never seen a battle of this magnitude. Even those with experience had nearly balked at the sight of the Dark Fae.

Thankfully, they'd stood their ground and it had made all the difference. They were succeeding, even if the body counts were rising more than he'd like.

Arianna exploded, her magic a majestic symphony that knew friend from foe with little effort—as though it had a will of its own.

She ducked, thrusting her sword up through a creature's jaw before twisting away. Rion grabbed her by the waist, spinning them both out of range of flying flames. His magic rose to dance with hers—testing, teasing—before colliding with another enemy.

Their magics knew one another as if they were old friends reunited.

They were one.

His chest swelled with pride. Their eyes met, hers exhilarated from the fight, before she dove back into the fray, and Rion followed.

It was a dance of water and sand and ice and steel. Teeth snapped at them but were stopped in their tracks. Claws reached out to rake down their flesh only to be cut off at the bone.

And his mate didn't balk once.

He'd seen her like this before. The day she'd protected him when she'd been sorely outnumbered. The day she'd stood at Talon's side, ready to fall defending Levea. The day she'd come for him, liberating him from being a captive once again. And the day Ruadhán had fallen.

Arianna's sword was out, her fangs bared, her body a living weapon.

A queen.

Rion ducked beneath a winged talon that reached for him and blasted the creature's skin right off its body. Arianna attacked another, a spear of ice flying straight through its torso. They kept moving toward the break in the wall.

Others saw and followed. Trees were growing where the wooden planks had failed. If they could just hold the line a little longer—

A scream echoed from behind and Rion pivoted, heart pounding, to find two Fae who'd been separated from their comrades. Arianna paused too, but the others kept moving, fighting back the creatures with everything they had.

"Rion." He heard his name at the same moment he felt her pull on the bond. He knew what she wanted.

Rion glanced toward the two being herded away. Everyone else had already left them to their fate. A fire wielding male and a water bending female. An unlikely duo fighting side by side to the death.

More of the Dark Fae turned their attention toward the pair. An easy meal.

Arianna's magic exploded, carving a path in their direction, but they both knew she wouldn't reach them in time. Even now he saw the male buckle.

"Get them," Arianna commanded, her fear reflecting down the bond.

Get them. Go after two complete strangers or stay at his mate's side. He'd already made his decision, but the pleading in her eyes had him reconsidering.

Arianna kept fighting to reach them, her magic blasting creature after creature. She'd never forgive herself if they went down. He knew that pain. The ache of being too late. The drowning guilt of knowing you could have done something but weren't strong enough.

"Rion," her voice echoed above the violence. Rion shoved another creature back, snarling as he ripped it apart. His eyes tracked their comrades' movements. They had to move. Now. They were too far away. Arianna was vulnerable. She hadn't spent decades on the battlefield. She didn't understand that some people just couldn't be saved.

"Rion," she screamed again and the absolute panic that shot down the bond somehow reminded him of the time he'd pushed her away and left her crying on her knees.

Rion looked back toward the two Fae who were fighting with absolutely everything they had. What if that were he and Arianna one day, left to their own devices, praying someone would intervene?

What if no one did?

Rion snarled and sent a wave of magic flying toward the couple. "Stay close to me." Her relief was instantaneous and she obeyed, keeping right on his heels as they ran through the narrow path he'd carved among the creatures.

His magic circled her, even as it ripped through any who dared to lunge for him or his mate.

The couple spotted him, but it wasn't fear that shone in their eyes at his approach. It was relief and hope. And it … startled him. These complete strangers *wanted* his help.

Rion propelled his magic outward. It circled the two Fae and blasted the creatures away, giving them an opportunity to flee back toward the wall and their waiting comrades.

The female wrapped an arm under the male's shoulder and hauled him to his feet. Rion held the line for them, following in their wake. He glanced behind and found Arianna smiling. He returned it. Then one of the fire-breathing creatures with large horns barreled right into her.

His world froze. Fractured. Shattered.

Too late, too late, too late.

Fear and agony radiated through him as he watched the beast's horn tear straight through Arianna's right side. He saw the depth of the wound, then the blood that rushed to fill it. Her smile faltered. Faded. Another slammed into her from her other side and she went spiraling forward. He was too late to stop her head from slamming into the ground. More were coming, just inches from sinking their fangs into her flesh and tearing his world apart.

A ringing echoed in his ears and the earth split at their feet. Rocks and dirt and everything he could command splintered apart, driven by some unseen force.

Boulders tumbled over one another and a chasm so deep he couldn't see the bottom split wide open.

Arianna plummeted into the fissure, along with the horde of Dark Fae rushing toward the scent of her blood.

Rion's body was already moving, but his magic was faster. It wrapped around her left arm and wrenched her to the side, away from snapping teeth and claws grappling for purchase.

Rion jumped for her, wrapped an arm around her waist, then lifted them both up and out.

His eyes raked over her body. She wasn't screaming. Wasn't moving. His magic kept fighting as he lifted her head, and his hand came away bloody.

He couldn't breathe. Every fiber of his body screamed for her. His magic spun in a violent circle, tearing the skin away from anything that dared to approach. He lifted the fabric of her torn shirt and a strange drowning sound escaped his throat.

Blood. It was something he'd seen a thousand times, yet it had his body trembling as if he'd never laid eyes on it.

Rion tilted her head and whispered her name, his voice cracking on the syllables. He tugged at their bond. Nothing. He pulled at it again, desperation overwhelming everything else.

Open your eyes, he willed. *Open them and tell me I haven't lost everything.*

The Dark Fae were increasing in number, battering against his magic. Their teeth snapped just out of range and Rion looked up at them, growling low as he clutched Arianna to his side.

He had to get her away from here. Protect her at any cost. Without her—without her, he'd unleash hell upon this world before jumping into the flames himself. She was everything, everything, everything.

Another lunged and Rion roared, rising to his feet with Arianna in his arms.

This battle needed to end. He had to kill them all so Arianna could get the help she needed. But they just kept coming, pouring from the darkness with no end in sight.

Panic seized his heart. Maybe if he got her back to the village— Zylah was there. She could help if—his blood ran cold as he turned around.

There was another hole in the wall, and he watched in horror as three more creatures barreled straight through the wooden structure. An entire section fell and the Dark Fae swarmed in like a dam breaking free.

He could feel Arianna's blood rolling down his arm now.

Lightning flashed on the western side and Rion's hope died in his throat. There was another wave coming they hadn't even seen. It was a speck in the distance, but Rion knew an army when he saw one. They wouldn't survive it, be it Niall or more Dark Fae.

Rion's eyes locked on a male still fighting on top of the wall. Talon. He shouted commands Rion couldn't hear. Not due to the noise, but the roaring in his head. Talon was pointing to them, but no one was available to obey his commands.

Rion's breathing accelerated and he stepped back. The creatures still surrounded him, but they were lighter on this side. If he left—he swallowed hard, his heart beating so fast he was sure it would stop.

He could run with her. Save Arianna from this fate. Maybe. She might still die anyway, leaving him alone.

They were all going to die. His mother. Saoirse. Talon. The villagers.

But Arianna. If he had her, maybe he could—

Rion stepped back again and let his magic pulse out from his body, knocking the Dark Fae back.

Nothing else mattered. Just his mate. He had to protect his mate.

Rion clenched his jaw, gave Talon a final look, then pivoted on his heel. He held Arianna tight, his heart thundering as he slammed through the creatures separating him from what he prayed was salvation.

Not for himself. He'd already been damned decades ago. But Arianna. Arianna deserved to live, even if it meant she'd ultimately damn him, too.

CHAPTER EIGHT

ELLIE

I am Lady Evelyn of Móirín and the future High Lady of Levea. I am the daughter of the High Lord of Storms. Sister to Arianna, The Queen of Alastríona. I have been trained to endure. To persevere. To overcome. I will not falter. I will not fall. I have a mate, Gavin from Pádraigín, but a half-breed with Móirín's magic in his veins has claimed my heart. I will protect Levea at any cost, even if that cost means my life. The people are everything. There is no home without them. I will remain their future. I will not allow myself to be manipulated. I will not break.

The door slammed open and an all too familiar scent had Ellie's stomach curdling. She could still taste the dry vomit on her tongue from earlier when—when—her head spun, pounding, pounding, pounding as she tried to pull her thoughts together.

A rough rug bit into the side of her cheek and she cracked one eye open to study the maroon fibers.

She hated this rug. This room. The High Lord's study.

It had become her second home. Second dungeon, more like. She much preferred the cold stone floors of the other one.

Candles flickered at various points in the room, none doing much to erase the darkness surrounding her. They merely made her remember things she'd rather forget. Things that caused her skin to crawl. Like the nauseating feeling of the High Lord's magic slithering through her mind. The feel of the iron shackles as they bit into her wrists and ankles. The piercing sound of Kirian's screams...

A shudder went through her too cold body. Goose flesh rose on her skin and her stomach rolled again, threatening to empty. *No, not yet*, she begged. If she didn't move, he wouldn't know she was awake. She just needed to stay still a little longer. She needed time to think.

Ellie cracked her eyes open again. Niall was here, though she hadn't heard him arrive. Maybe she'd fallen unconscious again without realizing it.

The two males stood staring at one another. They always did that. No, was that right? Maybe they never did it. Too many images were swimming through her head for her to sort through. She needed Kirian. He'd help her set everything straight.

She let her burning eyes close. Just for a minute. The room spun, bending and twisting like her memories. How long had she been out of the dungeon? How long had she been in captivity? Was Kirian okay or had she done something to earn him another round of beatings?

"I'm disappointed." The High Lord's deep voice floated through the room and inside her head, speaking directly to her subconscious. Ellie willed herself smaller, hoping to escape his reach. She didn't want to ever feel that magic again. It always felt as though he were rooting through her mind, shifting memories like loose papers scattered across a desk.

Ellie could visualize the High Lord bringing a stack of his own. He'd mixed them in against her will. They were tattered, frayed at the edges, and stained with oil. But they were getting lost in the stack until she could no longer distinguish one from the other.

Ellie forced her eyes open. She couldn't afford to cower. She needed to focus on the two figures in the room and collect information. She wasn't helpless. They'd give her something soon. They'd slip up, thinking her too weak to fight back.

Right?

A sob tried to rise to the surface, but she battled it back. She had to find a way to escape. She *would* find a way to escape. She'd get back to Arianna and Rion. To Talon and her father and her country. She'd warn them about everything.

Her pulse quickened as she recalled the information, and warning bells echoed through her head. They didn't know. They had to know. They had to know. They had to know—

"I made a mistake." Niall's voice. Not as sickening as his father's, but still slick with black oil. His voice made fire burn through her core, renewed anger simmering at the surface. His tone didn't carry an ounce of apology. He might as well have been talking about the weather.

The High Lord hummed in response and she cringed again, clenching her jaw at the sound. "You allowed yourself to get distracted."

Niall didn't respond right away. "I did as I was ordered and seduced the female."

Arianna. They were talking about Arianna. The memories began swimming again, fighting to the surface. They were plotting against her. No, not just her, the entire continent. *Wake up*, she screamed at herself, but her body was so tired, her mind even more so.

But she wasn't useless. She could gather information. She'd *been* gathering information, hoping it might prove helpful to ridding the world of this male and his ilk. Someone would come for her and when they did, she'd tell them everything.

The High Lord's voice turned darker and Ellie swore she could feel the room move and shift. Fear overwhelmed her and she shrank into herself further. She knew they'd be able to smell it soon. She didn't have her magic to help her.

"No, you took matters into your own hands. I specifically instructed you to bring that male to me."

"I had the situation under control."

"Clearly." His tone was laced with malice, but still, Niall didn't falter. How could he stand in the High Lord's presence and not be afraid?

Silence stretched for so long, Ellie feared she'd fallen back into that small room within her mind. The room where the High Lord's voice echoed from every corner, calling to her, dismantling her piece by piece only to throw her back together again. She still hadn't recovered from the first time, and he'd been in her mind dozens of times since.

She didn't feel … whole. As if the male was stealing pieces of her and covering his tracks so she couldn't reclaim them.

"If you'd tell me your plans—" Niall began.

"I have," the High Lord interrupted, "on a number of occasions." He bent to pick up a log and tossed it into the fire. Sparks shot out everywhere, fireflies dotting the darkness before disappearing again. Tiny beings winked out, dismissed by the darkness without a trace. "You always disappoint."

Niall stood in silence, but Ellie could sense his shock even if she couldn't focus on his face. "You've manipulated my mind."

"A time or two." Silence again. "Things might not have gone as planned, but you did manage to uncover a bit of truth I was blind to." The High Lord adjusted his robe. Ellie didn't understand how he could bear to wear the heavy thing when the room was so hot and stuffy.

"Which is?" Niall asked impatiently.

"I've always wondered why another Divine wasn't born. I thought that perhaps the gods had forsaken the land. I failed to realize it was my own actions and hatred of the previous king that kept her out of my reach."

"Are you going to be cryptic all day?"

Ellie thought she heard the High Lord chuckle. It held no mirth. "The male is always born first. He is required to grow to maturity in order to function as The Divine's protector. It's only when his magic is stable that the gods will allow the blessed one to descend."

"You've been reading your books too much."

"Tell me it doesn't make sense."

"I'd rather focus on what you meant by a time or two," Niall growled. "Who do you think you are—" Niall was cut off as the other male moved. Disappeared. He was in front of the fireplace one second, then had Niall slammed against the opposite wall the next. Long, slender fingers wrapped around Niall's throat, squeezing hard.

A crack raced across the wall and a sconce tumbled to the floor, embers rolling out to cover the very rug she was lying on. Smoke curled from the fibers, quickly filling the room. A flame flickered to life, but neither male showed an ounce of concern.

"I am your High Lord," he said, "and you'll do well to remember your place."

Niall choked and grabbed the male's arm with both hands. His father's arm, Ellie remembered. Adrenaline pulsed through her veins as she stared at the flames forming before her. Her eyes watered with the smoke, but it was the most clarity she'd had in days. Weeks.

Ellie scented their horrid magic crackling through the air. It reminded her of things she might have once loved. The breeze coming off an open plain. The sea air as it brought in a storm.

No longer.

Ellie tensed, ready for the two to brawl. She wouldn't be able to give them space if they did. Her chains wouldn't allow it. She'd be caught in the middle of—

"I apologize," Niall finally choked out.

The High Lord released Niall and backed away. Ellie could have sworn she saw a smirk on his shadowed face as his son rubbed his neck. Gods, would it kill them to light a candle?

"You don't mean it," The High Lord said. Niall didn't respond. "No matter. I raised you to be ruthless." He sighed. "I just didn't expect teenage-level rebellion to follow you around for seven hundred years. It's tedious."

Silence filled the room again, along with more smoke. Ellie resisted the urge to cough. Her lungs burned, but if she made a sound, they'd know she was listening.

Niall replied, his tone calm. "If you want me to capture the female, I can obtain her easily enough."

The High Lord waved a hand. "No, you can't. She's with her mate and their bond has grown strong. We have to proceed carefully if we want to keep it from solidifying, otherwise, I'll be forced to abandon this land altogether."

He tapped a finger on his chin and turned away from Niall, appearing lost in thought. "I have one more thing I want to try before that happens."

Niall opened and closed his fists several times. His jaw worked and it took several moments before he finally said, "You told me I was to be King of Alastríona. You've told me that since I was a child."

"It was a truth I needed you to believe. I didn't anticipate it taking so long for The Divine to be born into this world. She is the key to everything. If I'm to understand how to finally erase what's been made, then I need her."

"You're not making sense."

The High Lord looked at his son with the quiet judgment of someone who still saw a child. "You are no more the rightful King of Alastríona than I am. We are nothing. Warriors. Underlings to be used and discarded. But in my new world, we will be kings." The High Lord eyed him when Niall didn't respond. "Perhaps this time will be different. Perhaps you are old enough to bear the burden of the truth." Niall straightened as the High Lord approached. "I've tried this before. Twice. Both times, you turned against me. Understand, I won't forgive a third."

Ellie didn't understand how Niall held his ground. She would have run. She wanted to run right now.

Smoke still curled in the air and a flame was spreading, slowly consuming the fabric one strand at a time.

"Tell me the truth," Niall demanded.

A cruel smile spread across the High Lord's face. "I plan to break the mating bond."

Niall didn't so much as blink. "You can't break it."

"I can," his father reassured. "All I need are the first ones the bond was granted to. The Divine and her mate. With them, I can stop the curse. I can end it all. The bond is a cage. It traps Fae against their wills and puts shackles over their souls. I plan to free the world from those very shackles."

Niall opened his mouth and closed it again, thinking through his next words carefully. "What makes you presume it's unwilling? I've seen plenty of mated pairs."

"Have you not also seen those who suffer with a refused bond? Those who want nothing to do with their mated partner, yet are cursed to live with that pull for eternity? Have you not witnessed the unhealthy relationships where males and females alike justify everything their mates have done simply because their souls are bound to them?"

Niall didn't respond and his father turned back to face the fire, still ignoring the flame spreading through the middle of the room. His voice was softer when he spoke again. "Every once in a while, the bond gets it right. But for the rest of society, it leaves them crippled and hopeless."

"Were you caged once?"

The High Lord shook his head. "No, but someone dear to me was, and I couldn't save her."

Niall remained silent again, likely trying to absorb the impossible task, his mind working to sort through the how and why it was so important to his father.

"What's the plan?"

The male's gaze shifted to Ellie and she stiffened when their eyes met. "You'll see soon enough." He waved a hand and his magic swept through the room, extinguishing the flames and carrying the smoke toward the nearest window. It raced through, pushing out as if it couldn't escape the male fast enough.

She couldn't escape this male at all.

Ellie's body shook and she wondered how long it'd been since she last ate. She could barely rise to her hands and knees as she tried to drag herself, chains and all, away from Niall and the High Lord.

The male smiled at her and fear settled in the pit of her stomach.

Not again. Gods, please, not again.

She didn't want him in her head. She couldn't bear it. She wouldn't live if he dragged her back to that cold mental room.

Ellie whimpered when he stepped forward.

"It's not polite to eavesdrop, dear Evelyn." She met the end of her chains and clenched her jaw, hoping beyond hope that he might just leave her alone.

Rion had survived this. He'd suffered through the same mental prodding and come out on top. But was she as strong as him? Could she hold out and maintain a grip on her sanity?

"Don't look at me with so much contempt. We should try being civil, shouldn't we?"

"Go screw yourself."

The High Lord clicked his tongue. "Such foul language in the youth of today. It's disheartening to know our future sits in your hands." He paused to study the burned part of the rug, then stepped over it. He reached out a hand and white-hot pain speared through her mind, twisting like a sharpened knife.

Ellie screamed and screamed and screamed. The male plunged deeper. He took her back to that room. Slammed her against the cold metal wall, then tore at her memories, swiping through them, shredding them bit by bit.

Papers flew from the desk. Some she recognized, others she didn't. And there was a stack she could no longer distinguish from. They were all fraying at the edges. All burned and torn.

A tear slid down her face.

I am Lady Evelyn of Móirín and the future High Lady of Levea. I am the daughter of the High Lord of Storms. Sister to Arianna, The Queen of Alastriona. I have been trained to endure. To persevere. I will not falter. I have a mate, Gavin from Pádraigín, but a half-breed with Móirín's magic in his veins has claimed my heart. I will protect Levea at any cost, even if that cost means my life. The people are everything. There is no home without them. I will not allow myself to be manipulated. I will not break.

CHAPTER NINE

RION

The world had lost all its color. It was just darkness swirling around him, clawing at him, stealing little fragments of his soul that had allowed faded pigments to seep in from the edges.

His feet pounded against the rough ground. His magic took the brunt of the fight, never stopping. His breath escaped in jagged spikes, as if it, too, was trying to escape the nightmare unfolding before him.

The edges of his vision darkened, threatening to take him under. Had he expended too much energy? Had he never fully recovered from Niall's captivity? Had he been fooling himself all along?

Rion clutched Arianna tighter, listening to her heartbeat above the roar of the chaos. Her breaths were labored and the scent of her blood had his mind reeling.

Just like his nightmares. This was exactly what he'd suffered beneath Niall's spells. Did the male have him again? No, no, this was real. He had to remember this was real and that Arianna was really in danger this time. He was the only one who could save her. He just had to get away from these creatures first. Maybe he could find a village or—

Ice spread rapidly beneath his feet and Rion slid, turning his body so that his back collided with the hard ground. The Dark Fae lunged for him, but Rion's magic burst out, tearing their flesh from their bones. He spun and righted himself, baring his teeth at the foul creatures as he kept running.

He couldn't stop.

Arianna couldn't afford for him to stop.

A wave of fire came at him from his right and Rion ducked around it, always moving so his back was to the danger to protect Arianna from it. He felt the creatures hitting him from various sides. Claws and teeth that managed to get through his magic and nip at his flesh.

But he didn't feel the pain. He couldn't feel anything above the panic radiating throughout his body.

A spear of ice flew through his upper arm and Rion winced at that, but still didn't stop. He just sent another wave behind him, hoping it might catch the creature responsible.

They were thinning, if only slightly. Many gave chase, the pursuit a vicious game. Others prowled the woods, away from the main horde, and lunged for him as he sped through the trees.

Rion could see a set of mountains outlined in the distance. The mountains had always been a refuge. He could use them. He could get to them and hide and—then what? He knew how to stitch small wounds and care for burns and the like, but Arianna … Rion glanced down at her for a brief moment again. She rested in his arms, completely limp.

Gods above, what the hell was he supposed to do?

Rion didn't see the creature that grabbed his ankle. Its teeth sank into his flesh and Rion fell. He kept a tight hold on Arianna as he rolled across the forest floor, cradling her head. He should have prevented it from hitting the ground the first time. He never should have gone after those two Fae.

Stupid. Stupid. Stupid. Even if she'd hated him, she wouldn't be dying in his arms right now.

Rion got back to his feet and kept going, trying to dodge large groups amidst the trees. A distant command echoed from his right. Rion scented the air. Fae. Niall.

Shit.

He veered left, straining in the darkness to search for any signs of the enemy.

Another Dark Fae slammed its body into his and Rion fell again, barely keeping his hold on Arianna. His ankle twisted. Cracked. Rion roared and the rocks came to life, rising up to shred the creature to pieces.

Sweat rolled down his face. His body shook. Rion tried to stand again and nearly buckled from the pain radiating through his foot.

Panic overtook him again. He desperately searched his surroundings. Anything. Anything. *There.* Rion kept his magic ever moving as he ran with a limp toward a large rock jutting up from the ground. With barely more than a thought, he tore through the center of it, creating a hole large enough for him to enter through. The Dark Fae tried to follow, but Rion crumbled the rock entrance back in on itself, sealing him and Arianna inside.

Rion gritted his teeth against the pain and gently set her down on the hard stone. He couldn't see, but he could hear her breath and heartbeat. His hand found her wound and came away slick with blood.

She needed help now.

He had to do something *now*.

Rion cursed at the creatures bashing their bodies against the rock, chipping away at it piece by piece. He took those pieces and let them fly in random directions.

Rion placed his hand on the ground next and searched for their vibrations, catching all who stood anywhere near the wall in his clutches before crushing their bodies.

His head spun, exhaustion washing through him. This couldn't be it. This wasn't the extent of his powers. He'd held up an entire city only a few weeks ago.

And perhaps that was the problem. He'd been in captivity. His magic had been suppressed for over two months, then he'd unleashed it in a way he'd never done before. He'd trained endlessly afterward, trying to recover and process his anger.

Then he'd had to fight again, and now Arianna—

It was too much. Too much on his mind and body and soul.

Rion clenched his teeth and planted his feet. He shoved the pain to the back of his mind. Let it be too much, then. He'd let his body crumble before he let Arianna die in this makeshift cave.

Rion blasted the entrance open, using the debris as a weapon before he reformed the wall, closing his mate inside.

The Dark Fae lunged at him, but they were fewer in number, or was his addled mind just imagining it?

Rion tore them apart, whipping his magic around his body in a frenzy. He drew the only remaining blade he possessed and slammed it into one of the creature's eye sockets then let his magic do the rest.

He just had to make a path. Once these creatures were destroyed, he could figure out where he was and make a start toward the nearest village.

If the dark creatures hadn't destroyed that, too.

Rising voices sounded too close. Shit, he'd forgotten. There were Fae closing in as well. Likely not Niall, as he'd previously thought, but they could be his underlings. Rion could smell Pádraigín on the wind. He could smell them all, really. Or was it just a glamour meant to throw him off?

Rion didn't stop moving. He was a living storm. If he didn't make it out of this, then neither would she.

Images from his time in captivity plagued his mind. Pictures of Arianna's body withering before his eyes. Her lips slowly curling back from her teeth as decay took over and stole her from the world.

Rion roared again, fighting the sharp pricking sensation in his eyes and the way his throat suddenly burned.

A group of Fae rounded the corner. One stopped to look at him, their expression a mixture of awe and surprise.

Rion's heart pounded harder when they veered straight for him. They would know Arianna was nearby. If he let them catch her, she'd be subjected to Niall's torment just as he'd been.

And he'd die before he let that male lay a single finger on her again.

The Dark Fae were attacking the other Fae as well, which gave Rion a minor advantage as he waited for them to close the distance. He wouldn't separate himself from Arianna, not when so much could go wrong.

Closer and closer they approached through the thinning creatures. Another small group of Fae emerged from his other side.

Rion rolled his neck and stored the pain in the back of his mind.

Just another battle.

Just another war.

And he'd always won.

Rion stopped thinking and let his exhausted body move. His magic burned in his veins, sputtering and on the edge of giving out. He shifted to a halfhearted sprint and grabbed the nearest Fae by the throat, snapping his neck with his bare hands.

He could fight Fae with just a blade and his own strength. He'd save his magic for the dark creatures that could mangle a limb with a single bite.

The Fae's eyes widened as he let the male fall to the ground. They took note of his injury and Rion cursed again, letting the foul words fall from his lips like venom. He should have been praying, yet the gods had never seen fit to answer him before.

The Fae closed in, their eyes tracking him with the wariness of those facing something untamed. He scented their fear, something he was far too accustomed to. It fueled his rage. *Good.* Let them be afraid, let them see the monster that had been sleeping in his veins these last few months.

Four turned their attention to him, magic around their bodies and blades coated with blood. Their comrades continued the fight with the Dark Fae, circling around Rion until none could break through their line.

They thought isolating him would make him an easier target.

They were about to find out how wrong they were.

Three more shifted their focus to him. Three wielded fire; he could still see it sparking at their fingertips. One controlled water and at least one other was able to bend the plants to their will. That left two unknowns.

Until three more turned to face him as well.

One of the Fae stepped and Rion was already moving. Those surrounding him fell back a step as Rion used his magic to wrench the Fae's arm out of its socket. He sank his fangs into the male's neck, tearing the artery wide open. The male screamed and Rion shoved him toward his companions. Two caught him and the others were backing further away with—their hands were up.

Arianna's heart skipped and his did the same, fear consuming him as he relived the nightmare of listening to it stop over and over again.

When she was strangled. When she'd been beheaded. When his own magic had wrapped around her neck…

A growl tore from him and he launched at another male.

The sword fell from the male's grasp and he tried to hit his knees, but Rion had his fingers around his throat before his body could fall.

"Please, My Lord—" then his words were cut off.

Another ran forward and hit his knees. "We can help her." He turned his wrists up and desperately looked between Rion and the male suspended in his grasp.

One twist of Rion's arm, and the male would die. He didn't have time for words. He needed to move.

"Please," the Fae shouted again. "We came to help." His words were quick, voice shaking. "We're followers of The Divine. Please, My Lord, we're not here to cause you or your mate any harm."

Rion's eyes flashed toward the male on the ground, then he took a fraction of a second to register that none had turned their magic against him. At least not yet.

His heart pounded with a tendril of hope.

"She's hurt," the male said. "I can smell her blood. We can help her."

"How?" Rion growled again.

"We have a settlement nearby with medicine and healers."

Arianna needed both, but to trust strangers anywhere near her… to let them touch her…

No, they wouldn't have to, he knew how to dress wounds. He could just use their medicine himself and perhaps the advice of a healer.

Did he really have any other choice? The Dark Fae were still being pushed back and more Fae were joining them, their curious gazes staring at Rion and the magic circling his body.

Rion threw the male he'd been holding, then eyed those in the vicinity. "Anyone who tries to touch her dies."

"Understood," the male still kneeling said.

He didn't have enough time to assess them. All he knew was the male wasn't lying. He was from Móirín, or so his scent claimed. Arianna's heartbeat skipped again and Rion darted for her.

The scent of her blood washed over him the moment he let the rocks crumble away. His heart clenched at the sight of her and the wound on her side. Gods, she needed help and she needed it now.

This was worse than any nightmare.

This was reality.

Rion carefully scooped her into his arms and emerged with his magic still spiraling around his body. It fought against his control now, but he couldn't let them see that. His limp was bad enough.

The kneeling male slowly rose to his feet and stared at Arianna in awe for half a heartbeat before shouting commands for them to march north. Rion only hesitated a second before following.

"It'll be all right," he whispered to her. "I'm going to make everything all right."

CHAPTER TEN

RION

Time raced and stood still, coming in waves. Some moments felt like water crashing through him, dragging his mind beneath the surface while others felt like everything had frozen over. It left him wondering when the next crack would come or whether his reality would shatter entirely.

Those surrounding him whispered, more to themselves than to him, but there were a select few who were brave enough to speak to the unpredictable creature in their midst.

The group that had promised aid moved fast, yet it also felt as though they were trudging through mud, climbing a steep mountain peak after a fresh snow with no end in sight.

Somehow, the Dark Fae had disappeared. Rion remembered killing a few, sending his magic out to crush their bodies. The warriors accompanying them had seemed grateful, but he'd hardly paid them any attention. Not with Arianna fading.

No, she'd be fine. They'd get to this promised camp, she'd heal, then they'd escape back to the village to … to … Rion bit the inside of his cheek and tasted blood. Physical pain was the only thing rooting him in reality. That and the steady rhythm of Arianna's heartbeat.

They rode in a wagon now, the contraption pulled by two horses. Rion couldn't remember where it had come from. He'd hardly listened to the explanations. He didn't care. He just wanted to get wherever they needed to go. He just prayed that it wasn't directly into the enemy's hands.

Arianna's heart, though steady, sounded … wrong. He couldn't explain it. He only knew it wasn't right and she needed help as fast as these Fae could provide it.

His gaze roamed over the blood soaking her tunic, then the stains on his hands. There was more on his clothes, too.

Too much.

Too much. Too much. Too much.

Only one other person sat in the wagon with them. A female, her hands trembling and also covered in his mate's blood. Bruises lined her neck. He studied them, wondering if he'd been the cause. Rion searched for the memory, but there were so many others. He'd killed someone, maybe several of their comrades.

They only had themselves to blame. He'd warned them not to touch her. Or had he done it before?

A male remained nearby. The same one who'd stopped Rion from killing them all. He'd convinced Rion that this female could ease some of Arianna's pain. Possibly stabilize her. It was only after Arianna's heart had skipped another beat that he'd relented.

His hands shook. He couldn't heal her. He had no power here.

"Can you close the wound?" the male asked, his voice frantic. The others were worried too. Rion could scent it in the air all around him, and he hated it. He hated them. He hated himself for ever allowing this to happen.

"I'm trying." The female sniffled and Rion glanced up just long enough to see a tear roll down her dirt-stained face. A sliver of guilt trickled through whatever emotions were swirling around his heart.

He *had* hurt her.

Rion's gaze flickered back to Arianna. His chest tightened and his lungs constricted to a point where he could hardly draw breath. It felt like the vines of Brónach had come alive inside his body and were choking him from the inside out.

"Control yourself. Set your grief aside. She needs you." The male's hand rested on the female's shoulder in comfort. Rion's magic crawled over the male's arm. He couldn't control it, not that he wanted to. Anyone close to Arianna was a threat. He wouldn't let anyone else harm her.

The female held her hands over his mate, tracing symbols across her abdomen. Rion's magic snaked around her body, daring her to cause any more damage. He'd tear her apart.

The rest of their comrades walked beside the wagon, keeping a healthy distance, at least as much as they dared with the Dark Fae still lurking somewhere in the forest.

Rion risked looking up, trying to gauge where they might be headed. North, but north to where? Ashling? Niall? An iron cage?

Strange magic pulsed from the female's symbols that did nothing for his nerves. It twisted his stomach in strange ways. He'd nearly lashed out at first. Maybe he had. That might explain the bruises. But as he'd watched, he'd sworn he could see a slight change to Arianna's wound. It was still open, but the profuse bleeding had finally stopped.

Nothing made sense. Healing magic was supposed to be reserved for The Divine, so where was this female drawing her energy from and what did it mean?

Sweat beaded against her forehead and her teeth were clenched. "I can't heal this. I need Sive."

"We'll be there soon, just keep her steady."

The female cast a fearful glance toward him for a split second. "But she's—"

"It'll be okay. She'll know what to do."

Rion clenched his jaw. He wanted to grab them both and demand answers, but anything drastic might interrupt this female's concentration. He was afraid to imagine what might happen if she pulled her hands away from Arianna.

Rion hated the secrets and the unknown. He hated relying on others. And right now, Arianna was at their mercy.

His life was a living nightmare. Worse.

The wagon rolled on and on and on through an endless sea of trees. The female remained hovering above his mate, her back bent and both arms outstretched. The symbols glowed with a faint bluish light that flared before sinking into Arianna's abdomen. He wanted to ask a million questions, but he didn't dare to utter a single word. One slip, one miscalculation, and he might lose Arianna forever.

Then he'd be … he'd be … nothing. All over again, he'd be nothing. Less than nothing.

"Almost there," the male whispered, as if he could read Rion's spiraling thoughts. "You'll feel a barrier as we pass though, but it's nothing to worry about."

Rion's fists clenched. "A barrier for what?" His voice wasn't his own. It was dark and empty. Like he'd reverted back to his previous vicious self. Without Arianna, it was all he knew. It had made people from his past listen and obey.

"Pádraigín's magic keeps us hidden from the rest of the world." Rion's eyes went wide, but the male continued before he could protest. "We're a small group composed of every nation, much like Ruadhán was." His gaze roamed back to Arianna. "There are … younglings there. Fae and half-breeds. I know you fear for her, but please don't take your frustration out on the little ones."

Younglings. If there were younglings, then there wouldn't be chains. Right? Or was that only wishful thinking? Niall certainly hadn't had an issue with it.

"Then keep them away from me." The words tasted foul leaving his tongue, but it wasn't meant as a threat toward the little ones. He couldn't be sure of himself right now. He wasn't sure when his control might slip, and if Arianna's heart stopped—

The male's face paled, but he nodded and stepped away. Rion watched his whispered exchange with another. Two Fae glanced his way before disappearing through the trees.

They were running to warn someone. Running to announce their arrival and everything in him wanted to stop them for fear of what it could mean. They could lay a trap for him and if they succeeded, then Arianna wouldn't have anyone to protect her. But if he killed them all and ran—he looked at her again. If he ran again, she wouldn't make it.

Calm, he willed himself. *Breathe*. He just needed to keep a clear head. If he did that, then he'd be able to anticipate a trap before it was laid. He'd see through their intentions if—he wouldn't. Not right now. Who was he kidding? He'd lost his first battle when he'd been distracted by her mere presence. He'd failed to see Niall for the threat he was because he'd been too busy trying to please his mate and show her that he could be more than just a blood-thirsty monster.

Maybe change was the problem. Maybe holding himself back was what had caused half of their messes. If he gave up caring, he could easily rip the world apart and lay it at Arianna's feet.

Only … she wouldn't want that. She'd forgiven him for so much, but everyone had their limits. If he killed these people, would he finally find those limits?

"It's just ahead," the male said, his voice soft and coaxing. Just ahead. Hope? Salvation? Betrayal?

Rion's magic circled tighter and moved faster, pulsing in time to his heartbeat. His throat went dry all over again. The horses kicked their feet out, surging forward slightly to get away from the circling grains. He tried to keep his magic away from them, just so they wouldn't jostle Arianna any more than necessary, but it was so damn hard.

Another Fae stepped forward, taking the reins and whispering soft words of comfort to the restless animals. Rion tried to listen, too.

They won't hurt Arianna.

They won't hurt Arianna.

They won't hurt Arianna.

The words felt like a lie from a stranger.

Rion scented the magic before he felt it. It buzzed through the air and as they passed through, Rion felt it cascade over his skin like a thousand insects. He bent toward Arianna and the female tending to her leaned back.

Then the magic vanished just as quickly as it had come.

A line of Fae appeared before him on the other side, all watching with pensive gazes. He stood in the wagon, scanning each of them one at a time.

Nearly three dozen.

His jaw worked.

Then he saw the smaller silhouettes in the distance, each hiding behind more Fae.

The younglings. A village. Masses of eyes watching from every angle.

None had their weapons drawn. None had weapons at all.

The wagon veered left and Rion watched each person in passing. Their gazes were curious, awestruck even as they stared at his magic. Some rose onto their tiptoes, trying to spot something more. They whispered amongst one another and their fear was … different. It didn't carry the same harsh tang that he normally scented. Because it wasn't directed toward him.

"There's a bed waiting inside," the male said, interrupting Rion's thoughts. "We should—"

Rion spotted the small cottage the male had gestured to and was moving before he could finish his sentence.

The female who'd been tending to Arianna leapt from the wagon too, keeping close as Rion carefully scooped his mate into his arms. His ankle throbbed, nearly buckling as he put weight on it. Arianna groaned and his heart jolted at the sound.

"It'll be all right," Rion whispered, even if he wasn't sure he believed it himself.

The male opened the door and Rion stormed past him, thankful to find the interior void of more bodies. He immediately turned toward the bed and deposited Arianna on a soft, cream-colored quilt.

Once again, the female approached and placed her hands over Arianna's wounds. That unnatural light returned and Rion could only watch the strange magic in helpless anticipation.

The same male from earlier stood on the threshold. "Sive is on her way," he assured. The female at Arianna's side nodded.

"Who is she?" Rion demanded.

"Our best healer."

Rion gritted his teeth, then took in the layout of the room. There were two windows and the front door. Three points of entry.

His body itched to pace the length of the cottage, but he remained still, watching the female's magic for any sign of malintent. Those who'd greeted them hadn't carried any weapons, but were they gathering them now? Were they plotting the best way to separate him from his mate?

He couldn't calm his still-racing heart, and the female seemed to note his rising panic. Her gaze met that of the other male's, but that male only nodded in reassurance, as if saying anything might set Rion off all over again.

There were several here with the ability to use Pádraigín's magic. Would they try to knock him out? Steal the air from his lungs? How many were they willing to sacrifice in order to subdue him?

Rion's heart was pounding so hard the only thing he could hear was the racing of his own blood. He needed to calm down and—Arianna's heart skipped again and Rion hit his knees at her side, grabbing her hand, uncaring that the female tending to his mate could reach out and touch him with little effort.

Gods, please, please, please. He couldn't lose her. Not like this. Not when she was so young and had barely had any time to live.

More bodies gathered by the door. Rion swallowed a lump in his throat and turned to stare at the female that had stepped inside. A male stood behind her, one hand lightly resting on her shoulder.

Rion couldn't stop his magic as it glided across the floor, daring the new arrivals to take a single step. He scented the air and every hair on his body rose. Something about her was … different. Ancient. Her scent was similar to the female currently tending to his mate, but also different in a way he couldn't grasp. It reminded him of the way an older Fae smelled when they possessed more magic than their younger counterparts.

This was who they'd called to help his mate? Did they really believe he'd let someone like her anywhere near the anchor that rooted what was left of his soul to the world?

Did he even have a choice?

This female, Sive, took a step into the room and Rion growled, rising to his full height as he placed his body between her and Arianna. The male at the female's side grabbed her arm, trying to pull her back, but Sive gently rested a hand on his chest and drew a symbol there. It glowed for the briefest moment before disappearing.

The male's heartbeat slowed. His breathing eased, too. The pair stared into one another's eyes, seeming to have a silent conversation of their own before she turned back to face him.

No. Not her. Anyone but her.

Something was wrong. Different. Rion pulled his lips back from his teeth. He didn't want this female anywhere near Arianna.

Arianna's heart skipped again and Rion's throat burned. He tried to swallow it back, bury it down, but the tears formed anyway, lingering to cloud his vision.

He wanted them all out. He needed them out. If Arianna was going to die, then she'd do it in his arms and he'd go with her.

His breath came faster. Pain blossomed in his chest and constricted his ribs. He grabbed his shirt, willing the agony to pass. He couldn't breathe, couldn't breathe, couldn't breathe.

"What have they done to you?" His world paused at the sound of her ethereal voice. Blood thrummed through his ears. Pounding. Pounding. Pounding.

She gave him a sad smile then lifted one hand and drew a symbol in the air. "So much darkness. So much pain." Rion felt something in his shoulders give way. Like a tiny sliver had been chipped from the fear consuming him. "Has no one shown you kindness?"

His gaze wandered to Arianna. *Her*, he wanted to say, but his lips wouldn't move.

The female drew another symbol in the air between them.

The lump in Rion's throat thickened.

She drew another.

His lips parted and a strangled gasp escaped. His mind cleared another fraction, then he could finally put a name to the emotion swirling through him.

Not fear.

Terror.

Absolute terror.

Because if he lost her … if he lost her—

The female's features came into focus. Soft blonde hair hung down to her hips in gentle waves, the strands loosely held back from her face with a pair of twists that circled the crown of her head. Her eyes were honey colored and carried so much warmth within that he felt his own body relaxing even further.

She took another step into the room, her hands still moving in a slow, methodical motion between them. Rion stepped back and she paused.

"Is that better?"

"What are you doing to me?" His voice came out raw and broken.

"Nothing that will harm you. And sadly, nothing that is permanent."

He felt warm again, able to think clearly, too. She stepped again, closing the distance so that she was only an arm's length away. Her gaze drifted to Arianna lying on the bed behind him.

The female's other hand drifted to her stomach and he finally looked down, noticing the swell. She smiled at him, then Rion scented the air.

Not female. Woman. But her scent was strange, a mixture of something he couldn't place. Not a half-breed, but—

Her hand stopped drawing symbols between them. Grief flooded through his already fractured heart, as if she'd torn down every wall he'd built to hold it all back.

"Help her," he begged. It was a broken plea. He'd give her anything if she promised to save his mate.

Sive nodded, her face turning more serious as she turned and sat at Arianna's side. She placed a reassuring hand on her companion's shoulder. With a final look, that female fled from the room.

Three individuals waited by the door, but Rion wasn't even sure he cared anymore. He watched as the pregnant woman reached for Arianna and her hands began to glow. Rion settled himself on the floor beside the bed and took Arianna's hand, pressing it to his lips.

She drew a different symbol over Arianna's wound, staining her fingers with blood. Rion just watched his mate. Praying. Hoping.

As the minutes ticked by, a male crept through the doorway. Rion gave him a fleeting glance before turning back to Arianna. He couldn't very well blame someone for wanting to be near their partner, especially when they were carrying their youngling.

The male settled himself behind the woman, watching as she worked.

Time ticked by slowly. She drew symbol after symbol, each more complicated than the last. Rion only waited with bated breath.

Then Arianna's breathing eased a fraction. His mate's brow furrowed and she moaned. Rion was up on his knees in an instant, looking her over for whatever might be causing her distress.

The woman's voice was soft when she spoke. "Just as with her magic, healing is not a painless process. But rest in the knowledge that she won't recall any of this."

The woman, Sive, pulled away the fabric of Arianna's shirt. Rion grimaced at the soaked material but found himself watching the strange blue light circling his mate's wound.

It was healing. Gods above, it was actually healing, but it was different from Arianna's magic. Arianna was able to heal wounds in an instant, but this looked far more strenuous.

"Do not despair," Sive whispered. "She will live."

Rion had never heard three more beautiful words. A choked sob escaped him and he pressed Arianna's hand to his head, squeezing tight.

When he looked up again, he found Sive watching him. "One day soon, there will be a time for you to heal as well."

Rion's lips parted and as he stared at this strange woman, he had the oddest feeling that he was seeing one of the gods themselves.

His lips parted. "What are you?"

She smiled, easing the ache in his chest. "A Weaver."

Weaver. He didn't know that word or didn't have the sense to pull the information from his memory. "I don't understand."

She kept working, her eyes once again focused on Arianna. "I believe you call us witches on this continent. We find the name a little too barbaric for our liking."

A Witch. Weaver. His heart sped again. He had a million questions and a million more fears, but Rion swallowed them down.

"You … can heal."

She drew another symbol. "The earth heals. I'm simply the mediator that borrows and bends its power." Another symbol, then the wound on Arianna's stomach closed entirely, leaving behind a jagged pink scar. Another to add to her collection.

Sive reached for Arianna's head and drew a few more symbols before pulling back.

"Explanations can come later. For now, just know the two of you are safe. Rest, heal, eat, and we'll answer all your questions when your mate is awake and ready for them."

The female stood slowly, cradling her swollen stomach with both hands. Blood stained the silken fabric, but Sive didn't seem to mind.

"Thank you," Rion breathed. It was all he could say; words couldn't even begin to express the depth of his gratitude.

Sive dipped her head. "No. Thank you for finally coming to us. We are here to serve, My Lord. Whatever you need, you have but to ask."

CHAPTER ELEVEN

ARIANNA

A pounding echoed at the back of her head when Arianna finally stirred from the depths of unconsciousness. She refused to open her eyes as that same pain radiated throughout her entire body. It almost felt as if she'd been burned from the inside out.

Arianna tried to wet her lips and failed, then everything came back in a blinding rush. The Dark Fae, the battle, the pair that had been trapped. Rion running to their aid.

Arianna cracked her eyes open to find a very different scene surrounding her.

Dim sunlight filtered through a set of drawn ochre curtains, casting soft shadows across the worn wooden floor. A small table stood beneath the window with dried flowers in a vase, along with a tea pot and a pair of untouched mugs beside it.

The swirls in the wooden walls around her spoke of someone's home, though she didn't recognize anything. She prayed their previous dwelling hadn't been destroyed during the battle. Or maybe this little cottage gave Zylah easier access to her.

Arianna shifted slightly on the soft bed. She was wrapped in a thick, green quilt, but blood had stained the material. She grimaced, studying the complex stitching that swirled in a floral-like pattern. They'd never get the spot out.

Arianna strained to listen outside, but she only heard the slight rustling of distant footsteps. She loosed a breath. They'd won. It felt impossible and yet—a small smile tugged from the corner of her mouth. They'd won.

Her gaze drifted down to the male half lying across the bed, his arms extended over his head, one hand resting on her leg.

His brow was knitted with worry even in his sleep, but he looked whole. His clothes were fresh and he'd taken the time to wash up.

Arianna reached out and ran her fingers through his auburn hair. The slight touch was enough to jolt him awake. Rion's eyes flew open, his magic jerked, then his unfocused gaze scanned the space before he shifted closer to her.

Their eyes met, his red-rimmed and tear-stained.

"Hi," she managed with a weak smile. A surge of emotions flew down the bond, hitting her so hard that her own eyes misted.

Rion knelt beside her, took her hand, and kissed her palm, holding her fingertips against his cheek. His breath was ragged as he stared at her. Then he lowered his eyes. His shoulders shook and her heart ached.

Arianna clutched his hand. "It's okay," she whispered, her voice cracking.

Rion shook his head. "It's not. None of this is okay."

"What—" Arianna tried to move, then hissed as pain speared through her body. She groaned again when it didn't dissipate right away. Her muscles burned, fire pulsing through every fiber in her core.

Rion was up in an instant. He all but ran to the small table by the window and poured something from the teapot into one of the worn cups before returning.

"You're hurt." He was limping heavily on one foot.

"I'm fine." Carefully, he placed one hand behind her head and helped her sit up. "They said this will ease the pain."

Arianna sipped it once, then jerked her head away. "What unho-ly—"

"Drink it," Rion ordered, his tone firm. She peered up at him, then his hard expression shifted to something softer. "Please."

Arianna relented and choked down three mouthfuls before she turned away again. "I can't."

"It's okay." He rested her head against the pillow and set the cup aside. Nausea rolled through her stomach and Arianna closed her eyes, willing the spell to pass.

She licked her lips and the foul flavor hit her tongue again. "Please tell me you have something to wash it down."

He stood again and his leg nearly collapsed. She almost called him back, but Rion had already crossed the space, cup in hand.

He assisted her again and the spicy taste of ginger tea hit her tongue. Her head returned to the pillow and Rion sat in silence at her side. Gods above, she just needed the world to stop spinning.

Arianna opened one hand and Rion's fingers interlaced with her own. He was shaking. She peered at him again. His jaw was clenched as he sat there, staring at her, waiting for another command. Waiting to be of use.

"Why are you so far away?"

Rion didn't hesitate as he pulled the blankets back and scooted close to her. She shifted as much as her body would allow and Rion tried placing one arm beneath her head. He winced but wouldn't let her protest as he pulled her close, running his fingers across her scalp in soothing strokes. His warmth seeped through her chilled body instantly.

"Let me heal—"

"Later," he interrupted, pressing a kiss to her temple. Arianna let silence envelope the space. His racing heart slowed and she basked in the quiet moment. Arianna interlaced her fingers with his other hand and let her thumb rub across the back of his knuckles.

"What happened?" she finally asked.

Rion shook his head and pulled her tighter. Arianna tried to recall her most recent memory. They'd been surrounded by Dark Fae when she'd lost consciousness. She remembered a sudden searing pain in her side.

Arianna pulled her hand from Rion's and pushed the quilt down. Rion assisted her and she pulled the hem of her thin shirt up to reveal a jagged pink scar across her stomach. It was raised, and thick, and still warm to the touch.

Panic surged through her. "How long have I been out?"

"Two days." His jaw flexed against her temple.

Two days? But that wasn't nearly long enough for her wound to have healed this much. Her head throbbed and she allowed Rion to cover her up again. Maybe the blood loss was preventing her from thinking clearly. Or maybe she'd hit her head as well. That would certainly explain the pain.

A new sense of dread pooled in the pit of her stomach. If she'd been unconscious for two days—

"Is everyone okay?"

Rion didn't answer and his silence sent her heart into a gallop. She tried to turn in his arms, but he held her firm, almost as if he wasn't willing to face her just yet.

Oh gods—a lump formed in her throat as names filtered through her head.

Arianna couldn't keep the panic from her voice as she asked again, desperate to know and yet not wanting the answer. "Is everyone okay?"

"I don't know." His words were barely a whisper.

"You don't—what do you mean you don't know?" Surely he'd not kept himself confined to this little house for two days. But that's exactly what her mate had done. It's what she might have done too, if their situations were reversed.

Arianna wriggled out of his grasp and he reluctantly released his hold. She studied his face, her head still resting against the pillow, but he refused to meet her gaze.

"Tell me what happened."

"You need to rest."

"Please." Tears were forming in the corners of her eyes as she imagined the worst of scenarios. "I need to know. Are the villagers okay? Do they need me in the medical ho—"

"You aren't going anywhere." She bristled at his tone and the storm in his eyes. Rion's jaw flexed, then he rested his head against her shoulder in submission. "Please, just stay here and rest."

Arianna could hear the exhaustion in his voice. The desperation, too.

"Okay," she relented. His shoulders visibly relaxed. "But only if you tell me the truth."

He loosed a breath. "You won't like the truth."

"I can't just lay here and not know. Is there another attack coming? Are we safe? Was my father able to convince the villagers to finally move to Levea?"

"We're not in the village."

That brought her up short. "What do you mean? Where are we then?"

"Do you want something to eat first? A bath? Do you need—"

"Rion. Where are we?"

His jaw clenched again. "I don't know."

He didn't … she stared at her mate and studied the forlorn expression marring his anguished face. Her gaze ran over the black bags beneath his eyes and the way his hands kept clenching and unclenching.

Then Arianna finally noted the dirt all over the floor and the way the particles danced, poised to move at a moment's notice. Just like they'd always done at his cabin.

Her lips parted as she realized Rion was entirely serious. He had no idea where they were.

But how was that possible? She tried to recall the moments before she'd blacked out again. She'd felt a surge of happiness when they'd saved the pair of Fae. The two had run back to the wall with Rion clearing the way. The Dark Fae had surrounded them on all sides—

Arianna's gaze dropped back to her abdomen.

"You ran," she whispered. Rion's shoulders stiffened. "You ... left them." She could hardly believe the words. He'd just saved an entire city of people weeks ago. He'd been more than willing to sacrifice his life for theirs. But with her life on the line—"I don't understand. Zylah was there. You could have made a difference. What if," her voice cracked. "What if they all died because—"

"I don't care."

She blanched and he sat up, running one hand down his face. He stared at the curtains across the room, but didn't rise from the bed. Rion's magic shifted, moving in a pattern she'd come to know all too well. Arianna bit down her fear at the sight of it.

"You don't mean that," she tried. "Your mother and sister were there. So many people and—"

Rion whirled on her. "And I don't care!" His eyes were wide and wild and silver lined the corners. "Let them burn. Let it crumble. Let it all fall." His chest rose and fell, pain sparking down their bond in spirals she almost couldn't bear. Rion took a shaky breath, his heart racing. "I'd let this whole gods-forsaken world burn for you and I wouldn't think twice."

Silence filled the tiny cottage, save for the sound of his ragged breaths. "Two days," Rion whispered, his gaze now locked on the floor. "I've spent two days counting every breath. Two days wondering if the nightmares that haunted me during those months at that bastard's hands would all come true. Two days, Arianna, and I haven't left this room for fear that your next breath could be your last."

He was shaking and Arianna wondered if his body had done that for two days, too. She saw him now. He was balancing on the edge of a cliff and one gust of wind would send him toppling over the edge.

Maybe he'd already fallen.

"I'm not a stranger to fear," he continued. "I've lived with it for most of my life. It was always in the shadows whether I wanted to recognize it or not. I shoved it down for years. Decades.

"The first time I acknowledged it was when I found myself at the mercy of a beautiful female in my war camp. I had no allies. No one I could turn to. I was an abomination and yet she showed me kindness.

"The second time was when that same female was taken from me. When I scented her blood, I thought her dead." He paused, taking another breath. "I willingly gave myself over to that fear when I allowed her to place her hands on me.

"But those moments were *nothing* compared to the ones I faced at Niall's hands." Rion swallowed hard and she remained silent. They hadn't talked about his time in captivity. His voice lowered to a near whisper. "I witnessed your death over and over and over again. I saw you torn apart by our enemies. I saw your blood pooling at my feet." He shook his head. "Every single time, whether by my hand or another's.

"I tried telling myself it was just a glamour and that no such thing would ever happen. You were a warrior after all, you could defend yourself. I've watched you do it. So when we stood on that wall and the Dark Fae were closing in, I choked down the instincts screaming at me to hide you away." He paused again, his throat bobbing.

"Then you fell. You were hurt and I couldn't get to you in time. My nightmares became reality. Every image Niall had shown me didn't even come close to the pain I experienced in that moment." Another pause. "I *felt* you. As real as if the pain were my own. I—" he paused, shaking his head again. "I sat by helpless." He stared at his hand. "All this power and I was *nothing*. I could *do* nothing."

Arianna's lips parted, but no words came out. She'd almost lost him once too, and she'd nearly drowned in her own fear. She hadn't even known they were mates yet.

"You're all I have. I live for nothing and no one but you. If you fall, I go with you."

"Don't talk like that. Alastríona would need someone—"

"No." He said the word so harshly she might have flinched if she didn't feel his desperation right alongside it. "You will not ask me to do that. You will not command me to live without you. I've already lived a life with nothing but shadows for company. I will not be condemned to that fate again. If you leave this world, I go with you."

Tears blurred her vision. She knew she wouldn't be able to survive without Rion either. Life would be empty. Meaningless.

He finally looked at her again, then took her hand in his own. "You are my life, Arianna. Without you, I have nothing else." He wiped a tear rolling down her cheek and his face softened. "Don't cry." She couldn't help it. She hated Niall. Hated every foul thing he'd put her mate through.

Arianna swallowed hard. "The Fae. Thank you for saving them."

His jaw flexed. "Never again." She met his gaze. "Even if you hate me for it, I will never risk your life for another's again. No matter the circumstances."

She didn't say anything in return. Rion tried to pull his hand back, but she caught it. A familiar ache echoed down the bond. A lying voice that told him he was a monster and no one wanted him near.

"Your darkness doesn't scare me."

He let out a shuddering breath and peered down to the earth still circling his feet. "I'm not … calm right now."

"You don't have to be. I don't need a mask to love you."

Even through her nagging fear, she knew who Rion was and the harsh life he'd experienced. What she hadn't known was the full extent of the damage Niall had inflicted upon an already fractured soul.

Arianna tugged on his hand. "Come here."

Rion joined her in bed once again. He held her close, pressing his lips to her hair and breathing in her scent over and over as though reminding himself that this was his reality.

He was angry and hurt and needed a few centuries to sort through all the pain this life had thrown at him. But it didn't look like he'd get that any time soon.

Arianna clutched his arm. "How bad was it?"

His body shuddered. "Bad. The blood—" Rion's jaw flexed again and she felt the absolute gut-wrenching terror of the moment sweep down their bond. "They have healers here. If it wasn't for them—"

Arianna pulled away slightly. "Healers?" Clearly not the normal sort. She'd always been taught that The Divine was the only one who possessed the ability to heal with magic.

"Witches," he said. "Or Weavers, as they like to be called. One of them explained their magic is different from yours, but she mended you enough to keep you alive."

"Well, that's something." He nuzzled back into her. "Tell me what you *do* know."

"They promised us refuge. They've kept their word so far and maintained their distance at my request. The Weaver who healed you is the only one who visits, along with her partner."

The fact that Rion had let anyone near her at all was a miracle in itself. "What else?"

"I think we're north of Ruadhán. It was hard to keep track after—"

He trailed off and Arianna squeezed his arm. "It's all right. Have they told you anything?"

"I haven't given them much of a chance, honestly. I've made it clear they're not welcome to linger."

Arianna glanced around the room again. They'd been provided food and shelter and space, but even as she took in the clean sheets and pleasant surroundings, she couldn't help but ask, "Are we prisoners?"

"No," he said the word with so much malice that Arianna almost shrank away. "I'd rip this whole place to pieces before I'd let that happen."

"Then I suppose it's a good thing we don't have such intentions." Arianna's head lifted toward the door and the woman standing on the threshold. Arianna didn't know how she hadn't heard it open. Rion hadn't reacted either. Perhaps neither of them were in their best state of mind. Or perhaps there was more strange magic at work.

Rion sat up and positioned himself to Arianna's front. Earth rose to surround his body, but he didn't growl or show his teeth.

A male appeared at the woman's side, his brows knit with worry as he eyed Rion's magic. Arianna scented the air. He was Fae, but the woman wasn't.

"I thought you two might be hungry." She lifted the tray in her arms for emphasis before entering and placing it on the small table beside the window. Arianna noted the swell of her stomach and the way the woman's hand cradled it. She turned back to the pair. "Would you like me to look at your wound?"

A Witch. Arianna had heard of them, but she couldn't recall—another throb pulsed through her temple. Had she read a book about them or merely been told their history? She remembered enough to know that they could live among humans undetected for a time. They aged much slower, so they couldn't linger long. They were also said to only dwell on the northern continent, so why was one here?

"Just you?" Rion asked, eyeing the male behind her.

"He can come in," Arianna said. Rion bristled, but when her hand reached for his, he stepped back to take it. "She's carrying his youngling; you can't expect him to wait outside."

Rion's eyes traveled down to the woman's stomach again and he finally nodded.

The woman waddled over to Arianna's bedside and Rion's sand parted, moving aside to allow her through. The male followed, but stopped just a few steps inside. Rion moved back and the woman eased herself onto the bed.

"My name is Sive. It's so nice to finally see you awake." Her smile was infectious, carrying enough warmth to brighten the entire room. "May I check your wounds, Your Majesty?"

Arianna's lips parted slightly. She supposed she wouldn't need to worry about hiding her identity here. "Just Arianna."

Sive inclined her head. "As you wish." Rion helped Arianna sit up and move her shirt aside. He winced again, but then Sive's hands were prodding Arianna's tender skin. Then she began drawing symbols over the raised scar. Arianna's eyes widened when the symbols turned blue, glowing faintly before sinking into her flesh. Warmth spread through her and the pain alleviated a fraction.

"Those are the same symbols I saw under Ruadhán."

The woman's thin fingers paused a moment before continuing.

"Around Niall's captives, I presume?"

Arianna's heart skipped. "How do you know about them?"

The warmth in her gaze vanished. "I know many things, all of which we're more than willing to share." She eyed each in turn. "Were you—able to save them before…"

Tears pricked the corners of Arianna's eyes. "A few." She looked away then, shame flooding through her. They'd left so many behind; she only hoped that by severing them from Niall's hold, they'd found peace in the afterlife.

Rion seemed to reflect the regret. She wondered if he blamed himself, too. He'd tried as hard as he could to hold the city up longer, but his body had given out.

"Don't blame yourself. The fault lies with another. At least they're free now."

Arianna tried not to let accusation leak into her tone as she asked, "If you knew they were there, why didn't you try to free them your-selves?"

"Ruadhán is—was," she corrected, "a fortress. We did try, but our spies were always caught. All we can do now is pray for their souls and try to liberate the others."

"What others?" Rion asked.

Sive eyed him. "We have a long story to tell you. For the sake of clarity and questions, it should probably be done in one sitting and by someone who possesses more knowledge than I."

"Who?" Rion asked.

"Our appointed leader. He's ready when you feel up to it."

"Where are we, exactly?" Arianna asked.

"In a sanctuary near the western mountains where those liberat-ed from Pádraigín's influence have gathered to stand against the High Lord of Ashling. We've successfully uncovered the true history of the continent and have documented the atrocities committed by the High Lord in order to keep the truth hidden."

"What truth?" Rion asked.

"That you are our rightful king and have been wronged by a male who has been on a quest for vengeance for centuries."

Rion's lips parted and silence fell over the small space. Sive pulled her hands back from Arianna's stomach and rested them in her lap. Her partner inched closer, but Rion only offered him a passing glance.

"I'm not even sure how to respond to that," Arianna said, feeling her mind whirl. She already knew their history had been manipulated thanks to Eimear's revelations, but even Eimear hadn't been able to elaborate on the extent of it. "Before we meet anyone, can you tell us what happened at the village?" If they'd found Rion, then perhaps they would run to provide aid. "Is everyone okay?"

Sadness covered Sive's features again. "We don't have answers yet. Our scouts haven't returned."

"Why not?" Rion asked.

"It's hard to say. It could be due to the Dark Fae, Niall's warriors, a guarded patrol, capture. The world isn't as predictable as it once was."

"I need to know," Arianna pressed. She couldn't imagine a world without Talon. Surely she would have felt something if he'd—

Sive stood and her partner rushed forward to help her up. "I'll see what can be done. When you feel up to it—"

"I'm fine," Arianna interrupted, even as she winced. "I want to know everything. I—we need an explanation."

Sive nodded. "I'll send word to Conall then. Do you wish for him to come here?"

"No," Arianna said. "We'll go to him."

Chapter Twelve

Rion

Rion carefully helped Arianna slide a shirt over her head. She slipped her arms through the sleeves but winced when she pulled the hem down over her torso.

"You promised to rest," Rion said, watching as his mate stared at the pants still lying on the bed. She'd have to stand to put them on. She'd gotten up a few minutes ago to relieve herself in the bathroom. It had been a struggle that had left her panting.

"I know, but I can't just sit here." He understood. It was the only reason he wasn't forcing her to stay in bed.

Sive had left with her partner, giving Rion and Arianna privacy, and to inform their leader that they'd be arriving soon. The Weaver had reiterated that there was no rush, but Arianna was having none of it. She wanted answers. As did Rion. At the very least to know for sure whether they were safe.

Conall of Móirín. He'd never heard the name, but given this place's secrecy, that came as no surprise. The world was littered with secrets. Maybe today the truth would finally come to light.

Sive had promised the walk wasn't too far, but she'd still offered a wagon to assist Arianna. Rion had declined. Arianna would be safer in his arms where his magic could protect her. She was conscious now and he'd already seen frost crawling across her arms. Her magic had been pent up for two days and needed release. She might even be able to subdue them without his help.

"Foot," Arianna said, tapping the bed.

"What?"

"I want to see your foot. You can't carry me limping." He opened his mouth, but she interrupted. "Otherwise I'm walking." Both knew it was a false threat—she could hardly stand on her own—but Rion relented and sat beside her and propped his leg up.

Her hands prodded the tender flesh around his swollen ankle for a moment, then that familiar glow illuminated the room. Something cracked again and he gritted his teeth, but then warmth spread through the muscles, mending them quickly.

"Shoulder." He didn't argue this time. Instead, Rion pulled his shirt off, revealing the bandages he'd wrapped over himself. Arianna's fingers pulled them off to reveal where he'd stitched the wound. She went to work. On that wound and the small ones covering his body.

Her fingertips were like fire over his skin, igniting his blood and body. He never thought he'd get to feel them again.

Once satisfied, Rion helped her stand and pull her pants on. He lingered, staring into those cerulean eyes that had captivated him so long ago.

Rion brushed the hair away from her face. He hated the way her heart raced whenever his magic appeared, but the way she still stared at him with so much love in her eyes told him she'd forgive him later.

"We can stay," Rion offered again. Her body trembled despite the painkiller. Despite Sive's assurance, he'd still made someone drink it before it had even entered the little cottage, just to ensure it was safe. He'd refused to drink any himself. Not with Arianna vulnerable.

She placed a hand on his chest. "For how long?"

"Until you're healed." His voice lowered. "Until you can fight."

"What if it's too late by then?" He wanted to tell her it was likely too late now. Whatever had happened to Talon and the villagers was over and done. But Rion could still see the hope in her eyes, as if she believed some other force might have intervened on their behalf. "It'll be okay. If they'd wanted to harm us, they wouldn't have healed me."

Rion pressed his forehead to hers. He wanted to believe those words. They made sense, but the world had taught him not to trust anyone, even those who reached out a helping hand. The other hand could just as easily be carrying a knife. If they wanted something from Arianna, which was likely, and Arianna refused—his jaw clenched again.

"If we have to fight—"

"I have my magic," Arianna said. "We'll give them hell."

He glanced down at the particles around their feet. "I'm sorry. I know you're not comfortable with my ma—"

She pressed a finger to his lips, then drew Rion into a gentle kiss that had his blood racing. "It's okay," she assured. "I'll be fine." His grip tightened around her. He'd never forgive himself for hurting her, and once this was all over, he'd spend the rest of his life making up for his mistakes.

Rion's gaze traveled to the door. He could protect her this time. No one would harm her again.

"Ready?" she asked.

"No." But Rion placed one hand under her legs and supported her back with the other before lifting Arianna from the floor. She hissed in pain and Rion waited for her to tell him this was too much, that she needed to rest after all. But of course, Arianna just stared at the door, waiting for him to step through.

He could hear several people outside, but as always, they were keeping their distance. His magic reached for the doorknob and twisted it. Everyone who'd been whispering outside fell silent. He took one more moment to steady himself before stepping outside into the sun.

A warm breeze floated past, rustling the trees. It carried the pleasant scents of summer. The spring flowers that were fading. The smoke from interior fires. The food that was being prepared for all who lived here.

A line of trees stood off to their left, all tall and wide, seeming to have stood for a hundred years. A smaller tree sat nestled right against the cabin with pink flower petals littering the space around its roots.

Three warriors stood just ahead, all staring at the open doorway and the two Fae within. Rion's gaze traveled over their forms. None carried weapons, but Rion noted the swords and knives in the grass off to one side.

Their gazes roamed over him first, then drifted to Arianna. Arianna gripped his tunic, just as uncertain as he felt. His magic came up to surround them and one of the warrior's lips parted.

Movement from the right had Rion's eyes shifting quickly, taking in all he could while he kept a constant watch on the males before him.

A village.

Bodies moved back and forth along what appeared to be a well-trodden path. He noticed someone lounging in a rocking chair beneath a covered porch. Younglings played in the dirt, all chasing a ball with sticks in their hands. One screamed in delight while another stomped their foot in frustration.

One of the males stepped forward and Rion's attention snapped back to him. The male lifted his hands. "Sive isn't back yet. I could escort you if you wish."

Rion's jaw worked as he took in the male's broad shoulders. Rion scented the air and found Fiadh's flaming undertones. If he were a Shadow Weaver—

"It's okay, she sent me."

Rion nearly whirled as a female appeared. He stepped back from the threshold, clutching Arianna in his arms. A quick scan told him she wasn't carrying any weapons. Rion studied her features and the kindness in her eyes. It reminded him of—his lips parted. She didn't appear much older. Maybe thirty by human standards. She was still beautiful, her body fuller, healthier compared to all those years ago.

"You don't remember me, do you?" She rushed on without giving him time to answer. Just like she'd done in the past. "It's been a long time, but you liberated me and my family from Nàdair."

Rion studied her features, hardly believing his eyes, then his gaze dropped to her exposed wrists and the scars all former slaves carried. "Cara?" A gentle smile graced her features. "But you're supposed to be in Levea."

"I was, and spent several happy years there." She looked around, absorbing her surroundings with quiet appreciation. "But I've found myself somewhere new, where I can forward the kindness of a stranger onto others."

"But … you have a family."

"A happy one, thanks to you. Some are here with me, others are back home." Arianna had gone still in his arms, studying the female before them. "They thought you might be more comfortable if you saw a familiar face."

He glanced back at the three still standing next to the trees. They hadn't moved. "I'm not sure comfortable is how I'd choose to describe it."

Cara's smile didn't waver. "Strange how fate flips the tables, isn't it?" Rion opened his mouth to respond but closed it again. Was this really happening? Was she really here? Cara's smile faltered. "I trusted you once. I hope you'll be able to do the same with me."

"Cara was among the first of the slaves I liberated from Brónach," he explained to Arianna.

Cara's gaze shifted to his mate. "It is an absolute honor to meet you, My Lady. I knew your mother for a short time. She welcomed us into your beautiful city with open arms." Rion felt Arianna's emotions down the bond, but she appeared to be at a loss for words. Cara didn't seem to mind as she addressed Rion again. "I told you you'd find someone someday."

Rion recalled that conversation and the doubt he'd felt in that moment. One of the Fairy Folk had sat beside him, quietly echoing Cara's words. He looked down at Arianna and wondered if the little creature had known what his future would hold.

"I promised you refuge if you ever needed it back then," she continued. "This might not be my home, per se, but I trust these people with my life. They won't harm you or her."

"I find it difficult to trust anyone."

"I know." He hated the sadness in her tone. Cara gestured to her left. "Conall is this way. They'll have refreshments for you. Or, if you've changed your mind, I can have them brought here. Either way is fine."

Rion's foot drifted back. He wanted nothing more than to take Arianna back inside the cottage where he could protect her until she'd healed, but his mate had other plans.

"Lead the way."

Frustratingly stubborn female. Rion gritted his teeth and Cara bowed, an act that had him wincing. She should never bow to anyone ever again.

He followed her as she moved along the perimeter of the trees. The warriors followed at a distance, leaving their weapons behind. Some paused to stare at them in the distance. They placed their hands over their hearts in reverence, as if they already knew who he carried in his arms.

"Sive mentioned this place was a sanctuary," Arianna said after a beat of silence.

"It is. Those who learn the truth generally have nowhere else to go. Not unless they want to forget all over again." Cara kept a leisurely pace and peered back at them. "I heard about your unfortunate encounter with Niall and the fall of the royal city." She turned forward again. "Conall can explain things better, but from what I've gathered, Pádraigín's High Lord has been waging his own internal war against the continent for centuries. He'd altered minds, shifted our history, denied us our gods, and stripped our rulers from their rightful place."

"So he's not with Niall?" Rion clarified.

Cara stopped at that and turned, her brow furrowed. "You think I'd have anything to do with that monster?" He flinched at the word. "No, Conall isn't working with Niall or his father. We'll all rejoice when Ashling is finally destroyed."

He scented the truth in her words and Rion's shoulder sagged with relief. They were safe from one enemy, at least.

"But you have Pádraigín's magic protecting this place, don't you?" Arianna asked. Rion glanced at the trees beside them. He could feel the barrier nearby, like a void had been carved out in the world.

"Yes. Just because a leader is in the wrong doesn't mean a country's entire people are at fault. Not everyone shares his beliefs, and I'm willing to bet most aren't even privy to the information. They're nothing but disposable bodies to him."

"How many are here?" Rion asked, gazing out toward the village.

Cara looked too. "I'm not certain of the numbers. Conall keeps that information to himself. Just in case. I know there are at least two other settlements, and more people arrive every day."

"And how long have they been here?"

"Since the beginning. Since the High Lord decided to implement his will on everyone he could reach."

Rion felt hope trickle down the bond. He glanced down at his mate but couldn't read her thoughts. Perhaps Arianna believed they might be allies. Or could provide information that might help her get her sister back. He could listen to this Conall if that proved to be the case.

Another cabin came into view as they neared the other side of the clearing. Trees circled behind it and around it. Smoke curled from a stone chimney and the scent of food floating toward them had his stomach growling.

He'd refused to eat while Arianna was out, just in case. Nothing Sive did could convince him otherwise.

Arianna glanced up at him and even Cara peered over her shoulder. He knew Arianna was hungry as well, though she didn't voice her needs either. Maybe with Cara here, he could let himself relax a bit.

Beneath the trees, six wooden chairs stood around an old table with faded indigo cushions tied to each, a welcome sight considering Arianna's wounds.

Cara inclined her head to the male standing in the doorway. Rion studied him too, but when Arianna shifted in his arms and winced again, he moved to set her down first. Cara handed him another pillow, but didn't reach for Arianna, much to his relief. He wasn't sure he could handle even her doing so right now.

Cara scooted one of the chairs closer for him, then settled herself in one on the opposite side.

Silence fell over the space and Rion glanced up at the male again. No one dared to move. It felt as though the world itself had frozen.

The male swallowed hard, his throat bobbing as he took them in. Arianna seated in a chair, pillows propping her up and Rion standing at her side, ready to tear the world apart should it prove to be a threat.

A pitcher of water sat on the table with droplets rolling down the side. Rion noticed the way Arianna stared at it. Cara did, too. The female took it upon herself to fill three cups. She took one back to her seat and drank from it. Rion was silently thankful for the gesture.

The male still hadn't moved. He appeared both ancient and young. His cheekbones were sharp, making him both striking and formidable. A deep scar hung above his left eye. His skin was a shade darker than Rion's, as though the sun had permanently branded him with its rays.

Untamed dark hair curled around his pointed ears and his hazel eyes carried a weariness that Rion recognized all too well.

He wore practical clothes, comfortable with no weapon in sight. At least they were sticking to that part of their routine. The male's arm moved and Rion's eyes locked onto an object around his wrist.

Iron. Not a shackle, but a bracelet similar to the one his mother wore.

The male stepped down from the top step, keeping his movements slow. He carefully walked down the second and third. Rion's magic circled himself and Arianna. He gritted his teeth at the scent of her fear. She did her best not to show it, but Rion could feel her emotions down the bond as if she was reliving the moment he'd snapped her arm in half.

Another step and the male dropped to one knee, twisted his

wrists up, and bowed his head. "My King." He glanced up briefly, his eyes shining with unshed tears. "My Queen."

"You don't have to do that," Arianna said. Rion wasn't sure he was inclined to agree.

The male rose slowly, his hands never moving from his sides. "May I sit?"

Arianna nodded, but the male didn't move. He met Rion's gaze instead, seeking permission from them both. "Wherever you wish me to be, you have but to say the word."

Rion nodded toward the farthest chair across from them. The male crossed the space and sat, still watching the pair with a reverence Rion had rarely experienced. "My name is Conall. I am the present leader and organizer of the village you see before you and I'm more than happy to answer any questions you might have." He looked between them again. "I can't begin to tell you what an honor is it to sit in your presence. My sources have been bringing me regular updates on you both, but I never imagined I'd get to see you in the flesh so soon."

Uneasy silence filled the space as they all stared at one another. Cara sipped on her water, but before anyone could speak again, the cabin door opened and a female carrying a large tray emerged from behind the door.

Rion's magic retracted to circle Arianna, and Conall sat straighter. The first tinge of fear drifted off the male. It wasn't for himself, but for the female now staring at them as she noted the tension in the air.

"Am I too early?"

"It's okay," Arianna said. Again, Rion wanted to protest. He didn't want all these strangers around his injured mate.

The female's face beamed and much to Rion's displeasure, she practically skipped down the stairs, completely ignoring his magic as she placed the silver tray on the table. The female placed a chaste kiss on Conall's lips, then seated herself beside the male. She was a ray of sunshine that had just pierced through a cloudy sky. Completely out of place.

"Sorry," Conall murmured, staring at her. "She can be a bit

free-spirited."

"Well, we can't very well let them go hungry." She gestured to the food. "Help yourself. I'm sure you're famished."

Rion eyed the plate, then met her gaze. "You first."

The female's face faltered, all humor vanishing. "I would never."

"Remember what he's been through," Conall said, resting a comforting hand on her leg.

"Right." She tried to smile again, but it didn't quite meet her eyes. It was Cara who stood and took a cookie from the center of the plate before popping it into her mouth. Rion watched her as she sat again.

"I figured it wouldn't matter if they did it," Cara said. "Given that they prepared the plate and all."

Arianna's stomach growled and Rion's soon followed.

"Please," Conall said. "Help yourselves. We can bring you more if you wish. Some real food perhaps, instead of just pastries?"

"I'm fine," Arianna lied. The scent of it floated through the space between them.

"Bring them food," Cara said. "I'm not going to sit here and listen to their stomachs growl the whole time you prattle on."

"I do not prattle," Conall said, straightening. Rion noted how relaxed Cara appeared to be with one leg pulled up on the chair and the other dangling loose. She might be a guest among them, but it was clear she'd formed a deep connection with the community.

Conall raised one arm and someone else emerged from inside the house. He instructed them to fetch food from inside, then they disappeared again.

"There's a few people on standby, just in case you need anything."

Silence filled the space again. "Have you gotten any news from the village?" Arianna asked.

Conall nodded. "Most survived thanks to Brónach's High Lord. We're still getting reports, but—"

"Alec is there?" Rion interrupted.

Conall nodded, a slight smile on his face. "He is. He arrived not long after you left, actually. A small party of your companions is on their way as well."

Arianna's lips parted. "They're coming here?"

Conall nodded again. "We felt having a few friendly faces might ease any uncertainty."

Rion's heart sped. Friendly faces. Alec. They'd survived?

"When will they get here?" Arianna pressed.

Conall looked through the canopy of trees overhead as if trying to gauge the time. "Any time now."

"But—how, I don't understand—"

"You're sure it was Alec?" Rion interrupted again. He'd known Saoirse had sent their brother letters, but he never imagined Alec would show up personally.

"A few of our warriors were present during the siege."

"Why?" Rion demanded.

"We've been … watching you." Conall grimaced. "That sounds a lot worse than it's intended to."

"For how long?"

He winced again. "Your entire life."

Rion's hand flexed as he stared at the male. He clenched his jaw, searching for the words that were swelling with his anger. A peaceful village stood behind him. These people appeared happy. Comfortable.

"You claim I'm your king," he began, voice low and dangerous. "Yet you allowed me to live as an exile?" His magic jerked in agitation.

"It's … difficult to explain."

"Enlighten me," Rion demanded, enouncing each syllable.

Conall loosed a breath and eyed his female companion before leaning forward. He didn't back down from Rion's hard stare. "Lady Eimear is one of us."

Fire sparked through Rion's soul. "Bullshit."

"She knew who you'd become, but—"

"Do not bring my mother into this."

"She's part of it whether you want to believe it or not. She helped keep us safe as much as she could. Your mother is a seer. Any hold Pádraigín tried to have over her was fleeting at best. Her visions would show her the truth. That's how she found us."

"I don't believe you."

"I'm wearing iron."

"And you have people here with Pádraigín's magic."

Conall blanched. "I swear, we're not—"

"There's no way my mother would have willingly let me suffer the way I did."

"Of course not," Conall said. "That's why she disappeared in the first place. She was trying to find a way to prevent those things from happening to you. She was exploring different paths and possibilities. She—"

"Enough!" Rion's magic blasted through the table before them, shattering it and scattering the contents across the ground. Conall's bracelet was off a second later, water springing to life to wrap around the female at his side. Cara had summoned small trees with interlacing branches to protect herself.

Conall and the female finally stared at him like the monster he was.

Rion's heart beat wildly in his chest, stealing the air from his lungs one breath at a time.

His mother had been taken because of him? She'd suffered at Niall's hands because—because—

"Rion." Arianna's voice was too far away. Muted, as though she were underwater. He stumbled back, then stepped forward again, determined to stay close to her. He had to protect Arianna. He—his mother.

Something like cold water blasted through his fire from behind. He whirled, baring his fangs at whoever had dared to touch him. But—he wasn't wet. It wasn't water that had struck him. It was—the feeling hit him again, breaking through the wall of flames consuming his every thought.

"Be calm," another voice said. He saw the owner of it before him, a black silhouette against a blurry landscape. Colors shifted together, blending until they were too murky to distinguish the sky from the ground.

Rion shifted into a stance, his magic rising, moving faster and faster around his body.

"Rion." Arianna's voice again, only this time it was frantic. Afraid. He turned, trying to find it, needing to protect her at any cost.

That icy magic blasted into him again, sending Rion to one knee. He growled at the way it broke through his mental defenses.

"Don't hurt him." A beautiful voice cried out. But why? Why not hurt him? Why not end him? Why not—

The magic blasted into him again and everything froze. Sounds, colors, the buzzing in his mind.

It hit again. He'd lost track of how many times this was. But now it cascaded through his chest like warm water dousing a raging fire.

Rion blinked the world back into focus. A woman stood before him, her hands moving through the air. It took him a moment to realize she was the source of it all. Sive.

Rion turned to find the table broken, the chairs along with it. Arianna stood closer to the cabin now, Cara helping to hold her up.

His mate tugged on their bond, desperate and terrified.

Terrified.

Rion examined the ground at their feet and the way it had been overturned, leaving the grass bare in several places. Cold sweat trickled down the back of his neck.

"You're all right," Sive whispered. She made no move to approach. "Everyone is safe and you're all right."

He didn't feel all right. He felt too thin, worn out like an old piece of fabric that had nearly turned translucent.

"I—Arianna." He turned to face his mate. She watched him with her lips parted, body hunched over from pain.

"She's all right," Sive repeated.

"I didn't mean—" Gods, what the hell had just happened?

Sive drew another symbol and he clung to the magic that washed through him, centering him.

"The mind can only tolerate so much hardship."

Rion clutched his head. The mind … was he finally losing it? Is that what she meant?

"I told you to broach the subject gently." It took him too long to register that Sive was addressing Conall. Scolding him. Rion glanced over his shoulder to find the male rising to his feet, pulling his female companion up as well.

"I didn't think—"

"No, you didn't," she chastised, her voice harsher than Rion had ever heard it. Conall closed his mouth and took in the aftermath. Rion dared to look at Arianna again. She just stared, her heart slowing to nearly normal levels.

How many times was he going to hurt her, or nearly hurt her? Rion stared at the chair she'd been seated in. He'd obliterated it.

"I need space." What he truly wanted was to run, but even if he was a danger, he couldn't leave Arianna alone. But they'd said the others would arrive soon, maybe then—

"No, you need to rest. You've been awake for two days, have refused to eat, and saw your mate nearly die before your eyes. Group that in with months of torture, finding your mother, and struggling with the new truth of your heritage, I'd say it's a miracle you're still sane."

Rion collapsed to the ground and pressed his palm to his temple. "Maybe I'm not."

"You certainly wouldn't be the first." He peered up at her. "We rescue those trapped in the prisons. We see what it does to a person."

"And?"

"We can help. If you'll let us."

He loosed a weak laugh that bordered on the edge of hysteria.

Sive stepped closer and reached out. "Let me see your hand."

He stared at her open palm and imagined that she might have knelt beside him if she were able. The shadows in his mind whispered against trusting her, but Rion was tired of fighting. He simply gave in and placed his hand in her own.

Her fingers were warm and gentle. They prodded the skin around his wrist for a second before she was drawing lines across it.

Relief washed through him ten times stronger than what she'd been doing from a distance.

He wanted to fold in on himself. To bury his face in Arianna's shoulder and come apart at the seams. Maybe then his pain would ease. Maybe it never would.

Her hand traveled down his arm. "This will only last a short while. I need something to write the runes out in order to make them permanent."

"What do they do?"

"Remind your heart that this is your reality. It'll block out the most gruesome of the nightmares. You'll still remember, but they won't be able to torment you the way they have been."

"Do it," he said. "Do whatever needs to be done."

Chapter Thirteen

Arianna

Rion settled with his back against a tree and Cara carried a chair over for Sive to settle in. The female with Conall had fetched some ink and Sive was now working on drawing lines across Rion's arms. Arianna wasn't sure she liked the woman putting anything on her mate that might alter his mind, but after seeing what he'd done …

Arianna eyed the wreckage surrounding them. Rion had shattered four of the chairs, and the table was nothing more than tiny fragments scattered across the broken ground. Loose particles of dirt littered the area like a coating of fresh snow.

She gently tugged on the bond again. Rion glanced up, but it was only to ensure she was safe before he looked away again.

Her mate was suffering. Drowning. He had been for weeks, and now he'd finally gone over the edge.

"How are you doing?" Cara asked, kneeling in front of her.

Arianna stared at the female and bit back the tears trying to claw their way up her throat. Arianna just shook her head, then Cara handed her a glass of water.

"I can have another come to work on your wounds if you like; it might help ease the pain." Arianna caught the slight way Rion's head lifted at that.

"I'm not sure that would be a good idea." She'd been so eager for answers that she hadn't even bothered to consider how her mate would handle it. He'd seemed okay, if a little agitated, but he'd also asked her to stay. He'd been on edge already and she'd shoved him off that tottering cliff.

"What is she doing exactly?" Arianna asked, watching as Sive painted markings across her mate's forearm. She still couldn't believe Rion was allowing someone else to touch him.

Cara settled on the grass beside her. "They're runes. Weavers pull magic from the earth and weave them through those symbols to hold their power in place. It's an ancient language of sorts, said to have been developed by those who learned it from the gods themselves." Cara crossed her legs. "The histories in the northern continent are even more complicated than here."

"They wouldn't be complicated if it weren't for Niall."

"Niall is a monster, but his father is far worse. He's the one to really blame for the state of the world."

Arianna glanced around. "Where is Conall?"

"Inside. Sive felt it was probably best for him to give Rion some space until she's finished."

Arianna glanced down to Cara's wrists and the faint scars there. "Rion set you free?"

Cara looked at her then and offered a small smile. "He did. Me and my family." Cara paused. "It was … frightening at the time. He had a brutal reputation even then. But when he offered me a chance at freedom, well…" her gaze drifted to Arianna's wrists. "I'm sure you understand."

Arianna rubbed at one of her scars. Memories flooded back, reminding her of all the death, the whips, the wishing she could be anywhere else.

Arianna ran her hands over her pants, fiddling with a loose strand in the garment. "You said you spoke to my mother?"

Cara smiled at the memory. "I remember walking toward the bridge at the northern gate. There were warriors guarding the entrance. We weren't sure what to do when we saw them. We just stood there, staring until one ran off. Lady Lillian arrived within minutes. Honestly, we all nearly ran, but she promised we'd be safe. That night, we were all cleaned up and went to bed with full stomachs. She helped us settle in. Some decided to pursue an education while others took up a long-loved craft."

"And you?"

"I opened a tea shop."

"Which one?"

"It's near the river in the western district. My son told me it received some damage during the raid from Fiadh, but otherwise it's doing well."

Arianna's eyes went wide. "The Gilded Leaf?"

"You've visited?"

"It's my sister's favorite place." Arianna's voice lowered. "She loves the western district. Claims it has more taste than the eastern side." A weight settled in her chest. She wanted nothing more than to take her sister there again. See her smile.

Cara rested her hand on Arianna's knee. "You'll see her again soon."

Arianna paused. "What do you mean?" She hadn't mentioned anything about her sister yet.

"Conall wants to help you find her." At that, Arianna saw Rion's head lift. "He wanted to be the one to tell you himself, but given the situation—" She met Rion's gaze and Arianna saw a flicker of hope there. "He intends to raid Ashling and release the prisoners, your sister included."

"Don't give her false hope." Arianna turned to find Conall standing in the doorway. Her gaze darted to Rion, but her mate remained still. She sensed uncertainty down the bond but no hostility. Conall seated himself on the first step and folded his hands together.

"You can save her?" Arianna asked.

"Maybe. We've infiltrated Ashling before and have stolen a few of their prisoners. But we haven't dared to enter the upper levels."

"But you said you would," Cara pressed.

"For The Divine, without hesitation. But it won't be an easy feat. Lady Evelyn is likely kept in the upper levels. We'd need nothing short of a miracle to find her without alerting the High Lord himself and if we do it, it'll likely trigger him to act against the entire continent. He's already hell bent on revenge as it is. Rescuing her means this will be our last chance to grab the others and any information within his stronghold."

"You think it'll push him to war?"

"I know it will." He shifted, pushing one foot out in front of him to stretch the joint. "He knows about us. He's known since the beginning."

"And you've been the leader from the start?"

"No, no. I've had several predecessors. It's the group that has survived through the centuries and preserved its original ideals."

"Which are?" Arianna turned to find Rion standing on the other side of the wreckage. He glanced at her, his eyes full of shame and questioning. Arianna let her gaze drift to the markings along his arms.

Sive still sat in the chair behind him, her partner tending to her. Arianna wondered if weaving the magic was taxing on her body or if her discomfort was simply due to sitting in one place for too long.

Rion started toward the far side of the area, but Arianna tugged on the bond, beckoning him closer. He obeyed and settled in the grass across from Cara. The female smiled at him, then Conall continued. "We want to bring down the High Lord and set the continent free."

"But why is he doing this at all? What's the point?"

Conall clasped his hands together. "Did Niall ever tell you the previous Divine's story?"

"He told us she lost her mate then basically went mad."

"He told you the truth. The part that he omitted was that she had a previous lover."

Arianna's lips parted. It couldn't be. That was impossible. Improbable.

"But she lived so long ago."

"Approximately ten thousand years have passed. In his anger, the High Lord convinced himself the mating bond was nothing more than an invisible set of shackles. He believed the female he loved, The Divine, was forcefully taken from him. Due to those beliefs, he's set out to discover how to break an already formed bond. He's failed at every turn and now believes you might be the key to unlocking an answer he's sought for centuries."

"Then why the whole fiasco at the royal city?" she asked. "What was the point in trying to convince the world that Niall was really my mate?"

"To maintain the story he's written. I can't say what was going through his head at the time, nor what he might have been doing in the shadows, but my guess is that he had to make the story play out, if only for a little while."

Conall looked at Rion. "And he might have been enjoying the pain it put you through. He holds a very deep grudge toward the previous King. So much so that he made a point to kill all the ones that followed."

"So what made me different?" Rion asked.

Conall shrugged. "What indeed. My only guess is that you escaped a few of his attempts. Or maybe he uncovered the same information we did and finally realized you needed to live in order for The Divine to be born."

"Why not kill me afterward? Why take me prisoner?"

"That was Niall, not his father. Our sources tell us that Niall isn't privy to all his father's plans. At least he wasn't. It could be different now that the royal city has fallen."

Arianna rubbed her temples, trying to process the information. It all seemed so far-fetched. Like they were inside some messed-up, fevered dream.

The door opened behind Conall and his female companion

smiled at them, a little unsure as she stood there with another tray. "I thought I'd bring you all a few more refreshments."

Cara stood to retrieve them. She set the tray in the grass and poured their tea before passing a mug to everyone. She handed Arianna a soft cookie, then placed the tray before Rion. "Eat something, it'll make you feel better."

Arianna took a small bite. The sweet sugary flavor burst across her tongue and she inhaled the rest of it, earning a smile from Conall's partner before she sat beside him.

Rion finally took one and bit into it.

"If there's anything else you'd like—" The female trailed off.

"Get them both some food." Arianna turned to find Sive standing behind them, moving closer to sit in one of the cushioned chairs that hadn't been destroyed. "They need the nourishment."

The female disappeared inside again. A beat of silence filled the space.

"I apologize," Rion finally said, his gaze locked on the ground. "For my outburst."

"No, I apologize," Conall countered. "Sive warned me to choose my words carefully. I didn't mean to spring on the fact that your mo—" Sive cleared her throat and Conall stopped speaking. His jaw worked. "She's okay, by the way. She wasn't injured during the attack. Neither was your sister."

Rion glanced up, a spark of disbelieving hope in his eyes.

"How do you know?" Arianna asked.

"We're able to send small messages with the runes."

"Is my father okay too?"

Conall nodded again. "The High Lord only suffered minor injuries. Nothing to be concerned over. We'll have more information once your companions arrive."

The female emerged from the cabin, carrying a tray with two steaming bowls. Arianna's mouth watered from the hearty aroma. Cara stood once again and took the tray. She carefully held one bowl and offered it to Rion. He hesitated before taking it. Cara lifted the tray with the remaining bowl and balanced it in Arianna's lap.

Blocks of cut cheese sat to one side of the tray while crackers were neatly piled on the other.

Arianna felt Rion's uncertainty down the bond. Cara looked between them. "I can try it first if you'd like."

"It's okay," Arianna said. She spooned some of the broth and sipped on it, letting the flavors explode across her tongue. A moment later, Rion did the same.

"It's wonderful," Arianna said. "Thank you."

Conall shifted again and slipped the iron bracelet back on. The female settled down next to him.

Arianna's brows knitted. "Why are you wearing iron?"

"It was customary in past days to wear iron in the presence of royalty. It was a sign of complete submission."

If their current situation were different, Arianna wasn't sure she'd like the idea, but given that they still didn't know much about these people, she found the gesture … appreciated.

"You said my mother was involved. How?"

Conall peered over them all to Sive. "Are you sure?" Sive asked. "We can discuss her at a later time."

"I'm sure." Arianna studied her mate. He was calmer now than he'd been since they woke. She stared at the lines on his arm, wondering what kind of long-term effects they might have on him.

"Eimear found us shortly after she married your father," Sive said. "It was then that she adopted a façade that made the High Lord believe she was under his control. It was clear he kept careful tabs on her, therefore she had to tread with utmost caution when it came to this group. We've moved over the centuries, adopting one refuge after another. Eimear claimed we'd be safe here for a long while and we'd know when it was time to move. I'm starting to think she was referring to your arrival."

"Does this High Lord have a name?" Cara asked. "Or are we just going to keep referring to him by a title he doesn't deserve?"

"Vairik," Sive said. "And the previous Divine's name was Laoise."

"Do you think he followed us here?" Arianna asked, fear suddenly pulsing through her anew. She could barely move, if she had to run—

"I think we'd already know if he had; however, I doubt it will take him long to figure it out." Sive's gaze drifted to Rion. "He's always possessed an uncanny ability to locate those who came before you."

Rion swallowed hard. "You mentioned how she'd been captured …" He trailed off again.

Sive's face fell. "Her actions were ones that any mother would take for her child." Sive's hand moved over her stomach. "Eimear received her first vision of who you'd become when you were only three years old. We actually celebrated for an entire week, though she could only stay for a few hours. She'd even brought you along, though I'm certain you were too young to recall such an event."

"She dragged a child across the continent?" Arianna asked.

Sive shook her head. "We were closer to Nàdair back then. I think there was a lake house nearby." Rion perked at that. "Her visions … changed after a time, as if they were being manipulated by an unseen force. She grew frantic and honestly believed those from Ashling had figured out a way to manipulate her visions. She consulted with Conall's predecessor for years on what might be done. She considered putting you under his care, but the visions would shift again and they weren't … pleasant, to say the least.

"We were forced to move away from Nàdair and went south for a time before relocating to Móirín and finally here. There were less permanent dwellings along the way."

"So what happened? If she knew how Rion's life would turn out, why didn't she change it?" Cara asked.

"We believe she tried," Sive said. "The very night she vanished. She wouldn't tell Conall's predecessor exactly what she had planned for fear of the outcome changing again. From what we've pieced together, Eimear was on her way to Ashling. Our only guess is that the attack on Nàdair turned her around. Somehow, she was captured before she ever made it back."

"But wouldn't she have seen them coming?" Arianna asked.

"A seer's visions are not something they can call upon whenever they wish. They can focus and try to listen for whispers, but they're not always found. Eimear's gifts were strong, even for a seer. It's why she wore iron so often, otherwise they'd render her unable to function in daily life."

"So you knew her personally," Rion said.

Sive nodded. "I would love the opportunity to speak with her again. Perhaps help her if your family permits."

Rion glanced down at his arm, but Arianna said, "Wouldn't that make you over a century old?"

"Five centuries, actually."

Arianna's eyes widened. Five centuries. That was five times the age of Rion. Nearly half the age of her father. She was a mere—

Shouting echoed from behind and Arianna turned to find a group of Fae emerge through the trees. No—not emerge. They blinked into existence, popping into her reality one at a time.

Metal slid free from its sheath then a familiar face had a male pressed against a tree with a blade to their throat.

Conall jumped to his feet and slid the iron bracelet off, letting it fall into the grass. Arianna hardly noticed. She cared for little else when she'd spotted that familiar hair.

Talon. Talon was here. He was alive. And just like with every other time in her life—he'd found her.

Chapter Fourteen

Saoirse

Saoirse followed the strangers through the trees, keeping an eye out for any Dark Fae that still lurked along the road. Last night had proven there were more out there than she'd been willing to admit.

She rolled her shoulders, working the tension from her joints. It had been a fight, but nothing they hadn't been able to handle. She hoped it showed these warriors that if they were leading them to a trap, it wouldn't turn out well for any of them.

Such dark creatures. Their mother had told them stories when they were little, but those beasts were supposed to be trapped inside the forbidden forest that resided in the mountains. Yet here they were, running wild, killing any unfortunate enough to cross their paths.

Saoirse gritted her teeth. And now there was some rebel force taking them to gods knew where claiming Arianna and Rion were alive and well.

Talon, Saoirse, and Raevina had bound the entire group in iron to question them. None were lying.

Saoirse kept one hand on her weapon as they moved through the trees. Raevina walked on her right, flames sparking at her fingertips as she watched the space between the trees. Talon marched just ahead, a knife hidden in his palm, ready to let it fly at any given moment.

Zylah trudged along behind with a chained Gavin at her side. The male had begged to accompany them, claiming he could be of use should Pádraigín's forces meet them on the road. They were traveling closer to Ashling and in Pádraigín territory now. Saoirse couldn't fathom why Rion would take Arianna anywhere near their country. Especially when the High Lord already had Ellie.

But maybe they'd told him something she didn't know.

"It's just ahead," a male claimed. They carried weapons, but no one had dared to touch them. Everyone was pensive, waiting for the moment of betrayal.

Seconds later, Talon disappeared. One moment he'd been there, the next he was gone, vanishing into mist. Raevina's heart spiked and the female drew her sword, summoning flames to surround her body before she was running.

Raevina disappeared, too.

Saoirse growled and followed, yanking her blade free. Familiar magic washed over and through her like cold water only to vanish a second later.

Talon and Raevina reappeared and several scents hit Saoirse all at once.

Her eyes scanned the area and when Zylah materialized beside her, she backed toward the female, determined to protect her at any cost.

Talon had a male pinned against a tree with a blade to his throat. Wisely, said male had raised his hands rather than reaching for one of his weapons. Raevina had grabbed another and her flames hovered dangerously close to the male's face.

Two others stood with their hands up, staring at Saoirse, likely wondering which of them would be put in a precarious situation next.

But Saoirse took in the scents littering the space, then her gaze roamed to the houses in the distance. Smoke curled from the chimneys and people moved back and forth, completely unaware of the new Fae in their midst.

"Relax," the male in Talon's grip said.

"What the hell was that?" Talon demanded even though they all knew. Pádraigín's magic. Was she in a glamour? Saoirse glanced back to be sure Zylah still stood behind her. The female nodded, telling Saoirse she was fine.

Their relationship might still be a strained one, but neither could deny how well they worked together. When the village was attacked, Saoirse had fought like hell to keep the Dark Fae away from Zylah's patients. She'd refused to submit, even when the wall had fallen.

It had resulted in Zylah giving her fifteen stitches in her left arm. She'd broken a few in her fight against the Dark Fae. Zylah had silently tended to them again. The hopeful part of Saoirse wanted to reason it meant Zylah cared. Or maybe she was just being practical.

"We have to keep this place hidden from Pádraigín's High Lord," the male answered.

"You can use his own magic to hide from him?"

"I've used it to lie to him," Gavin said.

"No one asked you," Talon barked. The male partly blamed Gavin for Ellie's disappearance. Saoirse couldn't say she blamed him.

"The glamour prevents his spies from finding us. It keeps us safe."

"Why didn't you warn us beforehand?" Raevina demanded, never taking her eyes off the male in her grasp.

"I—" His eyes were wide. "I just assumed you'd know."

Right, because a rebel group wasn't exactly capable of operating in the open. Still, it was a stupid assumption on his part.

"Talon!" Their heads all turned and Saoirse watched the tension fall from Talon's shoulders when he spotted Arianna across the field. Saoirse's gaze wandered to her side and relief flooded through her at the sight of her little brother.

He stood without his magic. No weapons drawn either. Arianna sat in a chair beside him.

Talon left the male where he was and ran, his long legs carrying him across the space in record time. Saoirse glanced back at Zylah and the pair of them were moving a second later with Gavin in tow. She didn't look to see if Raevina followed.

Saoirse studied her brother, searching the space around him for that strange ripple Gavin had pointed out. They'd entered a glamour. Even with their friends supposedly before them, they needed to be careful. None of this might be real.

"Talon," Saoirse called out in warning. The male stopped, seeming to realize the same thing she already had. Arianna's face scrunched as she stared at them, but Saoirse addressed her little brother, or who she hoped was her little brother.

"Tell me something only you would know."

Silence filled the space between them. Rion's magic swirled lightly at his feet, nothing like the storm she'd expected. And … were those markings down his arms? She studied the symbols. They did nothing to ease her mind.

"You have cacti pajamas."

She nearly smiled. "Everyone knows that."

He remained still. Thinking. "They don't know about the stain on the left pant leg where you spilled wine one night. Or how you furiously scrubbed the material, refusing to let anyone else touch them. They also don't know about you meticulously resewing the bottom seam when it comes undone or the night you threw out a male because he tried to rip—."

"All right, all right," Saoirse said. "It's them." She didn't look back at Zylah—couldn't without her face burning. Saoirse wasn't sure why she didn't want the female knowing about her past lovers. Maybe she didn't want to give her any more reason to turn away.

Arianna stood with the help of a stranger. A female, not Rion. She found the gesture odd, but when Talon closed the distance, she heard the clear warning in Rion's tone. "Careful."

It was then that Saoirse took in the way Arianna hadn't fully straightened. Talon watched too and wrapped Arianna in a light embrace before pulling back to look her over. Talon had mentioned

Arianna's injured state before her brother had taken off.

Saoirse inched closer, her emotions flaring through her as she watched her little brother staring at his mate as if she were the only one who existed.

"You're alive," Talon breathed.

"I think that should be my line," Arianna replied. Had she thought them dead?

Rion's gaze turned to his sister. "Alec really came?"

She waved one hand. "Came. Saved. Conquered. The usual Alec dramatics." Saoirse tried to keep her voice calm, even as her body shook. "He showed up shortly after you fled." Abandoned them.

"So the silhouettes I saw in the distance—"

"Weren't more Dark Fae, thank the gods," Saoirse finished. She took another step, closing the distance. Arianna might have been hurt, but he looked well enough. "You're okay?"

Rion nodded. "Nothing I can't handle."

"Good." Then Saoirse slammed her fist into the side of Rion's face, sending him sprawling to the ground. Those in the vicinity drew their weapons and magic sparked through the air. She didn't care, but when Rion stared up at her in shock, the wall of pain she'd been holding back surged to the surface. "What the hell were you thinking?"

The temperature in the air plummeted as a male with dark hair stepped toward her. "How dare you."

"How dare I what?" she shot back.

"You will not strike your king."

King. She hadn't heard anyone else refer to him as such. Not beyond their mother. "I'm his sister," she countered. "I can do as I please, especially when he runs off and makes us worry whether or not I'd find him alive." Her voice broke and Saoirse gritted her teeth.

"I—"

"Stop," Arianna said. She winced and the other female was there, helping her settle back into the chair. Rion just watched, his magic still nonexistent.

"What happened?" Arianna asked after a beat of silence. "Is everyone okay?"

"Avalon is fine," Talon said. "We lost a number of villagers, but they're all relocating to Levea. Your father plans to expand the walls to combat the influx of Dark Fae."

"There's more?" Arianna's face had gone pale.

Talon nodded.

"What about our mother?" Rion inquired, still sitting on the ground. His lip had split at the bottom, but he made no move to wipe the blood away.

Saoirse refused to feel guilty. Instead, she reached out a hand and Rion allowed her to pull him to his feet. "She's with Alec. He wanted to come sooner but had to handle a few unfortunate issues in Nàdiar first. It feels like the entire world has been thrown into chaos."

"Is she okay with him?"

Saoirse's eyes softened. "She knows him. They had a happy reunion. I haven't seen Alec cry in years."

Rion scoffed. "I'm not sure he's capable."

"Oh, he is. Sobbed like a youngling once they were behind closed doors."

"Is Levea going to be able to hold everyone?" Arianna asked.

"Some are going to Nàdair," Saoirse answered. "We have the room, though the journey itself won't exactly be an easy one given all the foul creatures running amuck."

They all fell silent, taking in the changed state of their world. All because Arianna had shoved a piece of iron through Niall. It made her wonder what might happen if they did the same to the High Lord.

"Are you going to introduce us to your new friends or are we leaving?" Saoirse asked, glaring at the male that still had his magic aimed at her.

The frost vanished and his face paled. "You can't leave."

"Why the hell not," she challenged. Talon stood straighter too.

"You—" He glanced between each of them, clearly not accustomed to being the outlier. His gaze finally settled on Arianna. "At least allow us to tell you the full story. Let us present you with the truth if nothing else."

"Tell your warriors to stand down," Talon commanded, eyeing each in turn.

Conall gave a signal and each of them lowered their weapons and let their magic fade. "You'll have to forgive them. Many have waited decades to meet their king, and he was just—"

"Rightfully punched in the face by his sister. Deal with it," Saoirse said. "You didn't interfere for decades when much worse things were happening to him. Don't pretend to be heroic now."

Shame covered the male's face and the scent of it floated through the air. Saoirse let another tense moment pass before she stepped forward and wrapped her arms around Rion's neck, pulling her brother in for a tight embrace. Rion didn't move at first, then returned the gesture.

His heart still raced whenever she touched him, but Rion wasn't trying to pull away from her anymore. He was trying, working through his past demons. She appreciated it now more than ever.

She was fortunate. More fortunate than most. To have her family members continuously taken from her only to see them again. She was certain the gods were at work.

"I'll have more chairs brought."

"That would help get things started," she said. "Along with introductions."

"Conall," the male said. "And you're Saoirse of Brónach, and Raevina of Fiadh." He continued, going through each face in turn. "Talon of Levea, Zylah, and—" The male paused when his eyes met Gavin's. "You—you're the High Lord's grandson. Gavin of Pádraigín."

"Ashling," Gavin corrected. Conall raised a brow. "The current High Lord is a usurper."

"I've never heard you renounce the name."

Gavin's face heated. "Well, it's not like I can say such things in his presence."

Only royal Fae carried the name of their nation. The rest bore the name from their city of origin, wherever that may be. For Gavin to willingly give it up …

"Wait—" Saoirse said. "He's not the rightful High Lord?"

Conall shook his head. "He wiped out the royal family centuries ago. None are left to claim such titles." Fae emerged from the cabin carrying chairs and set them in a circle so that everyone would face one another. They also brought out a few more small tables and refreshments before disappearing again.

Saoirse found the entire display a little unnerving. They seemed more than willing to serve Conall. It reminded her too much of Niall and the way his servants had done the same. Was it fear or loyalty?

Gavin stepped forward, his chains rattled, and Arianna's gaze snapped to them. "Why is he in iron?"

Talon chose to answer. He'd been the one to command it, after all. "Because we didn't have the time or patience to worry about whether he could be trusted."

"Take them off."

"My Lady," Conall said, bowing his head slightly when she turned to him. "Perhaps it might be wiser to keep them on."

"Spoken from someone who's never had to suffer in them."

Conall's lips parted and he bowed his head further before his gaze drifted to her wrists. Sometimes it was hard to believe Arianna had ever been a slave. To think she'd spent over a year in chains herself and had still been kind enough to show her brother mercy. Saoirse glanced to Zylah, watching as the half-breed withdrew the key and unlocked the heavy manacles around Gavin's wrists. The male was smart enough not to summon his magic.

Arianna continued, "He's already pledged himself to me and …" her voice broke, "my sister."

"Why your sister?" Conall asked, his tone skeptical.

"They're mates," Saoirse finished. "And we have full intentions to use any information he can give us to get her back."

"We can help," Conall said. All heads turned to him. "Please, sit. Let's have a long overdue discussion."

CHAPTER FIFTEEN

ARIANNA

Conall filled their small group in on the details he'd already revealed, and Rion made introductions to the others. Saoirse didn't like the fact that Rion had runes on his arms, Raevina clearly doubted their sincerity if her tone was anything to go by, but Talon seemed to be soaking in the details, filing them away to consider later.

Thankfully, Rion had moved closer, though his gaze remained downturned, as if he were waiting for Arianna to chastise him. She'd reached out her hand, and he'd taken it, seating himself in a chair at her side.

Raevina's gaze traveled over the village. "So you plan to infiltrate Ashling with … this?" Her tone was condescending, dismissive, but Conall chuckled, not offended in the slightest.

"I'm certain it pales in comparison to the armies beneath Fiadh's great mountain." Raevina eyed him. "The bulk of our warriors will be arriving back any day now. They're finishing an assignment."

"What sort of assignment?"

"They're liberating prisoners from another set of Niall's prisons.

With his return to Ashling, we worried for their neglect."

"You free those imprisoned," Saoirse said, leaning forward. "You claim our mother worked with you, you want to free the continent of the High Lord's control, and yet somehow, despite claiming him as your king, you still managed to let my brother go decades without interference."

Conall's gaze softened. "We tried."

"Tried," she repeated, tasting the word. Her anger burned through the air, hot as Raevina's fire.

"When I told you the High Lord, Vairik, has a personal vendetta against Rion, I meant it." Conall turned to Rion. "He's been manipulating your mind for a very long time. Whenever we tried to interfere, he'd glamour us to look like an enemy or someone out to kill you."

"Lies," Saoirse hissed. "He'd have to be everywhere. He can't have followed Rion around his entire life."

"This entire continent is under a glamour that's beyond comprehension. He's employed thousands to his cause and has a special team that works with the councils and High Lords."

Conall paused for a breath. "We almost got through to Caol, but he was being watched too closely. It was … strange that Vairik seemed inclined to watch you suffer rather than eliminating you like the others. We can only speculate it's because you resemble the previous King he had altercations with."

Rion squeezed her hand. "If you're about to tell me I'm some kind of reincarnation—"

Conall waved a hand. "No, no, nothing like that, but the spirit of your predecessors—at least the magic they wielded—does live in your veins."

"Is that why it's been acting so strangely?" Arianna asked.

"How do you mean?"

"My magic has been … abnormal. We thought it was just my animal shift trying to take form, but—"

Conall's brows furrowed. "Animal shift? The Divine doesn't have an animal shift."

"She doesn't?" Saoirse asked.

"No, neither does the King. I thought you knew this."

"We knew about Rion, but …"

"Then why has it been so volatile?" Rion asked.

"It could have been due to Niall's presence. Or maybe with your mating bond in place, it can better sense the unnatural glamour in the land, changing things that shouldn't be changed."

"Her magic doesn't react to Gavin," Saoirse said.

"Because he isn't a threat," Talon added. Gavin didn't respond.

"He's also not working with the High Lord, or so you've told me." Conall still eyed Gavin uncertainly.

"You claim this Vairik is over ten thousand years old?" Raevina asked.

Conall nodded. "It's the reason he's so powerful."

"I understand anger," Saoirse said. "But ten thousand years seems like a ridiculously long time to hold onto a grudge."

"A few of you have mates, yes?" None seemed inclined to answer. Talon didn't even look at Raevina and Arianna wondered if the image of her with a knife to her throat still haunted him. "Imagine the one you love was taken from you and suddenly loved another. I'm not rationalizing his decisions, but he firmly believes his lover was taken against her will."

"So it's a breakup gone bad," Saoirse said, rubbing her temples. "And we're dealing with an overgrown teenager."

"If one believes the stories, Vairik and Laoise loved one another fiercely. That type of love isn't something one lets go of easily." Conall's hand moved to rest on the female's knee and she smiled at him.

"So why doesn't the Divine get an animal shift?" Arianna asked.

"From what we've deciphered of the ancient texts, the original Divine and her mate opted to trade their animals shifts for the power to protect their people."

"You know the original story?"

"Most of it."

"Haven't you had centuries to figure it out?" Saoirse said.

Conall nodded. "We have, but just when we think we've broken the code and things start to make sense, another passage proves us wrong. Entire pages are also missing, and I fear we'll never recover them."

Arianna shifted in her chair. "Eimear mentioned something about the statues holding secrets."

"We've been looking there, too. If we find anything, you'll be the first to know."

"Let's take a step back," Saoirse said. "I don't care how old he is, how has a male managed to erase the truth from an entire continent of people who are immortal?"

"If we live forever, why are we so young?" Conall asked. "Who's the oldest Fae you know?" He glanced around and Arianna's heart beat just a little faster as she thought of her father. A male who was only a thousand, yet considered a leader. One of the oldest …

"There were many Fae over the centuries who couldn't be swayed. Sadly, Vairik saw to their deaths. He took advantage of grief, war, and personal vendettas. It's true, there are a few fanatics, as they're called, who preach the truth. But they've been labeled fanatics for a reason, too. They're outcasts. And if one gets too much attention, Vairik puts an end to them."

No one spoke, so Conall continued. "It started with the small villages. He experimented with manipulating their minds until he perfected his technique, and then let it spread to larger towns, then cities until everyone was questioning the truth and their leaders.

"Wars broke out over their beliefs until the ones who knew the truth were either converted or eliminated. It was chaos."

"Isn't The Divine supposed to be born to stop that sort of thing?" Saoirse asked.

"She is, but The Divine couldn't come about because Vairik kept killing the one meant to protect her."

"You'd think the gods would bend their own rules for the sake of peace," Saoirse said.

"If a god makes a rule, are they capable of breaking or bending it?

Their laws are absolute."

"What's the point of being a god then?"

"Perhaps you can take it up with them in the afterlife." Conall paused, waiting for more questions before continuing. "Line by line, Vairik rewrote history until we had what you know today."

Conall's gaze traveled to Raevina. "The only place you might still find the truth is in the deepest parts of Fiadh." The female looked up, her braids falling around her shoulders. "They've always been the most difficult people to persuade, which is why we believe Vairik allied with their nation in the first place. It's also the reason so many are here. But you already know all that."

Raevina didn't speak.

"Anyone going to clarify?" Saoirse said, her tone impatient.

"Shadow Weavers are meant to be guardians to The Divine. Their ancestors devoted their entire lives to ensure her will was enacted upon the continent," Conall answered.

Raevina's willingness to kneel at Arianna's feet suddenly made sense. It was a higher purpose. A calling. Her honor was on the line. And unlike humans, honor was something the Fae craved to uphold.

"Okay," Arianna said, holding up her hands. "Just start from the beginning. Tell us everything."

Conall settled back in his chair. "It's true that we all came from the northern continent after being persecuted by the humans. Those stories have remained unaltered. The original Divine, before she became such, craved freedom for her people. Thus, she and her partner crossed the sea and arrived on the northern shores of what we currently know as Brónach."

"How did they get past the Sirens' territory?" Saoirse asked.

"Repeated crossings are what drew the Sirens in. They didn't occupy that portion of the ocean initially." He reached for a glass and drank deeply before continuing. "As you know, the humans pursued us, and our ancestors were forced to flee into the mountains. They remained hidden and built a small sanctuary, but what they thought was their salvation quickly turned into a nightmare.

"The Dark Fae emerged, attacking both humans and Fae alike. As you can imagine, the Fae had an easier time staving them off, but the cost was still steep. They were desperate and moved further south, hiding in the mountain forest that separates what you currently know as Brónach and Móirín.

"They did their best, struggling to live off the land while fighting the wicked creatures. They were already small in number. The original Divine and her mate wondered if they'd led their people to a worse fate.

"They built altars and every day, the pair visited the highest mountain peak where they prayed and begged the gods for mercy." Raevina snorted, but Conall ignored her and continued. "The gods answered and granted the male and female powers beyond their current ones. Afterward, the people collectively proclaimed them as their monarchs.

"The gods also brought forth what the male and female eventually named The Guardians. Fae that seemed dark yet weren't. Small creatures accompanied them and they formed a pact with the male and The Divine. They agreed to protect them from the Dark Fae if they used their newfound powers to help drive evil creatures from the land."

Arianna glanced at Rion. The Fairy Folk. The Fae in the mountains that hadn't attacked them. Suddenly the statue in the royal city made sense. She was surprised Vairik hadn't destroyed it. Maybe he enjoyed waving a piece of history in their faces.

"The gods also granted them a bond that would hold the pair together and let the other know if their partner was ever in danger."

"The mating bond," Arianna clarified.

Conall nodded. "It also helped Fae find those who would be better apt at producing offspring with one another. It wasn't a guaranteed thing and it wasn't the sole purpose of the bond, but after losing so many younglings, the Fae were glad for it.

"The world moved on as peacefully as it could. What you now call Nàdair was formed first as a stronghold while they beat back the Dark Fae. I'm sure if you looked in your underground libraries, you'd find pictures that detail the entire story."

"Nàdair doesn't have an underground library," Rion said.

Conall gave him a look that told them otherwise.

"Over time, the Dark Fae were driven back and the world expanded. Levea was built, then Purog, and finally Ashling. But the Fae weren't separated by magic back then. The world worked in harmony with The Divine and her mate as the reigning monarchs. They lived for many, many centuries in peace before fading from the land hand in hand. Or so the legend states."

Conall shook his head. "But even the Fae can be petty, sometimes worse than the humans they fled from. Without their monarchs to guide them, ridiculous skirmishes broke out and the four strongholds formed into their own countries. The Dark Fae began to reemerge, and another Divine was needed to bring about peace again.

"As I've already mentioned, the male is always born first. It was a joyous occasion. Once he reached adulthood, the entire continent began searching for his mate."

"How did they know this?" Arianna asked.

"The ancient texts. They were written by the gods through the original Divine as our instructions in case the world ever needed help again. The male was a benevolent king and used his powers to correct as many wrongs as he could before The Divine arrived. He was even the creator of Ruadhán."

"And this is the same Divine that Vairik is so bent out of shape about?" Saoirse asked.

Conall nodded. "The King found her in a market buying something from one of the stalls. Their eyes met and the bond clicked into place instantly."

"Again," Saoirse said. "I understand being disgruntled, but what he's done is—it's like he thinks himself a god."

"I think he does," Gavin said, startling them all. Gavin looked up, seeming to shrink into himself for saying anything at all. "He's … terrifying, to say the least."

Conall continued. "Vairik eventually killed the King. He did the same with The Divine once he realized she couldn't be freed from the bond. It left the world in disarray and allowed the Dark Fae to breed across the land."

"What then?" Arianna pressed. "If the Dark Fae were free, how come we haven't seen them before now?"

"Because he's been storing them away. Niall controlled some of the runes that kept them locked away."

"Ellie mentioned something about cages," Rion said.

"We fear he might be breeding them as well and using the strait along Fiadh's western coast as a transport."

"Hold up, what do you mean controlled the runes," Saoirse asked. "You haven't even properly told us what those are." Her eyes drifted to Rion's arm again.

Sive took the chance to answer. "Weavers, or witches on this continent, are able to manipulate the land's life force with written symbols we call runes. They're an ancient language of sorts."

"And anyone can use them?"

"Weavers are able to use them freely, but there are limits for everyone else. For Fae, the runes are directly tied to their magic. If that magic is cut off, the runes will cease to function."

"What if their magic returns?"

"It wouldn't matter, the tie has been severed. For humans, runes can only be used with their own blood. It's that way with most half-breeds as well. The magic pulls from their life force instead of the land's, which is why many human witches come across as sickly. Their runes cease to function when either the marks are erased or when their lives end."

Raevina rubbed her temples. "I feel like I'm in history class."

"I know it's a lot," Conall said, "but allow me to give you one more piece that's been twisted." Raevina waved her hand for him to continue. "The mating bond," he started. Arianna's heart jolted. She'd already been lied to once about the bond. "It's not a rare occurrence."

Saoirse eyed him. "You're going to have to explain that one."

"I already mentioned that the bond was a gift from the gods.

Their intention was for every Fae to find their mated partner, but those bonds are more likely to form between those with different magical abilities.

"Since Vairik despised the bond, he separated us into four distinct nations, thus alienating many pairs from ever meeting. It solidifies the notion that we're stronger when we're together, which was the reason Ruadhán stood as long as it did. The easiest way to bring down a people is to divide them first."

"Can magic … mix?" Arianna asked, wondering if there were Fae out there capable of using more than one element.

"No, not that we've ever seen."

"But how did the separation start?" Talon asked. "If children had already been born to parents with different magical abilities, how did—" Talon trailed off, clearly unable to voice the horrible acts it would take to achieve such things.

"I'm sure you can use your imagination. He's rewritten entire family lines just to get what he wants. He's started wars and strife among the Fae. He's separated brothers and neighbors. He's certainly not above taking children or eliminating them altogether."

So many things had never made sense. Wars. Separation. Conflicts with no explanation.

"If you've been together this long," Rion said, "why haven't you done something about it? Why didn't you eliminate him a long time ago?"

"We've tried." Conall looked away. "We've raged countless wars and we've been beaten every single time. The number of casualties is astronomical."

"You said he always seems to know where you are," Saoirse whispered. "Is it possible he has a seer?"

There couldn't possibly be a third. They were so rare. Seeing Whelan in the same room as Eimear was something they'd write about for centuries to come.

"No," Conall said. "If that were the case, I'm confident he would have found and eliminated us a long time ago. The unfortunate truth is that we simply haven't been strong enough. We also deal with issues from the public as Vairik has turned the entire continent against us."

"You're the ones he labeled as rebels," Talon said.

Conall nodded. "There are factions out there who are against the idea of The Divine, but most are slavers, and quite frankly, Pádraigín's allies. If any of us are captured, we're put to death without a trial."

"Because a trial would bring out the truth," Talon said.

"And could jar the memories of those they're barely holding onto." Conall's gaze drifted to hers. "Like your father."

Arianna swallowed hard. "So when Niall mentioned that my father was asking questions …"

"Móirín's High Lord discovered one of our books. He began digging after that, and Vairik needed a way to keep him subdued without killing him. Once he learned your father had a mate, he wanted to … liberate him from his affliction."

All eyes turned to Arianna. Her mother had been killed because of this monster. Because this Vairik believed the mating bond was some sort of cage.

"So what are you actually doing that's remotely helpful?" Raevina asked.

"We're freeing those imprisoned around the continent and rehabilitating them in preparation for the coming war. Now that you're here, I believe we have a chance of winning."

Talon furrowed his brow. "Why?"

"Because the gods will be on our side."

"Are you about to tell us Vairik manipulated everything regarding them, too?" Saoirse asked.

"Do any of you know the names of the gods?"

None spoke and Arianna realized she'd never even had a mind to question it. She remembered visiting the temples on occasion with her mother, but the details were … blank, as if she'd forgotten everything. She pressed her palm to her head. They needed to relearn everything. The entire continent had to relearn it.

"So what's his endgame?" Arianna asked.

"I told you: to break the bond. He's conducted experiments for years." She paled. "It's why we're so adamant about rescuing the Fae in his grasp. One doesn't come back easily from a severed mating bond. And when you add torture to the mix, sometimes they don't come back at all."

"What if he can't break the bond?" Raevina asked. "What's his plan then?"

Conall sighed. "We believe that's what the Dark Fae are for. He's never let them roam free like this. We fear he might be giving up on his initial quest, which would lead to the next unfortunate stage of his plans."

"Which is?" Raevina pressed.

"Genocide," Gavin whispered. They all turned to him again, but he still didn't look up. "It's why I left to get help. I overheard him speaking with Niall and—" Gavin clenched his fists. "I've stood by long enough. I can't keep blindly following him."

Saoirse cleared her throat. "Well, clearly he's not taken that route yet, so what's the alternative?"

"Capturing them," Conall said, nodding toward Arianna and Rion. "And seeing if he can break the bond from its source. We believe it's the reason he took your sister, to lure you in."

"Does he plan to kill himself, too?" Saoirse asked. "Just rid Fae from the world entirely?"

"No," Gavin said again. "He'll kill everyone outside the Pádraigín bloodline. The Divine only comes from the Móirín bloodline, right? And," his gaze drifted to Rion, "his only comes from Brónach's. If those two are wiped out—"

"Even with the Dark Fae, he can't possibly take on three countries at once," Raevina declared. "None of them would stand for it."

"No?" Conall questioned. "You're telling me if Levea fell, then Fiadh's High Lord would rush to their aid? And what if Fiadh fell, would either Móirín or Brónach come together to avenge them? He's already divided us, all that's left is to conquer."

"He'll target Levea first," Talon said. "Levea and Nàdair are allies.

They'd rally to stand against him, but if one is wiped out first, then the other wouldn't be as strong."

"And Levea doesn't have an entire mountain range to protect it," Raevina said.

"If he releases all the Dark Fae, how does he plan to control them?" Saoirse asked.

"He doesn't. He'll move to the western continent and start over as its ruler."

"You'd think after all these years, he'd just fade already."

"Maybe he will, but by then, it'll be too late."

Silence fell over them. There was still so much to learn, so many questions to be had. Arianna's destiny claimed she was to bring peace, but she'd been envisioning it all wrong. It wasn't just about peace between nations, it was peace from this monster and the abominations he'd created.

"We have to get her out," Arianna said. "I won't leave my sister in the hands of that monster."

"We can help," Conall offered again. "We've been inside before."

"Ashling is a port city, isn't it?" Talon asked.

"It is, but the maps of its location are wrong."

"Surprise, surprise," Saoirse said, leaning back in her chair.

"So where is it, exactly?" Talon asked.

"Just a little north of here on a small peninsula."

"So we infiltrate, kill him, and end this once and for all," Raevina said, flipping a knife in her hand.

"No," Conall said. "If we go through with this, we don't engage with Vairik whatsoever."

They all exchanged uncertain glances. "If we're already there, why wouldn't we bring him down?" Arianna asked.

"Because we're not capable. We've tried."

"You haven't tried with me," Rion said.

"We can't risk you." Conall's gaze moved to Arianna. "Either of you."

"Let me guess, you're going to ask us to stay behind." Arianna's temper flared. She was so sick of everyone attempting to protect her.

Conall balked. "Never. Your strength might be the key to getting everything we need."

"Which is what?"

"Our comrades, information, and destroying that city."

Raevina's frustration was nearly palpable. "You want to destroy the city, but not him. You're not making any sense."

"We can't destroy him. Not there. It's a city fortified with iron. It weakens our magic."

"Wouldn't it also weaken theirs?" Raevina challenged.

"It does, but the Fae there have iron weapons. Their magic is irrelevant. He has relations with the human kings and they wield weapons far superior to the ones that subdued our ancestors."

"But I thought he had human slaves?" Zylah questioned.

"And who do you think he buys them from?"

"Gods, there's nothing that race of barbarians won't do, is there?" Saoirse said.

Conall shrugged. "A profitable business is a profitable business, no matter how grotesque."

Arianna glanced at her hands and felt her magic spark beneath her skin. To infiltrate his stronghold and leave him alive … could she or Rion put an end to him? Were they strong enough together? "He really won't stop until he gets what he wants, will he?"

"I'm afraid not," Conall said.

Arianna stared between each of them. This wasn't just about conflicting countries anymore. This was a fight for their race and their right to the truth.

"Make the arrangements. Take us to Ashling."

"To war, My Lady?"

Arianna straightened. "A rescue. Then we expose the truth." She met each of their gazes. "Then yes, to war."

Chapter Sixteen

Arianna

rianna tried to stretch her legs and winced. She probably should have moved around sooner, but with all the information Conall was giving them, she hadn't wanted to interrupt.

Rion and Cara were both at her side a second later. "I'm fine," she assured them.

"May I be of some assistance?" Sive was already on her feet, carefully walking around chunks of rock and dirt. Arianna nodded, but Sive's gaze traveled to Rion, seeking permission from him as well. It warmed her heart to see someone take his comfort into consideration. They behaved as though his outburst hadn't even happened.

Sive carefully knelt with Cara's help, then proceeded to trace the glowing symbols across Arianna's abdomen. The relief was instantaneous. Their entire group watched the woman carefully, but it was difficult to feel threatened by someone who carried a youngling, especially one so far along. If anything, Sive's partner appeared far more uncomfortable than any of them. These were pensive strangers around the person he loved and his unborn child.

"You mentioned humans needed blood to draw the runes. Do Fae require a medium?" Saoirse asked.

"Only Weavers can draw and use the symbols without a liquid medium. The Fae require something, be it blood, water, paint, whatever will hold up for the length of time they need the rune for."

"So, could I do this to myself?" Arianna asked.

"You could. Your magic doesn't work on your own body, correct?" Arianna shook her head. "Then a few healing runes would do you some good, though they wouldn't be nearly as effective as your magic. They wouldn't even be as effective as mine. It takes time to strengthen the ability, just like any other. The more you use them, the easier it is to pull the magic from the earth and mold it to your will."

Talon stood. "I think we've had enough revelations for one day. You need to rest." Arianna nodded, though, what she really wanted was to soak in a warm bath.

Conall stood as well. "He's right. I fear that in our excitement, we might have kept you too long."

Cara helped Sive rise to her feet and the Fae male took her other arm. Sive smiled at her partner and patted his arm. "I'm all right." Arianna wondered how many times she had to assure him each day. Arianna smiled. A lot, judging from concern on his face.

Rion took Arianna's arm and bent to pick her up, but Sive interrupted them. "You." Arianna turned her attention back to the woman, thinking she was addressing her. But Sive's gaze was locked on Talon. "Who was your mother?"

Sive stepped forward and Talon involuntarily stepped back. "I—" He glanced to Arianna, then back to Sive. "Morgana of Levea."

"She's Fae?" Talon nodded. "And your father? Is he also Fae?"

"Yes?" Talon answered uncertainly.

"May I touch you?"

Everyone bristled at that, including Sive's partner. The male whispered her name in warning.

"I'll do nothing to harm you, I promise."

Talon exchanged a look with Sive's partner, who looked ready to carry the woman off and hide her from the world. His gaze dropped to her swollen stomach next, then he reluctantly nodded.

She approached slowly and placed two fingers on his brow. Arianna wasn't sure she'd ever seen Talon so uncomfortable.

Nothing happened for several long moments, then Sive's fingers began glowing with a faint blue light. "I knew it."

She lowered her hand and Talon stepped back. Arianna didn't miss the way Raevina's hand rested on a dagger in her belt.

"Pardon?" Talon said, just as bewildered as the rest of them.

"You have Weaver blood in your veins."

He blinked at her. "I'm sorry?"

Sive smiled. "You're young, aren't you? By Fae standards, I mean?" No one replied, but she continued, taking their silence as confirmation. "It explains so much. Haven't you ever wondered why your abilities are so advanced?" He exchanged a look with Rion. "Don't think we haven't all heard the stories about a male who stood toe to toe with our King. Not just once, but several times."

Conall cleared his throat. "Sive has been adamant about recruiting you to our cause. When we learned you were also close with The Divine, it just seemed like fate."

"But I'm not a half-breed," Talon said. He shot an apologetic look to Zylah, clearly not intending to offend the female.

Sive only smiled and tilted her head. "No, you're not. I'd say less than a quarter. Either a parent or a grandparent. But I wonder if it was from your mother's or father's bloodline. Did either of them have extraordinary abilities?"

"My father died in a skirmish at one of the boarders. My mother never fought."

"But her gifts are extraordinary?"

He opened his mouth and closed it. Arianna had never really seen his mother's magic. Not beyond how they played as children when she'd entertained them.

"The generals often tried to recruit her, but she wouldn't leave me."

"I wonder if she knows. Perhaps they kept it a secret." Sive almost seemed to be speaking to herself.

"Wouldn't that mean he has human blood in his genes?" Saoirse asked.

Sive's intense gaze lifted to Saoirse. "You think we're human?" Saoirse opened her mouth and closed it again. "We don't live as long as the Fae, but it takes five thousand years before we begin the aging process and given that there aren't many Fae who have reached that age, I'd venture to say we're more immortal than your lot."

Arianna's eyes went wide. She'd previously wondered if the Fae male would have to bid the Weaver farewell due to her short life span, but if they lived that long—

Sive continued, "There's a legend about a Weaver who claimed to be over thirty thousand years old, but we've never encountered them to confirm. If they're still alive, I imagine they live far, far away from the chaos of our current world."

"So—Talon's magic is different?" Arianna hedged. Her friend seemed to have lost the ability to speak.

Sive smiled at Talon. "A bit. He'll be the most apt at using runes once we begin teaching you."

"I thought we were infiltrating Ashling?" Raevina said.

"We are," Conall answered. "But we have to wait until our warriors return. We also have to formulate a plan and our queen," he nodded toward Arianna, "needs to heal."

"We don't have that much time," Arianna protested. "What about my sister?"

His face fell. "Missions as large as this one demand time. I'm afraid it can't be rushed. Rest in the knowledge that he won't kill her, at least."

"How do you know?"

"Because if you don't come willingly, then he'll use Evelyn as a lure."

Arianna felt her magic surge again, pulsing in time to her rapid heartbeat. She just had to sit here and wait while her little sister continued to go through day after day of torment?

"What can you teach us in that timeframe?" Saoirse asked.

"We have runes that will help block Pádraigín's magic. We can show you how to heal minor injuries, how to unlock doors, and reveal glamours that have been cast over an environment."

"And these will work on those from Pádraigín?" Saoirse asked. "We can really block out their magic?"

"So long as you don't encounter Vairik himself, then yes. I'm afraid his magic is far too advanced for runes to have any effect."

"Speak for yourself," Sive said.

Conall smiled at her. "Too advanced for most of us, then."

"All right, enough," Cara clapped her hands. "You two need to rest; we'll pick back up tomorrow."

Rion bent to scoop Arianna into his arms and those still seated rose. Her mate didn't wait for a dismissal. He was moving across the open field a second later. Talon and Cara followed with Raevina close behind.

On the way, Cara informed them about a community breakfast and extended an invitation. She explained to Talon how they grew their crops and how they'd organized groups to maintain clean water and fires. Arianna shuddered. It all sounded eerily like Ruadhán.

Arianna thought back to her brief time in the royal city. Conall claimed the place had been built by Rion's predecessor. She wondered if he'd also been friends with the tree-like creature in the forbidden forest. The guardian. Maybe that's why it had welcomed Rion so quickly. Did that mean it was as old as the original Divine? Were all the Fairy Folk that ancient?

"I can walk," Arianna protested in a whisper.

"You're in pain." Rion glanced down at her. "Don't tell me you're embarrassed about me carrying you."

She caught a slight upturn in his lips. A smile. After his outburst, she expected him to grovel for weeks. "It draws attention."

"Trust me when I say they're more concerned about my magic than you being in my arms."

"I don't know," Saoirse said, coming to walk beside her brother. Arianna peered back to find Zylah and Gavin following. "I think the two of you attract attention just for being you."

"Thanks for that," Arianna said, her cheeks heating. "What are *you* going to do?" Arianna asked. It felt wrong to just leave them alone.

"Don't worry about us, we can fend for ourselves. Get some rest." Saoirse turned to her brother. "That goes for you, too. I'll stand watch myself if that's what it takes."

Rion opened his mouth to protest but his gaze roamed to the runes Sive had drawn on his arms. "That might ... be nice."

Arianna eyed the intricate symbols. "Do they help?"

"Immensely." Rion paused. "It's difficult to explain how. It's like a constant stream of fresh water."

"And you're sure they're safe?" Saoirse asked.

"They're better than the alternative." He peered at Arianna again, his gaze apologetic, but not overly so. She wondered if the runes were helping with that as well. Or maybe almost dying had changed him entirely. He'd not been quite the same after the royal city's fall, either.

"We can show you all around, if you like," Cara offered. "You can see and meet the villagers for yourselves."

"We'll take you up on that," Talon answered.

Cara smiled but Arianna noted a female figure crossing the field. She veered toward them, keeping her head down. Rion's magic rose and Arianna's heartbeat with it.

Everyone paused, then Cara stepped forward. "Maya?" she

questioned. "What's wrong?" Fear drifted off both females.

The new one, Maya, addressed Arianna first. "My Queen." Her voice was shaking. "I know I have no right to ask anything from you—" She choked on the words and tears rolled down her face. "My daughter. The Weaver has tried, but—"

Arianna didn't hesitate. "Take me to her."

The female's face lit up. Rion almost looked ready to protest again, but he followed instead, his magic swirling around his feet as they neared the line of houses.

Rion leaned down and whispered in her ear, "Are you up for this?"

Arianna couldn't deny her overwhelming exhaustion, but she wasn't about to let a child suffer either. "It's fine. My magic needs an outlet anyway."

Rion nodded, his expression telling her he sensed it, too.

They walked farther and farther down the dirt street with many dropping to their knees as the pair passed. The children just stared, watching Rion's magic with a certain delight on their faces that their parents didn't seem to share.

The dwellings were simple, made of carved wood with mud caked between the slates and stones at their base for support. Gardens surrounded the entrance of each structure, with yellow flowers already in full bloom.

Tracks lined the main stretch of road, indented from wagons and people alike. Trees dotted the landscape, casting their shade over homes and storage buildings.

Piles of wood were stacked against homes, though many looked depleted, likely from the brutality of the past winter. She noticed other bags too, along with hay for the animals.

Arianna wondered if parts of the village expanded into the forest. Maybe more animals dwelled there, soaking in the rays that filtered through the canopy.

Maya gestured them inside a small cabin.

Saoirse entered first and held the door open for her and Rion.

Rion tilted his body to carry Arianna inside where a number of people conversed in hushed whispers. Their voices slowly died until all stood in shocked silence. One by one, those who were able sank to their knees.

An infirmary. A small one with beds lining the floor.

Arianna tapped Rion's chest and he carefully set her on her feet. The male outside squeezed his way in, following Maya as she crossed the room and reached for a small bundle being cradled by another female. Maya turned and stared at the tiny infant as if it was the most important creature in the world. She cooed to the youngling, tapping its back gently with her other hand before her gaze rose to meet Arianna's.

Arianna could hear the child's labored breathing. Every inhale was a struggled rasp while the exhale made Arianna fearful that it would be the infant's last.

Arianna limped forward and the female who had been sitting rose and gestured her to the rocking chair. Rion remained by the door, watching each of them. She could feel his pensive stare from here, but the space was too small for him to follow on her heels. That didn't stop his magic. It remained circling beneath her feet. She did her best to ignore it.

Once she'd settled, Arianna held her arms out for the youngling. The infant didn't cry or stir. Arianna cradled her close. She'd never held something so fragile. So innocent. She rocked the chair slightly, ignoring the slight tinges of pain that lanced through her core. Arianna placed one hand on the child's chest before closing her eyes.

The infant's lungs were weighed down with fluid and the tissues were so swollen, Arianna marveled that the child could still draw breath.

Arianna recalled the time she'd had to remove fluid from Rion's body. She also remembered the agony it had caused him. But she didn't have to rush this time, and she certainly wouldn't do anything that would cause the child harm.

Arianna began with the irritated tissues, letting her magic guide her as she soothed the inflamed airways. Then she began working on the liquid. Arianna pulled a few tiny particles together and brought them up through the youngling's airways before they exited through her mouth. The child didn't stir, and the particles were so small that no one else even seemed to notice as she let them roll to the floor.

No one spoke. They simply listened to the infant's breathing and watched the slight glow of Arianna's hands.

If the youngling had been older and stronger, Arianna likely could have healed her much faster. But she was so tiny. So frail.

Hours ticked by slow and steady. Arianna didn't stop. Someone brought her a steaming cup of tea. Rion didn't protest. Neither did anyone else.

Saoirse settled herself against the far wall beside her brother. There was a pause when the infant required nourishment from its mother. It drank greedily and with enough enthusiasm that Maya had tears rolling down her face once again.

Then the child was back in Arianna's arms.

Every minute, Arianna could feel a bit more tension leave the youngling's body.

Night descended. The fire dimmed to coals and the father drifted off to sleep. Arianna smiled when the infant stopped wheezing altogether. A tear leaked down Maya's face and she took her daughter back, cradling her to her chest, trying in vain to keep her sobs quiet so she wouldn't wake the child.

RION WATCHED Arianna throughout the night. Saoirse had been right, he was exhausted, but he couldn't nod off when his mate was surrounded by complete strangers, even if it was apparent they meant her no harm.

They'd be banging on her door tomorrow, begging for her help just like those from his war camp had done.

Arianna smiled at the youngling in her arms and cooed to it whenever the infant became distressed. It would settle again, curling into her warmth as if it felt safe even with a complete stranger.

Such innocence.

Talon's words from months ago came floating back. Arianna wanted children. It was something she'd discussed with her childhood friend. Even when she was young, she'd known she wanted to be a mother one day.

His jaw worked.

But how could he give her such a blessing after all the sins he'd committed? Even if Vairik was responsible for manipulating his life, the reality was that Rion had a target on his back. It was something he'd carry for years. Possibly even the rest of his life. If he chose to sire younglings, they'd inherit that very target. His past mistakes already haunted Arianna. He didn't want it to follow something so innocent, too.

He and Arianna had never broached the subject of children. Conall had informed them that conception was easier between mated pairs. And Arianna had never mentioned if she were taking a tonic. If she wasn't—

He felt his face pale. Arianna was beautiful with an infant in her arms. The way she held it and cherished this small life even though it wasn't her own. It was magical.

But to have something so vulnerable in the world. To know that one sleight of the hand could harm them, kill them.

He wasn't ready for it. Wasn't sure he'd ever be ready for it. Just like he'd told his mother, he didn't deserve such a precious gift.

But if Arianna wanted them—

The mother took her infant back and thanked Arianna profusely before Rion helped his mate stand. She was moving better after Sive's last healing session. He ventured a guess she might even be ready to travel in a few days.

If Rion was being honest with himself, he didn't want Arianna anywhere near Niall or Vairik, but he wasn't sure he had a choice in the matter. Arianna wouldn't leave her younger sister in their enemy's hands, and neither would he.

Talon and Ravina were both outside waiting for them. They, alongside Saoirse, escorted Rion and Arianna back to their cottage, promising to guard it while they rested. Saoirse mentioned something about a hot bath—no surprise there—but Rion wondered if she were more worried for the half-breed she seemed infatuated with. After what she'd experienced at Niall's hands, his sister deserved anything as a distraction.

The night was silent save for the crickets chirping in the grass. He glanced up at the stars, soaking in the stillness he'd been missing for far too long. It was here, in these moments, that he regained a sense of peace.

His gaze traveled back down to the markings along his arm. He wondered if he could make them permanent. Every time his mind tried to conjure its panic, the markings would trickle their magic into him. Sive said they worked by pulling energy from the earth. It was such a strange concept, especially compared to how a Fae's magic pulled from the body. He wondered just how powerful a Weaver could be. Maybe there was no limit.

They entered the cabin minutes later and Rion gently sat Arianna on her feet before helping her out of her clothes. He retrieved a bowl of fresh water for her to wash her face, then pulled on a pair of pants, leaving his torso bare. It had always been his preferred way to sleep, though if Arianna kept staring the way she was—

The fear of having a child returned to the forefront of his mind. Rion turned away from her, opting to retrieve some of the food from the table. Cara had already informed him she'd be dropping it off.

He returned to the bed and placed a small plate between them. Arianna nibbled on a cracker, her eyes boring into him.

"You've been quiet."

Rion clenched his jaw. Now was not the time to talk about

such things. They had too much to do, too many battles to fight. But that was exactly the reason he needed to talk to her. Because if they were on the battlefield or in the middle of the upcoming war—

Rion cleared his throat and stared down at the floor. "Talon told me once that you wanted children." He swore he could feel his mate smiling down their bond. It only made his heart sink further.

"One day. In the future. Preferably a future where we aren't at war." His hands clenched and unclenched around as he struggled for a response. "Do you not want them?"

"I don't know," he answered honestly. "I just—" He blew out a breath. "We're—together—a lot, and after what Conall said about mates and younglings—"

"I take a tonic," Arianna said. Rion looked at her then and the amusement on her face had the stress crumbling from his shoulders. "Zylah helped me with one when we were in the war camp. Others did the same whenever we could find the herbs. I've always taken one … just in case." She looked away and Rion gritted his teeth at the thought of everything she'd been through. At all the things he still didn't know.

"Then Myrna, my caretaker, helped to supply one when we were in Móirín. Ellie took over the job in Ruadhán. I wouldn't risk a child while we were in the middle of … all that, no matter the odds." She took another small bite. "And I don't really want younglings quite yet."

"But you *do* want them."

She looked at him again, but Rion couldn't bring himself to meet her gaze. "Would having a child be so bad?"

"No." His answer was too fast.

"Look at me." He couldn't disobey. Her brow furrowed with concern. "Do you not want children?"

"I want to make you happy."

"That's not what I asked."

"I—don't know."

She rested a hand on his and threaded their fingers together. "Then I'll ask you again in a few centuries."

"And if I still don't know?"

"Then I'll ask again in a few more."

His jaw clenched again. "I want to give you everything, but—"

Arianna set the plate on the floor, then scooted onto the mattress. She beckoned Rion closer and he rested his head against her chest. "Do you feel me down the bond?"

Rion clutched her shirt. "Every minute."

"Then you already know it's okay."

He nodded, then kissed her, helping her scoot under the blankets before settling in. Rion curled Arianna's body against his and held her, thanking the gods for the mate they'd granted him. He prayed they'd get those centuries just so Arianna could indeed ask him again.

CHAPTER SEVENTEEN

TALON

Talon didn't sleep that night, not that he would have been able to even if he tried.

He'd remained by the cottage door until Rion and Arianna's heartbeats had slowed enough to tell him both were asleep.

Alive. They were both alive, thank the gods. When Rion had run, Talon feared it might be the last time he ever saw either of them. The Dark Fae had broken through the walls from multiple sides and he'd been determined to go down fighting. Then a familiar horn had echoed across the field. It was a sound that had once triggered his instincts to fight. But right then, it was the precursor to their salvation.

Brónach's warriors had roared at the sound, their battle cries giving everyone a renewed sense of strength.

None had faltered after that. They'd beaten back the Dark Fae until Brónach's warriors joined, providing the relief they so desperately needed.

Afterward had been the usual cleanup. The laying out of bodies so they could be identified and put to rest. The burning of their enemy's corpses; in this case, the Dark Fae. And setting plans in motion to move everyone from the ruined village to a safer location.

Then a group of warriors had arrived claiming to know Arianna's whereabouts. After questioning them, Talon and the others had followed, praying for a miracle.

Talon circled the last small house, keeping his footsteps silent in the darkness. There were warriors stationed along the border, each watching him with curious eyes. The male who wasn't quite a Fae. It was a revelation he still wasn't sure he believed.

A Witch—no—Weaver. But what did that mean? Why hadn't his mother ever told him? Did she even know?

Talon let his gaze drift back toward the small cottage and imagined he could see the outline of a female in the distance. She blended effortlessly with the shadows, bending them to her will as she saw fit.

Raevina had once told him he'd been nothing more than lucky when it came to his encounters with The Demon. He'd almost believed her. But after sparring with the male over the last few weeks, Talon had reaffirmed his abilities to himself. Now he questioned those abilities all over again.

He'd always been stronger. More adept. He could do things that no one else could at his age. His magic was a force that rivaled many Fae ten times his age. He'd flown through the ranks, rising to take his place as a commander at an unusually young age.

All because he might not be a full-blooded Fae at all.

Talon inhaled the cool air and tilted his gaze to the stars. Wisps of clouds drifted by on a phantom wind. Crickets chirped in the stillness and nocturnal creatures scurried beneath the bushes and trees, trying to hide from his presence.

He saw an owl not far off, its large eyes watching the night sky with far too much intelligence to merely be an animal.

Talon continued moving. It was far better than standing beside Raevina in utter silence. He couldn't think straight in her presence and could barely function when she was watching him.

And her eyes hadn't left him since the Weaver's revelation.

Talon wondered what she thought about it and whether she approved. Maybe she found him revolting now.

Fiadh's hatred for half-breeds was well known. While Brónach kept them as slaves, Fiadh saw them as nothing more than animals. Lower than animals. They treated humans even worse.

Talon paused at the edge of the tree line and stared down a dark path that led toward the beginning of the mountain range. He shifted his gaze northward, toward Ashling's real location.

Ellie was there and they'd be on their way to finally rescue her soon. Conall and his companions seemed sincere in that truth, at least. It was the rest that had his mind whirling. Not just his, but everyone's. He knew the facts had been manipulated, too much just didn't add up, but the sheer volume of manipulation was staggering.

To think they didn't even know the names of their gods. They had statues and temples and priestesses, yet the entire continent was clueless. It was no wonder they seemed to have abandoned the Fae.

Conall wanted to gather information and destroy Ashling, but Talon knew he could speak for all of them when he vowed to kill Vairik before ever leaving that place, fortress or no.

Talon continued walking the perimeter. He explored the far fields and the animals within, knowing full well Cara might take him on a tour tomorrow.

Rion had freed her. He'd freed many of the slaves that now called Levea home. Talon had grown up believing the male was nothing more than a monster. Rion had lived his entire life maintaining that façade, never telling anyone otherwise. Even now he wouldn't defend himself against accusations.

Talon ran a hand through his hair. How different would their lives have been without Vairik's influence?

Dawn crept across the horizon and lights slowly began flickering to life within the windows. He'd gone back once to relieve Raevina. She'd wandered off, that strange look still on her face, then Saoirse had arrived to take a shift.

Now he watched as males and females, humans, half-breeds, and Weavers alike, all began their day.

The smell of sausage and baking bread floated through the air, making his mouth water. Some stared at him, their gazes curious, but none approached to ask questions. He knew what they'd inquire about. Arianna. And possibly Rion, given that the people here seemed more curious than afraid.

He wandered past a few more homes, then settled between a pair of storehouses, leaning his back against the wooden wall as he watched their morning unfold.

The scene reminded him of Levea. He hoped the next time they set foot in that beautiful city that it would be for good. Ellie and Kirian would be with them, both safe and sound.

"You're Talon?"

He startled slightly and tilted his head toward a woman standing a few feet away. She held a bowl of water between her hands. Chestnut hair hung down to her shoulders and wide, doe-like eyes watched him with a level of curiosity that had him standing a bit straighter. She wore a long dress, the material pulled tight around her middle by an apron.

"I am," he said in a questioning tone.

She tilted her head and a gentle smile spread across her face. He might have called her human if not for the revelation about Weavers yesterday. Now he noticed the otherworldly presence in the air surrounding her. It made him wonder if this was how the humans felt around the Fae.

"I'm Róisín. Conall told me to seek you out today."

"For what?"

"To work on runes. Didn't he tell you?"

"He mentioned we'd practice at some point, but I didn't think …" Talon trailed off.

"No better time than the present, right?" He didn't move from the wall and her smile faded. "Unless you're busy?"

Talon glanced around. They didn't have time to lose, especially if they were mapping out the rescue mission today. But he wasn't sure he wanted to be alone with her. Not when a Weaver's magic seemed limitless. He'd seen what Niall had done to the Fae under Ruadhán.

"Where?" he asked.

"Right here." She nodded to the ground, then held up the bowl of water in her hands as if that was obvious.

Talon quirked a brow. "Okay."

Her smile returned and she sat cross-legged in the grass, her skirt long and loose enough to accommodate the position. She waited for him to join. Though he was still uncertain, Talon sat across from her.

They were situated between two houses, out of the way of foot traffic, yet still close enough that everyone could see them in passing. Even so, he still felt too secluded.

"Conall told me you have Weaver blood in your veins."

Talon shrugged. "Maybe."

"You don't believe Sive?"

"I find it hard to believe no one in my family knew."

Róisín looked down at the water. "Perhaps they had their reasons for the secrecy."

"Conall said it could go back a generation?"

"A few generations. Sometimes the magic fades away, but it can usually be awakened with the right prodding."

"So, there's a possibility that I just have a drop in my veins."

"A drop is all it takes." She looked up at him. "Weavers are not Fae. We do not discriminate between those who are full-blooded and those who are half-breeds. If you have an ancestor, then you are a Weaver, that simple."

Talon glanced down at the bowl. "How do you plan to distinguish the power from my Fae magic?"

"I'll sense it," she assured. "It's kind of like how Fae can scent feelings or lies. It's not quite from your senses, it's something deeper than that." He raised a brow and Róisín waved her hand. "We have something called science on the northern continent. We study these kind of things."

"You experiment on Fae?"

"Only those who are willing. They're free to come and go. We don't force anyone to do anything they don't wish."

Talon looked at the bowl again. "What do you want me to do exactly?"

"Manipulate the water."

"I don't need to learn a rune?"

Another smile. "Not yet. Maybe not at all." He stared at her, waiting for an explanation. "We believe you already pull from the earth's magic without knowing it. It's why you were able to survive in the battles against your king."

Talon tried not to react to the title. King. King of the Fae. Of the very land he walked on. And he'd fought against him for years.

Róisín tilted her head. "Does his position bother you?"

Talon clenched his jaw, hating that his face was revealing anything to this woman. He should have slept for an hour, just to keep his mind alert. "It's a lot to take in."

"I'm sure. With your history—"

"Look," he interrupted. "I appreciate your lot caring for Arianna, but stop speaking to me as if you know everything about my past and our history."

Light faded from her eyes. "Right. I apologize. I forget that you've all been through a lot lately." She glanced around him and Talon followed her gaze. A pair of villagers passed with a child running ahead of them, twirling a fan in the breeze.

"The children have never known a life beyond these borders. You're all special to us. You're the main characters in stories we've been told our entire lives. You've given us hope where we saw none. We want freedom. We want to see the little ones roam the continent without falling prey to someone else's twisted manipulations and we'll do whatever it takes to get them there."

He faced her again, noting the sheer determination her face. "They're the ones who will ultimately guide our future. It's our responsibility to erase the obstacles from our time so they don't stumble when facing their own."

Talon gave a subtle nod. Another moment passed, then the

Róisín took a sudden breath and slapped her covered knees. "Right, shall we?"

Talon eyed the water again, then reached out and easily manipulated the liquid, pulling it up to float between them. Róisín studied the stream moving through the air.

"Freeze it." He did, and her eyes lit up. "There, I felt it as soon as you shifted the liquid to another form."

"Felt what?" He still wasn't convinced.

"All right, let's try something. Place the water back in the bowl." He did as commanded. "Now I want you to draw this rune." She traced a flowing symbol into the dirt.

"I thought you said I didn't need runes."

"You don't, but it's the only way for you to actually feel the difference in the magic."

Talon studied the symbol as she drew it again, then replicated her movements.

"Good, now dip your fingers in the water and draw it in the dirt slowly. You should feel the magic begin to form as you're drawing the lines. Feel free to do it as many times as you like."

Talon raised his brow again, but she remained still, watching as Talon dipped his fingers into the water, then hovered over the dirt. A droplet fell from his fingertip before he took a settling breath and drew the first line.

Nothing.

He continued with the second line, circling it around, tracing the original design with his eyes to ensure he got it right. By the third line, Talon felt it. A pull, but not from within himself. This one came from the ground at his feet, as if he were tugging on a gentle rope.

It was ... easy. Effortless. And familiar.

He'd always felt the magic from within himself, but he experienced a pull from the earth, too. Because he was drawing from two sources.

He'd always thought it was normal. That everyone felt the same thing. He'd even had multiple Fae stare at him in frustration when he tried to describe how to amplify their power.

And it'd been because they couldn't do the same thing.

Because he wasn't just a Fae.

Talon looked up at her with the rune faintly glowing beneath his hand. She smiled back, pride shining in her eyes. "You, Talon of Levea, are a Weaver."

CHAPTER EIGHTEEN

ARIANNA

Arianna opened her eyes to find Rion already staring at her. She blinked sleepily, her body heavy with exhaustion. Sunlight already filtered through the small windows, casting a pleasant glow across the floor.

She looked at her mate again. The bags beneath his eyes had faded slightly but were still present. She imagined they would be until they rescued Ellie and put an end to the mess their world had become.

Arianna wondered if they could rescue Ellie and end Vairik in one blow. Perhaps the gods would recognize all their past hardships and grant them that mercy.

Not likely.

Ten thousand. Arianna still couldn't wrap her mind around the number. How much knowledge had he gathered over the years? How much had he learned? How prepared was he for an infiltration?

They'd been lied to at every turn.

The Dark Fae in the forbidden mountains were actually their guardians. There were Weavers. Fae had been locked in prisons, held against their will for decades, possibly even centuries. And Rion …

Rion was the king of their people.

"It's too early," he chastised.

"Don't pretend you aren't thinking about it all, too."

His hand rose and cupped her cheek. Rion moved his thumb back and forth, drinking her in as if she were some sort of miracle. "How are you feeling?"

Arianna stretched her side and winced slightly. Rion's jaw worked. "Well, my head isn't splitting open today, so that's a pleasant change."

"Good." He didn't move.

"We can't stay in here all day."

Rion looked her over again, twirling the loose strands of her hair. "Not yet," he whispered.

She rested one hand on top of his and relished in his warmth. "I think I can hear your sister pacing."

"She can wait."

"What if I said I'm hungry?"

His eyes met hers. "Are you?"

"A little."

Rion threw off the covers and was dressed faster than she could even sit up. He got her clothes together too, then helped her scoot to the edge of the bed. She stood easier today, but despite wanting to walk, Rion was having none of it.

Saoirse was speaking with one of the guards when Rion opened the door. She raised a brow. "Are you planning to carry her forever?"

"Only until she's out of pain."

His sister made a face. "The Weaver's magic didn't help?"

"It did," Arianna answered. "She just said it'll take time. It doesn't work the same as mine."

"Not sure what good it'll do out on the battlefield then. They mentioned wanting to teach us, but if the results are that slow—"

"It saved her life," Rion countered. "That's good enough for me."

"You always were up for learning new things," Saoirse said. "Never could keep him out of the library when he was a kid."

Arianna liked the image that brought about. A small Rion, pouring over piles of books, perhaps even taking notes before running off to try something new.

"Where is everyone else?" Arianna asked.

"Talon and Raevina are already grilling Conall. Cara and Zylah are talking to the locals. Gavin is sulking in a corner."

"Meaning Talon won't let him leave his side."

"Mostly, though Zylah watches him when Talon is busy."

Arianna sighed. She knew Gavin hadn't had anything to do with Ellie's capture. Not really. He was just as much a victim as anyone else. But at least Talon wasn't demanding him to remain in chains.

They began walking toward Conall's cabin. "The villagers have been talking about what you did last night. For the infant."

"Is she okay?"

"Perfectly fine this morning. Screaming and crying like any other youngling." Saoirse grimaced, but Arianna saw the smile behind it. The relief that a young life could be spared and given a chance to grow.

"Are Conall's warriors back yet?" Rion asked.

Saoirse shook her head. "He claims they could be here any day. He wants to give them a chance to rest before we move out. I can't say from a commander's standpoint that I disagree." Arianna's stomach dropped.

"You think he has the numbers?"

"He claims he does. From what I've pieced together so far, the mission will rely on stealth, therefore numbers aren't what's needed, at least, assuming everything goes according to plan."

"And if it doesn't?" Arianna asked.

"Then we storm the place. Or blow it up, if everyone manages to get out safely."

"I wish you had brought more warriors," Rion said.

"We had to lay low, just in case Niall or his father was watching from the shadows. Those who escorted us here claim he has spies everywhere."

"It seems surreal, doesn't it?" Arianna asked. "To imagine a single person having that much control over the world?"

"One person controls a country. I'm sure his magic works the same. He likely has a council who closely believes in his cause and that council has trusted warriors under their belts. Those warriors have their own commanders, and the commanders have soldiers. It's all a line of power and if no one stands up against it, the power never shifts."

"But this is a continent," Arianna said. "The sheer amount of people—"

"Keep in mind he's had a few millennia."

Millennia. It was still an unfathomable amount of time. Arianna kept hoping she'd wake up from a dream. But that's exactly what they were trying to do. Wake everyone up and recover their lost history.

They arrived to find Talon, Raevina, and Conall leaning over a map. Talon was pointing to something, in the middle of a question when the trio turned at their approach.

Gavin was indeed sulking, though he sat in the same circle, watching with his hands neatly placed in his lap.

"My Lady," Conall said, standing before bowing at the waist. He didn't rise before saying, "My Lord. What can we do for you this morning?"

"Your queen is hungry," Rion declared, making her face flush. "And quite frankly, so am I. Where is breakfast served?"

Conall only smiled. "It's nearly done and will be brought out shortly. Do you need anything else?"

"A bath," Saoirse said, her tone just as clipped as her brother's.

"You two are horrible," Arianna grumbled.

The siblings exchanged a glance, then Saoirse snickered. Rion couldn't hide his smile either.

"Can you please aid us in satisfying our hunger and point us in the direction of a warm bath?" Saoirse mocked. She turned to Arianna. "Is that better?"

Even Conall laughed. "As I said, breakfast is on the way and baths can be discussed once we have a plan laid out."

"Don't stop on our account," Saoirse said before straddling one of the empty chairs backward. Rion helped Arianna settle into the one beside Talon, but Rion remained standing, his eyes already roaming across the detailed map and the points they'd marked.

"Once we're inside, our first objective will be sneaking into the lower dungeons to retrieve the prisoners. We're already aware many of the Fae will be in less than optimal condition, so we've made arrangements to sedate them to prevent any unnecessary outbursts."

"Do you think Ellie is in those dungeons?" Arianna asked hopefully.

Conall grimaced and shook his head. "We'd have to be very, very lucky. Unfortunately, being that she's your sister, she's likely kept closer to Vairik."

"She was," Gavin confirmed. "She was often in his study and when she wasn't there, she was in a cell below it."

A chill swept down her spine. "What was he doing to her in there?"

Gavin clenched his fist. "I don't know. I was never allowed to stay long."

"How are we supposed to get her out if you don't want a confrontation with Vairik?" Talon asked.

"Distraction. If something big starts happening in his city, then he'll have no choice but to investigate and handle it himself. If there's one thing we've learned about him, it's that he craves power and control."

"I don't suppose you're going to share the details about said distraction?" Raevina pushed.

"I have several in mind, but isn't that why we're here? To formulate the plan?" They all nodded and Arianna was surprised to find herself relieved. Conall wanted to build this mission from the ground up with help from her and her companions. She wondered if he knew how much that likely meant to them and the trust it bred.

Conall continued. "Getting past the guards and inside is simple enough. Navigating the lower levels is even easier, especially given that they're not routinely patrolled, but we've never attempted to go higher, which means," his eyes turned to Gavin. "Unfortunately, we have to rely on you for information."

Gavin straightened. "If it's for Evelyn, I'll tell you anything you want to know, but I have a condition."

Talon growled. "You're not exactly in a place to negotiate conditions. I thought you wanted to save Evelyn?"

"I do, but Conall mentioned blowing the place up. I just want safe passage for my mom and sisters."

Silence fell over the space before Conall said, "Your mom is Vairik's daughter. Niall's sister. Doesn't that mean she'll be protected by him, too?"

Gavin shook his head. "Vairik has many children. He … he picks females based on the power of their magic and breeds with them for the sole purpose of producing a strong heir. Very few have met his expectations, and his drive for … producing another has dwindled over the years."

"That's disgusting," Zylah said, emerging from Conall's cabin with a tray of food in each hand. Cara followed after, along with several others, and they placed the trays in everyone's laps.

"Agreed," Gavin replied. "They live on the outskirts. I just don't want them caught in the aftermath."

"They're not within the main city?"

Gavin shook his head and Talon sat back. "I'm surprised he doesn't keep you all close."

"He has Niall check in from time to time. I showed some promise a few years ago, which is why I'm there now instead of with my mother. I'm rarely allowed to visit, but I still know where they live." He looked between them. "They're not at fault for anything. I just don't want them punished along with … the others."

Conall's gaze softened. "We don't punish those who are innocent."

Gavin glanced down at the iron bracelet circling his wrist. "It shows."

They were all silent again. Arianna had never wanted Gavin in chains, but Talon and the others had placed cuffs on him and beaten him from the moment he'd arrived. They'd blamed him for things beyond his control. He'd grown up at the mercy of the oldest Fae on the continent and they had not given him the benefit of the doubt.

Gavin hadn't had a choice. Perhaps he'd never had one. Maybe his first independent choice had been running from Niall and Vairik. It was an action that had labeled him a traitor and prevented him from ever returning to his home country.

Even so, neither Talon nor Rion appeared apologetic.

"Your mother didn't take someone dear to us," Rion said. "You did."

"I didn't have a choice."

"Maybe. You aid us in getting Ellie out and we'll clear your name."

Gavin's eyes lit up. "You mean it?"

"So long as she doesn't tell us otherwise," Talon said. "If you did anything to hurt her—"

"Could you hurt Raevina?" Gavin countered, unfamiliar anger flaring in his eyes. Talon's lips parted and Conall stared at the pair, realization sparking in his eyes.

"Careful," Talon seethed.

"Then don't insult me. I'd never do anything to harm Evelyn."

"Are we finished with the pissing contest?" Saoirse said. "I'd like to get back to discussing the actual mission."

"Right," Conall said, addressing Gavin again. "We need you to draw a map with every detail you can think of. We need to know where guards are stationed, when rotations shift, and what magic they use." Conall pulled several sheets of paper out from under his current map. "We also need to know where the offices for his council are located and what time of day the council members are most likely to visit."

"You think I know all of that?"

"Just give us what you can," Arianna said gently. "Anything will help."

Gavin stood and crossed the space, taking the pen and paper

from Conall's hands. "I'll do my best."

"While Gavin's busy with that," Saoirse said. "How exactly are we getting inside?"

"There's a series of underground tunnels through the mountain that start just over the ridge there," Conall pointed. "And open up at the edge of the ocean, right beside Ashling. The exit point requires us to scale down the cliffs."

"Won't they notice us?" Saoirse asked. "I mean, you all have a barrier around this place. Don't they have the same?"

"They do, but the tunnels allow us to sneak past it. The High Lord, at present, doesn't know about them."

"Let's hope he hasn't made a recent discovery then," Talon said. "How do we blend in?"

"We'll enter a few at a time and pose as a security patrol. There are hundreds of them. As long as we keep our hoods up and don't make a ruckus, we can pass through the city undetected."

"They won't scent us?"

"It'll be irrelevant if they do; plenty of Fae from the various nations call Ashling home. Despite separating the rest of the continent, Vairik understands the strength of a unified city.

"Once we're beyond the perimeter guard and through the city, you'll find a channel of water that flows under the castle and exits into the ocean. It's where waste is discarded, but the channel is large enough to accommodate several bodies at one time. We'll use the current to move into the underground chamber. Everything is easy from there."

Talon glanced down at the map and followed an invisible line with his eyes, as if he were already following Conall's instructions in his head. "That seems like quite a vulnerable point to leave open."

"It's not open, there are guards, but those with Pádraigín's magic will blend us into the environment. There is enough of it already at work that they won't notice a bit more."

"Sounds simple enough, if not disgusting," Raevina commented.

"With enough room for a million things to go wrong," Talon

added.

"If they go wrong, we pull out and retreat to the tunnels. Veer toward the ocean if you have no other option." Conall turned to Arianna. "Your ability to control water will work to your advantage, but Fae from Móirín also guard the shoreline, so you'll have to be careful."

Arianna nodded. "I will be."

"Once Gavin finishes, we'll talk more. For now, I encourage each of you to learn as many runes as you're able. My warriors will also have additional insights and opinions upon their return."

Arianna stared at the map and the black castle that had been drawn at the edge of the ocean. It stood in stark contrast to everything else. It felt like a blight on the land.

"My Queen." Arianna glanced up at Conall. "We'll make every effort to rescue your sister. But if it comes down to losing everything or letting her go—"

Arianna's gaze turned icy and her magic sparked in her veins. Conall straightened, sensing the shift. "I will *not* leave without her. You do what you must for your people, but I'm staying as long as it takes to find Ellie."

"Even if it means the fall of the continent?"

"Even if it means the fall of the world."

Conall looked ready to protest but nodded instead. The action … surprised her. Most would have argued or threatened to leave her behind if she didn't comply. But this male didn't.

"Now, about that bath," Conall said. Saoirse's eyes sparked like a child who'd been offered a sweet. "We have natural hot springs nearby if you're interested."

"Hell yes, we're interested," Raevina said before anyone could object. "I haven't soaked in a natural spring since leaving Purog."

Conall chuckled then stood. "I'll have Cara lead the way then."

CHAPTER NINETEEN

ARIANNA

Cara arrived shortly after and led their entire group through the trees. None could hide their excitement at the prospect of soaking in a hot spring. They paused at a bathhouse along the way to clean the grime from their bodies. Rion helped her sit, but Arianna washed quickly, not wanting to make the others wait.

She wrapped herself in a plush robe and met her companions outside. All were dressed in a similar fashion, but none had left their weapons behind.

Cara paused at the entrance, a looming cavern with sconces flickering inside to light the way. "The halls might seem daunting, but everything is marked." She addressed Rion first. "Take the first right, then the second tunnel beyond that. It has the biggest pool. Just flip the little sign in front to indicate it's taken and no one will disturb you."

Arianna scented the air wafting from the cavern and crinkled her nose at the smell. She stepped forward, intending to follow the others inside, but Rion's body didn't move when she tugged on his hand. His heart began pounding and she turned to find him staring at the walls, his fear nearly palpable.

Arianna studied the cavern entrance again. It was tall, taller than any Fae, and wide enough that four could have walked through shoulder to shoulder and still had some room to spare.

Even so, her mate balked, staring at the stone walls like they were an enemy he couldn't conquer.

Arianna squeezed his hand and Rion looked down at her, his eyes slightly glazed over before they shifted into focus. "We don't have to."

Cara was the only one who lingered, but the half-breed attempted to busy herself and turned away.

Rion, despite his trembling body, offered Arianna a gentle smile before stepping forward without a reply.

Sunlight peeked through crevices in the rocks above and sconces that had been nailed into the wall chased away the looming shadows.

The air grew thicker. Water ran off the walls, trickling onto the floor before disappearing again into tiny cracks in the stone.

There were several forks in the road ahead. They followed Cara's instructions and veered right before pausing in front of the second tunnel.

A tiny wooden sign hung on a loose nail that had been driven into the rock. Arianna flipped it around so it read "occupied," then Rion pulled her down the narrow passage.

She might have been more nervous under so much rock were it not for the knowledge that her mate could quite literally lift the entire mountain by himself. He'd held a falling city, after all.

Or maybe that had been too much. His magic had been worn down for nearly a week afterward, barely rising to his call.

The tunnel opened to a circular room and Arianna's eyes widened at the sight of the steaming pool of blue water. It was far from uniform, bending and dipping with the natural stones. A large section of overhanging rock stretched over the backside of the pool with a small waterfall trickling down its smooth surface. Arianna stepped forward to peer up through a gaping hole in the ceiling that revealed traces of the cloudless sky above.

She released Rion's hand and knelt at the edge to test the temperature. "This is incredible. I never thought I'd get to see one in person."

Rion untied his robe and let the material glide to the floor. Arianna's mouth went dry at the sight of his reforming muscles. She looked away, cheeks heating.

Rion seemed to ignore her reaction. "It's about the most relaxing thing you'll ever experience." Arianna peered back over at him with her brow raised. "I spent time in Fiadh."

Right, because he'd been hunting her mother's murderer.

"It's hard to picture you ever relaxing. Especially out on a mission."

Rion smirked. "I'm not immune to the allure." He said it with his gaze on her in a way that made her blood heat all over again. The truth was there were still so many things she needed to learn about her mate.

Rion lowered himself into the water and a groan escaped him that shot straight to her core. He still didn't turn. Was he trying to give her privacy? It wasn't as though Rion hadn't made it his mission to explore every inch of her.

You're in control. She swore she could hear the words echoing down their bond. He always gave her a choice. Their bond still hadn't solidified, but it was close. So close, she was certain it would click over any moment.

Arianna let the robe fall from her shoulders and sat on the edge of the rock before jumping in. She hissed when the liquid hit her abdomen, the skin still new and pink. Without Sive's help, the wound would still be open. She'd be bedridden … or dead.

It had happened so fast. One moment she'd been smiling at her mate, certain their victory was at hand. The next, darkness had consumed her, pulling her under against her will.

Is that what dying would feel like? Or fading, when her time came?

Once Arianna submerged herself, Rion turned. He leaned against the far wall opposite her while the pleasant sound of trickling water filled the space. The bottom of the pool was smooth beneath her feet, though whether that was natural, she had no way of knowing. Arianna hedged that the ledge wrapping around the perimeter wasn't.

She walked beneath the small waterfall and let the warm liquid cascade over her hair, rolling down the sides of her face. Arianna drank it in, staying there for a moment before emerging to find Rion with his head leaned back and eyes closed.

Steam curled up around his features and for once, she didn't scent his magic. She wondered if the runes Sive had painted across his skin had something to do with it.

Arianna thought they might wash off, but whatever the Weaver had used possessed some sort of dye that had stained Rion's skin, giving the appearance of a tattoo. If something so simple worked for him, then perhaps they should be permanent. If that was something he wanted, of course.

Arianna's gaze slid down to his exposed throat. She paused at the pulse there and the muscles that flexed when he swallowed. Then her eyes dipped to his chest and the lines of muscle he'd been working to regain. He looked nearly the same as the first time she'd seen him shirtless. Only now, he carried far more scars, most Niall's doing.

"You're staring."

"Am I not allowed to stare at my mate?"

He cracked open an emerald eye and Arianna's body flooded with heat at the carnal desire in his gaze. Rion had refused to touch her while she was injured and while it had only been a few days, it felt like months. Years.

"Come here." It wasn't an order. It couldn't be with how breathless he'd gone, but Arianna obeyed the husky tone that promised to bring all her fantasies to life.

They could talk later. About the war. The mission. The future. But here, in this small space, they were free. It might only be a few moments, but she'd cherish them as if they were her last. Once they walked under that mountain and into enemy territory, there was no guarantee they'd ever come back.

Rion gently pulled her onto his lap. She ran her hands through his hair, wetting the strands.

"It drives me crazy when you look at me like that." Rion pressed a kiss to the back of her hand, then worked his way up her arm.

"Look at you like what?" she teased.

The heat in his gaze told her enough. "Can I kiss you?"

"Aren't you already?" Arianna leaned forward and Rion smiled against her lips. Then he devoured her. His hands traced up her back and he threaded one hand in her wet hair.

She wasn't dragging it out today.

Their bodies joined and Arianna kissed him over and over, relishing the taste and feel of her mate. She ignored the faint tinge of fear plaguing the back of her mind when his teeth grazed her throat. She ignored the pain when his hands traced her scars and wounds. She ignored everything and let Rion consume her body, mind, and soul.

Something about having the most dangerous male on the continent beneath her, worshiping her, had a thrill of excitement shooting through her body. She was the reason his eyes were half-lidded. She was the reason his breathing had accelerated.

He was hers.

Her mate.

Her everything.

Another strand of their bond knit together and Rion gasped before pulling her impossibly tighter. She could feel his emotions now, their intensity merging with her own, and it sent them both toppling over the edge.

Arianna kissed the side of his neck and Rion tilted his head to allow it, baring himself to her. Only to her.

"Arianna—"

"Shhh." She didn't want this moment to end. Not yet. Here, they were tucked away from the horrors of the outside world and everything that would come. Here, in one another's arms, they were safe.

Rion kissed her again and Arianna settled into the crook of his arm. The pair basked in the silence as the heat chased the tension from their bodies.

"When I was chained," he started. "I wasn't sure I'd ever make it out of there. It gave me time to think about every moment I regretted." Arianna tilted her head to look at him, but he was staring at the water. Rion's hand moved up and down her arm. "I'm sorry for what I've put you through. I kept pushing you away, hoping it might be better for you in the long run. Ellie helped me see otherwise." Arianna's heart clenched at her sister's name. "I kept thinking you deserved someone with less darkness in their soul. Yet you've accepted that darkness over and over again."

He angled his body toward her and cupped her cheek. "You're mine, Arianna, and I'm yours. I'm committed now. I'm not letting you go."

A wide smile broke across her face. "You think I'd let you at this point?"

A crooked smirk. "No, but before we go through," he tilted his head toward the exit, "whatever we have to face out there, I wanted you to know I won't disappear. I'll never leave you. I won't back down. As unbelievable as it still is, I've accepted that you want me."

"Took you long enough."

A breathless laugh. "I think Saoirse is rubbing off on you. You never used to be so … mouthy." His thumb traced her lip.

She shrugged. "Or Raevina. Both females seem to have an edge to them."

"I like it. The challenge is—" Instead of words, Rion leaned down and kissed her again, taking her lower lip between his teeth. "Enticing," he finished.

"Glad I don't bore you."

"Never. Not if we live a million years."

Arianna settled against him again, listening to his heartbeat as she watched the steam curl from the water's surface. But Arianna couldn't stop the intrusive images that followed. Steam turned to smoke and the fresh air shifted to a burning scent that left her throat raw. She closed her eyes to the memories, willing them away. No matter how much she wanted peace, they were about to encounter all those terrible things again. She wondered if she'd ever escape war or if it would follow her for the rest of her life.

Arianna threaded her fingers through Rion's and squeezed. "Do you think we can save her?" Arianna tried not to think about all the monstrous things Vairik might be doing to her little sister. She tried to push those images away too, but a memory of Rion when she'd first found him in iron and covered in filth refused to leave her alone. Ellie could very well be experiencing the same torment.

"I'll get your sister back." His unwavering resolve floated down their bond. It strengthened something in her and Arianna was silently grateful for her mate's confidence. Niall hadn't killed Rion, and Conall had already assured her that Vairik wouldn't kill Ellie either. But the torture—her sister had such a light spirit. Arianna feared that spirit could be crushed under the weight of too much darkness.

"Don't think about it too much," Rion said. "Just focus on getting her back."

Arianna swallowed hard, fighting the emotion rising through her. "You and she really connected over the spring."

A small smile crept to his lips and Arianna wondered which memory he might be reliving. "She's the only one who's ever treated me like a real person. Aside from you, of course."

"Must run in the family." He pressed a kiss to her hair. "Do you think we can trust Gavin? Do you really think Kirian is alive?"

"Talon made sure to strip Gavin of his magic before asking questions, so yes, I believe we can trust him. As for Kirian, I imagine they're using the half-breed to keep Ellie in line."

"Do you think they'll be okay after—" Arianna didn't finish her sentence. She didn't have to. Rion's nightmares were still a day-to-day struggle.

"I'll make sure she is." The words were a solid promise, even if they felt hollow. He was always giving too much of himself, willing to help others before he was even whole himself.

How had the world ever branded someone like him as a monster?

Rion shifted and she allowed him to turn her around. His hands moved to her shoulders and she nearly moaned when he began working the tension from her muscles. She noted how careful he still was around the scar on her neck.

He'd gasped the first time he'd seen it, and a fresh wave of overwhelming regret had washed through her. They'd both cried again, and he'd tried to kiss away the pain.

Arianna propped her elbow up on the rock ledge and rested her chin on top of her arm. "Tell me something."

He paused for a moment. "What do you want to know?"

She shrugged. "Anything." She knew they wouldn't have time for simple conversations once they crossed into Ashling. Probably not until the entire war was over.

"You can ask, you know."

She knew what he meant. But Rion relived those nightmares enough without her pulling at them, too.

"It doesn't have to be about that."

Silence enveloped the space as he continued working her shoulders. His thumbs moved down her back, right over the scars from her past. He was careful around the thicker bands. "I want to tell you everything. But I'm not sure where to start without questions."

Arianna studied a small pebble before her, staring at a swirl in the stone. "Did he … hurt you?" She inwardly kicked herself. What a stupid question. Of course he had. She could see the scars. Still, she hoped it had been a one-time incident. That perhaps Niall had merely been in a fit of rage when—

"Yes." Rion paused a moment and his voice lowered. "Over and over. Every time he visited."

Arianna's jaw clenched. She'd kill Niall. She'd wrap her hands around his throat and watch the light leave his eyes herself. Or maybe she'd deliver him to Eimear and the two could tear off his limbs together.

"How did you meet Kaylee?" The young half-breed had been doing better with other younglings around, but she still clung to Eimear as if the female were her own mother. It had made hiding Eimear's current state impossible, but Kaylee didn't seem affected by it. Perhaps Eimear had been the same way in her cell before Rion had released her.

"She was responsible for keeping the prisoners alive."

"But she's a child."

Rion tensed slightly behind her. "I know."

Kaylee was better now. She had more color to her cheeks and had gained a bit of weight. But Arianna couldn't get the image of the frightened, neglected child out of her mind. She'd been so frail, too.

"At least she's out of that animal's reach now."

"She told me she wanted to see the trees." Rion said. "She doesn't stop talking about them whenever I visit."

A smile ghosted Arianna's lips. Trees. Children were so simple in their delights. "Was she the one who told you about your mother?"

"No." Rion began working on her other shoulder. "That was Niall. He—" Rion hesitated, and Arianna noted the way he tried to block his emotions from floating down the bond. He did that a lot.

"You don't have to," she whispered.

But Rion took a breath. "She was always screaming. Niall wanted me to know who it was."

Oh gods.

"He never used her in his mind tricks, though. That was always you." Arianna froze. "I've watched you die a million times. In a million ways," he admitted. "And my heart went with you every single time."

"Rion." She turned then, and the way he stared at her had her own tears falling. Gently, she wrapped her arms around his neck and pulled him close. Rion's arms circled beneath hers and he buried his face in her neck, breathing in her scent as if it might steady him.

The prospect of her death was the very reason he'd run. Why he'd panicked and trusted strangers when left with no other alternatives.

"When this is all over, we'll go somewhere. Just us." She pulled back and brushed her hand through his hair. "I want a life with you. When we finally come out, I want you at my side and we'll rule this continent together."

Rion tenderly kissed her lips. "Haven't I already told you I'm yours?"

CHAPTER TWENTY

TALON

Talon opted for the tunnel on the right. He was silently thankful the corridors were long and walls thick. He didn't want to overhear anything going on between his friend and Rion. They deserved their privacy anyway. Both had more than earned it.

A short winding hall on his left led Talon into a small cavern with a pool at its center. He inhaled the crisp scent and felt his magic respond to the water. With Fiadh's and Móirín's rocky alliance, visiting had never been an option. He ventured a guess that this might be the last time for a long, long while.

Talon loosened his robe and folded it before setting it neatly on the floor by the entrance. He placed his weapons on top and leaned his sword against the rock before sinking into the hot water.

A flame in one of the sconces cracked. He eyed it, then waded to the far side and let his head fall back against the stone.

A resistance group. It seemed too good to be true. It was too sudden. A blinding ray of hope in the darkness.

Conall's explanations made sense even if Talon didn't agree with them. As a commander, he knew what it felt like to lose his warriors. He understood the guilt and the burden one carried as they played through different scenarios that might have resulted in a better outcome.

But Conall had simply chosen not to fight. He'd gone into hiding with the sole mission of freeing those held captive while they waited on The Divine. Not to mention how the male had virtually ignored Rion through the years.

Talon shook his head. Could this Vairik's influence really extend so far? Were they all still suffering from that male's magic, or had they broken it by learning the truth?

Talon clenched his fists. He didn't like the idea of Rion or Arianna walking into Ashling. According to Conall, Vairik desperately wanted both of them. The best plan would be for the pair to return to Levea and lie low. Avoid the masses. Maybe even go into hiding.

But he knew neither would agree to it. Especially with Ellie in that male's clutches.

A familiar sense of pain and longing washed through him at the thought. He wondered how she was doing.

Talon was no stranger to war or the hardships that accompanied it. He'd seen firsthand how horrendously the slaves had been treated. He'd witnessed bodies tortured beyond recognition. Fae begging for death with their final breaths. He'd seen others ripped open, their organs picked apart by the creatures of the forest. And he'd had no way of knowing whether death had granted them mercy beforehand.

Talon pulled the tie from his hair and slipped under the water's surface, letting the heat wash over his face before emerging again. He stared at his reflection as droplets rolled down his face.

Defeating a ten-thousand-year-old Fae wasn't going to be easy. They'd gotten lucky with Niall. More than lucky, and he was only seven hundred. Ten thousand—the number kept repeating in his head, but maybe that was the wrong thing to dwell on.

Talon could hear his old commander's voice in his head yelling at him to focus. He wished that male was here with him now.

No—he wasn't a child. He could formulate plans just as well as his predecessor. He just needed a few hours of sleep, then he'd reconvene with Rion followed by Conall's generals once they arrived. They'd finalize the plans, rescue Ellie, and kill Vairik before their world could erupt into another war.

Quiet footsteps echoed down the passage. Talon pushed his wet hair back and inclined his head to listen. His gaze traveled to the weapons he'd deposited on the other side of the room. He had the water. It wouldn't take but a few seconds to grab them.

But Talon nearly stopped breathing when Raevina strolled through the entrance. She paused just inside, eyes scanning the space before landing on him.

"You're alone." Her tone came out accusatory, clearly expecting otherwise.

"What are you—" His words died when she loosened the belt of her robe and let it fall to the floor. She stared at him as she tied her hair on top of her head then stepped forward, her hips swaying as she walked into the pool without an ounce of modesty.

His throat had gone dry. Closed up entirely. He couldn't form words. Thoughts were a distant memory.

"Do you always stare at women when they're undressing?" She settled against the opposite side of the pool and closed her eyes, oblivious to the effect she was having on him.

Talon bit the inside of his cheek hard enough to draw blood. He tore his eyes away and stared at the water, his face burning.

"I don't care," Raevina said.

"Clearly." His voice was too high. Talon heard her shift in the water, but he didn't look up. "Why are you here?"

"The other pools were taken. I wasn't about to join Rion and Arianna. Gods know that male's moody enough. Saoirse is busy guarding the pool with the half-breed, and the others are too small. I didn't think you'd object."

Object? He couldn't even move. Gods, was this female trying to kill him?

Silence filled the space. Talon had wanted to unwind in the heat, but it felt like every muscle in his body had coiled in on itself.

The water moved and Talon nearly jumped out of his skin when he looked up to find Raevina less than a foot away. She was standing, her torso fully exposed. He couldn't help it, his eyes traced over her body. The luscious curves and dips. And the scars. So many scars. He counted each one, then lifted his gaze to hers.

Raevina tilted her head and smirked. The movement reminded him of a predator who'd ensnared their prey. "Are you so reserved that you won't take a female who's clearly offering herself to you?"

Talon licked his lips then tried in vain to clear his throat. "You made yourself pretty clear last time."

She waved her hand. "I was tired and cranky."

His lips parted. She was—

"Don't play with me."

Raevina's smile widened. "It's true then, you haven't bedded a female before." She cocked her head. "You don't want the experience?"

His jaw clenched. "Some of us want the experience to mean something."

Raevina stepped closer and reached for a strand of his hair. She let it fall between her fingers before looking at him again. Her gaze heated. "And what do you want it to mean?"

His heart was going to beat right out of his chest. "More."

"More," she echoed the word, letting it roll off her tongue. Talon wasn't sure how his body remembered to breathe. "I don't do more."

Their gazes locked again. It would be so easy. So, so easy to let himself have this. To take her in his arms. Run his hands over her body. To satisfy the cravings plaguing him since the first night they'd danced.

But he also knew he'd be left disappointed when she walked away. He'd be nothing to her, just another notch in her belt.

"Then the answer is no." His words were confident despite how he felt.

Her gaze traveled down his torso and peered through the water before she looked up at him through her lashes. "Your body tells me otherwise."

Talon didn't respond. She stood there, staring at him, waiting, before she finally sighed and pulled away. She sank back into the water and seated herself on the adjacent edge of the pool. Her arms rested on either side and she tilted her head back.

"Shame," she said. "I was looking forward to a pleasant evening."

Talon could hardly draw breath. He peered at her from his peripherals, then averted his gaze at the sight of her bare chest. His heart was beating so fast. He'd barely maintained control and was already kicking himself for it.

"Will you seek that company from someone else?" Anger burned through him at the thought of another male's mouth anywhere near her.

Raevina lifted her head and quirked a brow at him. "Would that upset you?"

"About as much as it would upset you," he countered.

She smirked. "What?"

"I saw the way you walked in here. You were looking for the Weaver."

Raevina tilted her head back again. "I didn't want to disturb you if you were occupied."

"You hardly seem like the type to care."

She shrugged. The silence stretched. Water trickled down from somewhere nearby, then she finally said, "Would it be so outlandish if I were a touch concerned for your welfare? We're in unfamiliar territory, and after all that nonsense about you being one of them—" She waved a hand.

"It's true."

Raevina didn't lift her head. "Were a few parlor tricks all it took to convince you?"

"I felt the difference in my magic."

She scoffed again. "I thought you and your companions were smarter than that." She raised her head and Talon could see the fire in her eyes. "Trust no one, no matter what they tell you."

"Is that why you don't do *more*?" Talon asked. "Because you don't trust anyone?"

The flame in her gaze flickered and for a split second, Talon thought he saw shadows cloud in her deep golden eyes. They disappeared as fast as an extinguished flame. "I've learned many lessons the hard way."

He opened his mouth to push but stopped himself when she sank her shoulders into the water and rested her head against the rock. Talon changed the subject instead. "I trust that these people despise Niall and Vairik as much as we do."

"And how far do you think they're willing to go to destroy him? Do you believe, even for a second, that they care about Evelyn's fate? Do you think they wouldn't leave her to be tormented if it meant getting what they want?"

"Would you?" The question slipped out. Raevina had given her loyalty to Arianna, claiming she'd do whatever it took to protect her. She was the wild card in their group. The newcomer. The only one they knew absolutely nothing about.

Raevina was silent for a time, breathing deep before she said, "I would find the best solution for whatever situation arises."

"What's that supposed to mean?"

"It means none of us knows what we're walking into. If young Evelyn can be saved, then I'll save her. But if I'm presented with an opportunity to kill Vairik and free this entire continent, then I'm willing to sacrifice a few lives to make it happen."

"Arianna won't like that."

She shrugged. "Most don't like tough decisions, but they still have to be made. I swore to protect The Divine and that's exactly what I intend to do."

"So that's your loophole? You'd go against her—"

"I'm not against her," Raevina interrupted. "I'm here to ensure she lives, which is more than can be said of my predecessors. If they had done their jobs, we wouldn't even be here."

"You mean those who guarded the previous Divine?" She nodded. "That was centuries ago. We don't even know what really happened."

"They made a mistake and she died. That's all I need to know. I don't intend to do the same. We've waited centuries for her; who's to say we won't have to wait centuries more for the next one? What happens if we're not given that kind of time? Vairik is hell-bent on revenge, and that kind of rage is unpredictable. I won't see this land destroyed."

Talon's lips parted, then closed again. He'd never heard her say so much in one breath and as much as he was loathe to admit it, Raevina was right. If they failed, if Arianna or Rion died, Vairik could decide to do away with the continent altogether.

Talon clenched his fists. But if he had to lose Ellie in the process? He knew he wouldn't make the same decision. If it came down to Ellie or Arianna or any of them, he'd choose his friends first.

"Consider your own values and prepare yourself for the hard decisions." Her voice shifted to a whisper. "Others have died trying to be noble only for it to mean absolutely nothing in the end."

"You sound like you speak from experience." Raevina stared at the water for a long moment, then stood. Talon looked away, trying in vain to keep his heart from spiking all over again. "Where are you going?"

"To one of the smaller pools. Turns out they might be more pleasant after all."

She grabbed her robe and walked out without even bothering to put it on.

CHAPTER TWENTY-ONE

ELLIE

Ellie's eyes fluttered open in the dim lighting and for a fleeting moment, she feared she might still be trapped within that small room just waiting for that wretched male's next strike.

Her chest rose and fell evenly, but the racing of her heartbeat betrayed her. Ellie refused to move until she was certain she no longer felt his oily presence.

Seconds ticked by. Minutes.

Silence.

Comforting silence.

She breathed a sigh of relief.

Sweat rolled down her face and every muscle in her body ached as if she'd been ripped apart only to be violently shoved back together. Her eyes stung, her throat burned, and gods she was so, so tired.

Without moving, Ellie glanced down at her wrists. Her eyes widened a fraction more. Blood coated her hands. Her blood? Another's? She couldn't tell, even with the scent. It smelled foul. Old. Her stomach twisted and Ellie vaulted up despite the pain and vomited all over the stone floor.

Footsteps sounded behind her a second later followed by the rattle of chains. She spun, ready to defend herself. It didn't matter that she always failed. She wasn't going down without a fight. She wouldn't give him the satisfaction.

A feral sound she hardly recognized escaped her lips and Ellie's hands clamped around flesh before slamming a body against the nearest wall.

Her heart thundered in her chest. She had him. She *had* him. She'd finally gotten her hands on this vile male. She—

The room spun from the sudden movement, causing her stomach to lurch again. Ellie tried to focus on the pulse beneath her grip. *Rip out his heart, his eyes, his throat,* but just before she sank her fangs into his artery—

"Ellie."

She halted, freezing mid-movement.

That voice. It was soft and tender. That wasn't the voice of the High Lord. This was one she recognized. It was … It was …

Ellie forced her eyes to focus. Her vision blurred and tiny balls of colored light blotted her view. She scented the air instead, then a warm hand met her cheek.

She flinched from the touch, but those gentle fingers didn't pull back. His thumb moved back and forth until—

Oh gods.

Ellie yanked her hands away from his throat.

Kirian. She'd almost—

Her vision finally focused on a pair of eyes. His brows were knitted together, mouth slightly parted as he caught his breath. Bruises lined his throat. His arms.

Ellie sank back to her knees, her stomach twisting for entirely different reasons.

Kirian knelt at her side and wrapped a comforting arm around her shoulders.

"It's just me." His hand met her shoulder and a sob tore through her chest. Ellie collapsed into his embrace and let her pain and fear rise to the surface.

He was alive. Kirian was alive. She could touch him. Smell him. She didn't know how long it had been this time, only that it had felt like an eternity.

It always did.

The High Lord had somehow managed to create a little space in her head that felt like a prison. It was there that he kept her isolated, tearing through her mind one painful image at a time.

Ellie buried her face in Kirian's tunic. It was filthy and torn and stained with his blood. She didn't care. She just needed his warmth to chase away the cold and the nightmares. His scent made her feel strong again. Alive again.

Ellie steadied her breathing and focused on the mantra she'd developed to get her through every agonizing hour she'd spent in this place. It was the one thing the High Lord couldn't take from her.

Another breath.

She could do this. Just a little longer, a few more days and someone would come for them. They'd free her and Kirian, then she could return home and let herself sit in a hot shower for hours. The servants would serve her a warm meal and Arianna would give her a steaming cup of hot cocoa.

Ellie let the full image form in her head. She imagined herself curling up in a plush armchair before a roaring fire. She'd swap stories and give whoever was present all the information she could recall. Maybe she'd even talk to Rion about the High Lord's horrible mind magic. The vile images he'd conjured and the things he'd made her relive over and over again until she questioned whether the images were real.

Or maybe she'd keep all those gruesome details locked in her heart for eternity.

He'd convinced her that Kirian was dead. He'd shown her images of her sister's blood on her hands. Of Rion lying in the dirt, his vacant eyes staring up at a gray sky.

She'd seen her beautiful city burn to the ground, the flowers scorched and stone crumbling. He'd shown her that she was the one to do it.

The High Lord had convinced her that she was utterly alone and like a fool, she'd believed him. He'd broken through her mental barriers more times than she could count. And each incident allowed him to sink deeper. To taint more.

Ellie took another steadying breath, then tilted her head up. Kirian loosened his hold but kept his hands around her arms, the gesture a silent promise that he was here.

How many times had he done that now? Were any of the bruises lining his body her fault?

Ellie moved her hand and noticed the chains that held her. Thick iron manacles drowned her thin wrists and heavy chains connected to a pair of anchors bolted into the stone at the rear of their cell. They hadn't given her enough slack to reach the door.

The metal rubbed against her bruised bones. She remembered those. She'd yanked on the chains in an attempt to break them. And she'd done it for hours, refusing to give in until Kirian pulled her into his arms to quell her rage.

Ellie's gaze drifted to the single shackle locked around Kirian's ankle. She crinkled her nose at the swollen joint. He pulled his foot beneath him to hide it.

"What happened?" she asked, a strange bit of hysteria creeping into her tone.

"Nothing for you to worry about."

She tried to pry his foot out to get a better look, but Kirian held her firm. "It's nothing. I'm fine."

"They did that because of me, didn't they?" It was always because of her. His left eye was still bruised, though it had shifted to a yellowish color. There were still nearly black fingerprints around his arms. Those didn't include the ones she couldn't see. He wouldn't even be in this situation if it weren't for his involvement with her.

No, he'd be worse off. He'd be dead.

Or maybe he'd be back in Levea, spending his free time with

another female. One who would allow him to live a simpler life. There had been that one in school who—

"Whatever you're thinking, stop thinking it. I'm fine." He shifted her so she was sitting up more and Ellie winced from the movement. "Do you think you can eat?" Ellie shook her head, but Kirian reached for a bowl anyway. She tried not to look at the contents. The very smell made her stomach turn. "I know it's not the best, but it'll help keep up your strength."

Ellie relented and drank the water first, thankful despite the sour smell. Then she took a single bite of the gruel. Her entire body shuddered in response. It nearly resurfaced, but Ellie forced it down. Kirian was right, her body needed the nutrition. She couldn't allow her strength to wane, not if she hoped to fight off the High Lord.

Another shuddering breath rippled through her as she struggled to collect herself. Kirian made to brush her hair away from her face and Ellie snatched his wrist. He winced and she quickly released the swollen area.

She clenched her teeth. They'd hurt him. Again. She'd obeyed, hadn't she? She'd let the High Lord rifle through her mind, doing as he pleased with whatever information he found there.

Tears pricked the corners of her eyes and Ellie ran a gentle finger over the raised skin. "They promised to leave you alone."

Kirian offered her a weak smile. "It's okay. The guards were just frustrated. I wasn't taken anywhere."

A fresh wave of helplessness washed through her. *She* might be able to survive the torture and pain. She was Fae. She would heal, but Kirian's bruises from when they'd first arrived were still yellow. His ribs were still sensitive and despite how much he tried to hide it, Ellie caught him wincing whenever he moved.

Just like a human.

Just last month, he'd shown her he was capable of using magic. He wasn't able to summon much more than a handful of water, but it had given her hope that he might have inherited more aspects from his Fae heritage.

But watching the way his body was healing had her facing the painful truth. Kirian was far more human than she'd ever allowed herself to believe.

Tears burned her already swollen eyes. If they took things too far, if they punished him too much—Ellie's voice cracked. "What are we going to do?"

"Hey," he pulled her into a tight embrace and she listened to the steady rhythm of his beating heart. A lullaby that promised hope where she saw none. "It's going to be okay, you'll see. We'll get through this just like everything else."

He honestly believed it.

Ellie gave a breathless laugh that held no mirth. "We've never faced anything like this."

"Myrna can be pretty scary."

Ellie appreciated his attempt at humor, but it only caused a fresh wave of tears to rattle through her body. She just wanted to rest. She just wanted this nightmare to be over.

Kirian's hands brushed her hair back, over and over in slow, methodical strokes. "It'll be okay, you'll see. We'll get out of here and you'll have all the bragging rights in the world."

Ellie clutched his tunic, staring at the damp stone floor. Kirian rocked her back and forth, lightly resting his chin on her head.

Survive. They just had to survive.

She recited the mantra in her head again.

She wouldn't forget who she was or the things she was fighting for.

I am Lady Evelyn of Móirín and the future High Lady of Levea. I am the daughter of the High Lord of Storms. Sister to Arianna, The Queen of Alastríona. I have been trained to endure. I will not falter. I have a mate, Gavin from Pádraigín, but a half-breed has claimed my heart. I will protect Levea at any cost, even if that cost means my life. The people are everything. I will not allow myself to be manipulated. I will not break.

CHAPTER TWENTY-TWO

ARIANNA

Nine days passed before they were walking through the underground cavernous halls on their way to infiltrate Ashling. Her wounds had healed thanks to Sive, Conall's warriors had returned, and they'd each studied the maps, plans, and escape routes relentlessly. She could practically see Gavin's drawings every time she closed her eyes. He was quite the artist.

Said male walked just ahead of her, still wearing the iron bracelet at Conall's request. Most still distrusted him, but Arianna could feel his sincerity whenever he spoke. Gavin was a good male who'd grown up under the influence of the wrong people and ideals. If he were willing to learn and change, then she was willing to give him the opportunity.

Arianna lifted her gaze to the tall ceiling, watching as water dripped from the crevice that reached higher than their light could penetrate.

When Conall had mentioned tunnels, Arianna had envisioned tight, narrow passageways, but these were the complete opposite. The

Fae walked comfortably in small groups, whispering amongst one another with packs slung over their shoulders.

She glanced down at her wrist to the pair of bracelets the Weavers had gifted every single warrior embarking on this mission. The stones attached to the bands acted as a means to keep track of time, counting down to Ashling's destruction.

One bracelet for the journey there. Another for once they arrived. If everything went according to plan, they'd have around twelve hours to find her sister, free the prisoners, gather intel, then set the place on fire. Or blow it up as Conall planned to do.

Arianna traced her fingers over the six stones that had already turned dull. Each one had been imbued with a certain amount of magic. It pulsed until that magic faded and triggered the next to activate. Handy, given their mission, but Arianna wasn't sure twelve hours would be long enough to accomplish it all.

They had one shot. If they messed up—Arianna shook the thoughts away.

She pulled her sleeve back further to reveal the small rune painted on her skin. It would serve to help them resist Pádraigín's influence. Everyone had a similar marking, courtesy of the Weavers.

Conall led them personally, something that surprised her given that he was the leader of the resistance group. Arianna thought he might stay behind, but the male had assured her there were more than a few who could take his place should things go wrong, Cara among them.

Arianna glanced over at Rion, listening to the drip, drip, drip of water as it rolled down the sides of the tunnel walls. Those with Pádraigín's magic kept the air moving, just to ease those uncomfortable with thousands of pounds of rocks overhead.

But it did nothing to calm her mate's fears.

Sweat rolled down his face despite the pleasant temperature, and his heartbeat had been erratic since they'd stepped foot underground. Any time she took his hand, he gripped it like a lifeline, hardly seeming to notice how tightly he squeezed. Just like he was doing now.

She made a point to not let go if she could help it.

Arianna kept walking, following the line of hundreds that accompanied them. Each had their own assignments. Some were solely responsible for retrieving the prisoners. Others would secure their exit, ensuring no obstacles blocked their path. The mission had to be fast. They had to trust that everyone knew their roles and could act quickly if things went wrong.

Twelve hours was all it would take to change the direction of the entire continent one way or the other.

Talon had tried to convince her to stay behind. She'd told him she wouldn't risk losing another friend to the monster that called himself a High Lord.

Arianna watched one of the warriors pause and press their back against the wall as everyone else filed past. Another stopped beside them, both opening their water skins to take a long drink.

They were part of the team that would be helping prisoners make the journey back. All would remain unconscious until they reached safety. She just wondered how long it would take their minds to believe it.

The sound of rushing water grew louder as they kept pressing forward. Conall had mentioned the walls would carve around an underground river at the halfway point. They'd rest for a few minutes before crossing the final stretch.

Arianna tugged at her uncomfortable uniform. She wore Pádraigín's colors, with a heavy green cloak that she'd pushed back to leave her arms free. She hated the rough material and hated the colors even more. Niall had wanted to cage her in these colors. To combine them with the blues and silvers of Móirín. Even if it meant doing so against her will.

But even if she hated them now, these clothes were the only thing that would hide them once they crossed into Ashling. Rion wore the same colors, though if he loathed the material, he didn't show it. Or couldn't be bothered to care with the fear coursing through him.

Her mate's gaze flickered to the right where a bit of shadow had jumped along the wall. It had just been from one of the torches and yet even that slight bit of movement sent her mate spiraling.

The wall opened ahead, giving Arianna full view of the gushing water.

The line slowly came to a halt.

Arianna unclasped the heavy bag from around her shoulders and let it fall to the floor. She dragged it toward the back wall, leaning it against the rock. They'd told her she didn't need to carry anything, being that she was the queen, but she'd insisted she could help. As had Rion.

Talon was ahead alongside Raevina, but once again, the two seemed to be mostly ignoring one another. Arianna couldn't wrap her mind around the dynamic. They were magnetized to one other, even without speaking.

Rion had told her to stay out of it. She'd only pouted, knowing it was best to let them work it out on their own.

Rion placed his pack beside hers before leaning against the rough wall. He breathed deep and closed his eyes. Arianna watched his jaw clench. She could scent his magic as well, even if he tried to keep it hidden.

Most gave them space, opting to sit closer to their comrades. They were always watching. She wondered if they were afraid she'd vanish if they looked away.

Arianna sighed, then approached Rion slowly, gently tugging on their bond. He cracked one eye open. His lips parted, but Arianna spoke first. "Don't try to convince me you're okay." She kept her voice low, barely a whisper. There wasn't really any way for them to have privacy here, not with the wide-open tunnels.

Rion didn't move as she paused before him and laid a hand over her mate's racing heart. He sucked in a breath and watched her, his eyes wide and wild in a way that made her own heart race.

Arianna shoved her fear aside and someone to their left gasped when light began emitting from her palm. She ignored them. Rion's shoulders gradually melted beneath her touch, like ice beneath a warm sun.

Rion leaned forward, pressing his forehead to hers. "Thank you." He didn't need to elaborate. He'd been caged within walls with nothing but darkness for company for months. Being under the mountain sent those memories racing to the surface all over again.

Arianna just wished she could remove his pain permanently.

"I should have let you do that from the beginning," he murmured, voice raw.

"I tried to tell you." The words hung between them, heavy with the silence of the weeks that had followed Ellie's disappearance. The pain. The loss. It was all still there, gnawing at the edge of her thoughts. Rion and his mother ... they'd suffered far more than anyone should have to.

Arianna's fingers brushed the skin of his neck as she leaned in. "You're safe now," she said. "You're safe with me."

He relaxed further and wrapped his arms around her back, pulling her close. Arianna found herself wishing for the cabin again. For just another moment where they could disappear and forget about the rest of the world.

A throat cleared. "We're ready to move, My Lady."

Arianna pulled back, met the male's gaze, then nodded. "We're ready." She glanced down at the first bracelet. Half the stones were already dull. Once they reached Ashling, the second would begin ticking away the hours until they saw Ellie again.

The cavern came alive with sounds as everyone stood and began pulling their packs back over their shoulders. They murmured to their friends and heart rates spiked with excitement for the mission to come.

The line began moving, but Rion gently grabbed her upper arm and pulled her aside. "Are you sure about this?"

Arianna furrowed her brow, glancing around at those who filtered past at a snail's pace. "It's a bit late for me to back out now."

"You could." His voice was almost hopeful. "Talon and I can go. Conall already told me he'd give you a personal escort back to the village."

"And you'd just let me leave with complete strangers?"

"Raevina said she'd join you."

"And when did you all decide to have this part of the conversation without me?"

Rion looked away, shame filling him in a way she hated. "I never want to hold you back, but …" He gritted his teeth. "Conall spoke with us when you were working with the Weavers. There are things you're going to see in Ashling that won't be pleasant."

"I know." Pádraigín was the country that procured the slaves, after all. She knew the atrocities there would be far greater than anything she'd seen thus far. Though she wondered if those who sold their own kin were even worse. Perhaps they were the true monsters. She'd never understand how a human could sell another human without feeling racked with guilt.

"You won't be able to help them."

Her mouth went dry. She knew that, even if she'd been trying to avoid thinking about it. "I know that too."

Rion's jaw worked. "I know you—" His gaze traveled to her wrists. "I know you understand, but—" He gave her a playful smirk that didn't quite reach his eyes. "I've also seen you try to take on an entire unit of warriors for one slave."

"I had you to back me up." She touched his chest again. "You don't really want me to stay behind."

He laughed, more to himself than at her words. "No. I don't. I want you with me every second of the day, but I also don't want you in danger."

"You can't have it both ways."

"I know, which is why I'm letting you make the choice." Even after she'd nearly died in his arms.

"You already know my choice."

He smiled again and pressed his forehead to hers before capturing her lips in a longing kiss. Rion pulled away. "We'll get them out after," he promised. "Once we have Ellie, we'll get the rest out."

"How?"

He shrugged. "I'll improvise. Saoirse and I are good at that."

"Sounds like the two of you are just trouble waiting to happen," she teased.

He ran a hand through her hair. "Maybe." His face turned serious again. "But I have no intention of leaving anyone in chains. I just wanted you to know that."

Arianna glanced behind her, watching the backs of those who were already walking ahead. Some had hesitated, clearly unwilling to let her and Rion take up the rear. "Does Conall know about your plan?"

"Does he need to?" Rion glanced around, noting how the others were trying very hard not to listen in. He took her hand and began walking, filling the space from the gap in the line with long strides. "I have no intention of interfering with what he has planned. Once the prisoners are free, we'll go after the slaves. I'm sure he won't object to more allies for the war to come."

"Maybe we'll get lucky and Vairik will get caught in the middle of all this, then there won't be a war."

"Maybe." His voice was low, edged with something unspoken. She wondered if he wanted to be the one to end Niall and Vairik. "Promise me something," Rion murmured, his grip tightening around her hand. His gaze darkened, fierce and intent. "If you come face to face with Vairik … run."

Her breath caught, the weight of his words settling deep in her chest. "Would you?"

Rion's eyes flared with an intensity that could burn, the kind of fire that only came when everything worth protecting was on the line. "If it meant getting back to you?" His voice was soft but certain. "I wouldn't think twice."

CHAPTER TWENTY-THREE

ARIANNA

Crouched behind one of the mountain's jagged edges, Arianna stared down at the massive city below. City. Not village or town. The place was crawling with citizens and sentinels. Animals perched on the rooftops watched the crowd closely. The guards in their Fae forms were just as keen, their gazes catching every shadow that moved.

Her stomach twisted in knots as she watched the first few groups slip inside undetected. Someone from Pádraigín accompanied each small group, using their magic to blend them in with the environment. She'd been afraid of detection, but Conall had assured them the magic would blend in enough. There certainly wasn't a shortage of it, despite the entire place reeking of iron.

The oily magic crawled all over her, like a parasite trying to leach its way into her body. She'd experienced it so much without even realizing it, thanks to Niall. He'd made it seem pleasant, more like a butterfly's wing beat. Now it felt more like the slime left by a snail.

Her stomach rolled. She hated what Niall had done to her. She hated that she'd been so susceptible to it, and how easily she'd fallen prey to his suggestive prodding. Rion had suffered as a result. Perhaps his nightmares were her fault after all. If she'd just been more aware. More—

Rion's hand threaded through hers and Arianna shook the thoughts away. Later. Right now they were in the middle of phase one. Infiltration.

Another group moved into position, keeping close together as they approached the gate and the guards. Wind whipped at her hair, pulling on the edges of her tight braid as though even it were a spy just waiting to tell Vairik of their arrival.

The group of six slipped past the guards and blended into the crowded street moments later. Arianna's gaze lifted to Vairik's castle in the distance. It loomed above everything, tall and menacing. The structure promised twisting halls that would have them all second guessing their plans.

Tall spikes rose from the top, ready to impale anything that might fly in from above. Large crossbows stood between the spires, too. Arianna didn't want to imagine what kind of creatures Vairik might fear to have something like those in his arsenal.

Another group moved and Rion pulled her closer, crouching down as he watched.

They were next.

Her, Talon, Rion, and a male from Pádraigín who would lead them inside.

Arianna pulled her hood up, as did her companions. Once inside, they'd look like everyone else dressed in the faded green that almost appeared gray.

Raevina was accompanying Gavin and three of Conall's warriors. Saoirse had refused to leave Zylah's side. They would be joined by four others.

Arianna tried to calm her racing heart. They'd reconvene inside, but after the underground cells were empty, they'd separate all over again. She wished they could stay altogether, but they'd all agreed that solely relying on a group of strangers probably wasn't in their best interest.

Raevina and Talon would split off to gather information while Saoirse and Zylah would focus on securing their escape route. Once they had Ellie in hand, alarms would likely start blaring through the city. They'd have minutes before Vairik confronted them personally.

Arianna chewed her lip. There was a very real possibility that one of them could end up captured. Possibly killed. Her heart pounded at the thought. If she were ever put in a position to choose between Talon or Ellie, her heart might literally shatter.

Rion had gone still beside her, his eyes scanning the field and bodies below. He wasn't pensive like the others. No, her mate was steady. He was in his element here, ready to tackle the challenge of infiltrating one of the most guarded places on the continent.

The male accompanying them nodded, indicating they were about to move. Arianna tried to steady her breathing. They needed to blend in and go unnoticed.

Her gaze scanned the fence line again. This was a training exercise, nothing more. It was just her, Talon, Rion and a stranger running through a routine.

Her heart slowed and the male's magic sprang to life, circling them like a blanket before trickling over their bodies like rain. Her skin tingled and Rion stiffened at her side.

She waited for the magic to prod her mind, but this manipulation was different. It only acted on the outside of their bodies, blending them in with their surroundings. So long as they kept quiet, the glamour would go unnoticed.

The male stepped over the ledge they'd been hiding behind and Rion followed, pulling her along. Talon stayed close behind. Rion didn't release her hand and she briefly wondered who he was trying to comfort, himself or her.

They marched downward at a brisk, yet steady pace, directly in the line of sight of the guards. None stood to attention or lifted the long-range weapons that hung at their sides.

The contraptions looked like crossbows but promised iron balls in place of arrows. One hit and it would render a Fae's magic useless.

Thankfully, no one looked up.

They slipped through a narrow section of the gate that had been ripped open, carefully moving around the boards and metal to avoid making any noise.

She glanced behind, but Rion pushed her forward, keeping his gaze locked on the buildings just ahead. Within minutes, they were blending with the crowd, keeping close to one another as they followed the male from Pádraigín.

Their movements slowed as the crowd thickened. Arianna kept her gaze on her feet and the crooked cobblestones that promised to trip her any moment. Rion's hand never left hers.

It took far too long to enter the small storehouse. Their first checkpoint. The male from Pádraigín closed the door and removed his hood, though his magic remained in place.

"You remember where to go?" he asked.

Talon nodded. "We have it from here."

The male bowed at the waist, first to her, then to Rion. "Be careful and stay low."

"We will," she whispered.

She knew the rules from here on out. Absolutely no magic from any of them. Especially Rion. Hers was already crawling beneath her skin at the command, raging against being forced into silence.

Just for a little while, she promised, then clenched her fists. Just a little while, then she'd unleash hell on them all.

The male's glamour left with him, and a chill skittered across her skin. Talon met their gazes before peeking his head outside the doorway. Rion reluctantly released her hand and Arianna ran her fingers over her knives to assure herself they were still there.

Talon stepped outside and they followed.

A light drizzle had started. A blessing. Conall assured them they wouldn't have to worry, but Arianna welcomed anything that would help conceal their scents as they moved through the most dangerous city on the continent. She had to assume everyone present was an enemy who would turn her over to Vairik without hesitation.

The crowds closed in again and Arianna noted the scents from the four nations. Far more than she'd previously thought might be present. Clearly Vairik understood the advantages of them all working together.

But of course he would. He'd been born during a time when the nations functioned as a unit.

Arianna wondered if anyone here knew the real truth and what they might do if it was revealed.

The city itself was a dank place, with too much gray stone where life and greenery should have been. Drums collected rainwater on every other corner, but even it looked dark and unwelcoming.

The slanted roofs were all slightly crooked, each one with oddly colored shingles.

She wrinkled her nose at the scents that drifted by, the smoke and sweat and iron.

People walked through the streets with their shoulders hunched from the weight of their cargo. Some with wood, others with boxes or sacks of grain.

A loud voice echoed across the expanse as one Fae cursed another when a rope snapped and logs rolled everywhere. Another kicked the firewood, and none bothered to help the male who was scrambling to pick it all up.

Arianna studied their haggard faces. This wasn't a place of prosperity. It was a prison, and the holder of the keys held no love for its inmates.

They appeared to have adequate food, clothing, and shelter, but the fire had left their eyes—slowly chipped away by the rudimentary schedule of an unchanging existence.

For the Fae who lived forever, it was as good as dying. To never know change. To never travel and see the far places of their beautiful continent. Everything surrounding her was gray and colorless, like rain had stripped all the color away from a beautiful mural.

The winding roads continued in a maze, each building seemingly placed at various puzzling intervals that were designed to confuse any attempting to infiltrate. Gavin had said Vairik was rather proud of its construction.

Talon and Rion had memorized the paths, leaving her to follow their lead. She'd focused on memorizing the quickest exits, though if it came down to running, they all knew to head straight for the ocean. It would give them the best chances even with the dark creatures that swam in the icy depths.

A scream echoed across the expanse, and Arianna bristled against the sound.

Her first instinct was to run toward whoever might be in pain, but a light tug on the bond kept her walking.

To her utmost horror, no one else reacted. The citizens didn't even seem fazed by the sound. As if they heard it every day.

The world stilled again and the trio continued weaving through the maze-like pattern of the buildings. Talon veered down what appeared to be an alley, then emerged on the other side of a busy market. He turned again and she was certain they were heading away from the castle until another sharp turn had them moving in the right direction again.

Talon paused a few times, studying his surroundings. A ploy so they looked like a normal patrol. She resisted the urge to glance at the bracelets on her wrist.

The first one's beads had faded altogether, the rocks dull once more. They'd been late entering the city. Not by much, but enough that she wanted to run to that channel and get inside as fast as possible. Any minute they could spare was another minute to search for Ellie.

Another scream pierced the air. Arianna's head whipped toward the sound. There, in the distance between two buildings, she caught a glimpse of a group of people in chains.

Arianna couldn't tear her gaze away. Her eyes traced down their new clothes, their bodies that were still healthy as they pulled against their restraints and fought their captors.

Humans.

Humans that were fresh from the northern continent.

One hit her knees, begging for them to just kill her and get it over with. The Fae surrounding her laughed, pointing and jeering. Then a boot collided with the woman's ribs and she rolled through the mud.

Another human beside her lunged and grabbed one of the males, doing everything in her power to bring him down. She kicked and screamed and bit into his flesh. The scene felt all too real.

The Fae male sneered down at her in disgust but mostly seemed annoyed before he threw her to the ground. Arianna recognized that fire in the woman's eyes. The face of a warrior willing to die before allowing herself to be used like an animal.

The male drew his sword. Arianna took an involuntary step, but it was too late. The blade came down, severing the woman's head from her shoulders in one movement. Rion stepped into her line of sight before the woman's head hit the ground. Arianna still heard it. Her body shook with rage. The magic in her veins did the same, pushing against its invisible cage.

Rion guided her away, urging her forward through their bond. He willed a sense of calm through her, but it did nothing to ease that burning fire or the memories it dragged up from the recesses of her subconscious.

Just a few months ago, that had been her, kneeling in the mud, accepting her fate. It had been a miracle that Lan and hadn't killed her then. Miracle, or divine intervention.

Maybe the gods did look down on them. Maybe they'd brought her and Rion together on purpose so they could liberate these people from their hardships.

Maybe Ashling was exactly where she'd needed to be.

Arianna gritted her teeth and forced breath through her lungs. She tried to ignore the rattle of chains and the pleas for mercy. Soon, she promised. She'd free them all soon.

They rounded the next set of buildings and her heart sank all over again. Lines upon lines of humans and half-breeds filled the square. All were in chains. All were tied to one another, each waiting to step onto a platform where Fae would call out bids.

Men. Women. Children. It didn't matter.

A man stood on one of those platforms now, his shoulders sagging in defeat. He might have been in his mid-thirties. Nothing protected his bare torso or head from the rain. He was cattle on display for potential buyers.

A female below him watched with equally numb eyes. A look Arianna had seen far too often. Something she'd experienced, too.

It was better to be hollow, to be nobody, and let your mind drift off somewhere else.

Her gaze traveled from one soul to another, then a hand wrapped around her arm and gently pulled her back. She moved in a daze, letting the building block them from view once again.

How could she just leave them here? How could she face anyone if—

I have no intention of leaving anyone in chains.

Arianna glanced up at her mate and saw the sadness on his face. The ache down their bond mirrored her own. Rion had warned her. He'd asked if she wanted to stay behind because of this. He'd been in the field for decades. He'd seen the worst.

But if she chose to fight now. If she released these slaves and revealed them to Vairik, how many of the prisoners would die in their cold cells? How would her sister fare if she were never released?

Arianna clenched her jaw, but she couldn't stop the wave of tears as they burned down her cheeks. She knew what the right move was, even if she didn't like it. They had a plan, one that would free everyone from Vairik's control.

She was a queen. One who could make any move but was trapped into making only one. Go straight for the king and leave the pawns to their fate.

Her stomach twisted as she turned away from their plight.

Voices rose as numbers were called out, several bidding on the male standing on that platform. He'd be at someone's mercy within the hour. Arianna used her other hand to finger the bracelet around her wrist. Less than twelve and he'd be free. She'd never be able to erase what he suffered today, but she might be able to prevent what might torment him tomorrow.

Arianna steeled herself and tried to block her resolve from flowing down the bond. If she encountered Vairik today, she wasn't running, she'd fight and end it all today.

Arianna followed Talon and Rion as they wound their way toward the castle looming above them like a vulture on a perch. She was glad Conall planned to destroy it. Ridding the land of this foul monument would do it some good.

"You." A deep male voice shot a pang of fear through her so fast there was no way to hide it.

Chapter Twenty-Four

Arianna

All three turned as a unit to find two males glaring at them with their hands resting on the hilts of their weapons. "Identify yourselves."

Shit. Arianna resisted the urge to search for an escape route, recalling Conall's instructions to remain calm and speak as though they belonged there. Had she just blown their cover? Even now she couldn't get her heart to slow.

Had they scented them? Was it strange not to have someone from Pádraigín accompanying their patrol? Had they seen the way she'd acted around the slaves and chosen to follow?

Talon cocked his head and she wished she could summon as much bravado as he displayed with his next words. "And who are you that we need to identify anything?"

One of the males drew his sword. Arianna glanced around, happy to find them in one of the alleys with no one around. But that could change in a split second. If someone rounded the corner and raised the alarm—

"I don't recognize any of you." The male scented the air. "And I don't recall the High Lord releasing the recent recruits for duty."

Arianna cursed to herself again. Hadn't Conall mentioned Vairik recruiting all the time? Apparently he wasn't known for his patience, which resulted in many earning an early retirement.

Again, Talon shrugged. "Maybe you don't have the required rank."

The male smirked. "Maybe we'll just take you to the general and find out."

The two males advanced, their bodies swift and boots light on the broken cobblestone. Rion stepped to her front, then Talon launched himself forward and struck the first male in the throat. He gasped for breath, then Rion nearly vanished. In a blink, he was behind the other male, his arm wrapping around the male's thick neck before a loud crack rang through the air.

Talon finished the other in a similar manner and the males' limp bodies crumbled to the ground.

The rain picked up, pattering against their cloaks in the stillness. Talon jerked his chin at Rion and the two males dragged the corpses inside a nearby storehouse. Arianna stood by the door, doing her best to keep calm.

Someone walked by the alley and peered down, but she didn't make eye contact. They moved on.

Blood strummed through her ears, pounding in her veins. Her companions had moved before she'd even given it a thought. It just proved she was in over her head.

Act without hesitation, Talon had always told her. *Move before the enemy knows what you plan to do.*

Rion and Talon had done that. Arianna clenched her fists. She'd commit the lesson to memory.

The two emerged a moment later, their eyes scanning the area. "We have to get to the rendezvous point. Now," Talon declared.

Arianna nodded. She couldn't ask questions here, not without risking someone overhearing. It was a miracle no one had seen them just now.

The males pulled their hoods back up and kept moving, their pace faster than before.

More guards patrolled the area closer to the main wall, but thankfully, that wasn't their destination. When they'd originally made plans, Arianna had wondered if they might be able to enter hidden inside a caravan. Arianna watched the guards stationed at the gate open every crate. Another dropped to his knees in the mud, scanning the underside. Conall had been right in advising against it.

Talon marched away from the main part of the city toward the open ocean in the distance. Homes were replaced with storehouses and foot traffic ceased to exist, as if this section were somehow cursed and the people strove to avoid it.

Rion kept peering down at her, but he didn't risk voicing his thoughts nor sending anything down the bond. Death still wasn't something she was accustomed to, but she recognized its necessity now. She just prayed the gods had mercy on their souls should they deserve it.

Talon paused when he reached the final building at the end of the walkway. The cobblestone path ended here, replaced by sharp rocks and sand. Several boulder sized stones lined a hillside that separated the city from the roaring ocean just below. The water sprayed up, coating the rocks so they appeared nearly black against the already dark water.

The ever-moving wind carried the ocean spray toward Arianna, mixing salt with the rain. Its roaring power called to her, beckoning her toward the icy depths. Or maybe that was the Sirens' magic, trying to lure her in for their next meal. No wonder the citizens avoided this place.

Talon pressed his body against the edge of the wall and crept forward. They followed suit, waiting. Her heart began pounding again, wondering if they'd come this far just for everything to fall apart, but seconds later, Pádraigín's magic settled over them again. A female poked her head out from around the other side and nodded, giving them the go-ahead.

Arianna crept forward to see exactly what they'd be running into.

Just a short distance ahead, a gushing passage of water moved with each crest of a wave. It rose and fell, pushing water through the channel at incredible speeds. She grimaced, knowing that once they dove in, they'd have to keep themselves hidden underneath. If they drifted too close to the surface, they'd risk discovery. If they moved too close to the bottom, they'd scrape themselves on the jagged rocks below.

Arianna leaned her head back against the wall as they waited. She was responsible for keeping herself and Rion steady. Talon would propel them through, but they had to wait until they were fully submerged before summoning their magic. If the guards scented a little magic, they would just assume it was the work of the Sirens. If they scented a lot, the mission would end before it even began.

Arianna had asked Conall what would happen if the Sirens caught them. The male's face had gone deadly serious and he'd uttered three words that had chilled her to the bone.

Ensure they don't.

Talon made a hand gesture, then they were running. Arianna sprinted after him with Rion on her heels. Her heart thundered in her chest. Their feet hit the ground too hard, too loud. Then Talon was plunging in and she followed after him.

The cold water shocked her system and Arianna spun through the current, nearly losing her breath. She reached for Rion, using several tendrils of magic to pull his body close. Their hands clasped, then she eased the raging water around their bodies, holding them steady. Talon's magic had them rushing through the channel seconds later.

Arianna dared to open her eyes in the foul liquid and found Rion squinting, his face pained as they moved at a rapid pace. Her lungs cried out and her body balked against the cold.

A ringing echoed through her ears, then her body, pulsing through the water itself. It moved in a rhythmic fashion, like a hammer coming down on an anvil. She squeezed Rion's hand and he squeezed back.

Just a little further, she told herself. A little more and they'd be safe.

Time ticked. A slow painful thing. Then, just as fast as their plunge, they resurfaced.

Arianna gasped for breath and Rion did the same beside her. Talon had already pulled himself up and out of the water, his gaze scanning the rocky incline that led to a small opening in the wall.

Sconces lit the area, each burning bright as though they'd just been lit. She waded through the water, bile rising in her throat from the stench drifting up from the surface. With the bend in the channel, the pocket of water here was calmer, pulled away from the rapid current still gushing through the tunnel behind them.

A white thing bobbed on the surface beside the back wall and it took Arianna one horrifying moment to realize exactly what it was. A body, discarded and left to rot.

She pulled Rion toward the rocky incline and he helped her out before she wrung the liquid from their clothes and discarded it back into the cesspool at their feet. The smell remained. Arianna half wondered if their enemies would flee from that alone. She certainly might.

Rion studied the crudely formed entrance that seemed to resemble an arch. Arianna couldn't be sure if flooding waters had caused irreparable damage or if whoever had originally built it couldn't be bothered to finish the task.

Everything dripped with seawater and sludge. Barnacles and mollusks gripped the grimy edges lined with dark lichen. A distinct line marked where the tide would roll in, effectively covering everything they stood upon.

But nothing explained the humming she could still hear pulsing through the walls. Arianna crept closer to Talon, straining her ears. "Do you hear that?" Both him and Rion stilled, waiting for the sound. Neither reacted for a long moment despite its continued presence.

She stepped closer to the wall, but the sound didn't change. She was certain it was coming from within—

"Arianna," Talon hissed in warning, his eyes locked on the ground surrounding her feet. A light layer of frost coated her boots and the surrounding loose stones. Then she realized the hum wasn't coming from around her. It was *in* her.

Her magic was reacting, pulsing like an angry swarm of wasps ready to defend their nest. Because right in front of them, inlaid into the stone itself, was iron. Huge chunks of iron.

Conall had mentioned the metal covering parts of the city, but this place had been built long ago by the Fae themselves. Surely they wouldn't have constructed a stronghold that would only serve to weaken its occupants.

Unless … unless this place wasn't the Ashling they thought it was. Their maps showed the port city farther north and no one had set foot there in centuries. Maybe—maybe their maps *were* correct. Maybe a ruined city rested where the original Ashling had once stood. Did that mean this place had been built by humans, or Vairik himself?

"What is it?" Rion asked, standing beside her with a knife in each hand.

"There's iron." Rion followed her gaze and furrowed his brow at the sight. "My magic is … reacting to it."

"I'd venture a guess it's reacting to a lot more," Conall said, emerging from the water. Three others followed him, each grimacing at the stench floating in the air. Conall looked them over. "Everyone okay?"

"You never mentioned the castle had iron inlaid into the foundation," Rion said, a slight growl to his voice.

"I told you this was a city of iron. Vairik has taken every precaution. It'll weaken your magic, but you'll still be able to use it if this comes down to a fight."

"Unless we face Vairik himself," one of Conall's companions stated before lifting themselves out of the channel.

Conall's gaze darkened. "If it comes to that, I'm afraid we're all likely doomed anyway."

"Way to be encouraging," Talon commented, his gaze focused on the ever-moving surface.

Conall pulled the water from his clothes and let it fall to his feet. "I'm a realist. I do nothing without a plan and don't live for unrealistic expectations." Talon clenched his fists, but no one commented. Conall gestured toward the arched entrance. "Shall we?"

Arianna pulled up her sleeve to stare at the bracelet and the first stone that held a steady pulse. It was time to start phase two: clearing the underground prison.

Nearly one hour was already down. Less than eleven and she'd have Ellie back in her arms.

Talon gestured Conall to walk ahead. Arianna followed Talon, watching her footing as she climbed the steep slope. She wondered if the worn rocks had once been shaped into a set of stairs but then had been eroded by the water through the centuries. She supposed they might never know.

Rion took her hand again when they passed beneath the arch. Her magic gave another pulse, urging her to be careful. Uncertainty crawled through her as she watched the shadows dancing along the wall. She couldn't forget that Fiadh and Pádraigín were allies. Mostly. How easy would it be for a Shadow Weaver to walk the halls without their knowledge? She'd seen the devastation they could cause in Levea. Would Raevina be able to spot them? Were Conall's Shadow Weavers already searching?

"When was the last time you were here again?" Arianna asked Conall. She kept her voice low, but it still echoed along the walls.

"Just over three months."

"And you said they don't notice the prisoners that go missing?"

"We've only taken those from the lower levels. Most are left to die either from starvation or illness. When the guards bother to check on them, their bodies are deposited into the channel. The ocean takes care of the rest."

"There was a body back there," she said.

Conall nodded. "Which means they were probably down here yesterday."

"Will they come back?" Talon asked, suddenly watching the tunnels with renewed intent.

"It's possible. Which is why we have to move as quickly as possible."

Those who'd arrived ahead of them had already unlocked at least a dozen cells. Fae lined the halls, their clothes in tatters that barely covered their hauntingly thin frames. Arianna grimaced at their hollow cheeks and pale skin. Even with her magic, she wouldn't be able to ease the pain of hunger in their bodies, nor the ache in their limbs. Those were things that would come with time.

The prisoners all rested peacefully, rendered unconscious by those who possessed Pádraigín's magic. Arianna had helped to oversee Rion's mother; she knew it was best for both the prisoners and those setting them free. She still hated it.

They followed Conall further down the passage and he briefly paused beside a female who no longer drew breath. "It's a sadness." Conall bent to touch her pale hand, his touch a silent offer of comfort in the afterlife. "Such talent wasted."

His words twisted her stomach. Wasted talent wasn't exactly her first thought upon seeing the dead. She studied the frail Fae around her. Did he really expect these people to fight in a war? It would take months for them to recover. Longer. The war could be on their doorstep tomorrow.

Arianna opened her mouth to press the male about it when deep laugher had everyone freezing in place. Her eyes shot to Rion first, then a wave of Pádraigín's magic swept over the area, coating their bodies. Arianna braced herself against the magic, readying herself for the illusions that would follow.

Rion pivoted for Conall. The male only had time to raise one hand before Rion's fingers dug into his throat. He slammed the male against the stone wall and pressed a dagger to Conall's artery.

Conall lifted a finger to his lips, urging them to be silent even as he faced the brunt of Rion's wrath.

Arianna turned to Talon next, but he was assessing those fleeing into the tiny cells, tugging the bodies of those they'd just released inside. Arianna grimaced at the way their bodies scooted against the hard stone, knowing full well it would leave marks.

Doors closed on unnaturally silent hinges.

Light bounced off the walls as the voices drew closer, their boots echoing off the thick stone.

Conall pointed to the cell across from them and mouthed a single word. *Move.*

Rion didn't budge. He kept glancing down the hall then back to Conall. She sensed his magic writhing beneath his skin, ready to tear free. But if Vairik really did have something in place to detect it—

Conall dared to grip Rion's wrist and Rion's blade dug deeper. "Move," Conall hissed.

"No." It was single word marked with absolute resolve. There was no way Rion was going back into a cell, even if it meant discovery. Arianna quickly glanced around for another alternative. A crack, a crevice, an open place in the ceiling—too late.

The males rounded the corner and stopped, their gazes blinking as if they were seeing a group of ghosts. Perhaps, for a moment, they believed they were.

As though materializing from thin air, Gavin stepped from one of the cells. She hadn't even seen him enter. That meant Raevina was here, too. "At ease," he commanded, his voice surprisingly calm. "They're with me."

The males glanced between one another and Gavin continued. "We were told to clear the cells to make room for the others." Gavin loosed an exaggerated sigh. "It's tedious, as I'm sure you're already aware. Care to lend a hand while you're down here?"

One of the males opened his mouth to respond, then stopped. He studied Gavin, squinting in the dark. "Aren't you the High Lord's grandson?"

Gavin nodded, unfazed. She'd never see him look so … mature. "If you—"

"There's quite the price on your head, little lord." Gavin's face visibly paled. He'd mentioned Vairik's discovery of his betrayal. She supposed everyone knew now.

The guard withdrew a pair of shackles from his belt. "I believe he used the word 'traitor.'" The male clicked his tongue in disgust. "I wonder if he'll throw you into a cell with that little whore from Móirín. He said you'd grown quite obsessed with his new pet. What was her name again? Evel—"

The male didn't have time to finish his sentence. Arianna's magic broke free, racing across the space before she'd even commanded it. It cracked and spread, climbing up the walls, digging into crevices and engulfing their bodies within seconds. They hadn't even had time to scream.

White-hot rage burned through her body, igniting the magic even further. It crawled down the hall, extinguishing the flames one by one until everything before her was bathed in darkness.

Her breath came in shallow gasps, each exhale marked with steam. Anger pulsed through her that didn't feel like her own. It clawed at the very fabric of her being, begging to conquer. Begging for control.

"Arianna." The voice was both familiar and foreign, but a light tug on the bond rooted her back to the present. Arianna reined in her rage, willing the magic back into submission before turning to face those behind her. They all stared with mouths gaping and eyes wide.

"Beautiful," Conall whispered. Jagged spikes surrounded her feet, rooting her to the ground. Frost coated her hands and arms in a light layer. She melted everything with half a thought.

Rion watched her, his own breath ragged. They were both angry, ready for war, and she knew, right here in this moment, that if she chose to charge down the halls, he'd follow without a second thought. Judging from Talon's expression, he would too.

"We can deposit the bodies in the river." Conall offered. "No one will know the difference."

"Won't their higher ups miss their return?" Talon asked, still staring at the males that had been frozen with their mouths gaping.

"By the time they realize, it won't matter."

"I thought you said there wouldn't be patrols," Rion snarled, glaring at Conall, ready to do away with him right there.

"There usually aren't." He was surprisingly calm for someone pinned against a wall with a blade to his throat.

Arianna could feel her mate's anger down the bond. The fear. She stepped toward him and placed a hand on his arm. Rion's gaze slid to hers. "Let him go," she said. "He can't predict everything."

Those rage-filled eyes softened. He looked her over, as if assuring himself she was there, then let up and stepped back, sheathing the knife.

Conall awkwardly nodded his thanks. "Let's not waste any more time, then."

The magic buzzing through the air faded and it was just then that Arianna realized it had come from their allies. If Rion had hidden, then the two males likely would have passed by none the wiser. She stared at their frozen figures, her anger trying to surface again at their words. Maybe they'd deserved what they'd gotten.

Raevina emerged from the same cell Gavin had and Arianna could have sworn Talon's shoulders relaxed at her presence.

Without further distraction, they all set to work. More emerged from the water, including a cursing Saoirse and a very green Zylah.

They opened each and every cell on the first, second, and third floors. Some Fae screamed but were quickly silenced and placed into the line. Those with Móirín's magic were already transferring them to the channel and out into the open water. Another team would transport them back to the tunnels and ultimately to freedom.

Arianna prayed their minds wouldn't be as plagued as Eimear's, but given that Vairik enjoyed experimenting on mates, she wasn't hopeful.

She healed a few here and there, but made a point to preserve her magic. She thought her outburst might have left her drained, but it had done the completely opposite. She was invigorated, ready to tear the entire place apart one stone at a time.

But she wouldn't take that anger out here. She'd save it for Vairik himself. And his wicked son.

They entered the final hall. More lights flickered on the walls and a thick iron door stood before them, blocking the exit into the next area. From here, they'd be relying on Gavin's drawings and memory.

At Conall's command, the last few cells were emptied and Arianna watched the third stone on her bracelet fade.

Nine hours to go and they were about to start phase three: Split up and search.

Some had already begun, following specific routes laid out by Gavin in the search for information. Conall had assigned multiple teams to tackle various locations. He wasn't taking any chances on a single group. Arianna wasn't sure exactly what kind of intelligence he hoped to gather, but she supposed if they all survived, she'd find out then.

"You try anything," Conall said, glaring at Gavin, "you die."

Gavin rolled his eyes. "In case you forgot, I'm here for Evelyn too."

Conall's jaw clenched, but he didn't comment. The male knelt and pressed his ear to the door. Arianna glanced at Saoirse, then Raevina and Talon. They'd be splitting up from here on out. Saoirse and Zylah would head to the front to create a distraction for their escape. Raevina and Talon would help Conall's warriors infiltrate the council's offices and gather intel.

She, Rion, Gavin, Conall, and a few of Conall's warriors would all search for Ellie.

Arianna studied Gavin. He had seemed so childish the first time they'd met. Like a youngling who'd been excited to just be in the presence of his queen. Now, though still young, he resembled a warrior. A male ready to lay down his life for his mate. Even if that mate might never return his feelings.

She watched Rion next. He possessed the keenest hearing she'd ever seen in a Fae. If she trusted anyone to give them the signal to move, it was him.

Another moment passed, then Rion and Conall nodded. Gavin

twisted the door handle, and they all emerged into a long hall that stretched to left and right.

This was it. Saoirse met her brother's gaze and something passed between the siblings. An unspoken promise. Talon watched Raevina, but the female was already staring down the left hall, watching the shadows. Seconds later, Saoirse, Zylah, Raevina, and Talon were all sprinting down that very hall with half of Conall's warriors following in their wake.

Arianna's stomach twisted in knots. This could very well be the last time she saw any of them. She just prayed that trusting Conall wasn't the biggest mistake of her life.

CHAPTER TWENTY-FIVE

ARIANNA

Her friends disappeared behind a bend in the hall, then Arianna turned to face Rion and the others.

"Ready?" her mate asked. He was sturdy. Prepared. He'd been on missions before. As had Talon. Maybe she was the only one still questioning their decisions.

Arianna rolled her shoulders and refocused. "Let's go."

Conall gave Gavin the go ahead and they all ran down the opposite hall. Arianna refused to look back.

Various doors were already open, the contents within rummaged through by the previous groups who were already deep within the castle.

How long would it take Vairik to realize his castle had been infiltrated? Was twelve hours too long to hope they could remain hidden? He was a male with ten thousand years of experience. Was it possible they'd all walked right into a trap?

They rounded a corner and froze at the sight of a male relieving himself against the already damp wall. Conall lunged for him, knife drawn, and before the male could adjust his pants, Conall tore the blade across his throat, splattering blood all over the stone floor.

Conall wiped the blood on his pants before sheathing the weapon. She stared, watching the crimson sink into the crevices before following the line in the stones. Conall didn't pause. He simply gestured for Gavin to keep moving. Arianna noted the way Gavin's face had gone pale.

They kept running, climbing staircase after staircase and running down hallway after hallway. Rugs replaced the previously bare floors. Paintings and vases began lining the halls. Curtains hung over drafty windows. It seemed with every step, the entire structure came to life, spreading color and warmth that felt so at odds with the castle's outward appearance.

Gavin paused at a door and Conall crept forward. Voices echoed from the other side and Conall pressed a finger to his lips. He unscrewed a canteen and used a bit of the water to draw a rune over the handle. The mark glowed then the lock clicked and Conall cracked the door open to peer inside.

Arianna stepped forward and rose up on her tiptoes to look through the tiny top window.

A pair of Fae dressed in white cloaks emerged from another doorway, dragging a limp prisoner between them. Fae. The prisoner was Fae. But he was far too skinny, evidenced from his protruding ribs and cheekbones. He wore nothing more than a pair of torn, battered shorts. Chains dangled from his frail wrists and the look in his eyes. That damn hollow look—

Anger flared through her anew and hoarfrost coated the carpet at her feet. Conall backed away and no one reached for her as Arianna blasted the door wide open.

Those holding the male between them stared at Arianna in shock before she formed a spear of ice and let it fly straight through one of their skulls. His companion dropped the injured Fae and tried to raise his hands, but ice was already crawling up his legs, covering his torso, and finally his face.

Her body shook with rage. They didn't deserve mercy.

Conall approached slowly, giving her a wide berth. He knelt and withdrew a set of keys from the pocket of the dead Fae, then turned to help the injured prisoner lean against the wall.

The male's breath was ragged, his eyes open but not quite seeing.

"It's okay now," Conall assured him. "We'll get you out of here." Someone handed Conall a cloak and he draped it around the male's shoulders.

"Don't leave her." The Fae's voice was broken and raw. "Please," he rasped. "Don't let them throw her out like—like all the others." His shoulders shook, voice breaking.

Arianna stepped toward the room they'd dragged him from and peered inside. Her eyes widened, bile rose in her throat, and Arianna tore her gaze away, bracing one arm on the opposite wall as she struggled not to heave.

She covered her mouth with one hand, trying to shake the horrifying image of the Fae female inside. Her chest had been split wide open, ribcage sawed in two, and Arianna was pretty sure the red clump floating in the jar on the table was the female's heart.

Blood soaked the sheets and had dripped onto the floor. So much blood—Arianna vomited then Rion was at her side, rubbing circles on her back as he kept watch.

Conall peered inside next and cursed, slamming his fist against the wall.

The male still slumped on the ground didn't react to any of them.

Gods, what kind of monsters had her sister?

"Why?" She kept her gaze on the floor, willing her nausea to pass. "What was—" Arianna wasn't sure she could even form coherent sentences.

"He's searching for the link to the bond," Conall said, voice dripping with menace. "I told you, he'll do whatever it takes to be rid of it."

Arianna's gaze drifted to the frail Fae male again. The hollow look in his eyes wasn't due to the chains or any torment his body had suffered. It was because he'd seen the single most important person in his life torn apart. He'd watched his mate die and had been powerless to stop it.

Arianna turned away from him. The bond wasn't something physical, surely Vairik knew that by now. Was this to be her fate if he captured her or Rion? Would he kill them in front of one another just to see what might happen?

Every Fae who'd been blessed with the bond could tell him it wasn't something physical. It ran deeper. It was part of their soul, etched into the very fiber of their being.

Arianna strained to listen for more heartbeats. There were a few, but as she lifted her head to count the doors along the hall, she realized the corpses likely outnumbered those still alive.

She clenched her fists. She was going to kill Vairik. Him, Niall, and anyone else who felt it was acceptable to treat Fae like animals.

A deafening crash had them all starting. Arianna spun, her heart skipping a beat as she watched an iron door slam shut, blocking their way back down the stairs.

Her skin prickled, every instinct roaring at her to move as another door slid from the ceiling and slammed shut even closer.

Without a word, one of Conall's warriors grabbed the male from the floor and began running. Rion grabbed her hand as another iron wall slammed down, sectioning off each room one by one.

They sprinted down the hall, Gavin leading the way.

The doors kept slamming behind them one at a time, the noise grating against her nerves as she pushed her body to move faster.

Those carrying the male fell behind, then a cry split the air. She looked back, but Rion kept pulling her forward. Arianna's breath caught in her throat as she watched the bodies of the prisoner and Conall's warrior get caught in one of the cruel jaws of the iron doors.

An arm fell, severed from the body.

Conall cursed, she thought Gavin might have screamed.

Arianna's heart beat against her ribs as terror flooded through her. *Slam. Slam. Slam.* The doors gave chase, as though they were creatures of their own, reaching forward to devour them all whole.

Her nails bit into Rion's hand and they pushed. Faster. Faster. Faster.

Gavin crashed into the door at the end of the hall, desperately twisting a handle that refused to open. Conall slid to his knees beside them, summoning his magic. He drew a rune and the door swung open.

Two of his warriors followed, each sliding to a stop behind their leader. Rion kept pulling Arianna, tugging. She could feel his panic pulsing down the bond.

Another wall slammed behind her and Arianna swore she could feel the metal slide against her hair. They just had one more to get through. She threw her magic outward, knowing it might do little good against the iron itself.

"Hurry," Conall screamed, even as his magic joined her own.

The iron door let loose, then Rion's magic tore the stones apart, rushing to catch the wall before it fell. It slammed against his magic, another force pushing the iron down from the opposite side.

"Slide," he commanded and pushed her to his front. Arianna stared at the opening that was growing smaller and smaller. She didn't hesitate. Arianna pushed harder, then dropped to the floor, letting her body take the impact as she slid across the stones and directly under the heavy iron that was crumbling Rion's magic bit by bit.

Rion followed right after, his foot grazing the top of her head. Conall and his warriors grabbed them as they tumbled through the door, then Gavin slammed it shut.

Silence stretched out around them, their breaths haggard and hearts pounding. Gavin collapsed to the cold floor, the area once again appearing like the dungeons down below. Her pulse roared in her ears and she gulped down air.

"How do we get back?" one of Conall's warriors asked.

"We don't. We move on," Conall said. Arianna glanced between the two.

"But … what about the others?"

"They knew what they signed up for."

"But we can't blow this place if they're stuck in there."

"And what would you have us do?" Conall demanded. "Spare one life at the expense of thousands of others? If I were stuck in there, I'd expect no different."

One life.

One life.

Arianna was doing all this for one life.

And Conall had just confirmed that one life meant absolutely nothing to him. "You came all this way to rescue Ellie, but not your own people?"

His gaze turned to her. "I came all this way to destroy everything Vairik has built. If I'm able to rescue Lady Evelyn in the process, then I'll do it." Conall pointed behind him. "But there's nothing I can do for them now. We have limited time to do what needs to be done. There are dozens of people relying on me to ensure that happens. I know nothing about the mechanisms in those doors. I can't be everywhere all at once."

"I'll stay behind," his warrior offered. "I'll open the doors."

"Leo," Conall sighed. "We need you for—"

"I'm not leaving them."

A growl in the looming darkness had them all turning. They'd entered a strangely circular room with ceilings so high she could only just glimpse the rafters above. A steep staircase rose to her left, but to her right, the room expanded, cloaked in nothing but shadow.

Her skin crawled with something thick drifting through the air. Conall cursed and before she had time to question anything, dozens of wings unfolded from the shadows.

Rion moved, his magic rising to block the Dark Fae as they dove after them, talons extended. She joined the others with magic of her own, until the world around them was nothing more than a frenzy of water, ice, wind, earth, and flames.

It was over in minutes. Blood permeated the air, the acrid tang stinging her nostrils as they all watched the darkness in silence.

Her breaths were too loud in the large space. "Why were they here?" Arianna tried not to pay attention to the way the claws seemed to extend from fingers, nor the way these creatures resembled the Fae more than the ones she'd encountered in the village.

Judging from the experiments in the other room and the creatures lying dead before her, it was clear Vairik had been tinkering with more than just bonds over the years.

He was … creating things. Creatures. Fae. He was playing with their lives. But for what? Revenge? Boredom? Had he gone mad after all the years he'd spent plotting his vengeance?

Conall sniffed the blood at the end of his blade and recoiled. "A good way to keep those below from moving to higher levels if they were to escape, no?"

Guards. Free labor. The things they'd just killed were nothing more than slaves. Slaves to Vairik's will and slaves within their own mangled bodies.

More growls sent chills down her spine and Arianna glanced toward the staircase to her left before looking back into the shadows. Her heart ached, knowing there was nothing she could do for the Fae who'd had their bodies twisted against their will. She knew giving them a quick death was likely a mercy. Even so, she didn't want to be the one to do it. Not until they made sure there was no other alternative. If they'd been changed, then maybe, just maybe, they could be changed back.

"We can make it," she said. They all followed her gaze toward the set of stone steps that wound up the wall toward another door.

Conall stepped closer to the shadows. "You first."

She didn't hesitate. Arianna broke into a sprint right as the first set of mangled faces stepped into the light. Gavin followed on her heels.

Rion's magic ripped free and shoved the creatures back, causing them to roar in anger before his feet were hitting the steps too. She focused on her footfalls, ensuring she didn't trip as she bounded for the door.

Someone below yelped and Arianna turned to find the male who had wanted to return for his comrades being dragged down the stairs, one claw straight through his calf. The creature that had him sank its teeth into the flesh of his thigh before Conall launched a series of spears to impale the creature.

Another grabbed the male's arm, then yet another clamped their jaws around the male's neck, ripping the tender flesh.

Her stomach twisted in knots at the sight. Seconds. Mere seconds and one of their comrades was dead.

Her magic pulsed beneath her skin. She stared up at the door just a few feet away, knowing full well it was likely locked. The creatures would be upon them before they made it.

She stopped short and Gavin screeched as he passed her. "What are you doing?"

She shoved him forward. "Use a rune and unlock it."

He moved at her command and steady voice. The last of Conall's warriors ran by her, Conall too, his eyes wide as he stared at his queen.

Rion paused at her side, right as she let her magic burst forth. It raced down the stairs, enveloping everything in its path. The clawed hands paused mid-movement, the growling faces went utterly still with their mouths wide and gaping. Their wings were spread wide, ready to propel the creatures toward their next meal.

The world fell silent.

A lock clicked, then the door behind her opened.

Their breaths all hung in the frigid air as Arianna stared at the Fae before her, wondering what their lives might have been like before coming to this wretched place.

Vairik was angry that so much had been taken from him, yet he'd taken so much more. How could he not see that? How could he not care?

Arianna turned without a word and Rion let her pass before following.

Once again, they found themselves in another long hall, doors upon doors lining either side of the space.

Lights flickered overhead, likely powered by Fae stripped of their freedom. She'd have to find them, too.

There were so many that needed saving and just like with Ruadhán, there wouldn't be enough time to get them out. Conall had already known this. Accepted it.

Her stomach soured, but the plans were already in motion. She couldn't stop it even if she wanted to. Unless she and Rion said to hell with the plans and hunted down Vairik right now.

Arianna glanced at Conall again, wondering if someone he knew had faced Vairik before. Conall seemed confident they wouldn't stand a chance. But hadn't the gods gifted them powers to conquer the evil of the world? Would those gods stand with them against someone like Vairik, or would they remain silent as they'd done these past ten thousand years?

"Which way?" Rion asked.

Gavin's mouth opened, his breath still ragged. He stared at the door they'd just come through, then clenched his jaw. They all had a million questions. A million comments about the violation they'd just witnessed. But it was clear that now wasn't the time.

Gavin's eyes were wide and wild as he glanced down each hallway, trying to gather himself.

He'd been raised in these halls. He'd stood in his grandfather's presence and knelt at his feet. But it was clear he hadn't known the extent of Vairik's atrocities.

It was easy to conform to something you were raised in. Easier to ignore issues that glared in the face of others. It took someone brave and possibly a little reckless to upend the system they were born into.

The hall to their front rose in an upward slope, curving in a way that blocked their view. The hall to their left was short, with only a handful of doors on the right side, each made of iron. After the creatures they'd just encountered, Arianna wasn't sure she wanted to open them and find out what might lie within.

The hall to their right was long, once again hosting doors along its left side, all the way down.

Gavin pointed straight, but she didn't hear his words when a shadow moved to her right. Arianna's head whipped around and she nearly stopped breathing at the sight of a familiar face.

Arianna's lips parted and she slowly turned, studying the dark hair and bright blue eyes that stared back.

Her hair had been pulled back into a tight braid that crowned her head. Arianna had never seen her sister wear it in such a fashion. Her clothes were midnight black and Arianna swore she could see blades tucked within holsters around her thighs.

Ellie just stared, expression unreadable. Did she see her? Did she recognize her?

Arianna's heart beat wildly and she stepped forward, scarcely willing to believe.

The moment stretched on forever, then Ellie pivoted on her heel and disappeared around the corner.

Arianna sprinted after her. She didn't turn to check if her companions were following. They were always following, always watching. They'd scent Ellie and know. Hell, they'd hear her heartbeat and realize something was amiss.

But why was Ellie here instead of in chains? Why had her sister looked bathed and clean rather than dirty and tortured?

Arianna rounded the corner and found her sister waiting, staring at her again. Her eyes were strangely vacant, like she hadn't slept in days.

"Ellie," Arianna called to her, but Ellie just disappeared behind the corner again.

Arianna took off at breakneck speed, reaching the end of the corridor only to find Ellie disappearing behind the next and the next and the next.

Arianna couldn't catch up, no matter how hard she ran, but she wasn't giving up either. Not when her sister was right here in front of her.

She could grab Ellie and run. Flee from this place and reformulate a plan with Conall and his rebels at a later date. They could take on Vairik's entire army and destroy Ashling later. As long as she had Ellie, she could take on the world.

CHAPTER TWENTY-SIX

RION

Rion saw his mate take off and sprinted down the hall after her. Conall cursed and followed with the others close behind.

He didn't know what had made her run, only that something had grabbed her attention enough that a jolt had shot straight down the bond, nearly knocking Rion off his feet.

Gavin had pointed them in another direction, but the male had seemed unsure, as if he didn't recognize this part of the castle. After seeing his horror-struck expression, it was clear he'd likely never been here. Rion didn't recognize it as part of Gavin's drawing either.

The entire place was enormous with multiple floors and hidden rooms. Rion was certain there were more than a few secrets Vairik had chosen not to share with those he deemed beneath him.

Arianna sped around a corner, somehow pulling ahead of him. He could nearly feel her heart racing down the bond, beating with a desperate sense of urgency.

Rion furrowed his brow. He'd always been able to keep pace with her, but when he rounded the next corner, she was already disappearing beyond his line of sight.

A desperate plea fell from her lips that had Rion's heart racing with anticipation.

Ellie.

Had Arianna seen her sister? Rion scented the air, pushing his body harder as he struggled to keep up. His limbs were growing heavy and weak, like he was moving through mud and water.

Arianna's footsteps echoed ahead. Too far. She was too far. No matter how much he tried he couldn't catch up now.

No, what was he thinking? He had to catch up. Arianna was his mate, he couldn't just give up.

Rion glanced behind him, but Conall and the others had gone missing. Rion scented the air again, searching for him and Gavin. He strained to listen for Arianna's fading footfalls, but they'd gone silent.

Rion kept running and yanked his sleeve back to study the rune on his wrist. It was still there, still glowing faintly. Which meant he couldn't be caught in a glamour unless … a chill swept through him. Unless Vairik himself had discovered them.

But Rion hadn't felt the familiar blanket effect of Pádraigín's magic, nor had he scented any change.

He rounded another corner, his feet nearly sliding out from under him as he struggled to increase his speed.

The bright lights that had surrounded him moments ago had dimmed, and the shadows were far longer. Deeper. He slowed, then turned back from where he'd come only to find the stone darker there, too.

Panic surged through him.

Arianna was gone. Lost in this maze of a castle with one of the most powerful Fae to ever walk the land. Rion had promised to protect her. He'd already nearly lost her once and now she was beyond his reach.

He recalled the female's chest from one of the other rooms, the way it had been pried wide open.

Rion's breath came in heaving gasps. The walls closed in around him. He was trapped again. Helpless. No. No, he wasn't. He could handle this. Rion fought the invasive thoughts, shoving them down. He could choke on them later. Right now, he just needed to find Arianna.

If he lost control now, he'd be caught. Arianna would be caught. They wouldn't be able to rescue Ellie and everything they'd worked for would all be for nothing.

Rion forced himself to breathe. He glanced down at his weapon, focusing on the scent of blood from the creatures they'd killed earlier. He was a general, he wasn't new to missions or their complications.

But he was still new to having something to fight for. To having people to protect. They were relying on him, and if he let darkness take over, they might all fall.

Rion took another steadying breath, then began inching down the corridor again. If he was trapped in a glamour, then he'd be able to see it, he just needed to spot the shimmer Gavin had mentioned before.

Rion studied the cracks in the stones and the flickering lights that seemed to follow a pattern one minute and none the next.

The surrounding shadows moved at strange angles, stretching and lengthening as the corridor began to twist and bend in unnatural ways.

Water dripped from the cracks now, leaving a slimy texture against parts of the walls. The area almost seemed to age with each step he took, as if it had been abandoned decades ago. But the torches were still lit, which meant someone was down here. They had to be.

A rock hit the cold stone ahead, shattering the silence as it bounced down the passageway, tripping over broken stones in its path. Rion froze, watching, waiting for whoever might have thrown it to appear.

Nothing happened for several minutes.

There was the faintest possibility that the stone had simply fallen from parts of the crumbling wall, but Rion knew better than to chalk anything up to circumstance, especially where Fae were involved.

Rion inched further down the corridor. The torches were becoming fewer and farther between. Darkness threatened to engulf him. The walls were closing in, ready to trap him beneath the earth once again, only this time, he wouldn't come back out. He'd be left to starve or die of thirst. He—a roar echoed down the hall that had the hairs on the back of his neck standing on end.

Rion took off running toward the anguished sound, his feet pounding against the stone.

Another corner had Rion sliding to a stop, his heart beating wildly in his chest.

Talon knelt over a bloodied Raevina. The male reached out, clearly wanting to cradle her head, but pulled back, repeating the motion, unsure how to help her without causing further damage.

Raevina's entire body was covered in her own blood. Deep gashes lined every inch of her skin as if one of the flying creatures had tried to claw its way through her.

And her leg …

Rion grimaced at the sight of the mangled limb and the way it had been nearly severed in half. Her heartbeat was faint and fading.

Then Rion's gaze stopped on the familiar particles surrounding her body. Small bits of sand and dirt that had soaked up her blood.

Rion's breath hitched as Talon's gaze lifted to his. The absolute fury in those eyes had Rion retreating a step. He'd seen that kind of rage before, but something about this was different. Primal.

Talon's magic stirred around him, rising and falling with every breath. It spread through the cracks in the ground, freezing the crimson liquid surrounding the female.

Dying. Raevina was dying, and Arianna was nowhere to be found.

"Talon." The sound was nearly a plea, then ice crackled around the male's body before he lunged.

CHAPTER TWENTY-SEVEN

TALON

Talon guarded the door while Raevina sifted through the drawers, yanking papers out before tearing the entire wooden desk apart. They already had a handful of important documents stuffed into a bag. He'd scanned a few, but there wasn't time to read through the content. If it looked official, they grabbed it and moved on.

But Raevina seemed far more focused on this particular room, as if she were looking for something specific. She'd insisted on being part of the intel recovery team when they were making plans with Conall. He hadn't questioned her about it at the time.

"What are you looking for?" Talon asked, his gaze still locked on the long halls. They'd turned darker somehow after separating from Arianna. Maybe a Fae of Vairik's age couldn't be bothered with proper lighting.

The air in the castle was warm and stagnant. They currently occupied an interior portion that gave off the illusion of being trapped underground. He would've thought Fae who possessed the power to manipulate the wind itself would at least see to proper ventilation.

Raevina kept shifting through the papers and pulled out another drawer before shattering it against the desk. Bottles fell out of a hidden compartment and burst along the floor.

Talon grimaced, certain they shouldn't be making so much noise. Then again, if anyone showed up, he wouldn't let them live anyway. None of the scum in this castle deserved to. Not after what they'd seen in the dungeons and those other rooms.

He shuddered at the memory.

One of Conall's warriors peeked out from a doorway and met Talon's gaze. The two nodded to one another, indicating all was still clear as they kept rummaging through the rooms. There hadn't been much time to get to know them, but the little he'd seen made Talon confident in their abilities, at least. They'd run through a few drills, practiced runes, and memorized the layout before setting off.

He supposed he'd worked under worse conditions while hunting The Demon and searching for Arianna.

But Rion wasn't a demon anymore.

Talon sighed. If any of this went according to plan, it would be nothing short of a miracle. Hell, it was a miracle in and of itself that they'd gotten this far.

Talon stared up at the ceiling. Just a few more floors and they'd find Vairik's study. Ellie was nearby, he could feel it in his bones. Before long, Arianna and Rion would find his future High Lady, then they'd blow this hellhole to bits, hopefully with Vairik still inside.

He doubted it would end up being that easy.

Talon watched the other end of the hall. A chill swept through him. It was quiet. Too quiet for his comfort, like the world had taken a breath it hadn't yet released.

They'd dispatched a few guards and had waited countless minutes for more to appear. None had and whoever sat on the council hadn't come to collect their things either.

It wasn't a holiday or the solstice, not that Talon expected Vairik to honor such things. Still, he'd expected to find *someone* of importance. He'd wanted it, in fact, if only to have the chance to question them himself.

Talon checked the rune on his arm again. It remained, as did the bracelet that was still counting down. Only hours remained. He prayed they would have enough time to free the slaves outside. Saoirse and Zylah would create a distraction for their escape. He could break a few chains on his way out and urge them to follow.

Raevina's sudden pause caused him to glance back. She was reading a document, her eyes moving quickly down the page. Her face contorted in rage before she crumpled the paper and slammed her fist on the desk, splintering the wood beneath her hand.

"That bastard," she seethed.

"What did you find?"

She slammed her fist into the desk again. "He completely sold out. The coward gave up everything."

"What are you talking about?"

Raevina didn't answer. Instead, she stuffed the paper into her pocket, then spun toward the map hanging on the wall. Her eyes traced the lines near Fiadh and he noticed the pins that ran from Ashling all the way down the strait.

Talon glanced down the hall again, then joined her to study the various points. This map was different from the one he'd always known. Instead of Ashling sitting on the northern part of the continent, this map showed it slightly further south, at the edge of the mountains, right where Conall's maps had shown it, too.

He tried to memorize the marked points along various roads, then his eyes caught on a line running straight through the mountains. Talon's heart sank.

He knew. Despite Conall's beliefs, Vairik had known where the rebels were all along. Which meant he might already know they were here.

Shit.

He needed to find Arianna and get her out of here. It had been a trap from the very beginning. He should have known better; they all should have.

Talon stepped back, ready to move when another mark grabbed his attention. A red ring surrounded one place. Whoever had circled it had done it several times while also pinning a black flag over top.

Levea.

There was only one other location marked with a black flag. Ruadhán.

His mouth went dry.

They couldn't have. Avalon had just received messages from their capitol city before he'd left. They had Nàdair's royal army as back up. Vairik couldn't conquer two High Lords at once.

Could he?

No, it was circled in red. Ruadhán wasn't, which meant it was likely just in the plans.

But why Levea? Was it revenge for Ruadhán's fall? Did Vairik finally want to come out of hiding and stake his claim there?

Talon scanned the map again. Colors dotted the land and sea but he couldn't make sense of them. Talon wished he had time to write it all down. They couldn't take a map of this size with them, not with the markers remaining intact.

Talon glanced at Raevina again. "We already knew your father was working with Vairik."

Raevina whirled on him, her eyes flashing like molten steel. "You don't understand. Our mountain. Our jewels, the very land is sacred. It's meant to be—" She stopped herself, her fists clenched and body shaking. "He let the Dark Fae taint the land. He's using it as a breeding ground for those monsters. There are creatures *inside*. In the sacred bowels of our mountain. No one is supposed to go down there, we have—" she stopped herself again. "I'll kill him. I'll kill them both."

Talon had no idea what she was talking about. No one really knew much about Fiadh or the mysterious Shadow Weavers they kept hidden from the rest of the world. The only thing he knew about the female in front of him was her drive to restore her honor. Raevina took the failure of her ancestors very seriously.

Talon tried to get her to focus. "Did you get everything you need here?" They still had several rooms to sort through. Even with the rebel's help, they couldn't afford to linger.

She glared at him. "No, I still need—" The ground shuddered beneath their feet, and Talon grabbed onto the desk with one arm, wrapping his other around Raevina's waist. She reached for him in turn, one hand clutching his bicep as they waited for the spell to pass.

"The hell was that?" he asked, voice low and tense.

"We have to go." She rushed from his grip and Talon gave the desk a final look over before scrambling after her.

"What do you mean, what was—"

Raevina looked up and down the hall before bolting down one side, sprinting as fast as her legs would carry her.

Talon ran past an open door, half expecting to find their new companions within, but the space was empty.

He could have sworn—Talon didn't have time to finish the thought as Raevina darted around a corner and away from his line of sight.

"Wait," he called after her. "Where are you going?"

She didn't stop or answer. Raevina just kept moving as if she were trying to outrun the wind itself.

They passed another set of doors. The lighting around him shifted, turning darker. He glanced around, studying several sconces that had simply winked out. He blinked against the sudden shift, then drew his blade, ready to take on those likely hiding in the shadows. Even if those from Pádraigín couldn't manipulate his mind, they could still hide their bodies, blending them with the environment.

Talon passed another open door and did a double take at the desk inside. His eyes roamed over the papers littering the floor and the broken bits of wood scattered across the lush carpet.

"Raevina," he called in warning. She didn't stop or acknowledge him.

Talon cursed under his breath, yanking his sleeve back, relief flooding through him at the sight of the runes still glowing faintly. But too many had faded. Had they really wasted so much time?

Talon kept sprinting, turning right again. Then left.

The portraits on the walls seemed to mock him—smiles widening, eyes tracking his every move.

Another door ahead was open. The door to his right.

He glanced in upon passing.

Papers and broken wood.

What the hell was happening?

"Raevina," he called again, but she didn't answer, couldn't, not as something slammed into her from the cross section of the hall. Her body folded in half and she went flying. Talon's eyes went wide, then his magic broke free, flying down the hall to block the entire tunnel where the attack had launched from.

He rounded the corner and slid to Raevina's side, a sob already choking him.

Blood was everywhere, leaking out of her mouth, from her leg, from a wound to the side of her head, the hundreds of lacerations along her arms …

She coughed once, then Talon followed the trail of familiar magic to find Rion standing before them both, a look of confusion written across his face.

Something tore through Talon that he'd never felt before. A rage that consumed him.

And at that moment, he didn't give a damn if Rion was a king or Arianna's mate. He didn't give a damn about anything.

CHAPTER TWENTY-EIGHT

SAOIRSE

Saoirse and Zylah snuck through the outside gardens, watching the shadows as they bent with the torches that were barely still lit. A light shower had started minutes ago. Thick clouds overhead obscured the midday sun, making it seem much later in the day than when their mission began.

Under normal circumstances, Saoirse basked in the thrill of a mission, but with Zylah beside her, she just wanted to find Evelyn and get Zylah the hell out of here.

They crept between the old crumbling stones and walls, keeping close to the vines that crawled up through the crevices. Saoirse noted each and every one. The landscape was a perfect battleground for her should something foul decide to rear its ugly head.

Saoirse studied the gate in the distance. All they needed to do was reach it, disarm those who stood guard, and wait for the bracelets to count down. Or all hell to break loose.

Conall had warned her they might be sitting still for hours and that they shouldn't panic or rush to get into position. They had time, so long as the alarms didn't go off.

Saoirse wanted to be there in case they did. The faster she could secure the area, the better prepared she'd be to get her brother and everyone else to safety.

Zylah crept along behind her. The two had paired off from the rest of the group that was sneaking around the opposite side of the garden. Saoirse didn't like relying on near-strangers, but they needed the extra bodies. If they were captured, then it'd be their own fault for not paying attention.

"Remind me why I'm stuck with you again?" Zylah whispered as they rushed behind another crumbling wall. Everything looked so similar in the garden that it was difficult not to get turned around. And that was exactly why Saoirse was leaving small imprints of her magic within the greenery, just in case they took a wrong turn or someone with Pádraigín's magic affected their runes.

Saoirse glanced around, then veered off into what might have once been a pleasant veranda. But the chairs had nearly rotted away and the wood's stench floated through the space, mixing with the rot of everything else.

Saoirse stopped and peered up at the next level balconies. "Because your other choices weren't ideal."

Zylah watched too, her eyes nearly as keen as any Fae's. "And why is that?"

"Well, you could be stuck with Arianna, which would probably be the most ideal, but then you'd have to deal with my grumpy brother."

Another corner had them pausing, glancing around before darting past. "Or you could have been paired up with Talon and Raevina, but I think Raevina rivals Rion where decent conversation is concerned."

"Talon is pleasant enough." Saoirse looked at her, then refocused, but she caught Zylah's smirk at the suggestion. "Was that jealousy?"

"No, I know where you stand with males."

"I'm not sure you know where I stand with anything."

Saoirse made a noise in her throat. Footsteps sounded and Saoirse grabbed Zylah, spinning them both around a wall. Saoirse pushed Zylah's body against it with her own and covered the female's mouth with one hand.

They waited, their breaths ragged and too loud in the dark alcove. Saoirse calmed her racing heart, watching through a small crack in the stone as two guards ambled past. She expected them to be on high alert, but they kept their eyes downcast and moved swiftly.

Saoirse couldn't blame them; the entire space felt like a graveyard.

Saoirse didn't move even after they'd disappeared. She strained to listen to their retreating footfalls, then breathed a little easier once they vanished.

Her focus shifted to Zylah and the way the female's body heat had begun to seep through her clothes. The female's hands had clamped around Saoirse's arm.

Her mate.

And this mission could very well be the last time she ever saw her.

The reply finally came to her, but Saoirse didn't voice her words even as they echoed in her head.

I know where you stand with me.

Rejected. Again. She supposed it was a just punishment after all the pain she'd inflicted, or rather, had failed to prevent.

Saoirse removed her hand and for a tender moment, she stood there, staring at the female she might never have.

Saoirse sighed and stepped back, knowing full well the disappointment on Zylah's face was only her own imagination. Zylah had been kind to her for kindness' sake, nothing more. She might be attracted to Saoirse physically, but mentally, Zylah wanted nothing to do with her.

Saoirse had made Zylah a promise. To leave her alone and let her live her life however she wanted. With whoever she wanted.

Reality stung like a blade laced with poison.

"Let's go." Saoirse peered around the corner again. She let another sliver of her magic seep into the vines. They curled around one another, interlacing to form a triangle with a line that went straight through the middle. It blended with the rest of the structure so as to not be too noticeable. Only someone like Rion or Alec would pick up on it.

They darted across the courtyard, their footsteps light against the mossy stone, then paused again on the other side. Saoirse frowned as she studied the area. Her hands pressed against a wall and that's when her eyes drifted to the familiar mass of vines above them.

Her symbol sat among the greenery.

Saoirse straightened, turning to look back from where they'd come. They hadn't taken any turns. It was impossible to have gone in a circle. She'd memorized the map alongside her brother. She knew exactly how many statues and verandas they'd passed.

Too many.

She'd thought that perhaps Gavin had miscounted. It was easy to do and had happened to her before but—

"Something's wrong."

Zylah's gaze roamed over to the symbol. Saoirse hadn't been sure if the female had noticed them before now. "What do you mean?"

Saoirse turned again to study the layout. They'd passed through three sections so far, though Gavin had sketched five. She grimaced. All of them were run-down. Virtually identical. Statues of menacing Dark Fae reached their claws toward the delicate females across from them. They were all chipped, the females weeping. Many had their arms cut off at the elbows.

They were the same as the ones in the previous garden. At least … she thought they were. Something about them had shifted so they looked different, yet when she stared directly at them—

Saoirse opened her mouth to respond when sudden searing pain lanced through her side. Saoirse stumbled away, ready to reach out for Zylah when another blade swiped at her throat.

She gritted her teeth and her back slammed against the wall, distracting her enough that the same dagger plunged straight through her shoulder.

Zylah's eyes locked with her own, the half-breed's contorted with rage. Saoirse shoved her back, yanking the weapon from her shoulder.

"What in the seven hells are you doing?" Saoirse growled.

The half-breed's chest heaved and she lunged again. Saoirse moved to the side, around another wall, but the air whipped up, carrying bits of dirt that stung her eyes, momentarily blinding her.

"Zylah." The name was a warning as she stumbled back, swiping at her eyes as she tried to simultaneously listen for the female's movements. Wind blasted into Saoirse's chest, knocking her to the ground. She rolled, cursing again as she dodged another knife flying her way. "We don't have time for this; if you want to kill me, do it later."

Saoirse stared at the blurry figure before her. Dust moved at the female's feet, reminding Saoirse of her brother's magic. Saoirse swore the clouds above had thickened, blotting out the sun.

Whispers floated through the air and Saoirse quickly assessed their surroundings, wondering if a group of warriors was about to find them fighting. She needed to subdue Zylah and hide. She wasn't about to be the one to set off the alarms.

Saoirse tugged at the bond, hoping to throw Zylah off balance. It was barely a whisper of a thing, nearly a figment of her imagination. But—it wasn't there. No, it was further down the hall. Far away, as if—as if—

Damn it all.

Saoirse rolled away from another attack, then planted her boot in the female's gut. Zylah, or rather, whoever this was, crumpled in on themselves before stumbling back, coughing and hacking as they struggled to catch their breath.

Saoirse checked her rune to find it intact and cursed again. If her mind was being messed with, then it had to be Vairik or Niall, unless there were other guards who'd stood beside Vairik through the years. There was no telling how many others might possess his level of magic. Something they'd all taken into consideration before embarking on this suicide mission.

The female lunged again, her eyes darker and smile more wicked than she'd ever seen Zylah capable of.

Saoirse dodged the blade again, then slammed her hand against the female's elbow, pivoting before trapping her against the wall. The body beneath her struggled and for a split second, Saoirse considered slitting the female's throat.

But what if this was a glamour similar to the one Niall had trapped Rion in? It might not be Zylah, but what if it was Arianna or Evelyn? How would Saoirse know otherwise?

The female struggled and Saoirse slammed her head into the stone wall. The scent of blood filled the space. A scent Saoirse recognized half a heartbeat later. The distraction cost her and the female shoved back, slicing her blade across Saoirse's chest.

Saoirse only stared, her heart aching as Máili's beautiful face stared back. But—but she'd seen—Saoirse's eyes roamed down Máili's neck to find a red line across her throat. Then that line began bleeding. A small drip at first, then a flood of crimson.

Saoirse stared in horror, her body shaking as the female before her smiled before her head rolled off her shoulders and hit the ground.

The whispers grew louder, coming at her like a storm.

Saoirse's throat tightened as she held her weapon loosely in one hand. The body withered before her eyes, turning into a husk, then a skeleton, and finally crumbling into dust.

Someone walked through the doorway to Saoirse's right. Saoirse could barely focus as she locked her gaze on Máili's face again.

This one wasn't smiling. She glared in anger, an incurable rage blazing in those once beautiful eyes. "Your fault," the female said, her voice hoarse.

Then blood dripped from her throat. Máili rushed forward. Saoirse braced, but before she even made contact, Máili's head hit the ground, her mouth still moving in silent accusation.

Saoirse's body trembled and she stepped back, staring at the dead figure. This one didn't disintegrate; instead, the skin peeled back as if her body were being burned by an invisible fire. Muscle turned black, then the flames reached bone, consuming everything in its path.

Another figure stepped out from the shadows of a veranda. This one with tears streaming down their face.

Máili again.

Saoirse's breath shuddered.

An illusion.

This was an illusion.

It had to be Niall, he was the only one who knew about—

Máili stumbled forward, her body too thin and frail. "Your fault," she whispered again before blood began trickling from the slice in her neck.

Saoirse stepped back again, her heart racing, breath too shallow. She needed to get herself together … she needed … she needed—

A violent tug on the bond yanked Saoirse from her panic and shifted her focus away from the head rolling at her feet. Fear shot down the bond next. Fear. Fear from—the bond—the *bond.*

Saoirse pivoted on her heel as warmth flooded her soul, spreading through her body until she could feel her limbs again. But it wasn't that warmth alone that had her moving. It was the visceral fear pouring from her mate. From Zylah.

Saoirse sprinted down the winding passages, ignoring the figures that bled from the walls, white hands reaching, whispered echoes accusing. They didn't matter now. Let her nightmares haunt her. As long as Zylah didn't have to suffer at her side.

She followed the tug of the bond. Her magic raced across the ground, rising up and up. She sent the magic into the wall ahead and the stones exploded outward. Saoirse leapt through the hole, ducking around the still crumbling stones overhead.

More voices echoed behind her. Máili's. Rion's. Her mother's.

But her mother wasn't here. Rion wasn't here. And Máili—tears slipped down her cheeks. She'd never given herself time to grieve or come to terms with what had happened.

Máili had been her friend. Her partner.

Spy, a dark part of her whispered. Had anything between them ever been real?

Another surge of panic pulsed down the bond and Saoirse grabbed hold of it with everything in her.

I'm coming. How long had she been under the glamour's influence? How long had Zylah been fighting on her own?

The castle shifted, turning from smooth winding halls into straight, narrow passages lined with dim torches. Faint light trickling through breaks in the wall.

Hold on. Hold on, Zylah.

Saoirse barreled through another wall, rolling to her feet when she tripped over the broken stones. She ignored the cuts along her arm. Ignored her still wounded shoulder.

Only one thing mattered.

Zylah. Zylah. Zylah.

She'd make it. She had to make it.

Saoirse's heart raced as the bond shortened. The voices were a frenzy now, blocking out her ability to hear. She didn't need it. She just needed to reach her mate.

A gust of wind swept past Saoirse and a blade caught the light as she watched Zylah twisting around a knife aimed at her heart.

Zylah was covered in sweat and blood. Her blood. The smell of it pierced through Saoirse like a hot iron. Saoirse roared, even as she came face to face with a dozen Dark Fae.

Their gaping maws turned on her, fangs dripping with some dark liquid she didn't care to identify.

The vines sprang to life and shot for the beasts, some familiar, others slightly altered in ways that made them leaner, faster, and as she watched them dodge her attacks, Saoirse could have sworn they were smarter too.

It didn't matter. She'd brought down warriors with twice their experience. She wasn't about to let a bunch of wild animals bring her or her mate to their knees.

Not today. Not ever.

Sturdy wooden branches ripped through the wall and howls of pain echoed off the stone as the creatures went flying.

Saoirse left them behind, their teeth snapping, then fire erupted to her left, singeing the exposed skin along her arms and hand.

She screamed from the sudden pain, but refused to stop, even as more heat trailed after her. Zylah dodged another attack, but her breath was ragged, her movements slow.

Faster, Saoirse pushed.

Four more Dark Fae prowled from Zylah's other side, corralling her back until Zylah was pinned against the wall. She grimaced, fear consuming her as hope faded from her eyes.

Saoirse yanked on their bond and Zylah's head whipped toward her. Recognition sparked there, thank the gods. Recognition and relief.

Saoirse drew her knives and let them fly. They sank into the creatures' thick hide, effectively drawing their attention toward the new threat.

That's right. Look at me. Come at me.

Blood rolled down the side of Zylah's face. Saoirse bared her teeth at the creatures, then Zylah took advantage of their distracted state and sank her knife into the nearest one's throat.

Its teeth snapped too close to Zylah's arm when it spun around. Still, the female managed to dodge.

An ache formed behind her temple and Saoirse's vision went blurry. She bit the inside of her cheek, drawing blood, forcing her eyes to refocus.

Warriors exploded from the wall to her right, their swords drawn and magic tugging at their loose clothes in an angry frenzy.

Saoirse didn't wait for a command or explanation. She spun through the Fae with all the speed and precision she could muster. Now wasn't the time for arrogant swagger. No, this was the time to destroy everything in her path.

Another group of Fae emerged, pushing Zylah back.

Saoirse attacked, forcing those before her to go on the defensive. Zylah stepped back again then Saoirse saw the door. No, not a door, an opening in the wall, the structure crumbling from the top as if someone had blasted through it. Had Zylah done that? Had it always been there?

Zylah stepped back again. Chains rattled and Saoirse saw a renewed sense of fear cover her mate's face. It sent Saoirse into overdrive. She fought, kicked, let her magic burst out and pierce flesh. Even so, the very air turned against her and Saoirse hit the ground, scraping her leg against a sharpened blade.

Saoirse ignored the blood and fought to stand. She'd let a thousand blades shred her to pieces before she let Zylah be captured again.

One of the Dark Fae lunged for Zylah and the female's foot slipped over the edge. Their eyes met for a fleeting moment. Fear, so much fear, then Zylah disappeared over the ledge.

Saoirse roared again, fighting through the bodies blocking her path. Magic and blades tore through her flesh, but she didn't stop, even as she felt herself fading.

Chains rattled to her left. Someone stepped forward, but she lunged for the male, sinking her teeth into his throat and tearing his artery out before trying to run again.

Someone else reached for her arm, but she spun away, ripping the iron chain from his grasp. She wrapped it around his neck, yanked until his bones snapped, then kept moving.

Her vision blurred, faded, but Saoirse just kept listening for Zylah's final scream. Kept waiting for their bond to shatter.

Then iron clamped around her wrist. A foot collided with her knee from behind. Something in Saoirse's leg cracked, then blinding pain flew through her head and darkness engulfed her.

CHAPTER TWENTY-NINE

ARIANNA

Arianna sucked in sharp, uneven breaths, her legs burning as she continued pushing forward. Ellie was always just beyond her reach, waiting around corners or at the end of corridors that seemed to stretch on forever.

Arianna kept calling her name, begging Ellie to stop, but she never did. Was Ellie leading her somewhere? Kirian was the only logical explanation. Perhaps the male was being held somewhere Ellie couldn't access. Maybe he was hurt and there wasn't time to explain. Or maybe Vairik was watching her little sister, just as Niall had been watching Gavin back in Ruadhán. Arianna recalled the male's visceral fear at the prospect of being caught by his uncle.

The lighting within the halls remained dim, but her surroundings shifted from a cold dungeon to a space covered in lush rugs with pictures lining the walls that spoke of a history she knew nothing about. Heavy curtains hung over windows, effectively blocking the light from outside.

Arianna tried not to look at the pictures where eyes seemed to follow her every move. Childish fears resurfaced and she briefly wondered if the paintings might actually be alive. Perhaps they reported every-thing they saw to Vairik and his council.

Arianna shook her head and shoved those fears aside. Something like that wasn't possible.

She hoped.

The halls kept shifting in their structural makeup, as if the design-er couldn't settle on one artistic method of creation.

Some halls contained high arching ceilings while others were so low she could nearly touch them. Some corners were sharp while oth-ers were more rounded. Some were narrow, others wide.

She passed under one of the high arches and briefly glanced over her shoulder. Her heart sank.

She'd lost everyone. Even Rion, who had been on her tail and who had always managed to outrun her.

It didn't make sense, and she couldn't even pinpoint the moment he'd disappeared, as though the very ground had risen up to swallow him. One minute he was there, the next he was gone.

But she wasn't alone. Ellie was here. Once she caught up to her sister and freed Kirian, they could formulate a plan and escape.

Could she run to Saoirse and initiate the evacuation process early? Would it give Rion and the others enough time to escape?

Arianna nearly slid around the next corner. She caught herself on a dusty side table then found a large set of double doors closing just ahead.

Ellie.

Arianna lunged forward, gripped the thick brass handles, then swung the heavy doors open.

She paused on the threshold.

The lighting inside was nearly nonexistent. Small rays filtered through windows that were high up on the vaulted ceiling. Vines stretched around the shelves and reached for the sun above.

And covering everything were rows upon rows of books. The entire room might have once been as grand as Ruadhán's library, but it was clear from the smell of rot alone that these volumes hadn't been maintained.

Dust covered every surface, and stacks of books, loose parchment, and quills sat at the foot of several shelves, abandoned like their previous owners had moved in a hurry.

The roots from the vines had crawled into the books surrounding them, and a few shelves had broken altogether, the weight pressing down on the books below and bending their spines nearly beyond repair.

There were statues too—some broken, others intact—that sat trapped within the dust, just waiting for the day they might break free.

Arianna studied the space, straining to listen. Then a figure appeared at the end of the aisle. One hand rested on the edge of a shelf, her sister waiting in utter silence.

"Ellie." Arianna's voice cracked. "We can talk about it. Let me help you."

Neither female moved.

Arianna squinted in the dark, trying to decipher the emotions on her little sister's face, but the shadows were too thick. Almost as if they had a life of their own and were doing everything in their power to keep the two females separated.

Arianna scented the air, searching for anyone else who might be in the space, searching for Niall, but all she smelled were old books and rot.

She swallowed hard and her heart beat wildly as she took a tentative step forward only for Ellie to take off running.

Arianna cursed, her frustration growing as she gave chase once again.

Ellie pivoted left, diving down an aisle where the shelves reached higher than any Arianna had ever seen or thought possible. She tried looking up only to find the shadows obscuring the topmost shelf. They swirled like dark clouds, taunting her with their presence.

A scraping sound had her head jerking to her left then a thick, leather bound book flew out from one of the bottom shelves. Arianna skidded to a stop as it landed on the old lush rug that might have once been green in color. Dust flew up around the thick volume.

Arianna looked beyond it, only to find her sister standing at the end of the aisle again.

Had Ellie moved it? Was her sister trying to tell her something?

Arianna stared down at it again before carefully creeping toward the book. She watched her sister, ready to leap over the new object in her path.

Ellie didn't move.

Arianna flinched when the book flipped open of its own accord. Her magic responded, spreading from her body until it kissed the edges of the shelves and dusted the wood. The book—or whoever was responsible for the rapidly turning pages—didn't seem to notice.

The book stopped moving once it reached a middle section, and the world fell silent once again.

Arianna swallowed hard, then crept closer, her magic vibrating against her very bones.

Pádraigín's magic. It had to be, there was no other explanation. Only … she didn't smell or sense it.

Words written in another language covered the left page and a piece of art covered the right.

The sketched image displayed dark creatures crawling up a mound of bodies, each reaching long claws toward a female standing at the top.

Fire surrounded her, almost seeming to extend from her tendrils of long dark hair. Ice hovered in chunks around her body, some having already impaled the dark creatures causing them to tumble off the pile. The wind ripped at her clothes and vines lashed out from the base of her feet.

Arianna glanced up just as Ellie took off running again. She cursed, leapt over the book, and followed.

She ran and ran and ran, watching Ellie's back as they sprinted down the impossibly long hall.

Ellie finally turned and Arianna turned with her, swearing the shelves were growing taller while the aisles became narrower.

A sudden crash split the air and had Arianna spinning on her heel, heart hammering in her chest as she struggled to catch her breath.

Another crash and the ground shook beneath her feet. Then Arianna watched as one of the tall shelves leaned and leaned and leaned until the books were falling one by one. The towering structure crashed into the one beside it. That one leaned as well, crashing into the next and the next.

Thunderous noise echoed from her left and she stepped back slightly when the wood groaned too close.

She watched in horror as a massive bookcase slammed into the one beside her—then it started leaning, too.

Arianna pivoted and ran, her sister still ahead.

Books and shelves crashed behind her, filling the once silent space with falling tomes and splintering wood.

Arianna darted around another corner, hoping to find a way out, but she skidded to a halt when a shelf raced straight at her, floating on a phantom wind. Arianna spun on her heel again and followed Ellie down another path.

Books began flying at them, too. Not different books, the same book, over and over. They all landed at her feet, the pages flipping rapidly until they landed on the same one from earlier.

Arianna swore the letters were moving of their own accord, scrambling, attempting to fight their way off the page.

A shelf crashed to her right, impossibly close. She'd just looked and—

Arianna skidded to a stop but there wasn't time to backpedal as the shelf directly in front of her came down fast. Ice burst from her body, rising up to cocoon around her form and catch the massive piece of furniture.

Arianna's legs nearly buckled beneath the impossible weight. She could have sworn a massive hand was pushing down from the other side.

Her feet slid and she gritted her teeth against the weight, her magic writhing, pouring out, struggling.

A rush of icy wind hit Arianna from behind and she peered over her shoulder to find the floor—no, not gone. It looked like it had never existed. But she'd just come from that direction, hadn't she?

A tall cliff face had replaced the solid floors. A dark roaring ocean crashed against the rocks beneath, promising to devour anything that dared to land in the murky depths.

Arianna shoved against the shelf harder, trying to get her footing as she was pushed back, back, back.

Shelves toppled over the edge, splintering on the rocks below before being swallowed by the waves. She could see over the edge now and her pulsed raced when she glimpsed giant tails flipping within the current.

They swarmed around the books like—like—the books grew arms and mouths. Their agonized screams pierced the air, sending shivers down her spine. Arianna pushed against the shelf harder and peered back again to find the water red.

The books had vanished, replaced by bodies that were floating, fighting, struggling to get away from the serpent-like creatures racing for them.

Her feet hit the edge and the bookcase began to topple over. Arianna released her magic and grabbed one of the shelves, squeezing her way between the openings and pulling herself out the other side. She balanced on the wood, running along its edge in a desperate push back toward solid ground.

It tipped right as her feet hit the wooden edge and Arianna leapt. She hit the rocky cliff with her torso and slid a few inches before her hands found purchase. Something below roared, displeased it wasn't getting her as its next meal.

Arianna dug her fingers into the rock, breaking her nails as she clawed, then finally rolled her body back to safety.

A repeated drumming had her whipping her head around to find the shelves marching, tottering on their corners like feet. The books scrambled to jump off the shelves like their lives depended on it. She could hear their cries as they pleaded to be set free.

Arianna jumped to her feet and squeezed around two wobbling cases, the space barely large enough for her to fit. She leapt through the second, scarcely dodging as one of the corners came down too close to her foot.

Papers flew up, blinding her as she tried to fight her way through. They slashed across her body, leaving tiny cuts in their wake that burned as though they'd been coated in acid.

Nothing made sense. Time was a warp. Images and whispers and screams all flooded her very soul.

Then the world froze.

Arianna fell to her knees, her mind spinning as she tried to collect herself.

The shelves had stopped mid-movement, leaving most teetering on one corner. Books were suspended in the air, spiraling in slow circles. Pages floated as if an invisible string held them aloft.

The crashing of the waves vanished, taking all manner of sounds with it.

Arianna tentatively stood, her breathing ragged in the stillness as she spun in a slow circle.

She dared a step, but as soon as her foot touched one of the open books, gravity took over and it all came crashing down. Her magic sprung to life to cover her head as the thick books thumped against shelves and the stone floor. Spines splintered and corners dented as they all landed in heaps.

The shelves hit the floor with loud thuds that had Arianna wincing while the papers floated down slowly.

Arianna spun again, assessing the area.

Ellie.

Ellie had been right in front of her before the shelves had started falling. Her heart raced as the books' screams echoed through her mind. What if her sister had fallen? What if—

A lone figure stood down another aisle, an unknown dim light illuminating her round face. She didn't smile, but at least her little sister still appeared unscathed.

"Ellie," Arianna tried again. "Ellie, tell me how to help."

Arianna took one step toward her sister, but instead of running away, Ellie rushed toward her. Arianna stepped back at the sudden movement and lost her balance, nearly tripping over a pile of books.

Her little sister's magic sprang to life and Arianna's answered, blocking the sharpened spears with a wall. Ice burst in a kaleidoscope of white shards.

Ellie shoved through them without hesitation and grabbed Arianna's throat before slamming her against a shelf that hadn't been there a moment ago. Arianna's head cracked against the wood, then sharp pain lanced through her side. Arianna gasped for breath and looked to find Ellie gripping the knife she'd plunged into her sister's side.

Arianna reached down and clamped one hand around Ellie's wrist, freezing the joint up to her elbow to prevent her from twisting the blade further.

Ellie still tried to drive it deeper, pushing her body against the hilt.

"Ellie," Arianna choked out. Their magic warred against one another, but the creature within Arianna hesitated, as if it cared for her little sister just as much as she did.

"Evelyn," a voice whispered from the shadows. It slithered over Arianna's skin and gooseflesh rose as another figure emerged through the shifting shadows. Those shadows swirled around him, pulling back, submitting to their master's will.

Ellie's head cocked to the side like a defiant teenager.

"Play nice; we don't want to lose our best piece before the fun's even begun, do we?"

A terrible smirk spread across her sister's face. The ice melted away and Ellie withdrew the blade before backing up. She flipped the bloody knife in one hand before slipping it back into its sheath without even bothering to wipe it off.

"Good girl." He stopped too far away for Arianna to see his face, but some internal part of her knew exactly who he was. "We'll take her with us. I have a few other matters to tend to before we can play."

Arianna's magic nearly growled within her own body, but just as it was about to lash out, the shadows rushed in like a black wave.

Oxygen and light disappeared. Stolen. Arianna clawed at her throat, gasping for breath, and watched as her sister's form slowly merged with the shadows, like giant fingers closing around her body.

Arianna tried to reach out with one hand, but Ellie turned away, leaving Arianna to sink into oblivion.

CHAPTER THIRTY

RION

Talon lunged for him, ice crackling around his form as both body and magic slammed into Rion, knocking him to the ground.

Rion's magic blocked the deadly spears of ice, rendering them useless, but he'd barely blocked Talon's hands in time as they'd reached for his throat.

Talon roared, snapping his teeth and Rion grimaced before twisting beneath him and throwing him off. Talon pivoted, landing on his hands and feet like a feral animal before lunging at him again.

Ice snaked up the walls, branching out to surround Rion on all sides. Talon drew his blade and dove for him again, the ice following in dozens of sharpened spears.

Rion yanked the stones loose from the walls, crushing them with half a thought before encasing his body in a protective cocoon. Ice formed at his feet, forcing him to roll to avoid the next attack, but Talon was already there. He grabbed Rion by the front of his tunic and slammed him to the ground before pinning him with his body.

Rion's magic wrapped around Talon's arms, stopping the falling blade a mere inch from his throat.

Talon growled at him, his eyes full of rage and grief.

The very floor turned cold beneath Rion's body. He tore through the stone to their right and hit Talon hard in the ribs, knocking the male off balance long enough for Rion to regain his feet.

"Stop, I didn't touch her." Rion didn't know why he bothered trying. No one had ever believed him before. That familiar tang of rage resurfaced, reminding him of all the pain and betrayals. It was that very rage that had sent him on mission after mission until he'd earned a reputation for himself.

Talon had seen the changes in him. Talon had helped him train his body after Niall's torment. They'd finally started to build a bond. To trust one another as comrades.

But one misunderstanding and he was the monster all over again.

Rion growled, baring his teeth. The stones around him crumbled to dust.

Talon lunged, but this time Rion caught his ankles with sand and stone. Talon tried to twist from their grip, but Rion held firm and yanked hard. Talon's jaw hit the stone floor, then Rion threw him into the wall. Rion's magic engulfed Talon's limbs, rendering them useless. Then his hand snaked out and grabbed Talon by the throat.

Rage pulsed through his body. Talon was just another name to add to an ever-growing list of people who had betrayed him. He hadn't even hesitated.

Talon squirmed beneath Rion's iron grip, but Rion's magic tightened around Talon's arms, legs, and torso, grating against his skin, squeezing his ribs until they were ready to snap in half.

The male thrashed, his magic trying to break him free. Spears of ice flew from different angles, but the stones crumbled at Rion's command and blocked them each time.

Talon's face turned red as Rion cut off his air supply. He watched the desperation in Talon's eyes and relished in the feel of a life fading beneath his hands. It had been too long.

This isn't you.

Rion startled at the female voice echoing in his head. He turned, searching for who it belonged to, scenting the air in case they were trying to hide, but—no one was there.

Rion turned his focus back to Talon, ready to finish it and move on.

Don't let him steal another piece of your soul.

"Come out," Rion demanded. He released Talon's throat but kept his magic firm. He could deal with this other threat first.

She needs you.

Rion whirled again, searching for the voice. They were close. Whoever—

Arianna needs you.

Rion's entire body locked up and the rage pulsing through him shattered like a mirror disappearing to reveal the truth behind the reflection.

He spun to find Talon pinned against the wall with earth and stone, the male still gasping for breath. Marks lined his throat from where Rion had nearly crushed his windpipe.

He'd almost—

Rion stumbled back, his gaze roaming toward the female on the floor. She wasn't covered in blood anymore. Her leg wasn't nearly severed either. Raevina looked … normal. Rion blinked and the blood reappeared, scent and all. Another blink and it was gone again.

Shit. He didn't know who the voice belonged to. It certainly wasn't Arianna. The female sounded older. Wiser. Maybe Sive had placed another rune on him that he wasn't aware of.

Rion silently thanked the voice, then checked the rune on his arm. It hadn't changed, which meant whoever was controlling the glamour was stronger than the average Fae.

Was it Niall? No, Rion was confident he'd recognize that male's magic. Vairik? Wouldn't he already be dead in that case?

Talon finally stopped coughing and glared at Rion, baring his teeth in absolute rage. He pulled at the restraints and frost coated the dirt and stone holding his body in place.

"She's fine," Rion said, remaining against the wall opposite of the male. Talon's gaze darted to Raevina, a spark of hope there and gone again. He fought harder. The rock around his left arm cracked. "Look harder," Rion urged. "It's a glamour. Search for the bond."

Talon's heart pounded, but he stilled again, his gaze roaming over the female as if he barely dared to hope. Rion understood that fear and desperation. He'd do anything to protect his mate. All of them would.

"The bond," his voice was a hoarse whisper. "It's—where is it?"

"That's not her." Rion watched as Talon's face paled, then he stopped pulling at the bonds.

"Let me go."

Rion did, even as he pulled his magic up to surround his own body in case Talon changed his mind. He knew better than to underestimate the warrior despite his age.

Weaver. He had Weaver blood in his veins. It explained so much.

"Where is she?" Talon growled as he stared down at the female. Her image kept shifting, the glamour trying to reclaim its hold.

"I don't know."

Talon turned to him then, his face still a mask of rage. "And how do I know you're you?"

"You're not dead."

Talon scoffed, then shadows wrapped around the female. Her body disappeared seconds later, vanishing in a swirl of shadowy smoke.

"Where's Arianna?" Talon demanded.

Rion clenched his fists. "I lost her."

Talon's gaze snapped up. "Who's with her?"

"No one."

Cold silence drifted between them. The kind that told Rion they were all about to face their worst fears.

"Conall said Vairik wants you and Arianna, which means he won't kill her."

"If you knew half the things Niall did to me, that wouldn't comfort you." Rion's mind kept flashing back to the memory of that female lying on a table and how her chest had been ripped wide open. Then to the dark creatures that had resembled the Fae far too much for his liking.

"Do we split up?" Talon asked.

Rion ground his teeth. It had been so easy to turn them against one another. Would they be able to do it again? Did they risk it?

"No, we stay together for as long as we can. We se—"

The floor shook then turned to shadows beneath their feet before everything crumbled beneath them. Rion reached for something to pull him out, but every stone he grasped broke away. Talon cursed, trying to do the same.

Neither found purchase and they both fell into a darkness that consumed everything.

CHAPTER THIRTY-ONE

ARIANNA

*A*rianna's entire body trembled when she woke. Her breath clouded in the frigid air, and she blinked against the brightness of the room. White walls surrounded her, devoid of anything that might offer a scrap of information. She tried to move her arms, but her wrists and ankles were clamped down with thick metal bands. Another wrapped across her torso, locking her body in place.

Iron. Panic engulfed her. Her head pounded and her side burned, telling her the knife hadn't been an illusion.

Ellie. Gods, what had that monster done to Ellie?

Arianna twisted her head to take in the room. A single metal chair sat in one corner along with a small table with a clipboard resting on top. No pen or pencil.

The plain iron door across from her had a small window on the top. If she freed herself, she might be able to see who stood on the other side. Were her friends strapped to tables as well?

Was Rion?

Arianna reached for the bond, but Rion was silent on the other end. No pain. No movement. She hated that feeling. She'd spent weeks unable to reach him and had felt their bond unravel strand by strand. It had been excruciating.

Arianna tried to focus on the steady rhythm of his heartbeat. It took several moments, telling her he wasn't anywhere nearby, but at least he was alive. She'd rest in that small comfort for now.

Arianna tried twisting her wrist, hoping to force her hand through the small opening. She pulled, gritting her teeth against the sting of the metal. Arianna tested the amount of room between herself and the bar across her torso next. Not much, but perhaps enough for her to shift to the side for more leverage.

She tried, gritting her teeth as she pulled on her wrist, but only succeeded in bruising her hip and reopening the knife wound. Blood trickled down her side, then her movements became more frantic.

Arianna yanked and pulled again, straining against the clasps holding her in place. Her magic thrashed and bucked and Arianna set it free only to experience a familiar electrical shock that flew through her body like molten fire.

She stopped moving and gasped for breath. Tears pricked the corners of her eyes and she slammed her wrists against the shackles in frustration.

Trapped. She was trapped all over again. She'd be subjected to Vairik's madness with no hope of escape.

Would he make her watch as he tore Rion apart? What would happen to Talon and Raevina? Would he start with them instead and discard their bodies afterward? Would Talon be the next floating mass outside the dungeon, left there without recognition or a proper burial?

Arianna yanked at her restraints again, then pulled on her magic a second time, bracing against the electrical shock that pulsed through her system.

Rion hadn't given up. He'd broken his own chains in his determination to preserve their bond. He'd gone through hell because of her weakness. She couldn't let him go through it again or let her sister suffer any longer.

Her heart beat even faster as Arianna recalled the illusions that had felt entirely too real. She hadn't even questioned them. Had her sister been an illusion too? Was Ellie safe and unharmed, or was she locked in a cell? Was she even alive?

Arianna yanked again, letting her magic free, but the current bit back even stronger. She arched off the table, teeth gritted in pain before collapsing again.

Arianna struggled to catch her breath. Magic wasn't going to work here. She needed to use her own physical strength if she hoped to escape.

She'd pushed her body in the weeks Ellie had been missing. They'd all trained religiously, preparing for anything the gods might throw their way. She could do this, she just—

A latch in the door clicked and Arianna froze. Muffled voices floated in from the other side. A set of keys jangled, then the heavy door swung open to reveal a familiar face she'd hoped to never see again.

"That's very distracting. Some of us have other assignments to attend to."

Arianna bared her teeth at him, a low growl escaping, but Niall laughed it off as if she weren't a threat. "Seems I'll have to arrange my schedule then." He stepped inside and let the door close behind him. Niall rolled up a sleeve then reached for the clipboard. His eyes scanned the page before he turned to her. Two long strides had him across the room in seconds. He reached out a hand.

"Don't you dare touch me."

Niall paused and that familiar smile crept across his face before falling away again. Instead, he turned and grabbed the chair, letting the legs scrape across the floor before he seated himself far too close for comfort.

"Perhaps explaining my intentions will relax you a bit."

"Where is Rion?"

"Where he needs to be. Shackled like the dog he is."

She growled again.

"Don't you want to know what we plan to do with you? It's what half the other prisoners beg for."

"Why would I listen to you? All you've ever done is lie."

He smirked. "I suppose I deserve that. But rest assured, I was lied to as well."

She furrowed her brow at him, but didn't give Niall the satisfaction of asking questions. He continued anyway.

"You see, I was led to believe I would rule the continent and that you were the key to obtaining that dream. But it was all an illusion. My father has kindly explained why it was necessary and though I'm still sore at him, I've come to accept we have bigger goals."

She wanted to ask what. To know if they really did have an army, but Arianna just glared at him.

Niall laughed again then ran a disgustingly long finger down her forearm. "You see, I don't need you anymore. My father does, but just for a short while. Once he's done, I'm free to exact my revenge." He gripped her arm painfully. "And I will most certainly be getting my revenge."

"It was your own fault for underestimating me."

"Perhaps it was. I didn't think you had so much fight in you, especially when you fell to my glamours so easily." Niall shook his head. "I was honestly disappointed you didn't put up more of a fight, but when you did," he whistled. "You actually caught me off guard. I really thought you'd finish the job." He leaned forward. "Too bad for you, you didn't."

"I had a city to save."

"Yet you've abandoned the continent to come look for a sister who doesn't want to be found."

She jolted at that. "Where is Ellie?"

He smirked and stood. "I'd tell you, but that would ruin the fun. Perhaps I'll fill you in once my father is finished with you. Rest assured, what I have planned is far worse so enjoy his company while you can."

Niall reached for her forehead and Arianna thrashed on the table, yanking at every restraint until she felt the metal bite through her skin. "Go ahead and fight, little dove, it'll just make this more fun."

Niall's clammy hand pressed against her forehead and pain exploded behind Arianna's eyes. She screamed and thrashed for what felt like an eternity before her world fell into darkness.

ARIANNA'S HEAD was still throbbing when Niall came back the second time. She couldn't even see past the black dots swimming across her vision, nor remember exactly what he'd done.

Arianna tried pulling at her restraints when he left again, but her efforts were futile. Her body wouldn't respond. Someone offered her water. A female, but Arianna refused it, certain it had to be poisoned.

She breathed in and out, trying to gather herself. Talon needed her. Rion needed her. Ellie needed her. She had to get out of here.

Her vision faded in and out. Time was a meaningless concept. She tried to pull her wrists from the cuffs again and winced. Both were raw and bleeding. She didn't remember how or when it had happened.

Memories assaulted her as she drifted through a meaningless void. Arianna recalled the first time iron had been clamped around her wrists. She'd already hidden herself within her half-human form, per Talon's instructions. She had remained in the boat, floating there for hours.

None of them had heard the slavers before they'd rushed in and slit her attendants' throats. They'd shoved a bag over her head. She'd been so distracted. So young and stupid.

The cracking sound of whips echoed through her memories next. She remembered the first one, but even that hadn't stung as much as Niall's penetrative magic.

Footsteps echoed outside the door and Arianna's heart sank when Niall walked through. She turned her head to glare at him, but couldn't muster the energy for much else. Even her magic had fallen silent.

"Judging from the look on your face, you still know who I am."

She didn't answer. Couldn't from how tired her body had become.

Niall drew closer again and Arianna turned her head away. He gripped the sides of her face with bruising fingers and forcefully turned her back before diving into her mind.

Arianna screamed and thrashed again, her head splitting from the tendrils that raced through her thoughts and memories. They were venomous barbs tearing through the core of her being, ripping her to shreds from the inside.

She didn't know when he left, only that she was panting, her throat raw and eyes heavy.

Arianna hoped that was the end of it. That he might leave her alone long enough for her to recover and formulate a plan. But he returned a third time.

Then a fourth.

By the fifth, Arianna drank the water.

By the sixth, she was numb.

It wasn't until the seventh time, when her mind felt as though it had been wrung out, that Arianna heard another voice. This one deeper and slick like oil.

Niall said something she couldn't decipher, then his hands were on her again and she fell and fell and fell.

CHAPTER THIRTY-TWO

ELLIE

"Do you remember the day we first met?" Kirian's voice was a soft murmur, drifting through her, easing the jagged edges of her mind. He pieced together the broken fragments she couldn't stitch, though something always remained missing—an emptiness she couldn't place.

A soft smirk played across her cracked lips. She tried to wet them in vain. Ellie couldn't remember the last time they'd given her water. "It's hard to forget. You completely wrecked my escape plan."

"That's not how I remember it." Kirian pulled her closer then pushed her dirty hair away from her face. She'd given up trying to tell him not to touch it. They were both filthy anyway.

"Right. Because you weren't following me or anything."

He laughed again, the sound equal parts hollow and warm. The only bit of warmth they could get in this dank, dirty cell. "How could I resist? After seeing you leap from the window on the first day of the school year, I had to find a way to get to know you."

"So you resorted to stalking," she snorted.

"I resorted to discovering your hiding places. The teachers never could find you."

"Neither could you."

He chuckled behind her, his voice comforting in the cold stillness. "What better way than to follow you mid-flight?"

"You got us both caught."

He shrugged. "It's not like you suffered a worse punishment than any other time."

"My father's methods were far worse. I had to read an entire historical text and make a twenty-page report on the previous High Lords of Móirín. Do you realize how boring that was?"

He laughed again. "I almost got expelled."

"I wouldn't let that happen. To anyone."

"My mother was mortified. If not for you, she might have moved out of Levea. I was grounded for three months."

"She never seemed upset when I visited."

"Because she liked you. Whenever you left, I was sent right back to my room."

Silence fell between them as Ellie reminisced about the first month they'd gotten to know one another. She'd needed a friend, even if she'd nearly bitten his head off.

"I'm glad you found me that day," her voice was lower now, lacking the playful tone she'd had a moment ago.

His arms tightened around her shoulders and Kirian rested his chin on her head. "I'd never seen you cry before."

She felt that same lump rise in her throat now. It had been the anniversary of her mother's death. A death she now knew had sparked a pointless war. A death that likely ran far deeper than she ever wanted to learn.

A hot tear rolled down her face. Kirian had been there for her. He'd rushed toward her instead of backing away and had folded her into his arms. He'd felt like home. She hadn't even fought after that. She'd just crumpled in on herself and cried into his shoulder.

And now he was here, holding her so she wouldn't break, just like he'd done back then.

Memories kept swimming in and out of focus, as if she were peering at them through a heavy layer of mist.

"I can't remember her face," Ellie choked out. "I can't hear her voice anymore."

"You will," Kirian assured. "Once we get out of here, you will." But she could hear the crack in his voice, too. Because maybe it wasn't just the torture. Maybe the High Lord was doing more to her mind than merely sifting through it for information.

Ellie gripped his arm and squeezed harder. He didn't flinch away. She took a breath.

I am Lady Evelyn of Móirín. I am the daughter of the High Lord of Storms. I have been trained to endure. I will not falter. I have a mate, Gavin from Pádraigín, but a half-breed has claimed my heart. I will protect Levea at any cost, even if that cost means my life. I will not break.

Chapter Thirty-Three

Arianna

When Arianna woke again, she wasn't strapped to a cold metal table. Instead, she found herself seated in a plush armchair before a roaring fire, her skin aflame and her body entirely too warm. The hearth stretched along the entire length of the wall. At least she wasn't shivering anymore.

Arianna let her eyes adjust to the dim lighting in the room. Tapestries hung on the walls around her, each depicting a different scene she couldn't quite make out. Old leather-bound books lined the shelves built into the walls. She shivered at the memories they invoked and studied the various trinkets that stood alongside them.

A thick rug covered the space beneath her feet, and Arianna noticed scorch marks in the maroon fibers.

She tilted her head, trying to work the tension from her shoulders. The fire popped, a spark shooting out into the room. Something moved to her right.

Not something. Someone.

Arianna let her gaze rise past the small, round table to her right, and her body went rigid at the sight of a male sitting in the chair across from her. He had one leg crossed over the other, his thick robes obscuring his legs, leaving only his boots visible.

Arianna noticed the runes along his robes first. Familiar symbols she couldn't read but now knew all too well. His scent wafted toward her, carried by the cool breeze at her back. He smelled like an old library, like he'd been caged inside a room too long.

His face, though young and fair like all the Fae, carried evidence of a thousand wars. A hundred lifetimes. His light golden hair was pulled back on one side, twisted around so that it was out of his face. The other side of his head was bare. He carried thick scars along that half that dragged all the way down his face, as if a creature had tried to tear it off.

He was blind in one eye, though he didn't wear any sort of patch to cover the cloudy opaqueness.

Even with his imperfections, there was something other-worldly about him. Something that seemed to draw her toward his presence. Or maybe that was just another of his illusions.

Vairik was a master of them, after all.

He didn't speak. Instead, Vairik watched her, seeming to study everything from the way her chest rose and fell to where her eyes wandered. Arianna's gaze traveled back to the table where she found a glass of water and chocolates arranged neatly on a plate.

She couldn't help herself. Arianna lunged for the water, hearing the familiar rattle of chains as she did.

Arianna ignored the iron around her ankles as she let the liquid ease her parched throat. She knew it was likely laced with something, but she couldn't bring herself to care. How long had it been?

Arianna's eyes snapped to her wrist. The bracelets were gone, which meant she had no way of telling how much time had passed. Nothing had exploded yet though, which meant Conall and the others hadn't enacted their plan. But ... did that mean the others had been caught as well? Had everyone failed?

Arianna looked back up to find Vairik still watching her. His gaze flicked between her wrist and eyes. She didn't have to turn her hand over to know the rune was gone too. Niall or that mysterious female had probably gotten rid of it as soon as she'd been captured.

Arianna carefully set the glass back on the table, resisting the urge to fling it at Vairik's face.

His voice was dark and silken when he spoke. "I'll offer you more in a few moments. It wouldn't do any good for you to vomit all over my clean floors."

Her magic reacted to his voice so violently that Arianna audibly gasped and clutched her chest. It leapt behind her ribs, trying to claw its way to the surface. She couldn't hold it back and leaned forward when the iron sent a pulse of electricity straight through her.

She tried coaxing it back into submission, begging the creature to calm down. Vairik was right in front of her. She needed to ask him questions and find a way out. Passing out on the floor wouldn't exactly help her do that.

It took Arianna several moments to ease her racing heart and quiet the creature. It resorted to pacing back and forth.

Vairik was studying her, a sharp curiosity in his gaze. Then he turned to watch the flames dancing in the fireplace. He still sat with a relaxed posture, his hands neatly folded in his lap, long fingers interlaced.

"You're the High Lord of Pádraigín." Her voice cracked, throat raw and aching. Not that he deserved the title.

A smile tugged at the corner of his mouth, pulling at the scars along the left side of his face. "And you're the sacred queen, our bringer of peace. Arianna, wasn't it?"

Her magic jolted again, vibrating against her sternum, growling from within. Arianna tried to swallow, but it did nothing to ease the fire in her throat. "That's what everyone keeps telling me."

Sharp eyes tilted toward her, penetrating down to her core. She half wondered if he could see that raging creature within. "You don't believe in your own destiny?"

Arianna opened her mouth to reply then closed it again. How was she supposed to respond? She'd done nothing but doubt herself from the beginning. "It's complicated."

His gaze turned back to the fire and he shifted slightly in his chair, as if an old pain were suddenly making itself known. "Most things centering around destiny are."

Arianna waited for him to continue or to say something else. After a few minutes of silence, she finally asked. "What have you done with everyone?" If he had her in his clutches, he had to have the others, too.

His jaw ticked, the first sign of agitation. "Worried for your mate?"

Arianna recalled Conall's words and the story he'd told about a male scorned by the female he'd loved.

Vairik spoke again before she could reply. "Tell me honestly, do you believe you would have fallen for such a male if it weren't for the bond pulling you together?" Before she could reply, Vairik leaned across the table. She shrank away, but he only grabbed a pitcher she hadn't seen a moment ago. He carefully refilled her glass then placed the pitcher back on the table. It disappeared again.

Arianna counted the seconds before reaching for the glass. Vairik interlaced his fingers again and leaned back, clearly waiting for her response.

Rion. Her mate. A male she'd die to protect. Would she have fallen for him without the bond? She'd been terrified of him in the beginning. She'd heard all the stories and she'd witnessed his ruthlessness firsthand.

But despite all that, she'd still chosen to save him. She'd done that because of her mother's teachings and because she couldn't bear to see anyone suffer.

But when she'd run to the river, something had pulled her back. She'd felt a connection to Rion she couldn't explain. The bond had stopped her from running. Without it, she would have dived into that water without a second thought.

"I don't know."

The male raised a brow. "He was a creature that swept across the land killing your own people and you don't know?"

"It's not like he would have done those things if it weren't for you."

The male chuckled, the sound mirthless. "Maybe. Or maybe it was always in his nature." Silence stretched between them. "Conversation is a rarity for me these days, humor me with your answer."

Arianna chewed the inside of her cheek. "I think it would have depended."

"Oh what?"

"The situation. Fate. Circumstance."

He smirked again. "You know what I think? I think without the bond, that male would have ripped you apart the moment he scented you were from Móirín. I think the bond is the only thing that stilled his hand. And yours." Arianna met his gaze. "I know your story. I know his, too."

He leaned forward slightly, resting his chin on his hands. "I know you once cared deeply for another of your companions. I know he's now plagued by the same bond. A perfectly good match ruined due to unnatural interference." Arianna wasn't sure if he wa speaking to her or to himself.

"Talon is free to love whomever he wishes."

"Is he?" Vairik's brow lifted. "The gods have shackled him to another with a ruthless nature. A female who was supposed to end the life of his proclaimed best friend and yet he forgives her intention so easily. As do you. A complete stranger."

"People can change."

"Just like that? What if I decided, right here, right now, to give up my endeavors, would you forgive me?"

"You're a monster."

"By your definition, so are they."

"What do you want me to say?" Her heart was racing with the truth of his words.

Vairik leaned back again. "Nothing, I suppose. It wouldn't matter either way."

Arianna watched him for another long minute. She tried to picture this male in his youth, back before the scars of the world had hardened his heart. He'd loved once. And that love had betrayed him because of the bond.

He'd mentioned changing his mind. Was part of him aching for a reason to let go of his anger?

The creature within her writhed again. Arianna tried to take a deep breath and quell it into submission.

"I think," she said, trying to choose her words carefully. "Given the proper circumstance, I might have fallen in love with Rion without the bond."

"Really? And what circumstances would those be?"

"A world without you. A world where he was never marked as a demon. One that saw him as the son of a High Lord instead of a creature of death and destruction." Vairik snorted, but she kept going. "Our countries were allies, we would have met eventually. You manipulated his fate, just like you claim the gods manipulated the previous Divine away from you."

A real smile slowly spread across his face. "My, how the tables turn. Who would have thought I might grow into the very thing I loathe." He rested his chin on his right hand, one finger over his lips as if he'd suddenly become lost in thought. "Perhaps it's no longer worth my time. Maybe peace is on the other side of moving forward."

Arianna wasn't sure she liked the sound of that. "Moving forward how?"

His gaze roamed to hers. "You already know my plans, or did Conall not inform you?"

Her heart jolted at the name, but she supposed she shouldn't be surprised. "So your solution is to just kill everyone?"

"It would be the easiest at this point. I've spent plenty of time trying to change it."

"You're talking about murdering innocent people. It's not their fault they have a mating bond."

"It's their fault for being complacent in it. It's their fault for not rising up."

"You want them to rebel against the gods who created them? The bond was a gift. The thing they feel for their bonded partner isn't something bad. It feels real to them. It feels right."

"Only the young can say such things. You've never come across someone unhappy with the bond, have you?" She didn't respond. "I consider myself fortunate to have never experienced it. To not be shackled and forced to call it fate."

Another beat of silence passed, then he stood and every cell in her body sprang to life. The creature inside her prepared itself, ready to spring despite the iron shackles.

Vairik crossed the space and leaned down, placing his hands on either side of the armchair. Arianna shrank back into the old cushions, her heart beating wildly as that eye studied her. She could fight, shove him back, lift her legs and kick him across the room, but something told her it wouldn't matter, that if she so much as shifted a muscle, his magic would lash out.

"I can smell her on you." His gaze traveled down to Arianna's chest, right over her sternum where her magic buzzed beneath her skin. "You're still here, aren't you dear Laoise?"

Arianna's magic jolted at the name, flaring beneath her skin. The iron around her ankles sent a violent shockwave through Arianna's body that had her arching off the chair. She gripped the edges, her fingers tearing into the fabric.

The creature within her beat against the cage over and over again, sending wave after wave of pain through Arianna's body.

Stop, Arianna begged it. *Please stop.*

"It seems we've both been trapped in a hell of our own creation."

"What—are you talking about?" Arianna breathed through the aftershocks racking her body.

He leaned impossibly closer. "Can you not feel her writhing within your bones, struggling to cleave her way into your world and set it on fire?"

"What?"

"The magic, dear girl. Do you think that fire in your soul is yours alone?" He smirked again, hanging his head and shaking it slightly. "And all this time I assumed you were in the afterlife with that bastard. It's almost reassuring to know I haven't been the only one suffering."

"I have—she's inside me?"

Vairik's gaze returned to her. "Her essence is. It seems she's defied the gods in her own way as well. I suppose that explains why my son made no progress with you. Laoise always was resistant where mind manipulation was concerned. No matter, I'll take care of you myself."

Cold fear trickled down her spine.

"Don't worry, I won't kill you. I want to play one final game before this ends." His gaze twisted back to her chest. "Thank the gods they didn't make you look like her, otherwise this would have been much harder."

"Wha—" His hands moved fast and those slender fingers gripped her like a vice.

Blinding white hot pain seared through her mind and Arianna screamed all over again, feeling the seams of her reality split into a million pieces.

The creature, Laoise, fought, but even it wasn't enough to stop Vairik's invasion.

He dove deep into her mind, swimming through it and tearing her apart with barbs on every surface of his mental body.

Vairik didn't stop until he found the moment she and Rion first met. The day she'd knelt on the cold cabin floor with The Demon standing over her. Arianna relived the fear she'd experienced at that moment, then it wisped away into darkness, fading like smoke carried away by the wind.

Vairik shifted through her memories, flipping through them like the pages of a book until he found the moment she'd first made Rion soup, hoping to placate his anger with her cooking. That image dissolved too, the colors blending together until they were nothing but darkness.

He moved again, sifting until he found the memory where Rion had stumbled in injured. He let it play for a moment but jerked it away before she could offer Rion—what had she offered him?

Arianna found herself standing before a red-haired male in a cabin next, her hand glowing against his chest. Her own heart was heavy with emotions she didn't understand. She tried to look up at his face and study it, but the image burned before her eyes, then the flames consumed her as well.

She loosed a silent scream as she fell into another image of a male being tormented by her father. Her body moved and she intervened, but Arianna couldn't remember why she'd bothered. She'd screamed a word and had growled at her father. She never growled at her father. The word was lost. She didn't resist when that one turned to ice and shattered into nothing.

Images of herself with the male, their bodies entwined blinked from existence. Pictures of her hand in his, the way he'd looked at her, the gentleness in his voice, it all flipped off, like a light switch, leaving her in a cold dark room.

There was still a light in the distance. Arianna ran toward it, trying to flee from oily hands chasing after her.

Arianna slammed open the thick door and dove inside a room that resembled a small temple. A golden braided rope sat within, reaching through the floor and ceiling. A tether to someone she couldn't remember.

Hands beat against the door and Arianna pressed her body against it, fighting to keep the shadows from breaking through. They'd ruin it. They'd destroy this beautiful thing before her.

The shadows slithered in from beneath the door anyway. She tried to stomp them out, to use her magic to keep them at bay, but the magic wouldn't answer her call. The creature within her was gone, locked away, hidden.

The shadows beat against the door again, splintering the wood.

Tears spilled down Arianna's cheeks as she watched those shadows stretch toward the glowing rope. Dark fingers wrapped around the strands, digging at the edges until they frayed.

Pain lanced through Arianna's chest and she dove forward. She clawed at the shadows, desperate to pull them away from the rope, to protect it at any cost. But they slipped through her fingers, continuing their assault.

Then the door burst open and those hands reached in, wrapping around the rope, pulling at it from both ends while the shadows slipped through the threads, digging, digging, digging.

No, no, no, no, no.

She began screaming the word, unsure why it mattered at all. Unsure why this room was so important.

The walls crumbled around her, the ceiling falling in great heaps around her body as she crumbled in on herself.

Then the rope snapped.

Her body was yanked from the room and Arianna covered her face with her hands as she plummeted into icy blackness, her chest raw and bleeding.

Something warm wrapped around her then. Something hot, nearly scolding. It stitched the fabric of her torn reality.

The pain eased little by little, stitch by stitch until it vanished entirely and she was left to hang, just like those old tapestries with fibers that were too old to mend.

Color returned, though the various shades seemed duller than before. Still, she reached for them, floating and clinging to things from her past.

Then her body and those colors drifted off to a land where her head didn't pound. Where cold shackles didn't hold her prisoner and she was finally safe at last.

CHAPTER THIRTY-FOUR

ELLIE

My name is Ellie. I am the—
My name is Evelyn.
My name is Evelyn.
My name is Evelyn.

Chapter Thirty-Five

Rion

Rion woke to his body being dragged along a cold floor. His arms were above him, wrists pulled taut with the familiar bite of metal. Of iron.

But that was nothing compared to the searing agony lancing through his chest.

He tried to keep quiet and fight the blinding pain that felt like a hot iron had severed through—through—Rion's eyes snapped open.

No.

Where was it? Where was his—

Rion wrapped his hands around the chains and yanked hard enough to drag his body upward and simultaneously knock his captors off balance.

Arianna.

Rion slammed his fist into the warrior's jaw on his right. He yanked a small knife from its sheath at the male's waist and threw it into his companion's throat. The male collapsed, gripping the blade as he choked on his own blood. Rion struck the one below him again. Again. Again. He wrapped the chain around his fist, slamming it against the male's face over and over until he no longer drew breath.

Rion fell back, blood drenching his hand. He gasped for breath, reaching for something that was no longer there.

The bond. The bond. The bond.

Did that mean Arianna was—he couldn't even think the word, not without choking on it. The image of an open chest with the heart ripped out haunted him, only this time it was Arianna's face twisted in agony.

Rion vomited all over the floor.

His mind spun, his world with it. Arianna was gone. She was gone. She was—his fists clenched. No. She couldn't be. Vairik needed her, right? Was this just another glamour meant to throw him off?

Rion gripped his tunic right over the empty void in his chest. He couldn't breathe. He needed her for that. He needed the comfort of the light she'd brought into his life. Without her—

His vision blurred, but Rion blinked away the tears before they could fall. *An illusion*, he told himself. This was all just an illusion. Arianna wasn't gone. She wasn't—Rion's body shook against his will and he clenched his fists, fighting back the emotions pulsing through his body.

He sat there for several moments, breathing through the pain. It wouldn't dissipate. He'd had knives shoved through his body, magic too. He'd experienced the pain of heartbreak and betrayal, but none of it compared to this.

Don't let him steal another piece of your soul.

Rion recalled the words of that strange voice. Is that what Vairik had done? Was he just trying to break him?

Alive, Rion tried to convince himself. Arianna was alive. She was somewhere in this castle and still needed his help. If he stayed here and wallowed in grief, he might really lose her forever.

And if she was really gone—no. He wouldn't stop until he saw her body. He wouldn't stop until he took her back to Levea. Breathing or not.

Rion forced his eyes open. He stared at the metal around his wrists, then tore through the pockets of the dead Fae beside him. Rion found a ring of keys. His hands trembled as he fumbled through the set, trying one after another until the latch clicked and the iron fell to the floor. Rion kicked it across the stone before unlatching the other.

His magic surged, moving in a frenzy that matched the storm raging in his chest. It tore at the stones, breaking them into pieces that floated around his body.

Rion blinked, trying to clear his head. The bracelets were gone, which meant he had no way of knowing exactly when Conall would blow this place to hell. His rune was gone too, though if he were facing Vairik, then it was irrelevant anyway.

Rion forced himself to stand. Bubbling vials of blue liquid lined the hall. Each was about the size of his torso and contained … something within. He didn't pause to study them. He didn't want to know.

Rion looked up and down the quiet space, counting the doors that stood between the vials.

Rion ambled toward the first door and pushed it open to find a large cylindrical chamber attached to the back wall. It stood empty with shackles inside that looked like they'd clamp around a Fae's wrists and ankles. A mask hung to the side with a large tube attached to it.

Rion's stomach twisted and his world tilted. He stumbled back, gripping the doorway to keep his balance as the pain continued radiating through his chest.

He needed to get himself together. Rion tried to remember what he'd been doing before his capture. The images blurred. He'd been chasing Arianna down a long corridor until—Talon.

Shit. Rion's head snapped around and he darted back into the hall. He risked glancing at one of the objects floating in the vials and his heart skipped. It looked just like a heart. Bile rose through him again and he looked away. He'd know if it was Arianna. Some part of him would know.

Rion scented the air, hoping to find the male, but an acrid stench filled the space, blocking out everything else. He tried again, dragging himself down the hall with his hand still clenching his chest.

Another door opened and a group of Fae emerged in deep conversation. They froze upon seeing him. Their eyes widened, but Rion was on them before they could even cry out.

He slammed his elbow into the jaw of the first, then snapped the male's neck. Rion ripped the blades from the male's belt and launched them at the others. Two hit their mark.

Glamours rose, trying to pierce his mind, then wind tore through the space, stealing the air from around him.

Rion dove for the one wielding it and sank his teeth into the male's throat before tearing it out. He turned to the final one. Knives clattered to the floor as the male raised his arms in surrender.

Rion grabbed him by the front of his tunic. "Where is she?"

"I—I—" The male trembled, his entire body seizing up in fear.

Rion shook him and slammed his back against the wall hard enough to crack the stone. "Where is she?" Rion repeated. He'd be damned if he let Vairik trap Arianna in one of those contraptions. She wouldn't be someone's experiment. He wouldn't let anyone touch her again. Ever.

"Down the hall," the male managed. He lifted one hand to point. "The other doors." The lie's burning scent hit Rion hard and he snapped the male's neck before throwing him to the side.

The searing pain in his chest wouldn't stop. It made him want to curl in on himself and let it all end. Let Vairik have him. Let death sink its claws into his soul.

But he had to see for himself. He couldn't give up until he knew for sure.

Rion stumbled into the room they'd emerged from and studied the cylindrical container before him. The door on this one was shut and that bluish liquid from the vials covered the small front window.

Rion snarled and ripped the door from its hinges. Warm liquid came gushing out, spilling all over his feet and legs. Without it, a body hung limply from the shackles within. Rion didn't recognize the Fae, but he still reached for the keys hanging on the side of the chamber. He unlocked their ankles first, then caught the body when he did the same for the Fae's wrists.

Rion carefully removed the mask from their nose and mouth.

Their skin was strange, wrinkled and loose and the creature in his arms gasped for air and looked around as if they couldn't quite see. Rion leaned them against the structure.

"Can you stand?"

The male didn't answer. He simply sat there, gaping like a fish out of water. The Fae began shivering. Rion caught the Fae's head as he fell to the side and curled into himself. Sympathy tugged within him, but Rion didn't have time to waste. He had to find Arianna.

Moving as fast as his aching body would allow, he rummaged through a set of cabinets and found a pair of cloaks. Rion draped one over the Fae's shoulders and folded the other beneath his head. His breathing and heart rate were erratic and Rion doubted the male would live long.

With no other alternative, Rion left him and moved on to the next room, still trying to ignore the bubbling vials along the walls.

Another cylindrical container stood against the back wall. This time, Rion peered through the small window slot first. Another Fae male floated inside, his hair floating around his body like dead pond grass.

Rion debated releasing him, but the first Fae's heart was already fading. Pulling him out would only result in an agonizing death. Rion was certain the creature had suffered enough at Vairik's hands.

Rion moved on, his heart racing each time he peered through a small window. Part of him hoped to find Arianna, another part of him didn't want her anywhere near this place.

When he stepped into the next room, Rion caught a familiar scent and bounded for the metal chamber. He ripped the door off its hinges and the blue liquid rushed over his already soaked boots. Talon fought against his restraints and Rion cursed before grabbing the keys hanging off to one side. He ripped the mask off Talon's face and the male gagged, gasping for breath as Rion unlocked each shackle.

Talon nearly ran him over as he stumbled out of the contraption.

The male collapsed to the floor, shoulders heaving, swiping at his face as though the mask was still there.

Talon's eyes were glazed over with fear. More fear than Rion had ever seen in him. Talon retched, then looked up through dripping hair to focus on Rion.

Rion just clutched his chest, willing the excruciating pain to subside.

Talon tried to clear his throat but his voice was hoarse. "Where are the others?"

"I'm looking."

Talon tried to rise, fell, then stumbled to his feet, his back hitting the wall and knocking half a dozen metal tools to the floor. He tilted his head back, chest still heaving as if unable to catch his breath.

They stood in silence, waiting for someone to come investigate the sound. None did.

"Come on." Rion began combing through rooms again. Talon followed, neither male moving as fast as Rion would like.

Rion wanted to find the stairs and tear his way through the castle until he came face to face with Vairik. But if he left and Arianna was trapped in any of these rooms, he'd never forgive himself.

And if they ran out of time—Rion clenched his jaw. It would take a split second and the entire place could come crumbling down on top of them. If he had Arianna, he might be able to survive, but without her—Rion pressed his fist against his chest, still fighting the pain.

He stumbled through door after door after door. Talon didn't try to release the Fae within. Maybe he already knew what the outcome would be. Or he just didn't care right now.

The corridor stretched on and on. Had these Fae been used for Vairik's experiments? Was he siphoning their magic? Did Vairik have others plans and intend to—

Talon took off sprinting down the hall, his movements still unsteady as he leaned too far one way then over corrected, zigzagging down the corridor. Rion followed, his breath shallow as he tried to keep up.

Talon had already torn the container's door off its hinges before Rion stepped over the threshold. Raevina tore out of the chamber roaring and swinging. Her fist collided with the side of Talon's face and she pinned him to the ground, snarling as flames circled her body.

"Raevina," Rion called. The shadows stretched around her, darkening the space as those fierce eyes snapped up to him. Liquid dripped from her long braids, but recognition sparked and her magic guttered. She looked down at Talon, then let herself roll off and collapse next to him.

"Are you okay?" Talon asked.

"Does it look like I'm okay?" she snapped, then sat up again, holding one hand against her head and wincing. Rion had no way of knowing how long the female, or Talon, might have been trapped. "Get this shit off of me."

The scent of Talon's magic drifted through the air and he did as Raevina commanded, pulling the strange smelling substance from her body before doing the same to his own.

"I'm going," Rion said.

"We'll be right behind you."

Rion only nodded before half running down the hall again. Several doorways later and Rion roared before ripping another container apart. He desperately yanked the mask off and unlocked the shackles. Saoirse fell into his arms and Rion sank to the floor with his sister's limp body.

Her heart beat, but her chest wasn't rising. She wasn't—she wasn't breathing.

Rion quickly laid her on the floor and pressed his hands against her chest. Talon and Raevina flew into the room, their magic poised to strike. Rion didn't bother looking at them. He wasn't sure how much his heart could take. He put his hands together and pushed down on her chest over and over again. Raevina slid to the floor beside him, pinched his sister's nose and blew breath into her lungs.

She didn't move.

"Saoirse," he called, voice desperate.

Raevina did it again.

Again.

Saoirse's body convulsed and Rion grabbed her shoulder, pulling her toward him as she coughed and sucked in breath after breath. She grabbed Rion's arm, clinging to it with an iron grip. He bowed his head, thanking the gods as a trickle of relief washed through him.

"Where—" Saoirse struggled to catch her breath, fighting her shaking body. "Zylah. Where?"

"We haven't found her yet." But if she was inside one of these containers, Rion wasn't certain the half-breed would survive. He wasn't sure if Vairik would even bother to keep a half-breed, magic or no. He hadn't found any yet, which just solidified the theory that the male might be using these Fae for their magic.

Talon pulled the liquid from Saoirse and Rion's clothes, then Saoirse leaned on her brother as she rose to her feet. He could feel her trembling beneath him, her body on the verge of collapse.

But his sister stepped forward. "Zylah. I need to find—" she retched, just as Talon had done, but Rion held her up.

"We don't have time," Raevina said. "We have to find Arianna and get out of here. We don't know when Conall—"

Saoirse hissed and turned on the female. "She's my mate, I will not leave without her."

They all stood in shock for a moment, then nodded in understanding.

Thankfully, it didn't take long. Talon called out from down the hall and Saoirse went running. Raevina found Gavin a few minutes later and dragged him inside the room where Saoirse was running her hands along Zylah's body, searching for injuries.

They all split up after that, searching room after room after room until they reached the end of the hall.

"She's not here," Talon said.

"Because Vairik likely has her. If we find Arianna, we'll find Ellie," Saoirse said, her gaze still locked on the half-breed.

"Can you tell where she is?" Zylah asked, her voice just as raw as the rest of them.

Rion's throat suddenly went dry. None had inquired about his injury, not that it was one they could see. He gripped his chest tighter, fire burning through him with every heartbeat.

"No," he said, voice cracking.

His sister straightened, staring at him. "What do you mean, *no?*" His body shook all over again and Saoirse stepped toward him. "Rion, what do you mean, *no?*" she repeated.

"I—It's gone."

"What's gone?" Raevina demanded.

"The bond."

They all fell silent and Rion scented the shock that flew between each of them. He knew what they were thinking.

"She can't be—" Zylah's voice trailed off.

"She's not dead," Talon said with so much certainty that Rion looked up. "She's here, somewhere, and we're going to find her."

CHAPTER THIRTY-SIX

ARIANNA

Arianna's eyes fluttered open and a pulse beat against the back of her head, echoing throughout her entire body. Her stomach rolled, but when she tried to turn over, she found her body once again bound to the cold table.

Niall.

The male's very name sent a pulse of anger strumming through her.

Tears still stained her cheeks from the pain he and his father had inflicted on her mind. She wouldn't forget either of them anytime soon. Them or their magic.

Arianna never wanted it to touch her again. As soon as she got back to the rebels, she was going to demand Sive teach her every mind blocking rune in existence no matter how complicated. She'd tattoo them across her entire body if that's what it took.

Anger pulsed through her again, burning hotter than anything she'd ever experienced before.

Arianna yanked at her restraints, then slammed her head against the metal table in frustration. A fresh wave of pain and nausea swept through her. She tilted to the side and vomited onto the table. Half of it splattered onto the floor while the other half covered her hair.

She rested her head against the table once again. It didn't matter. She was already covered in her own filth. Trust the males from Pádraigín not to care about a prisoner's physical needs.

Arianna squeezed her eyes shut, then opened them to stare at the bright light overhead. It hummed, pulsing with magic. Her skin prickled from the sound.

A chill had gooseflesh rising on her arms and legs. Arianna clenched her teeth, then her magic rolled, moving from the top of her head all the way to her feet. It spread a blanket of warmth through her, as if trying to both comfort and urge her to take action.

Action against what? She was wrapped in iron with no hope of escape. Her skin burned hot enough to tell her that she'd already tried multiple times.

But the creature within her writhed, commanding her to try. If she didn't—what? Urgency rippled through her. Was Talon in trouble? Had he been captured, too? Was something about to happen to her sister?

Ellie had a mate. Would Vairik experiment on his own family? Of course he would. They meant nothing to him. Arianna recalled that experimental room and fear engulfed her. If he did that to Ellie … if he ripped open her body …

The creature inside her pulsed again, twisting like a snake trapped inside a too small cage. It pushed against her, begging her to find a way.

Something else was wrong. Something far away. She needed to get out, break free, do whatever was necessary to ensure she escaped this room.

A pulse of adrenaline shot through her.

Let me out, it cooed softly

Set me free.

Hurry, hurry, hurry.

She wanted to. Gods, she was so tired of these chains. So tired of being treated like she was weak. Tired of acting like it, too.

She'd promised to lock the weak version of herself away and yet here she was, vulnerable all over again. A scared youngling trapped against her will.

Arianna slammed against her shackles, thrashing like a feral creature trapped in a cage. Fighting just like the magic pulsing beneath her skin. She raged and gritted her teeth. Metal bit into her flesh, bruising it as she twisted and turned.

She strained again, pushing, pushing, pushing before letting her body fall slack.

The creature within her paced.

Back and forth. Back and forth.

Arianna stilled. She closed her eyes and took a long, slow breath. She wasn't a frightened youngling anymore. She was a queen and after today, she'd make damn sure the world knew it. That Niall and Vairik knew it, too.

She just had to wait, bide her time for the perfect opportunity.

Arianna settled into herself and began counting.

One.

Two.

Three.

She let her body relax. Her magic did the same, curling up and conserving its power.

Four.

Five.

Six.

Once she attained freedom, Arianna would burn this whole place to the ground.

CHAPTER THIRTY-SEVEN

ELLIE

. . .

CHAPTER THIRTY-EIGHT

ARIANNA

Five thousand five hundred eighty-nine.

Five thousand five hundred ninety.

Five thousand five hundred ninety-one.

Arianna waited, keeping her breath and heartbeat steady as she counted in her head.

Five thousand five hundred ninety-two.

Five thousand five hundred ninety-three.

Five thousand five hundred ninety-four.

The door latch clicked. She let her eyes drift shut.

Five thousand five hundred ninety-five.

A female scent drifted over her. The same female who'd offered her water and seemed to be responsible for her care whenever Niall wasn't around.

Now that she wasn't in excruciating pain, Arianna recognized the scent. It was the same female she'd briefly met in Ruadhán. The one Niall claimed was his assistant because she didn't possess magic of her own. Maybe that had been a lie, too.

Upon seeing Arianna, the female cursed, likely due to the vomit all over the table, floor, and in Arianna's hair. She disappeared again, the heavy door clicking into place.

Arianna just kept counting.

The female returned and immediately began cleaning the floor. Arianna listened to the water slosh as the female wrung out a rag. Arianna didn't know why she expected the female to clean her up first. She assumed at least one person might possess a shred of empathy, but perhaps everyone in Ashling was rotten down to their core.

The female cleaned the table next, shoving Arianna's hair aside as she wiped up the mess. The cold rag met her shoulder, but Arianna didn't move.

The female left and returned again. Water sloshed onto the table as she began wiping the vomit away from Arianna's hair. The puddle had drifted down her arm and under the iron clasp. The female cursed again then pulled out a key.

Five thousand six hundred seventy-three.

It slipped into the lock and with a small twist, the iron shackle popped open. The female lifted Arianna's wrist and wiped the metal clean first.

Now.

Arianna's eyes flew open and she grabbed the female's shirt, yanking as hard as she could. The female's body flew over the table, her face slamming into the wall. The female screamed and struggled, reaching for something in her jacket.

Arianna saw the flash of a knife, a thin instrument that was probably more suited for removing precise sections of flesh than it was for fighting.

Arianna released her grip and snatched the bottom end of the handle. The two wrestled for several seconds as the female fought to regain her balance. A knee dug into Arianna's thigh. A palm into her shoulder. Metal bit into Arianna's skin, but she refused to loosen her grip.

The female leaned forward, trying to force herself into an upright position, but Arianna headbutted her, sending her right back down.

The female lost her grip on the tiny knife, then Arianna plunged it into the female's stomach.

She did it again and again, tearing through flesh and clothes, refusing to stop. Crimson stained the female's white coat and she cried out, frantic and desperate to escape.

She braced and tried to rise again, but Arianna sank her teeth into the female's neck, holding her in place. The iron burned her other wrist, her ankles, her legs, and torso as her magic danced, ready to break free, but held itself back.

It crackled beneath her skin, a raging beast as feral as she felt. Arianna plunged the blade into the female's stomach again and drove it as deep as she could without losing her grip.

The female thrashed, but Arianna didn't release her hold with either her teeth or the blade.

"Please," the female pleaded. "Please, don't kill me. I have a family. I have a youngling."

Arianna released her neck, then slammed her forehead into the female's again. She didn't care how much it hurt.

"The key," Arianna demanded, blood rolling down her chin.

"I—I can't." Arianna withdrew the blade and sank it deeper. The female cried out. "He—he'll kill me."

"And what do you think I'm going to do if you don't?" Fear shone brightly in the female's gaze, but Arianna didn't waver. She was tired of the same excuses. She had people to protect too, and she'd kill to get to them if that's what it took. "Your choice."

"Y—You won't make it down the hall. There are guards—" Arianna twisted the blade and the female cried out.

"Unlock. Me. Now."

"My pocket," The female choked out.

"Get it." The female reached down slowly, her hands shaking with pain, and withdrew a small silver key. "My chest first."

The small round key entered the lock and twisted. Arianna threw the offending bar aside, then grabbed the key, popping it in her mouth before shoving the female off the table. Her body collided with the hard floor and Arianna quickly unlocked her other hand, sat up and freed her ankles.

Her magic exploded.

In seconds, ice coated the entire room. It had spread from her body in a violent wave, crawling up the walls and covering the female's body even as she tried to scramble away.

The female screamed, but Arianna reined the magic in, preventing it from doing more than coating her skin in a thin layer of frost.

She hid in the corner, her teeth chattering as she looked Arianna up and down.

"Will this key open the other doors?"

The female nodded, her body shaking violently. Maybe an old version of herself would have healed the female despite working for Niall, but Arianna felt no such compassion now.

She slid from the table, her bare feet hitting the ice. Anyone else might have recoiled, but warmth floated through her, wrapping her body in a pleasant embrace.

Her magic crackled in the air and creature within her hummed, ready just as she was to tear everything apart. Tiny spears of ice materialized around her head, floating as she crossed the room.

"You won't make it."

Arianna tilted her head back. "I will and I'm hunting down that piece of shit you all claim as a High Lord."

Arianna turned away and peered through the small window at the top of the door. People were racing back and forth. Their voices were muffled, but she knew they'd likely heard the female's scream.

Arianna yanked it open and stepped into the hall.

Five males and three females stood on the other side, some with shackles in their hands, others with vials that likely held some sort of concoction to render her unconscious.

She nearly smirked. As if she'd let that happen.

Arianna let the creature within burst free. Hundreds of icicles surged forward, impaling each one with enough force to send them crashing to the floor.

None rose again.

Her magic tugged Arianna forward, begging her to hurry, hurry, hurry. She took off running. Ice crackled at her feet with every step. It spread to the walls, seeping through the cracks, diving deeper and deeper, racing toward their destination.

More doors slammed open and Arianna ducked around weapons and magic fired at her. Arrows, flames, small balls of what she could only assume were iron.

None hit their mark.

She saw everything with unnatural clarity, her magic reading the movements and relaying them faster than her brain could process.

She closed the distance. One male reached out with his hands and Arianna gripped his wrist, tearing the water from his entire limb before solidifying it into a spear and firing it at his companions. She ducked around fire as it spun toward her and froze the flames midair. They crashed to the ground, shattering into hundreds of tiny shards.

A vine lashed out next and Arianna engulfed it in ice, stopping it in its tracks before sending it right back at the female.

Arianna threw the remaining few against the wall then sprinted down the hall again, that pull tugging at her very soul.

She didn't know what it meant or how to make sense of it. She just knew if it vanished, the world would fall and everything she'd been fighting for would cease to exist.

CHAPTER THIRTY-NINE

TALON

Raevina was fine, thank the gods. Zylah and Gavin only carried minor injuries, though neither had spoken much since their release. He understood the haunting fear on Gavin's face. He'd experienced it himself. To think that Vairik really would discard one of his family members as if they were nothing—Talon shook his head, regretting for the first time the way he'd treated the young male.

Talon placed a hand over his face, right where that mask had been. He'd felt the contraption, whatever it was called, pulling at his magic, stealing it from his body as he floated there completely helpless. A quiet humming had engulfed him, suffocating him. He'd lost count of how many times he'd passed out.

It was the first time Talon had ever experienced iron. The first time he'd ever felt so … defeated.

Talon's gaze drifted to Saoirse. She was the worst of the lot. Someone had stitched the wounds that needed it, but she'd ripped them open while looking for Zylah. Zylah was currently looking her over, ensuring the female wouldn't bleed out. He didn't fully understand the forlorn expression on Saoirse's face, but he noted the way she wouldn't meet Zylah's gaze.

His eyes moved to Rion last, looking the male up and down as he leaned against the far wall, still clutching his chest. Rion watched his sister, concern etched across his features along with unrelenting pain. His breath was ragged, as if whatever he was feeling was nearly unbearable.

He'd said the bond was gone. The fact weighed on all of them. But Vairik wanted the pair to rid the world of the bond. He'd been waiting centuries. He wouldn't kill either of them so easily, which meant he'd done something to Arianna.

Talon clenched his fists. The two were thwarted at every turn. Just when they thought they were about to reach a place of happiness, outside forces came along to break them apart.

To know that Vairik had targeted Rion for his entire life—Talon had his own apologies to make. When he'd seen Raevina on the ground, he'd attacked Rion without reservation, ready to kill him once and for all. His actions were inexcusable, even if Vairik had been manipulating him.

Talon had spent so much time fighting against The Demon that his mind hadn't realized Rion was a separate person. That The Demon had been a façade to ensure his survival over the years. And that some of the deaths might not have even been his direct doing.

How many times had Rion's mind been manipulated into believing an innocent person was an enemy? How many of those deaths belonged to Vairik alone?

"We're wasting time," Saoirse said. She tried rising from the floor and nearly fell.

Zylah caught her and draped Saoirse's arm over her shoulder. "You shouldn't be moving."

"Yeah, well, I don't have a choice, do I?" Saoirse looked up at Rion. "Let's go find her."

"Here," Raevina handed Talon a pair of daggers along with a holster, then passed out a few more. "It's all they had. We can grab more along the way."

Talon buckled the belt around his waist and inserted the two daggers. They were meager compared to what he usually carried, but some weapons were better than none. They had their magic, but judging by the way Rion's kept jerking, he'd be leading their path of destruction anyway.

Rion pushed off the wall and they moved down the hall as fast as Saoirse could manage. Zylah had done her best to treat Saoirse's injuries with runes, which seemed to relieve some of the pain, but just as Sive had mentioned, it wasn't as fast acting as Arianna's magic.

The group paused before a set of staircases. One led up, where Vairik's study was likely to reside. The other led down, back to the dungeons.

"Which way?" Raevina asked.

Rion gripped his chest harder as they all turned to him. "I don't know."

"You do," Zylah countered. "Focus past the pain. Even with a severed bond, you'll still be able to find her."

Talon saw the way Rion's throat bobbed. Fear drifted off him. If he couldn't find that tether, no matter how small, then that would mean—

They all fell silent as Rion stared at the floor, his gaze vacant. The seconds ticked by and Zylah used the time to continue tracing runes over Saoirse's leg. If they could get her running, it would make getting to Arianna easier. Faster.

Talon glanced down the hall again, eyeing the bubbling vials lining the walls. His stomach turned, knowing the body parts within were likely all Fae. He just didn't understand why they'd been kept. Did Vairik believe he'd found pieces of the bond in them? Could he siphon a Fae's magic even in death? Or was he using the bits to incubate something more sinister?

"Down," Rion suddenly said and Talon whirled to find Rion's magic flaring, tearing at the stones in the corners. A fierce determination flashed through his eyes, replacing the hollow grief from earlier.

"She's down."

The male practically sprinted for the stairs and the rest of them followed. A small smile spread across Talon's face. She was alive.

Hold on, Arianna. We're coming.

Chapter Forty

Arianna

*I*nstead of fighting, Arianna quickly left the chaos behind. Fae were screaming and howling in pain as she let her magic cover everything in her wake. She didn't have time to see who died or survived. Not with the urgency pulsing through her, urging her down, down, down.

Run.

Hurry.

Something was pulling her into the depths of the castle, drawing her in with magnetic force.

Something.

Or someone.

She kept sprinting, bounding down staircase after staircase, weaving through halls, and passageways until it all just … ended.

Arianna carefully stepped into the silent, dark hall. The sconces lining either side only held a small flame, telling her they might blink out any moment. She scented the air, tasting blood and fear.

Large cells spread along the walls, each door torn through as if some giant creature had burst free.

Arianna inched forward on silent feet, keeping her breathing even. She peered into the first cell and covered her nose, trying to block out the stench of rot and decay. Straw littered the floor in a corner. A nest. Bones were scattered around the enclosure as well, with flies buzzing between chunks of flesh that she didn't want to examine too closely.

She should creep right back up those stairs, find a different route, but Arianna couldn't turn away, not when her magic was begging her to move faster. It promised that whatever she sought waited right at the other end of this hall.

Arianna crept through the gloom, staying close to one of the walls. As her feet scraped across bits of dirt and unknown debris, Arianna found herself thankful she'd stolen someone's shoes, even if they were a bit too large.

Something crunched just ahead and cold dread swept through her like a biting winter wind. She paused to listen, then crossed to the other side of the hall. Whatever it was resided in the cell just ahead.

Rustling, then the sound of something tearing had Arianna cringing. She shuffled forward, bent slightly to make herself smaller, then peered around the edge of the wall.

A thick muscled frame stood hunched over near the rear of the cell. Tufts of black fur jutted out at awkward angles. It stood on all fours like a giant dog. Its head pulled back again and she heard the distinct sound of bones crunching between its massive jaws.

Bile rose in her throat when she glimpsed a limp hand laying in the straw.

Now she understood exactly why Conall had wanted to rescue the prisoners. If they weren't experimented on, they were used for fodder. Arianna hoped the victims had been brought in dead. She doubted Vairik would be so merciful.

Arianna had encountered a similar creature when the Dark Fae had attacked the village, back when she'd been standing beside—beside—she shook her head. This one looked even bigger. It was at least six times her size with enough muscle to rip her to shreds with little effort.

Arianna looked past the cell. It was only a matter of time before the beast finished its meal, then went searching for the next. Her eyes traveled to the open door. The latch appeared intact. If she moved fast, she could close it and trap the creature inside long enough for her to sprint down the hall.

She craned her neck to listen, hoping the other cells were empty. Maybe Vairik had summoned them to attack another innocent village. Her fists clenched. She needed to destroy them, but she needed to get to Vairik first.

Perhaps that was where her magic was leading her. It seemed to hate the High Lord more than she did. Arianna recalled the conversation she'd had with Vairik in his study. What had he called her magic? Laoise?

Arianna returned her attention to the door as another crunch resounded through the silent space. She prayed the beast wouldn't be very agile with a full stomach.

Arianna loosed a quiet breath, then moved, sprinting on nearly silent feet. She grabbed the door and yanked, slamming her full body weight against it. The hinges let out a shrill shriek that had the creature spinning to face her. It charged without hesitation. Arianna grabbed the latch and dropped it into place right as the beast slammed against the thick door with a resounding thud.

Arianna fell back, landing on the dirty floor as she watched it relentlessly pound against the door over and over again.

The iron bent inward and Arianna staggered to her feet before sprinting down the hall. It roared after her, its fury sending a spike of fear straight down her spine.

She didn't slow and passed cell after empty cell as she kept running. The hall split, but her magic urged her left and Arianna followed it, squinting in the dark. No cells here, just a long corridor with the same barely lit sconces.

Something prickled against the back of her mind and Arianna skidded to an abrupt halt. She cursed beneath her breath and searched for any signs of a glamour. The cracks were still on the walls and the sconces hadn't changed. Had she entered some sort of barrier?

Arianna growled into the gloom, searching for anyone who might be hiding in the shadows. Her magic reacted too, coating the area around her feet. It crawled up the walls, forming thick, jagged spears of ice.

She kept moving, following the guide of her magic one step at a time.

Click. Click. Click.

The hair rose on the back of Arianna's neck. She pressed herself against the damp wall and stared down the hall from where she'd come.

Click. Click. Click.

A shadow grew along the floor and Arianna's heart beat faster. A low growl echoed off the walls, then the creature from the cell prowled around the corner, pausing and turning its head as if it knew exactly where she'd gone.

Click. Click. Click.

Arianna's heart sank as another appeared beside it, standing twice as tall as the first. The broken doors suddenly made sense.

Arianna didn't move, hoping beyond hope that they might not see her in the shadows. But the larger one sniffed the air then something dropped from its mouth. Whatever it was slapped against the stone floor. She shuddered.

The larger of the two sank back on its haunches then barreled straight for her. Arianna's magic exploded.

A shield of thick ice covered the entirety of the hall and she shoved it forward, hoping it might knock the creatures back. The large beast burst through the thickened glass with little effort, sending shards flying in every direction.

Arianna sent ice skimming along the floor, and the beast slipped, slamming its massive head on the ground before scrambling to its feet. The smaller one chased it, followed by several others that had just appeared.

She quickly formed several large spears, launched them at the creatures, then ran in the opposite direction as fast as her legs could carry her. Arianna kept freezing the ground in her wake and her magic shot out from the walls in thick jagged spikes. She prayed the spikes would slow the creatures down.

The clicking behind her didn't cease. It grew closer and closer and Arianna swore she could feel their hot breath against the back of her neck.

She covered the floor ahead in a thin sheet of ice, then dropped down to slide around the next corner right as one of the beasts dove for her. It collided hard with the wall and one of its claws cut the bottom part of Arianna's leg. She cursed from the pain but forced her body to keep moving.

Arianna peered behind her to find more beasts colliding with the first, stopping them all momentarily as they clambered over one another to rise again.

Her magic pulsed beneath her skin, the creature within her rising as if it had been holding itself back; for what, Arianna didn't know.

She spun and let the magic burst from her very bones. It coated the hallway in seconds, then crawled over the beasts, freezing them into a heap of solid masses that didn't move again. Arianna collapsed, breathing hard as she stared at them. At least a dozen. Gods, what was Vairik breeding down here? Had they previously been Fae or were these the dark creatures she'd been warned about as a child?

A burning sensation pulled her focus down to her leg and Arianna twisted it to examine her calf. Blood poured from the wound. She grimaced, then dipped her fingers into the crimson liquid and drew one of the runes Sive had beaten into her brain.

It glowed, then part of the skin stitched itself together. It did nothing for the pain, but at least it wasn't bleeding as much as it had been.

Crack.

The sound sent a chilling wave of dread through her.

Crack.

It echoed against the walls. Arianna stood, watching in horror as spider web cracks spread from one end of the frozen Dark Fae to the other.

A chunk fell off, revealing the largest one's mouth. It snarled, then its front leg exploded from the frozen mass.

How? She'd never—another piece of ice broke off, then Arianna turned and sprinted down the hall. Maybe she'd find a narrow staircase somewhere that they couldn't follow her through. She'd seen enough small doors and nearly hidden steps to tell her the castle was littered with them.

But the walls were solid here, as if the creator had only intended there to be one way in or out.

A roar echoed from down the hall and Arianna turned to find the large creature bounding toward her. Her magic swelled and rose before darting out to encase the creature again.

The resounding silence was short lived as the ice began cracking again.

Arianna stepped back. Everything that had ever been hit with her magic had been frozen inside and out. Were these creatures impervious to magic entirely or just hers?

She didn't have time to think as the others slid around the corner.

Arianna took off running again, throwing spear after spear of ice in her wake. It was only now that she realized they weren't hitting.

She sprinted around another corner and nearly cried at the sight of light flooding the end of the tunnel. She could escape. As soon as she entered the room ahead, she'd find another door, hopefully one more narrow where they couldn't follow.

Arianna sprinted faster, her heart and lungs burning. She could feel the pull just ahead. She was close. So, so close.

Arianna glanced behind and gritted her teeth. She summoned her magic to her fingertips and with one big pull, Arianna spun and let her magic burst from the center of her body.

It grew from the floor and ceiling, one part of a wall rising up while the other raced down until the two collided, thickening as it spread back to the wall, then inward again.

She knew it wouldn't hold. It didn't matter. She just needed enough time to make it down the hall.

Arianna kept her magic flowing, growing the wall thicker and thicker until the first body slammed against it.

 Just a little further.

In seconds, she emerged from the dark passageway and shielded her eyes against the offending light. She squinted up toward a balcony, right where her magic had led her.

And stared straight into the eyes of the High Lord of Pádraigín.

Chapter Forty-One

Arianna

Arianna stood in an underground colosseum. It was the only way she could think to describe the large circular space with a high ceiling and rows upon rows of stone benches that lined the area above.

Before her, nearly a dozen of the creatures she'd just escaped were chained to the back wall with short leashes and thick collars holding them in place. Five Fae stood evenly disbursed between them, just out of reach of snapping teeth. Their hands were clasped neatly behind their backs and they stood with their shoulders squared, awaiting instruction.

But it was the Fae male slightly above them that drew her attention. Not Vairik, the one hanging below the self-proclaimed High Lord.

His body hung from the wall, pinned there with swords, knives, a spear, and a thick spike of wood that had been driven straight through his heart.

Lacerations covered his body and shards of glass protruded from every inch of his flesh as if he'd been dragged across a mirror.

Conall.

His heart no longer beat and his body carried a scent that told her he'd been dead for a while. Her mouth gaped. Gods, how long had Vairik tortured him? How long had she been in captivity? Had Conall's warriors been captured as well? Is that who the beast in the cell been—

Gods. Gods above.

Arianna's gaze shifted with movement to her left. Her eyes misted when she spotted Talon. He was safe, but judging from the blood on his clothes, he'd had his own battle on the way here. Had Vairik's presence drawn them in as well?

Raevina stood beside him, weapon in hand, her furious gaze locked on the male above. Zylah had Saoirse's arm draped across her shoulder. She looked like the only thing keeping Saoirse on her feet. Gavin's face was paler than she'd ever seen it as he stared at Conall's lifeless form. And beside Gavin—

Arianna's breath hitched when a triumphant roar echoed down the hall accompanied by the sound of thundering feet. She spun around and her magic wrapped around her body, ready to defend herself no matter how futile. She should have grabbed weapons off the Fae she'd incapacitated. They would have done more than her magic.

A set of thick iron bars slammed down from the top of the open passageway and the creatures rammed right into them, the impact hard enough to shatter bone. They roared again in frustration biting and clawing at the iron. The sounds sent the other ones into a frenzy. They bucked and thrashed against their chains until Vairik's voice rang out above the chaos.

"Enough." A violent wind tore through the area. It hit the chained Dark Fae first and the massive creatures whimpered before cowering against the wall. The Fae between them didn't move, as if they were statues guarding the invisible line separating the beasts from freedom.

The violent air kicked up mounds of dust and hit her so hard she stumbled back. Arianna shielded her eyes with one arm.

The biting air hit the creatures behind the bars next and they quickly backed away, lowering their heads but never taking their eyes off her.

Arianna's gaze moved back to Talon, then snagged on the other male. His eyes were full of—something. Concern? Relief? His lips were parted and his gaze ran up and down her form as if counting every scrape across her skin.

Her magic jerked toward him and she furrowed her brow in confusion.

"Well, my son certainly didn't do a good job at containing your lot."

Arianna bared her teeth, but her face quickly fell slack as a lone figure ambled into view from the opening in the wall behind him.

She was dressed differently now, in brown leather instead of the black but her hair was still up in a braid that crowned her head. Arianna's eyes scanned her little sister's body. No chains. No marks.

"Ellie." The name slipped from her like a plea.

Another figure limped behind her, the unmistakable sound of chains rattling with each step. Kirian's face was haggard, his face hollow and worn. He kept his eyes on the floor until he caught sight of them. Arianna heard his heart jolt.

"Get out of here," he screamed, his voice hoarse. Neither Ellie nor Vairik reacted. When Arianna didn't move, Kirian yelled again. "She's not right, you have to—"

Ellie spun and planted her elbow in Kirian's solar plexus. The male gasped in pain and doubled over coughing, then sank to his knees on the cold stone balcony.

"How many times have I told you to keep your mouth shut?" Arianna blanched at her sister's harsh words. Ellie just stood again, her lips curled in disgust. She'd just—was it all an act? Was she being forced to serve Vairik in order to keep Kirian alive?

A wide smile spread across Vairik's scarred face.

"Evelyn has quite a temper, as I'm sure you're aware." His hands wrapped around the railing, one finger tapping it in a slow repetitive motion. "Now what are we going to do with you? Every single one of you escaped, which leads me to believe my warriors are just as incompetent as they've always been." He sighed. "I suppose I should have known better than to leave *him* in anyone else's hands. He did escape once, after all. It's my own mistake for assuming it wouldn't happen again."

Arianna followed his gaze to the other male in the room. Sweat rolled down his face as he glared at Vairik, those fierce green eyes pinning him in place.

"And you," Arianna refocused on Vairik when he addressed her. "I suppose you have her spirit. Laoise was always … unpredictable." He said the words with pride and Arianna's magic surged and shot toward him, but it wasn't Vairik who blocked the attack. Ellie held up one hand and her magic collided with Arianna's, exploding in the center of the space. Shards of ice rained down over their heads.

The beasts growled and backed away, snapping their teeth at the offending magic. Saliva dripped from their massive canines and their claws dug into the ground with impatience.

Ellie growled, her gaze darkening as she glared at Arianna. The magic within Arianna hesitated, pacing within her as if it hadn't expected this outcome.

Was this just another of Vairik's illusions? Was Ellie really in front of them or was it someone else?

No, this wasn't an illusion, it couldn't be. She'd been subjected to various glamours already. She'd felt Vairik in her mind, tearing through it as he pleased. This was real, which meant Ellie needed her help.

Arianna searched her sister's gaze, hoping to find some hidden plea behind her eyes. Did she want them to run or fight? If they got Kirian to safety would she cease this façade? Or was there something else holding her back?

But Ellie's hard stare was unflinching, filled with a darkness Arianna didn't recognize.

"Let's not drag this out," Vairik said. "As you can plainly see, Evelyn is in good hands, so be good little experiments and get back in your cages before something happens that you'll regret."

Vairik lifted one hand and the five Fae beneath him drew their weapons. Flames and shadows rose to surround Raevina. Ice materialized around Talon. Saoirse, despite her injured state, summoned the plant life from beneath the stone. Wind whipped around Gavin and Zylah. And that male, that strange male summoned the very stone at his feet. It rose up to circle his body, winding around him and her friends.

Earth. There was only one Fae said to be able to use that kind of magic. Only one cursed to wield nothing more than dirt and rock.

Arianna's heart thundered in her chest, but Talon wasn't running from him and neither were the others. Had they—she didn't have time to finish her thought as the Fae rushed forward. More jumped from the balcony above with magic, steel, and iron in their grip.

The creature within her roared and Arianna let it burst free. It was angry, so very angry.

Water shot toward those still falling and wrapped around four, shifting to ice in an instant. They shattered like glass upon hitting the ground. The beasts lunged for any pieces that rolled in their path, crunching the frozen chunks of flesh between their teeth.

Sand and stone shot across the floor and grabbed the legs of six others, crushing them faster than she could blink. They screamed out in pain, grasping at the limbs that would never function again.

She turned her head to him again, studying the male. His eyes drifted toward her, seeming to carry an apology she couldn't decipher. Their gazes broke as more Fae joined the fray.

Raevina surged forward, melting skin from bones as she fought, stealing knives and launching them at opponents across the colosseum floor. She shifted into a small bird, diving around another body before shifting back and sinking a blade through his neck.

Talon followed her, hoarfrost coating everything he touched. He grabbed a Fae's arm and ripped the water from his entire body, rendering him nothing more than a husk before reaching for the next.

Zylah was tracing runes over Saoirse's leg, over and over again while constantly looking over her shoulder. Saoirse looked ready to explode, but she stood back, using her magic whenever one of the enemy came too close. Gavin stared up at Ellie, his mouth gaping, but the young male quickly collected himself and helped Saoirse keep their enemies at bay.

One of the chains broke and a beast charged straight for her. Arianna braced herself, her magic sinking deep into the floor, then deeper, parts of it veering from her grasp.

A rock jutted up suddenly from beneath the beast, impaling it straight through. The creature kicked its feet and howled in pain. Arianna's gaze met The Demon's. He nodded to her as though they were allies.

But ... why?

More chains broke and each of the Dark Fae focused on a target, almost as if they'd been directed. Fire bubbled in one's mouth and fear flew through her as she remembered the Dark Fae that had attacked the village. A brief glance at Vairik told her he was enjoying their distress. But Ellie—Ellie was smiling, too.

Kirian had righted himself, but Arianna was forced to look away as she dove to the side, avoiding a stream of molten fire. She cringed from the heat that had narrowly missed. Earth rose around her body and Arianna rolled, separating herself from the monstrous magic. She glanced up at the male, wondering if he was playing both sides. Or maybe he'd been working for Vairik all along.

Talon hadn't turned, but he was also focused on Raevina and his own fight with two of the beasts who seemed immune to his magic as well.

The male stared back, his brow furrowed, clearly confused by her reaction. Then sorrow covered his face. Sorrow? No, that wasn't right, a creature like him couldn't experience such a complex emotion.

The Demon's magic reached for more of the creatures, crushing their bodies in seconds. She did the same, shooting her magic at any that drew too close to her or her companions.

It was chaos. All of it. The Fae fighting, doing Vairik's bidding.

The Dark Fae from legend, breathing fire. The Demon, tearing everything apart, aiding them.. Her sister enjoying the show at Vairik's side.

Ellie jumped from the balcony and Arianna watched her sister's rapid descent. One of the beasts turned on her when she landed and Arianna's heart jolted. Ellie ducked, then slid under the creature's belly, dragging her blade along the entire length of it. It curled in on itself like a dying spider then thrashed, rolling across the floor in agony. Ellie stood without looking back, her attention fixated on Arianna.

"This is taking too long."

Vairik didn't stop her, but he said, "We must learn patience, dear Evelyn." Ellie gave him a vulgar gesture over her shoulder.

A wicked smile Arianna didn't recognize covered her sister's face. Ellie adjusted the grip on her blade, then rushed forward.

Arianna barely had time to react to Ellie's speed as she ducked around her sister's blade and danced back. Ellie moved with her, step after step after step. It took every ounce of concentration to keep out of range.

"What are you doing?" Arianna demanded, but her sister leapt, closing the distance. Arianna summoned a thickened spear of ice to block the blade aimed at her neck. It slipped off the ice, but Ellie brought it up again with lightning speed. Ellie's magic zigzagged across the ground before suddenly spreading. Arianna slipped, then Ellie was on top of her, pressing her long knife down on Arianna's spear of ice. Arianna thickened the blade.

"Submit," Ellie demanded. "So we can all be free."

Arianna gritted her teeth, pushing against her sibling. "What are you talking about?"

Ellie cocked her head in a way that had a chill sweeping down Arianna's spine. "Didn't he explain the new world to you?"

Ellie pushed harder, but Arianna bucked her sister off and rolled to her feet. "What's the matter with you?" Arianna lowered her voice. "Talon can grab Kirian, we can escape. You're fr—"

Ellie shot forward, closing the space again, but instead of her sword swiping up, Ellie slammed her head into Arianna's. Stars shot across her vision, then the ground yawned open between them. Ellie jumped back, as did Arianna, determined not to let that male's magic catch her within its grip. Talon had warned her to avoid it at all costs.

"Get out of here!" Kirian's voice rang out again. "You can't win. He's too strong. He has Ellie in—"

His air was cut off as Vairik snatched Kirian's neck and lifted him from the ground. The world paused. Kirian kicked his feet, tugging at Vairik's hand in vain. Then Vairik threw him over the edge of the railing.

Talon lunged for Kirian, his magic racing across the ground, but one of the creatures snapped their teeth too close to Talon's arm, breaking his concentration. Talon pivoted around the beast and shot his magic out again.

It slowed Kirian's fall, but not enough. The half-breed's leg snapped when it hit the ground, the bone protruding at an awkward angle. Kirian howled from the pain. He braced against it, forcing himself up to meet Arianna's gaze.

Ellie darted for him, jumping over the creatures and rubble.

"Knock her out," Kirian bit out through gritted teeth, forcing himself to stand on one leg. "It's the only way she'll go. Distance will help and—"

His voice cut off again. Not due to Vairik or the creatures, or the remaining Fae, but by Ellie.

Their entire world froze and Arianna's mouth fell open as she stared at the blade that had been plunged straight through Kirian's gut.

Kirian grasped the long knife, staring at it wide-eyed. He looked up at Ellie next, then Ellie drove it deeper, twisting the blade before yanking it straight up through the male's torso.

Talon roared, Raevina and the others with him as they fought with renewed vigor, as if to defy the inevitable. But Arianna had frozen, staring at her sister and the absolute fury in her eyes.

Kirian's arm shook as he raised a bloody hand to Ellie's cheek and smiled at her. "I love you," he whispered, breath ragged. "And when you wake from this nightmare," his body jerked, "know I forgive you."

Kirian leaned forward, his head angling up, lips ready to brush against Ellie's—his body collapsed, his head falling to her chest instead. Ellie let the blade slip from her hands. Kirian's body hit the ground, his heart stopping on impact.

Ellie stared at him, unmoving, but a single tear slipped down her cheek. She didn't even bother wiping it away before she kicked his body into the reach of the Dark Fae.

Arianna watched in horror as the creatures tore Kirian's limbs apart. She shuddered at the sound of his tearing flesh and clenched her teeth with the noise of crunching bone.

Kirian. Kirian was gone.

Ellie turned away, looking at them as though she hadn't just killed the only male she'd ever loved.

"Release them all," Ellie commanded.

The remaining Fae didn't even bother confirming with Vairik before unlatching the rest of the chains.

Arianna stared at her sister, stared and wondered if this was all just a horrible nightmare. In a minute, she'd wake up and they'd all be back in Levea, surrounded by peaceful waterfalls and familiar faces. Arianna would walk out her door and see Ellie and Kirian hand in hand, laughing with one another as they walked down the estate halls.

Kirian would kiss the back of her sister's hand and Ellie would blush before he moved her hair back and told her how beautiful she was. Arianna would find them in the library after lunch, pouring over books and documents that neither should have access to.

Then she'd find them under the waterfalls, resting in the grass as they watched the sun set below the horizon. They'd laugh and lie awake for half the night watching the stars.

The beasts lifted their heads from their finished meal and stood behind Ellie, blood dripping from their stained maws.

Ellie's eyes were vacant. She was devoid of everything. Everything aside from the strange anger brewing within those blue eyes. An anger that wasn't her own.

The Demon stepped forward and his voice shook. "And you have the audacity to call me a monster."

Vairik clicked his tongue. "What a rude thing to call our dear Evelyn."

Another tear rolled down Ellie's face, but she only adjusted the grip on her weapon again.

Arianna's body shook as grief and anger flooded her heart. Tears spilled over, trailing down her cheeks.

She turned toward one of the fallen Fae. Her magic wrapped around the hilt of a blade and Arianna pulled it to her hand.

The iron gate lifted behind her and the creatures burst out, all charging at full speed.

Arianna twisted to face the new enemy, keeping an eye on her sister who looked ready to join the fray.

The Demon's magic lifted too, then shot toward the beasts, capturing three of them in his grasp.

Arianna felt her magic resist her call, too taut to respond. She focused on the surge that was still making its way underground, digging past the rock, creating an entrance where there was none.

A Dark Fae jumped past The Demon's magic. He cursed, but she summoned her own magic and threw a handful of shards at the creature's face. It howled and stumbled back, scratching its eyes. Arianna ran forward, blade in hand, and sank the sword straight into the creature's foreleg.

It stumbled back again but Arianna's magic raced for the wound, entering the slit she'd just created. The water moved inside the creature, heating hotter and hotter until the beast's very blood began to boil.

It fell on its side, thrashing and clawing at itself until Arianna sent her magic straight to its heart and squeezed tight.

The beast fell silent and though snapping teeth and clanging steal still surrounded her, Arianna glanced up at Vairik. Niall stood beside him, entertained by the events unfolding below.

The floor rumbled beneath her feet, nearly knocking her off balance. Arianna cursed, then dared a glance toward The Demon, wondering if he was the one responsible. His gaze was locked on Vairik. She'd never seen so much malice from a single person before.

Not allies, then. Had Vairik brought The Demon here to experiment on him?

More iron grates lifted, the heavy chains creaking as if they hadn't been moved in a few human lifetimes. Beasts and Fae trickled in and Arianna's heart sank.

They were just going to keep coming. She was certain Vairik wouldn't run out of Dark Fae or warriors anytime soon. Not with how many centuries he'd had to plan everything out. He would watch them fight until their last breath, then clamp iron around their wrists and do as he pleased.

He'd make Talon watch as he tore Raevina apart. He'd kill Zylah for being a half-breed and Gavin for being a traitor. Saoirse would likely be used as a pawn against Brónach.

Arianna shot a glance toward the hall from where she'd come. If she combined her magic with The Demon's, they might have a chance at escape. Unlikely allies for a time, sure, but they were out of alternatives.

Arianna watched the creatures prowl in, one after another. But it wasn't just the fire-breathing beasts this time. These creatures possessed wings and elongated fangs. Barbed tails and deadly claws.

Ellie merely stood in center of them, uncaring about the danger that lurked right behind her. She was like a puppet on center stage.

Arianna's gaze flicked back to The Demon. She might be able to rely on his need for survival, but Talon was the only one she could trust to get Ellie out alive.

Knock her out, Kirian had instructed.

She gritted her teeth, ready for the fight, but something below her was building, draining her energy against her will as magic kept pouring from her body.

Then the colosseum floor split in two.

CHAPTER FORTY-TWO

RION

"What have you done?" For the first time, Vairik seemed unsure of himself as he watched the earth split the entirety of the colosseum in half. Everyone turned to face him, but Rion lifted his arms. He was as clueless as the rest.

Another crack and steam burst from the fissure, rising up to coat the air. The heat from it had Rion shielding his face with one arm.

Arianna.

Rion looked at his mate. He could feel her magic pulsing through the droplets in the air, each one under her control. A queen ready to make her final stand even if she had to bring down the castle itself.

His gaze traveled to her injured leg and Rion's blood boiled at the sight. But it was her strange behavior that concerned him the most.

She'd been afraid of his magic since the day he'd hurt her, but she'd never outright fled from it. He wanted to help protect her, yet she wouldn't allow it.

And when she'd first seen him in the colosseum, she'd barely glanced his way. But none of them had time to address that now. Not when Ellie had just killed the male she loved and Saoirse was barely on her feet. And certainly not with Vairik's sinister plan in mind.

Another crack in the floor and Rion's magic strummed through his body, answering the call of Arianna's magic. It had always done that, but something about this moment was different. It felt like their energies were two sentient beings conversing. Plotting.

The ground shook beneath their feet again and another crack crawled along the left wall before more boiling steam burst into the room.

Vairik gripped the railing above, his brow furrowing. Then Rion scented his anger, a blast of ancient magic rising up from his body.

Arianna's magic was more volatile than even his own, fed by an equally ancient rage he'd never seen from her. If she suffered from the emptiness of the bond, she didn't show it.

Rion clenched his jaw and resisted the urge to reach for his chest. Even with Arianna standing right beside him, he could scarcely breathe.

But she *was* beside him. She was safe and alive and the most beautiful thing he'd ever laid eyes on. A few moments alone, a few days and the bond would rebuild.

But first they had to get out of here. Alive and with Ellie.

The Dark Fae lunged, plunging their world into chaos. He kept an eye on his mate, trying to stay as close to Arianna's side as she'd allow.

She kept backing away and avoided his magic at all costs. He caught her eyeing him, her gaze wary as if he were the enemy.

Rion glared at Vairik. That blasted male had tampered with Ellie's mind; there was no reason to assume he hadn't done the same with Arianna's.

One of the beasts lunged and his heart broke all over again when Arianna cried out in pain. He blasted everything surrounding them and ripped the hound off her body with his bare hands.

Earth and rock crushed the creature before it even hit the ground. He knelt at Arianna's side, his knees scraping against the hard stone. He reached for the wound, ready to draw a rune with his own blood, but a thin layer of frost crawled up his arms, and Rion stilled.

She crawled backward before stumbling to her feet, her chest heaving.

She'd never done that before. Not even when she'd been terrified of his magic.

Rion's heart thundered as he recognized the look in her eyes. The same look everyone else always gave him.

The floor cracked beneath their feet, along the walls, across the continent and in his heart.

"Stop," Vairik bellowed, a tinge of fear in his voice.

Another burst of steam and Rion struggled to see beyond himself and Arianna. Then the entire castle shook, threatening to topple from its foundation. He felt it with his magic first, a burning fire rising up, up, up until molten rock spewed from the crack directly below Vairik. It consumed the dark creatures and Fae who were unfortunate enough to be standing too close.

Ellie stepped away, her face a twisted grimace at the sudden interruption.

He didn't know how Arianna had done it or why or if she was even aware. But when another crack crawled up the wall, Rion realized she'd just sealed this entire castle's fate.

"It's time to go, Evelyn," Vairik commanded. His voice was far too calm for someone who knew everything they'd worked for was about to come crashing down.

Rion looked up at Conall's lifeless body. Whatever information they'd hoped to gather, whatever people they'd hoped to free, it had all been for nothing. They'd died for absolutely nothing.

Ellie huffed but obeyed, pivoting and craning her next back to stare up at Vairik's retreating form.

Rion's heart jolted. If she left with him now, there was no telling if or when they'd ever see her again. That monster had already made Ellie do something that would haunt her for the rest of her life. If he didn't grab her now, there might not be an Ellie to bring back at all.

Rion had lived his entire life doing unspeakable things because of this monster and his games. He'd be damned if he let Ellie suffer the same fate.

Another fissure erupted and Raevina stepped into the path of the fiery blast, using her magic to bend the spraying rock in another direction. He felt Arianna's magic race across the space to subdue it.

Ellie crouched and ice spread around her feet.

Now.

She jumped but Rion sent a tendril of magic snaking after her. It wrapped around her ankle and yanked her right back to the ground. She landed on her hands and knees before flipping over and baring her teeth at him.

Rion looked up again, but Vairik and Niall were already gone, leaving their new pawn to either live or die. The male likely didn't care either way. She was just another tool in his game. Another piece he could move or discard without much thought or care.

Ellie's magic shot across the space, but Rion summoned his own only to find the molten rock itself responding. He yanked it up to block the ice. It sizzled between them, and more steam clouded the air. Rion winced again from the heat, his skin feeling like it would melt right off his bones.

He sprinted across the space, turning the molten liquid beneath his feet to solid rock. It did little to ease the heat and he swore the bottoms of his shoes were melting into his flesh.

Ellie's eyes widened and she tried to step back, but Rion was faster. He snatched her wrist and forced it behind her back. Ice jutted from the ground, aiming for his body, but Rion summoned the earth to block it strike for strike. She swung her other arm around, but Rion grabbed it too, then shoved her to the ground. He grimaced when her face collided with the hard earth.

Ellie screamed and bucked. Frost crawled up his hands and her fingertips reached for him. Rion encased them in earth. One touch and Ellie would disable him for the rest of his life.

The ice just kept coming and the frost on his arms was spreading. He couldn't wait for the others. As much as he hated to do it, Rion gripped her hands with his magic, then slammed the side of her face against the ground. She went limp and the magic faded.

Rapid footsteps had Rion looking up in time to see Arianna charging for him, fury written all over her face. "Get away from her," she growled. Rion didn't hesitate. He released Ellie and took a single step back with his hands in the air.

"She's fine. Kirian said to knock her out." Arianna just stared at him, her eyes moving back and forth between his own. Did she not—

The entire area shook again, the ceiling cracking above. A large chunk plummeted down, landing to his far right. The floor cracked beneath its weight, then collapsed as more molten fire spewed forth.

Ice suddenly coated the floor and Talon skidded to Ellie's side, pulling the young female into his arms. "We have to go. Now."

The floor cracked beneath their feet but Rion grabbed it, calming the fiery stone below. It writhed beneath his grasp and nearly pulled free. "Go," he roared. Arianna didn't move until Talon had Ellie draped across his back. Gavin stood beside them too, his eyes wide, struggling to grasp the events unfolding around him.

Talon ran and Arianna followed. Raevina curled her arm underneath Saoirse and she and the half-breed ran with his sister between them.

They made it past the center crack, his and Arianna's magic holding everything at bay.

A rock crumbled from the ceiling above and Rion shoved his magic forward, jutting portions of the stone out to block it. Arianna looked back just as he was crossing the space himself. Her eyes were still—strange. As if she was surprised he was helping them at all.

What remained of the Dark Fae were running, many getting caught in the fire themselves. Their screams still echoed throughout the space. The Fae had fled behind Vairik.

Rion dodged and leapt over falling rocks. He caught up with the rest of them, still knocking falling debris away from their bodies. Wind whipped around the space, telling him even Zylah was using her magic to toss the stones aside.

The entire floor behind them collapsed and Rion spun to find the lava spraying up. It spilled over the edge, racing for them, consuming everything in its path. Rion yanked at the rocks around him, pulling the stones together until they formed a wall to block the molten rock. Rion gritted his teeth when the lava hit and began melting the stone from the other side.

"Out," he yelled.

"No staying behind this time," Saoirse called.

Rion stepped back, pulling more and more stone to replace the chunks in front of him that were disintegrating. He winced, feeling the heat beneath his feet again, searing against the burns that were already there. Then ice coated the ground around his feet and reached up to form a wall. Rion backed away as it thickened, retreating into the tunnel.

He turned to find Arianna standing with one arm outstretched, her wide frightened eyes meeting his in silent understanding. No matter what was going through her head right now, they had to survive. They'd figure out the rest along the way.

He nodded to her and the lot of them took off sprinting down the long, dark hall.

CHAPTER FORTY-THREE

ARIANNA

They zigzagged through the passages, running at break-neck speed, everyone following Arianna as she made her way through the halls and back up the stairs. Alarms blared in the distance.

It was the very sound they'd feared might signal their capture and defeat. Now it was a countdown to destruction.

Arianna wasn't certain exactly what had happened. She only knew her magic had been digging into the earth for some time. She wondered if the creature within her, Laoise, had known about the fire that rested within the earth.

She gritted her teeth. A lot of good it had done. Even if they destroyed Ashling, they still had Vairik to contend with. And that was if they even got out of here alive.

Talon had moved Ellie onto his shoulder. Someone else had slipped an iron bracelet around her wrist. Saoirse was nearly running on her own, though her limp was heavy. Even so, she looked more determined than any of them.

Arianna faced forward, refusing to meet The Demon's gaze.

Fae ran in all directions, scarcely passing them a glance as they sprinted down the halls, carrying things they deemed important enough to risk their lives for. She wondered if Vairik would punish them for leaving certain items behind.

The ground rumbled beneath her feet and Arianna nearly tripped but righted herself again. Emotion welled in her throat and she clenched her teeth knowing the Fae they hadn't rescued were all about to meet a gruesome end. She wondered how far it would spread, if the slaves she'd vowed to rescue would be caught up in it too.

They ran up another level and she nearly breathed a sigh of relief upon seeing sunlight through the far window. An explosion echoed from behind. The walls splintered and several cracks raced along the stones. A blast of heat surged from down the hall, nearly knocking Arianna off her feet again. She saw The Demon grab Saoirse's arm, keeping her upright as they continued running.

Arianna pushed faster and scented The Demon's magic at work as he held the walls up around them. She didn't know why she'd saved him, nor why he bothered helping at all. He'd rendered her little sister unconscious and hadn't killed her, almost as if he cared. Her magic had reacted of its own accord, desperately reaching out for him. Maybe their survival depended on it.

Now wasn't the time to ponder his reasons. Not when a portion of the ceiling crumpled before her. The Demon's magic shot out again, holding the rest of it up as she jumped around the fallen stones. Arianna glanced behind her for a brief moment just to ensure everyone followed.

She continued toward the sunlight, then a wave of molten rock exploded from around the corner ahead. Arianna skidded to a halt, throwing her magic down the hall to stop it in its path. She could already feel the scorching heat.

The Demon slammed his hand through the stone to their left, opening a new path. Sweat poured down the sides of his face as he met her gaze again before jumping through. They all followed, racing forward as they jumped through wall after crumbling wall.

Arianna kept knocking chunks of it away, determined to keep herself and her friends safe.

They kept running, kept pushing. Arianna dodged around another piece, then the entire ceiling came down around her. She used her magic to quickly shove Talon and Ellie out of the way, then something slammed into her back. Her chin hit the floor, her leg cracked, and Arianna didn't even have time to scream before her world went black.

CHAPTER FORTY-FOUR

RION

Rion cursed and spun around. He'd hit the wrong wall. The entire structure crumbled behind him. Talon was shoved forward, and Ellie fell from his grasp, her body bouncing across the hard floor. Rion reached out, catching the crumbling stone before it could fully bury his mate beneath the surface.

The others stopped briefly, gasping for breath as they watched him pull Arianna's limp body from the rubble. He checked her breathing, then cradled her in his arms before taking off again. They were all nearly ready to collapse. If they didn't find an exit soon …

He'd expected to face hell eventually; Rion just never foresaw it rising to claim him itself.

The ground rumbled, quaking, just waiting for the chance to snatch them all with its flaming grasp.

"How much further?" Talon panted.

He didn't know, and without an answer, he could feel the collective fear pouring off them all. Everyone's magic helped to stave off the castle itself as the walls closed in. Even Gavin had regained himself enough to help. He seemed to be keeping the air clear enough for them to breathe, at least.

If they vanished from the world, would Vairik wait for another Divine, or would he destroy the continent before moving on? Was someone like him even capable of moving on?

Faster, faster, faster.

Another chunk of rock crumbled, revealing sunlight through the rubble ahead. Rion nearly cried out in relief, even as another chunk of the wall fell and hid the light from view.

Rion carved a path straight through it. He didn't even pause to see where it led before he jumped through the opening, the others leaping right behind him.

Rion's magic surged outward, giving them a foothold as they fell from the side of the castle. Talon's magic did the same, slowing their decent as much as he dared. Saoirse summoned vines and trees. They raced up from the ground below, forming a steep ramp. Rion's feet met a trunk and he struggled to match the pace of his fall.

One of the castle's towers landed directly to their left, a large crossbow releasing a sizable bolt that swept directly in front of him, narrowly missing his body. Saoirse kept her magic forming, guiding them until their feet hit the rocky ground below.

No one stopped.

Burning rock surrounded them on all sides, pooling around the castle like a fiery moat. Rion cringed at the heat as they closed in, but Talon was already wrapping them all in ice, covering their skin with a thin layer in an attempt to keep them cool.

Raevina seemed to be dimming the flames themselves, the rocks turning black in small patches. Rion raised the earth there and they flew across it, wincing from the blistering heat.

The scene around them was complete chaos. Dark Fae were pouring from the crumbling castle, but without magic, their bodies disintegrated when they tried to run through the molten rock.

Good riddance. Let them suffer in hell.

More Fae were fleeing the area, each somehow knowing exactly what he did. Any second now, the entire place would explode. The castle already appeared higher and it buzzed with intense energy that demanded to be set free.

"Don't stop," Rion breathed.

"We know," Ravina chided. He wondered if she felt it, too.

They raced as fast as their legs could carry them. Rion felt the break, the sharp release of pressure and barely had time to wrap his magic around them all before they were shoved forward so fast he lost track of his bearings.

They tumbled and Talon's magic joined his own, as did Saoirse's and Zylah's and Gavin's and Raevina's. All fought to keep them shielded and Rion just clung to Arianna as they slammed into rock again and again, his head spinning with each strike.

CHAPTER FORTY-FIVE

TALON

The world was on fire, consumed by the fury of the mountain itself. Talon vaguely wondered if this was the land's revenge on Vairik for every foul thing he'd ever done or created. Every surface surrounding them was coated in flames. Thick smoke hung in the air with ashes and embers still raining down from the sky. It was only by the grace of the gods that they'd survived at all.

The mountain had exploded and their combined magic had pulled them all together, cocooning them in a tangle of bodies as they'd struck the earth over and over before rolling right into the ocean. Talon had quickly used his magic to push them away. Rocks had rained down, splashing into the raging ocean, but he hadn't relented.

Thankfully, the sound had scared away any of the creatures Conall had warned them about. For now, at least. Talon knew they couldn't linger in the water long, but it was hard to look away from the space where a looming castle had once stood. Now, it was just a mound of gushing red liquid.

The water surrounding them was almost too warm and Talon was using his magic even now to keep it at tolerable levels. Still, they needed to move.

His gaze roamed to where the city had been. Molten rock had cascaded over it in a wave. He'd heard the citizens' screams of terror and hadn't been able to do anything about it. He prayed some had survived and that someone would help those injured. He couldn't be that person today. Not when they needed to lay low. If Vairik had managed to survive as well, then the High Lord needed to believe they'd been caught in the blast. It would buy them time to heal and plan their next moves.

No one spoke as Talon carefully moved them through the currents. A tingling sensation fell over his skin and he met Gavin's gaze.

"I figured you wouldn't mind."

The male's voice was hoarse. Blood trickled from the side of his head. Talon only nodded. A glamour was exactly what they needed right now. It enabled Talon to keep them close to shore as he steered them around the chaos.

The wind above their heads moved, pushing the ash and embers away and Talon caught Zylah's attention on it. Saoirse's magic snaked through the water in the form of seaweed and bits of debris drifted closer.

Rion was the first to wrap his arm around a charred log, clinging to an unconscious Arianna as he did so. She was breathing at least, as was Ellie. Talon reached for what looked like half a door and rolled Ellie's body on top of it. He studied her hollow face and too-thin frame.

She seemed so normal now, just like the Ellie he'd always known. And yet he'd watched her—grief rose through him, but he bit it back. She'd never forgive herself. Even if she woke and Vairik's magic no longer controlled her mind, the Ellie he knew might never return. Kirian had been everything to her. She'd been planning to marry the half-breed, to even ask him herself. She'd never been one for tradition.

The eight of them floated through the water, watching the fire fade in the distance. Conall had mentioned helping Fae return from their worst nightmares. But Conall was gone and the rebels' hideout had been marked on the map, leading Talon to believe their village might not even be there anymore. He wasn't even sure if those they'd rescued had made it to the mountain. Maybe Vairik had been waiting at the tunnel entrance. He shuddered to think what their fate might have entailed.

Talon sent out another pulse of his magic, searching for anything swimming through the dark waters. Nothing, thank the gods above. He wasn't sure they could handle another battle.

The shoreline grew closer. Ash rained down from above, falling like ominous black snow.

None spoke as they crawled among the rocks, lifting their tired bodies from the water. He gathered Ellie in his arms. Rion did the same with Arianna, and Zylah helped Saoirse limp her way to shore.

Everyone collapsed beneath the cover of trees. Talon pulled the water from their clothes, giving them the small comfort of being dry, at least.

Zylah was the first to stand. She knelt at Rion's side, studying Arianna's wounds. Zylah checked her up and down, grimacing at her leg. "Lay her down." Rion did without hesitation. Zylah prodded at Arianna's leg, then drew a rune over the area. This one had more complicated lines and swirls. Something in Arianna's leg shifted and she grimaced. Zylah quickly drew another over Arianna's chest. "To keep her sedated."

Rion didn't argue, neither did the rest of them as Zylah drew a few more, then sat back. "Not to state the obvious, but we need to find somewhere to lay low. She needs to heal. So do Evelyn and Saoirse."

"I'm fine," Saoirse argued, though she made no move to stand. Zylah shot her a glare that had the ambassador of Brónach looking away.

Raevina stood, catching his attention. "I'll be back."

"Where are you going?" Talon demanded.

"To find shelter."

He stood too, leaving Ellie in the grass. "Not alone, you're not."

"You can't keep up, stay here and protect them."

Talon clenched his fists at the insult but relented. Raevina shifted into a small bird of prey, then took off into the air at breakneck speeds. His heart beat wildly as she disappeared into the clouds above.

"She'll be fine," Zylah said, then crossed the space to work on Ellie. The half-breed only drew two marks over his future High Lady. One that looked like it might be for healing while the other mimicked the one she'd traced over Arianna's chest. It was probably best to keep her sedated for a while anyway.

Zylah returned to Saoirse, but the female waved her off. "Save your energy for when we need it."

"I need you to be able to run."

Saoirse didn't argue again.

MINUTES TICKED by and Talon counted every single one of them. His leg bounced and caught Gavin's attention, but the male didn't comment. Talon vaguely wondered if the male's silence was due to Talon's constant threats over the last several days. A tinge of guilt washed through him, especially as he watched how the male kept his steady gaze on the rise and fall of Ellie's chest, as if he feared she might never wake again.

In light of waiting, Talon understood his worry. It didn't matter how outrageous it seemed, one couldn't help but worry for their mate. It was the only negative aspect he could see when it came to the bond. He still couldn't wrap his mind around Vairik wanting to be rid of it forever.

A screeching cry piercing the air had Talon back on his feet, turning to the sky. Raevina swooped down, her wings tucked in around her body as she dove. She pulled her wings out at the last second to slow her fall.

A blinding flash and she stood before them in her Fae form, her breath ragged. "There's a house not more than a mile off. It's secluded and surrounded by trees."

"How many are there?" Rion asked, already scooping Arianna into his arms.

"Just two Fae. A male and female who look like the owners. Judging from the surrounding tracks, not many come and go. Their scents tell me the male is from Pádraigín while the female is from Móirín."

"Why is someone from Móirín all the way out here?" Talon asked.

She shrugged. "Not sure it matters right now."

"Let's go," Rion said, already moving in the direction Raevina had pointed. Talon picked up Ellie under the watchful gaze of Gavin, and Zylah helped Saoirse to her feet, once again pulling the female's arm around her shoulder.

Gavin's magic settled over them again. Talon shuddered, hating the feel of it, yet knowing it was necessary. Even Rion didn't protest.

They crossed beneath the trees at a steady pace until a two-story house entered their line of sight.

Talon kept his voice low. "Do we need to worry about the one from Pádraigín?"

"Only until he's subdued," Raevina said, reaching for one of her blades.

"We're not killing innocents."

"None are innocent as far as I'm concerned."

"Some are," Gavin said, his voice low. "Not everyone has a choice."

Talon watched the war in Raevina's gaze before she turned to Gavin. "Then it's your job to get the male in iron before he becomes a problem. If I have to deal with him, it'll be at the end of a blade."

Gavin furrowed his brow. "And how, exactly, do you expect me to put him in iron? Evelyn has my bracelet."

"She's subdued." Zylah said. "Take the bracelet. If that doesn't work, we'll knock them out and figure out what to do next." Gavin obeyed and slipped it from Ellie's wrist.

Raevina rolled her eyes. Talon knew those from Fiadh were said to be ruthless, but he never imagined they'd be willing to kill civilians when they'd done nothing wrong.

"They're inside," Rion said. "Both are walking around on the bottom floor." Talon watched him, realizing now exactly how he'd out-smarted all of Talon's plans. If he could tell where people were walking from this distance—he loosed a sigh and followed the others.

Raevina didn't bother with stealth as she marched right up the stairs and kicked in the front door. The wood splintered and the door slammed against the interior wall, bouncing so hard Gavin had to catch it as he followed.

Talon entered after him with Ellie hanging limply in his arms.

The male jumped in front of the female, using one arm to push her behind his body. He grabbed a large kitchen knife from the table and pointed it at no one in particular, his eyes flashing between each of them as they entered.

"I scent even a spark of your damned magic," Raevina hissed. "And you're dead." Flames circled her hands. The male's dark face turned a shade paler.

Saoirse limped in, still carried by Zylah. "We're not here to hurt you. We just need a place to rest."

Rion entered last, magic spilling in and coating the floors. The male's eyes widened and he stepped back. The knife clattered to the floor. "She needs a bed. Now." The male pointed to the stairs and Rion went up without looking back. Zylah left Saoirse's side to follow.

"There are three rooms," the female said, stepping forward to rest one hand on the male's shoulder. "If your other companion needs rest as well."

"Do you have anything that's made of iron?" Talon asked.

The male blanched and his voice shook. "No, we don't—why—"

"It's fine." Talon turned to the stairs, making his way up with Gavin on his heels. Talon could see Rion adjusting Arianna on the bed in the first room. He chose another down the hall.

He shoved the door open and a small bed stood inside a tiny room. Furs and rugs lined the space with everything decorated in warm fall tones. He gently laid Ellie on top of the quilt, then turned to Gavin. "The bracelet."

"You don't want it for the male downstairs?"

"Has he used his magic?"

"Not yet."

"Will you be able to tell if he does?"

Gavin raised a brow. "Suddenly willing to trust me now?"

Talon pinched the bridge of his nose. "I'm exhausted. If you want a half-assed apology, I'll give you one later." He pointed to Ellie. "Put the iron back on and watch her. If she wakes, call for me."

Talon bounded back down the stairs. Saoirse had taken a spot on the couch and was bent over, wincing as she struggled to unlace her boots.

The male and female still hadn't moved. Neither had Raevina.

"We need bowls of fresh water and rags," Talon said, doing his best to keep his voice gentle.

"Everything you need is upstairs in a closet." The male said, still guarding the female behind him. "Take what you need and leave us."

"We're not here to rob you." Saoirse pried her other boot off. "And we apologize for the sudden intrusion on your beautiful home." The male didn't reply, his jaw only clenched as he stared between each of them.

"My name is Saoirse. I'm Brónach's ambassador. My brother is the High Lord and I assure you, you will be more than compensated for any hospitality offered." She reached into an interior pocket and pulled out a small purse before tossing it onto the table. "Consider this a down payment."

The male stared at the bag, then back to Saoirse, his lips parting slightly. Then his gaze drifted to the window. The ash was falling thicker now. "Did you have something to do with all that?"

Saoirse sighed and leaned back, wincing with the movement. "Ashling is gone. The volcano beneath it exploded."

The male's lips parted. "Gone ... what about the High Lord?"

She shrugged. "Let's pray our luck is good enough to assume it killed him, too."

"So, you all escaped?" the female asked.

Saoirse nodded. "More or less." She tilted her head toward the stairs. "I don't think my brother needs introduction, but the female with him is The Divine and the other is her sister. Both were captured by Vairik and both need rest."

"The Divine," the female breathed. "Has fate truly graced us with her presence?"

Saoirse nodded, then pointed to Talon. "This is Talon of Levea." She pointed to Raevina next. "And Raevina of Fiadh."

The male's brows rose and he turned to Raevina again before bowing his head slightly.

The female stepped around her partner. "Is the future High Lady of Móirín truly upstairs?"

"Upstairs and uncuffed," Raevina said, staring at Talon in disapproval.

Talon nearly growled. "I am not putting her in chains after everything she just went through."

"So you'll have her wake up and put us all in danger? What if she escapes and runs right back to Vairik? You think he wouldn't make her do worse things?"

"She's my future High Lady."

"Who attacked your queen," Raevina shot back. "You need to think carefully where your loyalties lie and stop letting emotions get in the way."

"At least one of us is capable of emotions," he snapped.

Raevina's eyes darkened. "You're acting like a child."

Talon's fists clenched, but Saoirse interrupted. "I think that's enough. We're all tired, and arguing isn't going to get us anywhere. The fact remains that Evelyn killed someone close to her and also attacked Arianna. She should have restraints until we can assess whether or not she's in her right mind."

Raevina turned away, crossing the room to sit across from Saoirse. Half a second later she waved a hand at the fireplace and a flame ignited there. Talon wasn't sure whether the female was actually cold or just wanted to watch it as a distraction.

Talon's jaw worked. "We need to get back to Levea as fast as we can and warn Avalon."

Saoirse nodded. "He'll likely hear about it before we can get there, but he needs to know everything else, too. I need to inform my brother as well."

"You said Levea?" the female questioned. Talon had nearly forgotten they were there, but he looked at her now and studied the way her heartbeat had quickened.

"Yes," Talon said, hoping she wasn't about to ask to come with them. He had enough to worry about without throwing two civilians in the mix, though if Vairik went on a rampage, Talon wasn't sure it was safe to leave them either.

"You can't go to Levea," the male finally said. The female ducked her head and turned away.

"What do you mean?" Saoirse asked.

"Levea was attacked two days ago."

Dread washed through him. "By whom?"

"The High Lord. He took his armies there. The dark creatures, too."

"How do you know this?" Saoirse asked.

"People talk in the towns and news travels fast," the male said. "And we all watched as his armies and those filthy abominations marched out of Ashling. It's why we came here. He declared war on Móirín and we were afraid—" he wrapped one arm around his partner.

"Then we go to the rebels for help," Saoirse said. "Conall might be gone, but he said there were people stationed at other locations, too. Cara and Sive will know how to reach them."

The female took a single step forward. "You don't understand," she said, her voice shaking. "Levea … is gone."

Chapter Forty-Six

Arianna

Arianna woke in a warm bed with a heavy blanket draped across her torso. Her chest hurt, throbbing as though something had pierced her heart. She sat up slowly, her back aching from a wound she couldn't remember.

The room was strange yet comforting. A chair sat beside her bed with a wrinkled blanket laid over the armrest. Someone had been sleeping there. She sniffed the air around it, but didn't recognize the spicy scent.

Her gaze shifted to the wooden table at the bedside. A glass of water rested on top, condensation rolling down the sides. Arianna didn't dare reach for it. Pictures hung from the walls depicting images of the forest and the various animals within.

She was definitely in somebody's home, but at least she wasn't nursing a nearly fatal wound this time.

Arianna prodded the tender area on the back of her head and neck. No broken skin or lumps, which meant someone had likely been using runes to treat her. Zylah? Sive? Were they back in the rebels' camp?

Images of the last few days came rushing back. She remembered being chained to a table. She remembered escaping and finding Ellie with Vairik. But the rest—Arianna cradled her head. Had they gotten Ellie out? Had they killed Vairik, or—or was she still at his mercy?

Kirian …

Tears welled to the surface and Arianna covered her mouth. Gods, Kirian was gone, and the way Ellie had looked at him. Her stomach twisted. Did that mean her sister was gone, too? Had Vairik corrupted her mind beyond repair? Was there any hope?

The door creaked open and Arianna started. She gripped her blankets, staring at a male she didn't recognize. Thankfully Talon followed right behind him. Her shoulders relaxed a fraction.

Talon had cleaned up, changed clothes, and had his hair pulled back in his usual fashion, but both were staring at her with concerned looks on their faces.

"How are you feeling?" the male asked. He moved closer, but carefully, as if afraid to startle her. Was he a healer? A Weaver?

"What happened?" Arianna asked.

Talon sat at the foot of the bed and clasped his hands together. "What's the last thing you remember?"

She tried to bring the memories to the surface, but it was … difficult. Impossible. Each slipped from her grasp, one after the other.

"I remember Ellie," Arianna clenched her jaw, fighting to prevent the tears from falling. "And Kirian." Talon nodded, but she saw the emotions in his gaze. The grief. "I remember the Dark Fae and—how did we escape? Is Ellie … did we get her—"

"She's in the other room." The way he said it had dread settling in the pit of her stomach.

"Is she okay?"

"She's … resting and alive. We don't know what Vairik might have done to her yet."

"I want to see her."

"Okay, but can you rest a bit first? Maybe get something to eat?"

Her stomach growled in response. "Are we safe?"

Talon nodded. "For the time being. We're hoping Vairik believes we were all caught in the blast."

"What blast?"

"You don't remember running?"

She pressed a palm to her temple. "It's coming back, but … I think I blacked out at some point."

"Ashling is gone. Apparently there was a volcano under it. It erupted."

"The timing seems a little convenient."

"We think your magic triggered it. Saoirse mentioned something about pressure building beneath the surface."

Arianna did recall her magic burying into the ground, digging deep, but when she reached for the memories it was like a white-hot poker slashed through her brain. She grabbed her head again and winced. The stranger in the room stepped forward, then paused.

"Don't push yourself," Talon said, then exchanged a glance with the other male. "When we were separated, do you remember where you were?"

"Yeah," Arianna said, a familiar anger rising to the surface. "They caught me." The male stiffened and she clenched her fists. "I can still— he was in my head. They both were." She hated the lingering oily feel of Vairik's presence. A shudder ran through her body.

"Both?" Talon questioned.

"Niall and Vairik."

"And you feel okay?"

Arianna met his gaze. "I think so." After seeing what Ellie had done, Arianna understood perfectly well what he was asking. Could Vairik have altered her mind without her being able to tell?

"You think he did something to me?"

"It would be surprising if he didn't."

"Do I seem different?"

Talon hesitated and her stomach sank. "When we escaped, you were behaving … oddly. Even now …" he trailed off and looked at the male beside her again.

"How, exactly?" If Vairik had done something to her mind, she needed to puzzle through it as fast as possible.

"What do you remember about," Talon hesitated again, "about when you were taken?"

"Taken?" She tried to clarify.

"When you were a slave. How did you escape?"

Arianna blinked at him, confused. "I'm not really sure why that matters."

"Indulge me. Please."

"I was taken from the celebration—" she started.

"And how did you escape?"

"You came and blew up the camp. You got us out."

"Who is us?"

"Me and Zylah and the other slaves."

His jaw clenched again. "And afterward?"

"You took me back to Levea. Father threw a celebration then Fiadh attacked and Brónach came to our aid."

"*Why* did Brónach come to our aid?"

"Because they wanted to rekindle the alliance."

"Because?"

Arianna threw up her arms in frustration. "What does this have to do with anything? Because I'm The Divine, I guess. Isn't that why everyone comes to help?" She gestured toward the stranger in the room. "And why is he standing here gawking at me?" She lifted her gaze to the male. "Who are you?"

Arianna had never seen two males go so still. Both stared at her, but the stranger gasped as if she'd physically struck him. Something like sorrow tugged deep in her heart but was quickly washed away by shadow.

Then Arianna scented magic drifting from him. Not the usual sort, this was something different. Something that demanded she rise to attention. Particles skittered across the floor then around his boots, moving in a slow jagged pattern.

Particles of … earth.

Arianna's heart began pounding faster as she lifted her gaze to study the male's auburn hair and piercing green eyes. She'd scented the trace of Brónach on him before, but—

Memories of their escape came flooding back. The Demon.

Arianna scooted her legs up and winced from the pain in her back. The Demon's hands clenched and her magic strummed through her veins, pulsing in time to her rapid heartbeat.

Talon was saying something, but she couldn't hear him above the roar in her ears.

"Arianna." Her name fell from his lips like a plea. Like she were the goddess he worshiped. But she knew better. The Demon took a single step forward and Arianna sent him flying back, her magic exploding out of her with half a thought. His body slammed against the wall and she scrambled off the bed. Talon's hand reached for her, but she shoved him away with another burst of ice.

Arianna stopped at the doorway, turning to ensure she hadn't hurt her friend. She needed to get him out of here, too. If he stayed— Talon stood slowly and brushed the ice from his hand. Why wasn't he panicked? Why wasn't his magic out? Where were his weapons?

The Demon remained on the floor, staring up at her with devastation written across his face.

"He's not going to hurt you," Talon assured.

Arianna gaped at him. Not going to hurt her? What did he mean? Talon extended one hand and melted the ice from The Demon's body. The male still didn't move, as if she'd actually frozen him to the spot.

But Talon knew exactly who he was. He'd been the one to tell her stories about the creature that tore through battlefields without remorse. He'd been the one to warn her to steer clear of him at any cost.

Talon stepped, but not toward her. He placed himself between her and The Demon. Her lips parted.

But—but—

Gods, was Talon a traitor? Is that how they'd escaped? Had Talon made a deal with Vairik? Was The Demon working with him, too? Was her sister even free, or were they using a glamour to fool her? Maybe she wasn't even really in a house. What if this was a dungeon and they were all still inside the castle?

Arianna stepped back.

Talon spoke in a near whisper. "You're safe. Give me a chance to explain."

Her heart wouldn't slow. She couldn't breathe, couldn't breathe, couldn't—

Not Talon. Talon wouldn't—he couldn't—

"You're helping him." Her voice broke.

"I'm just making sure you don't do something you'll regret."

Regret? What the hell was he talking about? Arianna stepped back again and darted a glance toward the stairs. The Demon placed his hands on the floor, attempting to rise. Would he chase her down? Could she even outrun him?

Ellie. She needed to find Ellie.

The Demon's magic flickered to life and Arianna bolted. She took the stairs three at a time, each impact jarring her body so much it threatened to collapse.

She had to get to her father. He would know what to do. She wasn't strong enough as she was now, but if she could make it to Levea—

Talon's voice followed her down the stairs and Arianna paused upon seeing Raevina seated in the room with a glass halfway to her mouth. Saoirse sat across from her, but she'd half risen, her eyes wide as she stared at Arianna.

Arianna veered for the door. Tears stung her eyes. Talon was a traitor. They were all traitors. No, that wasn't right. Raevina had pledged her life to her, hadn't she? Unless they'd all turned together. Did she have no one? Was this even real?

"Arianna, stop." She didn't. She raced straight into the trees, just like she should have done when she'd first been taken into slavery. She just needed to find a water source. If she could do that, maybe she could lose them.

Talon's footsteps closed in, as if he was purposely making noise, but then The Demon appeared in front of her, easily cutting her off. She skidded to a stop, panting from the pain radiating through her back and neck.

Gods, he was going to kill her. One strike of his magic and she'd be dead.

Arianna backed away a step, but Talon and Raevina blocked her path.

"It's all right," The Demon whispered, his voice a strange sort of music that called to something in her soul.

Arianna shook her head and spun to find Talon too close. "Stay away from me," she shouted before summoning magic to surround her body. She morphed each droplet into a tiny spear.

Talon backed away and lifted his hands. "No one here is going to hurt you."

"What did you do to me?" she shouted again. Something was wrong. Something was missing. She needed time to sort through the facts and figure out exactly when it had happened.

"Please, Arianna," Talon pleaded. "Just come back inside. I'll explain everything, I promise."

"Explain him!" She jerked her head toward The Demon.

"I'm your mate."

Arianna scoffed, then anxious laughter bubbled to the surface. "You'd like that, wouldn't you? To be crowned king over the land after everything you've done." He visibly flinched.

Talon stepped and she shot four icicles at his feet. "Have you been working with Vairik this whole time? Are you the reason Ellie was taken?"

Talon furrowed his brow. "No."

"I don't believe you." She looked around. "Is Gavin hiding around the corner, ready to twist the truth for you?"

"Gavin is upstairs with Ellie."

Her lips trembled as she desperately tried to scent the lie. If they had Ellie, she couldn't leave. She had to get to her sister first. But she wasn't strong enough.

"I want to go back to Levea. I want to see my father."

More pain covered Talon's face. "We can talk about it, but you have to calm down first."

"Please, Arianna."

She whirled on The Demon. "Do not say my name." He hadn't moved through the entire exchange. She might be able to kill him, but Talon? She couldn't fight the male who'd always been there for her. She couldn't—she couldn't—

Her chest rose and fell faster than she could draw breath. Her mind spun, the colors around her blurring. Spinning. She needed to run and yet couldn't. They were going to put iron on her, use her for their own gain.

Arianna faltered and Talon dared a step closer. "Let me get you back inside."

"I don't—" Air. She needed air. Arianna gripped her chest, doubling over. Everything was moving too fast, too fast, too fast. "Don't—" She tried again.

"Let me assist you, My Lady. Tell me what you need." Arianna looked up. Raevina. Could she trust Raevina? Was she with them too? But … there was no one else. No one—

"Keep them … away." Then breath left her entirely.

ACKNOWLEDGEMENTS

First and foremost, a HUGE thank you to my readers. Your unwavering support has meant the world to me, especially during the challenging times. When I lost eight weeks of writing time due to an unfortunate issue with my special editions, your encouraging words kept me going. You've stuck by me, and I can't express how grateful I am for your patience and enthusiasm.

To my amazing husband, Kyle Reed, my developmental editor—thank you for everything. You've truly brought my male characters to life in ways I never could have imagined. You've spent countless hours, often at the crack of dawn, powering through edits to meet our tight deadlines. Your dedication and insight have been invaluable, and I couldn't do this without you.

To Dawn, my proofreader, thank you for dealing with my sometimes chaotic, disorganized self and still welcoming me back with open arms. Your attention to detail and commitment to making this book shine have been a huge part of its success, and I appreciate you more than you know.

To Story Wrappers, my cover designer, thank you for turning my vision into reality. When I first published, my self-made cover was far from ideal. You brought this book to life with stunning covers that have caught the eyes of so many wonderful readers. I'm beyond grateful for your creativity and talent.

To my cat, Tigris, thank you for wreaking havoc in my office, knocking things over, and generally being a little terror. Your rare moments of cuddles on my lap are *almost* worth the chaos you cause—almost.

To my family and friends, thank you for your unwavering support and belief in me. Your encouragement is what keeps me moving forward, and I am forever grateful.

And to my son, Rowan—the absolute light of my life—thank

you for being my biggest inspiration. You're the reason I push so hard to make this career successful. I cherish the freedom this career gives me, allowing me to drop everything and play with you when you come into my office. These little moments with you while you're still so small are priceless.

And of course, to the characters who have yet to finish telling their story—thank you for keeping the adventure alive.

Here's to the next chapter.

AUTHOR BIO

J.E. Reed is the #1 bestselling author of The Fae of Alastríona series. Reed loves writing magical stories full of love and adventure. She believes everyone deserves a happy ending.

Reed currently lives in Ohio with her husband, her son, and orange tabby cat who, she is certain, used to be a Viking in another life. Her latest series has enabled her to pursue a full-time writing career, and she plans to bring readers more heart-wrenching romance.

Visit Reed's website at www.jereedbooks.com
Follow her on Instagram: @jereedauthor
Follow her on Tiktok: @a_writers_quill
Follow her on Facebook: @J.E.Reed.author

www.ingramcontent.com/pod-product-compliance
Lightning Source LLC
Chambersburg PA
CBHW031201310726
48969CB00001B/176